Also by Jacci Turner

YOUNG ADULT

THE TREE SINGER SERIES
Tree Singer

THE BIRTHRIGHT SERIES
The Cage
The Bar
The Lamb

STANDALONE
Cracker
Snapped

MIDDLE GRADE

THE FINDING HOME SERIES
Bending Willow
Stretching Willow
Finding Willow
Willow's Ride
Willow's Roundup

STANDALONE
Shipwrecked

ADULT

Love Virus
Tumbled People:
Deconstructing and Reconstructing Your Faith

Triggensfeld
Castle Keep
King's Forest
Forest Clan
Ocean Clan
Table Mountain
Sun Clan

WIND CATCHER

JACCI TURNER

To my dearest friends who have become faithful readers.
You are the wind beneath my writing wings.
Thank you!

PROLOGUE

Flurry leaned on the deck of the *Lady Grace*, feet planted firmly on the rolling deck, and struggled to drive away a growing sense of unease. She licked salt from her lips and listened to the song of the ship with its creaks and pops. She loved the ship and the songs it sang. Those songs always settled her anxious thoughts, lulling her to sleep at night.

Overhead, the ship's three sails billowed with wind her parents caught and channeled. The wind kept her short brown hair permanently spiked like the hedgehog she'd seen on this last trip. Prior trading ports had been interesting, but this trip to Caspia was her favorite. She'd never seen so many people crowded into market stalls along the shoreline bartering for the goods the *Lady Grace* brought from Triggensfeld.

Her mind wandered back to Caspia, where the smell of unfamiliar spices had tickled her nose, and the food—mostly vegetables and fish over rice—was tossed in savory sauces. Her stomach growled. Ship food was uninspired at best. Beans and dried fruit, things that wouldn't spoil.

She longed to be able to move beyond the shorelines into the land and cities, but her parents kept her on a short mooring line, allowing her older brother and sister to wander further inland.

She loved exploring lands with people who looked so different from those in her island home, loved seeing the differences and the similarities, hints of where her people had come from.

A loud snap from the sails warned her of a course adjustment. Flurry took hold of the rail and widened her stance, keeping her knees flexible, absorbing the motion of the sails shifting again, directing the bow to port. The deck rose and fell to the rhythm of the waves as the ship settled onto her new course.

Flurry relaxed, letting her body sway with the ship. A gull cried overhead and—was that a crow? They weren't that close to land, were they?

She squinted at the waters ahead, looking for a dark shadow rising above the horizon. Her heart skittered in anticipation. Even though she couldn't see it, she knew her home—the island of Triggensfeld—had to be just over the horizon.

During these voyages, she'd learned so much about herself, her family, and her ancestors. Over the centuries, voyagers had landed on Triggensfeld for different reasons. Some had been slaves, some explorers, others political prisoners. Natives welcomed the newcomers. Some of the newcomers stayed, moving about the island and intermarrying, their skin taking on various shades of brown.

Flurry's parents and closest-in-age siblings had the darkest skin on the island, their bodies muscled like the slaves from Ropia whose ships had crashed on the island long ago. Those slaves had been freed by the island natives.

Yet she and her oldest brother had lighter hair and skin along with the thin, tall bodies of the prisoners who'd been exiled to the island from Sapia before her grandparents' parents arrived.

"Whatcha doing, monkey?"

Her brother Theo poked her in the back, humming a tune she knew all too well.

She scowled at him. "Why do you sing that song all the time? Are you in love with it or something?"

"Not the song." He grinned, a mischievous glint in his eye. "Just her. Someday I'll marry the tree singer."

"Sure," Flurry said, "and I'll marry the prince."

He looked her up and down, brows furrowed deep enough to hold dirt. "Not unless you get some lady parts soon!"

She smacked his arm, blinking back the tears that seemed so ready to breach her eyes these days.

He held his hands up in surrender and sang louder as he walked away. "We share the song of one who sang through fear, and foe, and pain . . ."

Why did his words always hurt so much?

She missed her oldest brother Cal. Not only was he like her in looks, he was quiet and thoughtful, qualities she could identify with. Sometimes he'd take her with him when her family explored new lands, but not on this trip. He'd stayed home to prepare for his joining ceremony with the king's daughter, Cherry.

How he'd ever gotten the courage to talk to her in the first place was beyond Flurry. He was more tongue-tied than she was. Though she tried not to, Flurry resented Cherry—not because she wasn't a nice person. Because she was taking away the only member of the family who didn't treat her like a baby or tease her when she said the wind spoke to her.

Cal didn't call her a monkey when she climbed the rigging like Theo did or laugh at her when she asked to learn to catch the wind as her sister Sirocco did.

Cal believed her, listened to her.

And now he was leaving her.

Soon he'd be joined with the king's daughter. Soon he'd have his own ship.

Leaving her at the mercy of her parents. And Theo.

She had just turned thirteen, practically a woman, but they still treated her like a child. Flurry brushed away tears, angry at herself. Angry at Theo, though she wasn't sure why.

It wasn't the song, not really. Flurry would love to meet the fabled tree singer. She was supposed to be only a few years older than Flurry herself.

But she knew how to listen.

Listen to trees, silly. She doesn't know anything about listening to the wind.

It couldn't be all that different—listening to trees versus listening to wind. Maybe the tree singer would understand.

What she'd heard from the wind frightened Flurry. Messages both dark and disturbing.

But what could she do?

The land was suffering and her parents just said she had an overactive imagination.

If she ever got the chance to meet Mayten Tree Singer, she would share the wind's images. See what the tree singer had to say.

CHAPTER ONE

Training tree singers for the king's new school was turning out harder than Mayten thought it would be. Six children ages four – eight followed her down the path leading to her homestead. Behind them came her mother with a group of older students.

Red and gold leaves blanketed the ground. A lone leaf edged in gold floated to the ground, rising and falling on a late afternoon breeze. She drew in a breath of the musky autumn air. To the side of the path grew a small patch of orange poppies still in bloom, perfect for one last demonstration.

"Gather round." She beckoned, waiting for the boys and girls to cluster close.

"When you want to encourage a plant to open and grow, it's best if you get down on its level." She kneeled next to the flowers, resting a finger on a bud that had not yet opened. "Touch the plant gently, and picture joining your energy with the plant's, sending it love and encouragement."

She closed her eyes. "Sometimes it helps you focus if you hum." She hummed low in her throat while picturing her energy joining with that of the poppy.

Startled by a collective gasp, Mayten opened her eyes to find the bud standing straight and tall in all its bright orange glory.

"Wow," Acacia said. The four-year-old was Mayten's favorite student. "I want to try it, I want to try it!"

She reached toward the plant.

Mayten grabbed her small hand. "Wait, Acacia, let me find you one to try."

She led the girl further along the path, the other students following like ducklings, until she found what she needed—a budding dandelion.

"Remember what I said. Touch it gently, and send it your love and energy."

Acacia squatted near the weed and put out her finger, her brows knitted together in concentration. Her tongue pressed through the gap where her front teeth were missing. All of the children fell quiet.

Mayten's stomach tightened. Had she explained the process right? Her mother was such a good teacher—

The plant shivered. The look on Acacia's face changed from determined to confused and then to sheer terror as the weed began to shrivel, then bend.

Acacia jumped back. Tears rolled down her cheeks. "I killed it! I killed it!" she shrieked, clutching her stomach and falling to her knees. "I'm sorry. I'm sorry. I'm sorry."

Mayten slipped an arm around Acacia's shoulders. She wanted to soothe the girl, knowing exactly how she felt, but she remembered her training. It was important not to diminish this moment. A trainee should be—needed to be—allowed to feel, really *feel*, the death of a plant.

This is why young trainees practiced on weeds. Accidentally draining the plant's life energy—any plant's life energy—and seeing it die was devastating to a singer. A child usually did it once. That was enough.

Finally, she hugged the sobbing child close. "Never forget this feeling."

Acacia looked up, eyes streaming, nose swollen, and nodded. "I killed it. I *took* the energy instead of giving it mine. I killed it."

Mayten tightened her arms around the girl's trembling body. "Yes, you did. You'll never forget this, right?

Acacia nodded, sniffing and wiping her nose with the back of her hand.

Mayten stepped back from the hug and looked at each of the children in turn. "What just happened to Acacia happens to all of us. Remember that the next time you touch a plant."

She waited a breath, then repeated. "It happens to all of us."

She placed her hands on Acacia's shoulders, then pulled a twig from her tightly curled black hair.

"Remember," Mayten continued to address the group of nervous-looking children, "I told you this happens to everyone when they are learning to sing. Even our chief tree singer, Castanea, the best singer in Triggensfeld. The same thing happened to her during her training."

As one, the children looked back at Castanea and her group further down the path.

"Did it happen to you?" Acacia's voice wobbled. "'Cause Ma says *you* are the best tree singer, you even got to level seven. You saved the trees."

Mayten's cheeks warmed. She was still not used to the way her reputation had changed after her quest last spring. She had been a nobody, a fifteen-year-old initiate tree singer trained only to level three, when she'd been asked to find out what was sucking the life from her beloved forest.

Just thinking about it made her stomach squeeze and sent a shiver running up her spine.

This was why trainees were allowed to experience the death of a plant. Once they had experienced that pain, that devastation, they would never want to feel it again. It tore a deep pain in a tree singer's gut to feel something die. She'd never understand how that evil singer could stand that feeling, could actually *kill* trees.

And had done so for centuries.

Though the quest had been only months ago, it seemed like years had gone by. She'd been forced to use skills she hadn't even been taught when they left on their quest to save the trees, but she still had so much to learn. Helping her mother teach the younger boys and girls made her realize how much knowledge she was lacking.

"Even me, Acacia. And the reason it hurts so much when you accidentally kill a plant is that you're feeling the plant's pain. You'll be careful not to take essence again. Our goal is to help the trees and plants grow, not to take their energy. Helping living things grow is an amazing gift and I think you will be very good at it."

Acacia nodded, swiping at her tears. "I'll never, ever kill another plant."

Mayten stood and pulled the girl into a firm hug. "Just remember, I'll never push you to do anything until you're ready. The same goes for all of you, understand?"

The entire group nodded.

Acacia gave her a weak smile.

Mayten looked at each child in turn: Acer, who was always trying to make the others laugh; Betula and Celtis, the twins; Picea, the shortest; Julans, the quiet one; and Acacia, the youngest of the group. "Your folks should be coming up the path soon. You'd better get to them before Anatolian does."

The children ran laughing and screaming toward Mayten's homestead. This was a game they played every day, trying to beat the dog to the parents who had delivered them to the homestead that morning for training.

Not all of the Forest Clan members were singers. The clan also had healers, questers, woodworkers, shipbuilders, and growers. She didn't know exactly how each of the other giftings were trained but imagined training for other gifts was similar to the way singers were trained—by watching and learning from their elders.

Acacia's father was coming up the path as they neared, smiling broadly. Acacia sprinted toward him just as a huge blonde dog with a black face and curled tail came dashing around the side of the homestead. Mayten's heart warmed at the sight of the large home with long wings that had been added as Mayten's family grew. The front of the homestead was bordered by the flowers her da sang. In the back grew the fruits, vegetables, and trees her brother and her ma sang.

Acacia shrieked in glee, trying to outrun the dog as she jumped into her da's arms. The man was taller than most men in the Forest Clan but Anatolian could have tapped his face with a paw if he'd wanted. Instead, Anatolian stuck his wet nose on Acacia's leg and gave her a lick, eliciting another shriek. She giggled as her da rubbed Anatolian's huge head, receiving tail wags in return.

Anatolian would never hurt anyone, though he kept their homestead safe from snakes and bears. She'd been fortunate to have him along on their quest. Not only did he comfort her when she'd been missing home, he'd helped bring down a mountain lion. He loved children but he was so big some of the little ones were afraid of him.

Acacia and her da waved as they headed back down the path to their own homestead. Mayten felt a flush of satisfaction as she watched her other trainees find their parents—and older siblings who'd been training with her ma—and head home, some to houses in the town center, others to homesteads like her own snuggled among the trees with other hill family homes. She still found it hard to believe there were over two hundred families in the Forest Clan.

The sun's disappearance left a distinct chill in the evening air. Mayten felt a hand on her shoulder and turned to see her mother's narrow face, a face almost identical to her own. Same skin the color of walnuts, same brown spirals of hair that refused to be tamed.

"Are they all gone?" her mother, Castanea, asked. "Was that crying I heard?"

"Acacia drained a dandelion."

Ma shook her head. "I'll never forget that feeling."

"Me neither." Mayten had learned tree singing at her mother's knee. They'd wandered the hills together, her mother pointing out plants and teaching little lessons along the way.

"Come on," her mother said. "I think your da has a snack for us and after this week of training we could both use a bit of food and a chance to relax."

She grabbed Mayten's hand, pulling her up the steps to their home. Mayten marveled at how close she and her mother had become since the quest. It hadn't always been so. Not only was Castanea a powerful woman in their clan, she was an elder on the clan council, had six children from infant to teen to care for, and she was also chief singer.

The chief singer's schedule wasn't the only thing that had created distance between them. Mayten had always respected her mother. But that respect turned to bitterness and anger when her mother had *insisted* her teenage daughter go on the quest.

She hadn't told Mayten she was going in Castanea's place. Or why. Mayten had learned her ma's "little secret" during the quest. It had taken quite a while to get over what felt like a betrayal.

After the trees had been healed and the king had agreed to begin cross-training students in all their gifts, she and her mother reconciled, becoming united in their purposes.

Now, they had two years to train students who would be sent to Castle Triggensfeld for further training. Of course, they wouldn't be sending those as young as Acacia. Only the top students who were twelve or older would go to the castle to complete their training. They would also receive exposure to other gifts, like healing, questing, and hunting.

The king's daughter would even be teaching them botany, combining science with their giftings.

Her mother cleared her throat. Mayten glanced up and saw her holding the door, eyebrows raised. Her face flushed with warmth. She'd been daydreaming. Again.

They stepped inside and were greeted by the warm smell of cinnamon. Heat from the kitchen was welcome after the chilly evening air.

"Da, you made rolls!" Mayten smiled at her da. His rosy cheeks reflected the oven's heat. There had never been any distance between Mayten and her father. He'd always had her heart.

Da's eyes crinkled as he smiled back. He knew cinnamon rolls were Mayten's favorite and never passed up a chance to bake them for her and the rest of the family. "I thought you two might need something extra after a full week of training."

He kissed his wife's cheek. "How did it go?"

"They are definitely starting to understand." Ma took a chair at one end of the wood table that dominated the kitchen. "I feel like it's getting a bit easier to train them all. Wouldn't you agree, Mayten?"

Mayten wasted no time finding her place on the bench facing the oven so she could watch Da portion out the rolls. "Oh yes, much better now."

Though she didn't feel as confident as her mother, she didn't want that lack of confidence to show. Her mouth watered in anticipation as Da placed a steaming roll along with a glass of cold milk in front of her. This was the best part of her day.

Mayten breathed deeply as other family members funneled into the kitchen and began taking their seats. With her family surrounding her, her job well done, and the warm delicious food her da made, she was glad the king had given her time to be with her family—

A knock on the door interrupted her thoughts. Everyone looked up, expecting the door to open.

But the door remained closed.

Mayten glanced at her mother. It was unusual for anyone to knock and not walk right in. Up here on the hill, the homesteaders always knocked and walked. Any of their friends from town would do the same.

Da went to the door, opened it, and spoke in a voice so low, Mayten couldn't hear. A moment later he closed the door and turned to them with a note. "It's from Solis."

Mayten frowned. Clan Leader Solis must have thought the matter urgent to have used a messenger.

Ma held out her hand.

Da paused, his brow wrinkling. "It's for Mayten."

The table went silent. Fear clenched Mayten's chest. What could the clan leader possibly want from her?

She took the message from her father and opened it. It was short and to the point. "She wants me to come see her in the morning. Ma, what's this about?"

Castanea shook her head. "I don't have any idea. We've heard something is going on in the Sun Clan, some kind of sickness, but we're still gathering information. I don't know why that would involve you."

Mayten lifted a brow. Was her mother telling her everything?

"I promise, Mayten," her mother insisted. "I have no idea. You'll have to find out in the morning."

CHAPTER TWO

After breakfast, Mayten dashed out the door and whistled for Anatolian. He trotted up to her with a grin, his tail creating a small breeze as it waved in anticipation. She scratched his broad head as they jogged along the well-trod path toward the center of town. "Good to be away from Taiwania's whining, isn't it?"

Anatolian gave a soft woof.

"Thanks for coming with me," she added, heart pounding as she thought about her upcoming meeting. "I might need your support."

Anatolian wove in and out of the trees, along the forest path, sniffing at plants and hoping to find squirrels to chase. She never tired of this run through the forest path down to town, no matter what mood she was in. Soon the tang of eucalyptus, the sight of leafy ferns, and the sound of birdsong gave way to the smell of fresh-cut lumber and the press of people going about their day.

Anatolian hugged close to her leg. A shipbuilder tipped his hat as he passed, and a baker smiled from her bread stall. This recognition had come about after the quest, and she was still not used to it.

The center of town was paved with stones and she slowed to a walk. Small houses stretched out from the circular center in rows, separated by cart paths. The houses were painted in pastel colors and flower boxes flourished under each window. If she could see the town from the sky like a bird would, it might look like the center was a square sun with rays stretching out in a horseshoe pattern behind it.

Cather's house was small, with a sign that read "Healer" over the door. The beautiful window box was filled with bright orange and yellow sneezeweed. Why did such pretty flowers have such an ugly name?

She knocked on the door, trying to slow her breathing from the dash down the hill.

Cather answered, her beautiful heart-shaped face drawn tight with strain. Strands of straight brown hair escaped from her loose bun.

"I need to talk to you," Mayten said. "Also, you look exhausted."

Cather smiled, giving Anatolian a pat. "I'm glad the week's over. You don't look so good yourself. Wanna sit outside? I've got to enjoy this weather before it turns colder."

Cather grabbed a sweater and slipped it on as she closed the door. They'd grown used to spending a few hours at the end of each week catching up. Cather's family were all healers and Cather promised to be one of the best healers in the clan. While Mayten had been charged by the king to train young singers, Cather's charge was to train healers for his program.

Cather took Mayten's arm and together they walked toward the river, Anatolian exploring along the way. Water glistened through the trees up ahead, sending a shiver of excitement through Mayten.

Since returning from her first quest to save the trees, the river always seemed to beckon, its tumbling waters whispering an invitation to adventure. The river ran past the lumber mill,

where the barges docked. She loved watching the barges float-
ing downriver to the sea, laden with furniture and other wood
products or fruits and vegetables to sell or barter to other clans.
Often she envied the barges their freedom to come and go.

"Away from the mill, please," Mayten said, itching to share
her news but not wanting to be in the middle of town. "I don't
think I can take any more noise."

She rubbed at the ache starting in her forehead.

Cather laughed. "The trainees are loud, aren't they?"

Mayten nodded. "I don't know what's worse. The girls and
their shrieking when we come across a snake or the boys and
their constant bragging about who's the bravest."

Cather grinned. "At least you get to be outside with them.
We do most of our training indoors."

She led Mayten away from the mill to a stretch of aspen
trees lining the river. The slender trees lifted delicate arms to
the sky, their leaves like silver coins dancing in the breeze. A
bench had been built there with a beautiful view of the bend of
the river. They settled on the bench and Mayten relaxed, breathing in beauty and tranquility. Anatolian left off exploring and
sat by her feet, his warm side pressed against her leg.

The river always made her think of her two oldest sisters,
twins who lived with their Ocean Clan husbands. They were
merchants, gifted in art and handicrafts.

"Are you thinking of your sisters?" Cather could practically
read Mayten's mind. They'd been friends since they were barely old enough to walk.

Mayten nodded, absently scratching Anatolian's ears. "And
their babies. They've got to have real personalities by now. I'd
love to see them."

The Ocean Clan was at least a two-day walk. Busy as she
was with the king's charge to train young singers and his

deadline of two years, a visit to see the twins and their new babies wasn't in the near future.

The twins had come home when Mayten left on her quest, worried that she might never return. They'd both been heavily pregnant and stayed to have their babies after Mayten arrived home. The boys would be three and a half months old.

"You should have heard Taiwania complaining this morning," Mayten said with a frown. "You'd think she was the only one who ever had to watch the littles."

Their family had lost two of the youngest during the year of the fever winter. Her favorite sibling, sweet Wollemi, was eight now. Taiwania always complained if she had to watch the littles—a little brother who toddled around pulling Anatolian's tail and generally causing havoc, and a baby sister.

During the fever winter, when so many children died, the clan leaders made a rule that children couldn't be named until they turned two years old. It was a silly rule as far as Mayten was concerned. It seemed superstitious, as if not naming the child made you less attached to them or protected them in some way. Maybe decisions made from grief weren't always logical.

And so her youngest siblings were currently unnamed. Privately, though, she thought of the littles as Aster the Toddler and Baby Maple.

Mayten pulled Solis's note from her pocket and held it out. "This came by messenger to our door after class yesterday."

Cather took the note, gave Mayten a glance, then read. When she'd finished, she handed the note back without saying a word.

Mayten could see her own concern—and confusion— mirrored in Cather's eyes.

"What could that be about?" Cather asked.

"I don't know. I don't think I've done anything wrong."

"Maybe she wants to tell you what a good teacher you are." Cather rolled her eyes. Solis was not known for doling out compliments.

Mayten laughed. "That would be the day."

"What did your ma say?"

"She swore she didn't know anything about it."

Cather chewed her bottom lip. "If your ma doesn't know, it can't be that important, right?"

Mayten nodded. Cather was probably right. Maybe Solis wanted to see how the new training program was going. Maybe Cather would get a note as well.

Cather laid a hand on Mayten's arm. "Come by after you talk to her. I'm dying to know what she wants."

"Me too."

Cather was the steady one in their friendship. She seemed older than Mayten though they were the same age.

Mayten breathed deeply, stretching out her feet as she gazed at the flowing water. Cather was right. This was not going to be a big deal.

Cather grabbed Mayten's arm. "I forgot to tell you. Tray might be home soon. Maybe even today or tomorrow!" All weariness left her face.

Mayten couldn't help but smile. Cather had been in love with Tray since they were little, but Tray had been clueless about her feelings until the three were called on the quest together. Now they were all googley eyes and giggles whenever Tray was home from his training as a quester.

They still had a year before they could stand at the big clan gatherings and announce their intentions but that didn't stop them from making plans.

Mayten suddenly felt awkward.

Cather winked. "I heard Kai might be with him."

Mayten's face warmed. Kai, the king's son. They'd seen each other very little since she'd returned from their quest. She was busy training singers, and he was off training as a quester with Tray and Tray's uncle, Adven.

If he came home soon, they might have a few days to spend together before training started up again or he was called off on another quest.

She thought about her brother Oleander's glowing face as he'd left to go see his intended after breakfast. Would she ever feel that way about someone?

Her first meeting with Kai hadn't been a good one. He'd come across her and Cather washing off road dust in the king's pond—a big no-no, though they hadn't known it at the time. He'd been sent with them on the quest and they'd gotten to know each other. Surprisingly, she'd found herself enjoying his company. He was pleasant enough most of the time—as long as no one called him "Thomas."

His father, King Thomas Redmond, had named all of his children after himself, then given them fruit-based nicknames.

Kai's nickname was Ki, short for Kiwi. When he told her his nickname, he'd sworn her to secrecy, so of course she'd told Cather immediately. He'd eventually forgiven her, accepting the nickname, though he insisted that everyone call him Kai.

Just thinking she might see him soon made her stomach flutter. "You'll let me know, won't you? If they do come home."

"Of course."

"And you'll come to Aster's naming day?"

"Wouldn't miss it. Do you think they'll choose your name for him? What if they decide on something other than Aster?"

"I don't know, but I've whispered it to Da, so I hope so."

Cather gestured at the sun slipping through the trees. "It's getting late. I've got to go help Ma."

Mayten jumped to her feet so suddenly Anatolian woofed. He cocked his head, concern in his dark brown eyes. She gave him a pat and a smile of reassurance, though her nerves were strung tight as a fishing line.

Where had the time gone?

"I've got to run too. I'll see you after I talk to Solis."

CHAPTER THREE

Solis kept a small office in the left wing of the community center, a long building on the far side of the town center. At one end of the building stood the bell tower that sounded morning and evening.

Mayten had been to Solis's office once before when the questing team had been summoned to speak with the clan elders before leaving on their journey. That had been nerve-wracking, but at least she'd had Cather and Tray with her.

Anatolian pressed his cold nose into her hand. "Yes, I have you this time, though I don't think you should come inside."

His soft whine seemed to echo her nervousness. Taking a deep breath, Mayten relaxed her shoulders and approached Solis's door which stood open. She gestured for Anatolian to lie down and wait, then tapped on the door frame.

"Come in, Mayten." The leader's resonant voice always reminded Mayten of the woman's clan singer days.

Solis stood behind her desk, white curls framing her coffee-colored face. "Thank you for coming so early." She gestured to a chair across from her desk and they both sat down. The clan leader studied Mayten, then smiled. "Relax child, you're not in trouble."

Mayten blew out a breath. "That's good to know."

Solis laughed and Mayten smiled. It couldn't be anything bad if Solis was laughing.

The clan leader picked up a packet of parchment tied with a ribbon and handed it to Mayten. "This came for you. From the king."

"For me?" Mayten took the package. What on earth could the king have to say to her?

"Of course I peeked." The clan leader tilted her head as though expecting Mayten to object.

Mayten settled the package on her lap. She was more worried that the king might have moved up the timeline for starting the new school than upset about the clan leader reading her messages. "Triggensfeld tradition," Solis continued, "holds that any family elected to leadership can only rule for three generations. In fact, it's more than a tradition—it's a rule. Most people don't realize King Redmond's family is in its third generation."

Mayten knew about the rule, but she'd never thought about what that would mean for King Redmond, the only king she'd ever known.

Good thing his eldest son, Kai, was not interested in being king. He wanted to be a quester.

"King Redmond is still young." Solis tapped her desk with a finger. "But the training for future leaders, kings or queens, can take decades. I have not been alive for this kind of transition, but the records and songs tell us there is to be a 'competition' of sorts to find appropriate candidates—men and women, age fifteen and up—who are interested in training for the position."

"A competition?" Mayten's stomach flipped. The king wouldn't want her in the competition, would he? She wasn't interested in ruling over the three island clans.

"Yes, a culling, one might say, of eligible candidates from all the clans." Solis leaned forward. "The king was very impressed with your leadership and dedication in solving the blight problem. He has chosen a team of people to plan the competition, one from each clan. This team will find worthy candidates who will come to the summer solstice gathering for a final interview. Those candidates will then meet with the king. Those he deems worthy will move to the castle to begin training. After a year, the king will choose the most likely candidates to be his future replacement and present them to the clan leaders."

What did this have to do with her?

"He has chosen you to represent the Forest Clan," Solis added as if reading her mind.

Mayten's mind reeled. She had trouble sorting through what Solis just said. Her brain was like a saw, jammed in a tree, refusing to move.

Solis sat very still, watching her.

Mayten swallowed hard, trying to wet her mouth so she could speak. "I'm sorry. Could you explain that again?"

Solis sat back in her chair, her face as serious as Mayten had ever seen it. "I called you 'child' when you entered my office, but last spring at the calling ceremony, you became an adult in the eyes of the clan. By saving our trees from the blight you proved you are no longer a child."

Mayten jammed her hands between her knees and tried not to panic. The office that always seemed so large suddenly felt smaller than Anatolian's doghouse.

Solis gave her an encouraging smile. "The king goes into great detail about what is required in the message you hold in your lap. He is trusting that his three representatives— you included—will be able to fulfill this mission. You have proven yourself to the entire clan. I want you to know as clan leader, I have faith you are worthy of being trusted with this great honor."

Honor? This felt nothing like an honor. Impossible and terrifying were the words that came to mind.

Mayten's head spun. "But the school. Ma needs my help."

"I will speak to Castanea. We'll find help for her. One of the older students might be able to help with the training. If that's not enough, we'll lighten her clan duties for the season. I suggest you go home and read the packet. There is a lot of planning to do. You will meet the other two team members when you reach the Ocean Clan. Santana Merchant is from there and Anteny Weaver will come over from the Sun Clan. You three can plan how to proceed, but the king wants you to do a lot of preparation before you go."

The clan leader stood, looking directly into Mayten's eyes. "Will you do as the king asks?"

The question reminded Mayten of her calling ceremony when Solis had asked if she would join the quest. She had desperately wanted to say no then, and she desperately wanted to say no now.

When Solis made a request, however, there was only one right answer.

She'd learned the same thing about the king.

A king usually gets what a king wants.

She gulped and nodded, afraid to try her voice.

"Good. Come by tomorrow morning with an update."

Mayten stood at the obvious dismissal. Her whole body trembled as she moved toward the door. "Thank you, Solis," she managed to say before stumbling out the door.

Anatolian bounded to her side and she laid her hand on his head for support. "What am I going to do?"

"Mayten, wait!"

Cather's voice brought her out of her trance. Anatolian pressed close to her leg while she stopped and waited for her friend to catch up.

"We just had a meeting with our healing trainers and when it ended, I saw you coming out of Solis's door. What did she say? You look positively pale. Are you in trouble?"

Mayten looked into her friend's worried eyes. "Worse than trouble. King Redmond . . . He sent this package . . . Do you have time to read this with me? I don't know if I can do it alone."

Cather turned Mayten toward the river. "Let's go to our quiet spot. You look like you might need it."

CHAPTER FOUR

Cather sat on the bench while Mayten threw a stick for Anatolian who happily splashed in and out of the river to retrieve it. The sun was out and beginning to warm them. The rich, earthy smell of woodsmoke danced on the breeze. They'd read every word of the king's message twice.

"Each member of the team is to come with a list of questions," Cather said. "So step one—you make a list of questions for likely candidates."

"Can I ask for help making up the questions?" Mayten turned to the side as Anatolian—fresh out of the water—shook, spraying her with cold river water.

"Yes, it says you can have advisors from your clan," Cather said, scanning the pages in her hand. "And the candidates can be males or females, aged 15 and up."

Mayten frowned. "And the only requirements are that a leader must be of good character, strong of mind, body, and known for integrity."

Cather nodded.

Mayten threw the soggy stick before turning to her friend with a frown. "That's not much to go on."

"I know." Cather turned a page. "After you do the interviews, you and your team will create challenges to further reduce the number of candidates."

Mayten ran both hands through her rebellious hair and plopped down on the bench. "You will be one of my advisors, won't you?"

She hated the pleading tone in her voice.

"As much as I can." Cather flipped a few pages back. "I won't be able to travel with you to the other clans, though. I'm supposed to be training healers. Besides, I think your advisors should be older, like your parents or Solis or maybe Adven."

Mayten nodded. She gently tugged the stick Anatolian offered. The dog tugged back. "This is crazy. Let's back up. What's after the interview?"

Cather flipped pages. "After you and your team choose the best questions and hold the interviews, you three plan how you will determine final candidates by making up some challenges."

"He lists some ideas, right?" She clenched her teeth as Anatolian threatened to pull the stick from her hands.

"Yes, several. Physical games as well as talking to friends of the candidates to determine their trustworthiness, but he also says you don't have to use any of his suggestions."

"You'd better believe I'll be using his suggestions—if the rest of the team agrees. That's it? We go from clan to clan, ask questions, and pull off all these competitions? Then winners come to the clan gathering this summer, and the king does the interviews?"

Anatolian dropped his stick and shoved a wet nose in her lap. "It feels like too much, Cather. I was just getting the hang of teaching."

Cather put her arm around Mayten's shoulders. "It is a lot. But you don't have to do it alone. You'll have two other people. Remember what we learned on the quest? How do you walk ten miles?"

Mayten blew a stray curl from her eyes. "One step at a time."

She slumped back against the bench and stroked Anatolian's wet head. She wanted to crawl into a hole and hide. She wanted someone else to take the king's list and magically make everything happen. "I could choose to delegate, right?"

Cather scrunched her lips to one side and flipped to the last page, reading out loud. "'Mayten, I charge you with this project as I trust your intuition to help bring me the best candidates.'" She looked at Mayten. "That part is written in the king's hand."

Trapped. Just like she'd been trapped last spring when she'd been called to go on the blight quest. This felt worse somehow. This time she had an idea how big the king's request was. Last time, she'd been clueless.

"Cather!"

Mayten recognized Tray's voice. Cather leaped to her feet and raced around the bench as Tray rushed into her arms.

Mayten grinned. Tray's brown eyes sparkled with joy as he grinned at her over Cather's shoulder. He broke the hug and came around the bench, Anatolian barking and prancing around him.

"Mayten!" He pulled her to her feet and gave her a hug.

She pushed his spiky black hair out of his eyes. "You need a haircut."

He had to be at least an inch taller than the last time she'd seen him.

"Soooo glad to be home," he said, beaming. "We're dying for some home cooking."

Leave it to Tray to be thinking about food. Wait . . . "We?"

She tried not to look anxious.

Kai jogged up, smiling broadly. His golden-brown skin had darkened since he'd left the castle and started questing. His wavy black hair was pulled back from his face. A face she'd once seen as stern and haughty with a nose too big for the rest of his face. His eyebrows joined in the middle when he scowled . . .

But when he smiled, she saw perfection. His smile faded as he studied her face. He came to her, taking her hands in his, and looked at her so long she could feel her face flush with heat.

Tray moved back to Cather's side. "Your ma said you were out, and I figured you'd be here. We're starved and have stories to tell. Who do you think would feed us?"

Cather laughed, her face glowing with joy. "I'm afraid there'd be no food at my house. My folks had two emergencies at the mill today. A bad accident." She glanced at Mayten who nodded.

"It's almost time for the midday meal. Everyone will want to hear your news and we have news of our own. Let's go."

She headed up the path, startled when Kai took her hand. She glanced at him, noting his raised eyebrows.

Was he as insecure as he looked?

Mayten smiled and gave his hand a squeeze. Just having him near, her cold hand tucked into his warm hand, helped her relax.

As the king's son, surely he'd have some ideas about how they should approach this crazy assignment. Maybe he'd even be allowed to go with her.

CHAPTER FIVE

It took all afternoon, but Mayten's family finally helped her come up with a plan to present to her team.

"Are you feeling a little better now?" Kai asked as he and Mayten strolled through the orchards behind Mayten's homestead. The sun was about to go down, casting long shadows in the evening light. The smell of ripe apples filled the crisp air.

Mayten loved her brother's orchards. He had fruit trees, nut trees, and acres of vegetables as well. But the growing season was winding down and the trees were beginning to sport beautiful yellow, orange, and red leaves. Fall was Mayten's second favorite season after spring, but it came with a bit of melancholy as the trees prepared to hibernate.

She missed their happy spring voices.

"I think I am." Mayten realized most of her anxiety was gone. "Having everyone together and discussing the king's mission made me feel less alone."

After eating, her parents had stayed at the table for two hours, helping Mayten work out a plan. "Having that huge task broken down into priorities makes it feel less daunting."

"Your mother was good at wording the letters to send to the clan leaders."

Mayten nodded. "She definitely understands how clans operate. I wouldn't have thought to send letters in advance so the clans can gather candidates before we arrive. I hope my team likes the idea."

Kai stopped and turned toward Mayten, the setting sun turning the sky orange behind him.

"I'd love it if you could come with me." Mayten's face warmed. "Cather and Tray, too. Wouldn't it be great? It would feel like an adventure if we could all go, less of a chore, less—lonely."

Kai smiled, showing the gap between his front teeth that she loved so much. He brushed a curl off her cheek, sending a shiver down her spine. "It would be wonderful."

Was he going to kiss her?

He dropped his hand and turned back to the path. "I have no idea if Adven would agree to let me go. You know how he is."

Adven could be impossible when he set his mind on something. During the quest he'd been so eager to reach the castle, he'd barely let them stop for meals. She'd had to beg him for time to listen to the trees, a vital part of that quest.

"Maybe if *you* ask him?" Kai looked hopeful. "He's got a bit of a soft spot for you now."

Mayten laughed. Adven had despised her when they'd begun the quest—or so she'd thought. She still couldn't believe they'd ended up friends. Or something close to friends. "I'll ask him. It couldn't hurt."

The sky was darkening, and it was almost time for Thanks-Giving. Mayten led Kai back toward the front of the homestead where her family would be gathering.

"I never really understood what happened during that quest that brought you two together."

Mayten pressed her lips tight, unsure how much she wanted to tell Kai. When they'd been battling the traitorous tree singer, energy flowed between them all. During that time, she received a flood of memories from each person. That's how she'd known Kai was attracted to her.

That's when she learned Adven had once been in love with her mother and that he'd agreed to lead the quest only if Castanea did *not* go along. Turned out Adven's mother had been a tree singer and had run off with another man, leaving the family with a father who drank too much.

She sighed. "Let's just say we found out our differences didn't matter that much."

They walked along the side of the homestead, each lost in thought. Mayten let the peace emanating from the grass and late-blooming marigolds soothe her jangled nerves, breathing in the scent of healthy growth tinged with a hint of fall.

Finally, Kai patted his stomach. "It was nice of your family to feed me two great meals in one day. It makes my stomach very happy." He grinned at her. "I never feel full when we're questing. And it helps me miss my family less when I spend time with yours."

Mayten smiled, remembering all his siblings. He'd been so eager to leave, to train as a quester, she hadn't thought about how he must miss them.

"I appreciate the invitation to Thanks-Giving," he added.

"When you're home, who do you give thanks to?" She'd never shared Thanks-Giving with the king's family. There'd been no time. Plus the queen had been sick at the time.

"To the Great Leader." Kai gave her a wink.

Mayten gave him a wry grin. Everyone on the island said thanks according to their gifting and his family was gifted in leadership. Of course, they'd thank the Great Leader.

Leadership, though, was not a gifting one had to be born with. Like several other giftings, leadership could be learned.

"My family likes having you around." Mayten squeezed his hand. "So do I."

Kai turned toward her again. Her heart skipped a beat, then started racing.

"I just wish we had more time together." He bent closer.

Mayten closed her eyes, heart pounding against her ribs.

"Mayyytennn." Her mother's voice echoed through the apple trees. "It's time for Thanks-Giving."

Mayten's eyes flew open. Her cheeks burned as she led Kai around the end of the log building. They reached the porch and took off their shoes and socks, before moving into the circle barefoot to join hands with the rest of her family. The cold grass between her toes sent a shiver up her spine.

Taiwania raced down the porch steps and the circle was complete.

Her mother had baby Maple strapped to her back and Da carried little Aster on his shoulders. Wollemi clung to Mayten's hand. He grinned up at her, face alight with excitement. He'd always loved Thanks-Giving.

Evidently, Oleaster was off to his love's house. Soon he'd have a wife to add to their family. She smiled, enjoying the feel of Kai standing on one side, Wollemi on the other. Two of her favorite people.

Da gave Kai a welcoming nod. Then he cleared his throat and looked lovingly at each face. When Da raised his arms, they all lifted their joined hands toward the twinkling stars.

His warm voice filled the air. "Our feet are planted on the earth from which we came. Our hands reach to the stars that give us hope. We thank you for all that we have. And we trust you for all we have lost."

Da's voice broke as it always did when he remembered the two children who had died during the fever winter.

A lump grew in Mayten's throat. Her beloved friend, Hunter, had died during their blight quest. She'd led his last Thanks-Giving, one of the hardest things she'd ever done.

"For everyone and everything between the earth and the stars," Da continued, "we give you thanks, Great Singer."

"Great Singer," everyone in her family echoed.

"Great Leader," Kai said.

A tear rolled down Mayten's cheek. *"Great Hunter,"* had been Hunter's last words.

After Thanks-Giving, Kai thanked everyone for the second time. Then Mayten walked him back to the path. He'd been staying in the village with Tray's family.

"You'll talk to Adven tomorrow?" he asked.

"Sure."

Kai glanced at something behind her. Mayten turned to see her da standing near the porch with an oil lamp.

"I'll look for you tomorrow then." He dipped his head and started down the path.

Mayten sighed. Would she ever get a chance for that kiss? She walked back to the homestead and joined her da by the porch.

"He's a nice young man," Da said.

"Yes, he is."

"The king has given you a big responsibility."

Where was he going with this?

"I think you will need all of your time and energy for a while." His eyes, so serious, held hers.

Mayten stayed quiet, hoping he'd say more.

"You remind me so much of your mother at your age."

Mayten looked at him in shock. "Mother has always been strong and confident, a real leader. I'm more like you. I like to be home with my trees and my friends."

Da chuckled. "That might have been true before the blight quest, Mayten, but you've changed. I see all her traits in you. When it comes time, you need to find someone who is willing to let you lead, who will support you, be your champion, and lift you up when things go wrong."

Now she could tell what he was getting at. "Kai's like that."

"Kai is the son of a king. He's been trained to be a leader all of his life."

"Kai doesn't want to be king. He wants to be a quester."

"Love," Da placed a hand on her shoulder. It felt warm and heavy and reassuring. "He's trying this gifting on like a new set of clothes. Being a quester is new to him. Who's to say he won't miss being in charge when the shine wears off? Two strong leaders in one family might be—well, fighting for space is one way to say it. I just want you to keep an open mind. You are about to travel outside of our clan—"

"But—"

"I know, you've already made a journey to the castle and to the dying trees. Remember how it felt at the time. How you said it expanded your view of the world."

Mayten nodded. Everything had felt new and different. She'd learned so much. She'd grown.

"Well, now you'll get a chance to meet the Ocean Clan and the Sun Clan, each with a culture and ways unlike anything you have ever known. Keep your options open. You have plenty of time for romance." His eyes grew wistful. "Let yourself enjoy everything about this adventure. Soak it up, really let yourself live it. I'm so thankful your mother and I had a lot of adventures before settling down. We have no regrets."

Mayten hadn't heard much about her da's adventures, only vague references to his time on a ship. He'd eventually decided wind catching was not his gift.

"Why—?"

"You have an amazing opportunity here. I don't want you to go into it feeling tied down to one person, that's all. Just stay open."

She wanted to resist, to push back. But Da was wise, and he loved her.

Da squeezed her shoulder. "Just think about it." He turned, setting the lantern on the porch before climbing the stairs.

Mayten sat down on a step. Maybe she was being hasty. Maybe she *should* stop worrying about Kai. So much needed to be done.

CHAPTER SIX

Mayten woke up groggy, rubbing sleep from her eyes. Her dreams had been disturbing—trees trying to warn her of something . . . dark. There was a girl involved, but when Mayten tried to remember specifics, the details slipped away like mist in the sun.

The feeling of dread lingered as she walked slowly down the path to the village. The tree shadows seemed deeper. A breeze whispered in her ear, but she couldn't understand what it was saying.

She'd left early, intending to get her thoughts in order before facing Solis but found herself distracted by the shadows and breeze. She wore a woven lavender satchel from her sister Acerola slung across her shoulder. In the satchel were her letters to the clan leaders, her list of candidate questions to share with the team, and posters to advertise the competition—a different poster for each clan.

Between her dreams and the king's new order, she'd barely slept. At least she was prepared.

If things went as she hoped, the team would agree to start the selections here in her Forest Clan. Not only would she be among people she knew, the team could work out any problems before traveling to the other clans.

After her meeting with Solis, she'd track down Adven and ask if Tray and Kai could go with her when she traveled to the other clans. And if Cather could come—

Her confidence grew and she lifted her head, nearly breaking into a skip as the village drew close.

Tree shadows and whispering winds were all in her imagination, she decided. The morning was crisp, and the day would be fine.

She was ready for this.

People moved in and out of buildings, waving to friends and stopping to chat as they went about their day. Mayten waved and kept moving, not wanting to get caught in conversation before her meeting.

She was halfway across the town center, cobblestones warm beneath her deerskin shoes, when the door to Cather's house slammed open. Cather ran out, eyes red. She was hiccupping.

Cather never hiccupped.

Unless she'd been crying.

Cather stumbled down the steps and ran to Mayten. "You're not going to believe it, but Ma said I can't go with you. I can help when you're here if it doesn't interfere with the school, but she won't let me leave. I'm so sorry."

Mayten's heart dropped. Cather was the calm one, the one who kept her from losing her mind. Knowing they wouldn't be traveling together felt like someone had gut-punched her when she wasn't looking.

She struggled to keep her disappointment from showing. "It's okay. I plan to ask Solis if we can hold the first competitions here. If she agrees, I'll have you and my folks to help. At least you can help me get started. I'm sure I'll feel much braver after we've done it once. Don't worry."

Cather didn't look convinced. "Are you sure? I feel so bad."

"We have weeks before anything happens. Who knows, maybe your ma will change her mind."

"I hope so." Cather threw her arms around Mayten in a fierce hug. "Are you going to see Solis now? I'll walk with you."

They walked arm-in-arm the rest of the way to the community center, ignoring the growing hustle as the village woke up. When they reached the clan leader's office, Cather squeezed Mayten's shoulder and turned to go with what would have been a reassuring smile—if Cather's lips weren't trembling.

"I'll see you later." Mayten said.

As usual, the clan leader's door was open. Mayten tapped on the doorframe and Solis looked up.

"What have you got for me?" Solis waved Mayten to the chair in front of her desk.

Feeling more than a little awkward, Mayten stepped over to the desk and pulled papers from her satchel, laying them out in stacks.

"Questions," Mayten said, pointing to the single page on the left, then moving to the other two stacks. "Possible posters and letters."

"So organized," Solis said.

Mayten couldn't tell if the clan leader had just complimented her or was teasing.

Solis went through the questions, brow furrowed. Sunlight slipped through the door, highlighting the woman's tight silver curls. Mayten wished she could read the clan leader's expression. Stomach churning, she took a seat and struggled not to fidget.

Solis took her time, apparently studying each question. She moved on to the posters, setting each one aside after she'd finished reviewing it. She paid closer attention to the letters, one to each of the clans.

After what felt like an eternity, she set the last letter down and folded her hands. "This is a good idea—letters first, then posters, then meet with the team. Did Castanea help with this?"

Mayten nodded. "The king said I could get help, advisors."

"I'm glad you did. She knows how clans work. I will make sure these go out." Solis scooped the papers into a pile.

"Shouldn't I wait to ask my team?"

"No, as clan leader—and advisor—I can make this call. The clan leaders will appreciate it. I only have one correction. I believe the king implied you start with the Ocean Clan when he suggested you meet there and I think that's a good idea. Start with the Ocean Clan first. Then move to the Sun Clan. The Forest Clan should be last."

Mayten thought she must have misheard. "But I thought—"

"If you start here, you will be distracted by the school, your family, and your friends. You will rely too much on other people. I want you to rely on yourself and on your team. Therefore, you will go first to the Ocean Clan. I'll send these letters out today. Be ready to leave on tomorrow's trading barge."

"Tomorrow?" Mayten's heart clogged her throat, making it hard to breathe. She couldn't possibly be ready by tomorrow. "I need more time. Today's my brother's naming day, and tomorrow is school and Ma—"

"Your mother will be fine. I've found a girl to help with your younger siblings and there's not another trading barge for a week. Santana Merchant and Anteny Weaver will be meeting there too. They will make up your team. You have family in the Ocean Clan, don't you?"

Mayten blinked. "Yes. Two sisters, Acerola and Zigba."

"Fine, I'll send a note telling them to expect you. I've got things to go out on the mail barge today and will include the letters and the posters in my package. Now, you'd better go pack." She handed back the list of questions and waved a hand dismissively.

Mayten walked out into the sunlight, blinking as her eyes adjusted, unable to take a deep breath. She wanted to run back to her homestead, beg her parents to ask the clan leader for more time.

Perhaps her parents could come with her.

They'd never agree, of course.

Her only hope was Adven.

Adven lived with his two brothers and their families, though she had no idea which brother he was currently staying with. One of Adven's brothers was Tray's father. She would try Tray's family homestead first, on the outskirts of town, a bit up the hill.

She walked as though in a trance, replaying the conversation with Solis over and over in her mind. Loud squawking startled her from her contemplation, causing her to glance up. She found herself in front of a sprawling homestead with a large chicken coop standing close by.

Tray's homestead.

She'd met Tray's uncles and aunts and cousins, all living on the homestead along with Tray's mother, father, and three brothers.

A lot of mouths to feed.

The house was built in the tradition of the Forest Clan—low roof and an assortment of additions, expanding as the family grew. Unlike her own homestead which was built of logs, the building in front of her had wood-plank siding. Nice enough, but she loved the feeling of a log home.

She wasn't sure where she'd find Adven. She'd only visited Tray.

Taking a deep breath, Mayten climbed the porch steps and knocked on the front door, setting off a riot of barking. The door swung open, disgorging two medium-sized dogs, black and white with bobbed tails, eager to say hello.

"Hi Fritz, hi Frats," she said, scratching their ears. Both dogs grinned at her, their bodies wriggling with excitement.

"Mayten." Tray's mother stood in the doorway, looking surprised. Then again, the quiet woman always looked surprised, as if she was shocked to be surrounded by so many loud men and boys. "Tray's not here."

"Actually, I'm looking for Adven," Mayten said. "But I don't know which door is his."

The woman waved a brown dishtowel, darkened to near black in spots where it was wet. "None of them are here. They're all at the lodge."

"Thank you." Mayten turned away as the door closed, corralling the dogs inside.

Each clan provided a lodge for travelers and questers who had no family to stay with. According to Tray, the questers also used the lodge for meetings to discuss upcoming quests and share information they'd gathered. Kai could have lived there but Tray let him share his room at the family homestead.

She continued up the road, following a fork that led deeper into the forest, arriving at the lodge sooner than she'd expected. The log building fit her idea of what a lodge should be, sturdy and spacious. The forest grew close to the building itself, helping the manmade structure fit into the natural surroundings. Brush that sprouted sweet-smelling blooms huddled around the trees. A stone path led to steps and the front door.

She grinned, remembering how she, Tray, and Cather used to chase each other around the tables in the dining room. If the upstairs sleeping room was empty, they would make forts with blankets over the bunks until someone came to kick them out.

Voices rose and fell inside and she paused at the door to look in. A woman she didn't recognize was giving a report. She stood at the far end of the dining room, Adven leaning against the log wall next to her and several other questers gathered around. Tray and Kai sat with their backs to her, listening intently.

Mayten couldn't help but smile at the sight of the quester's grizzled face. His long, stringy hair brushed his shoulders and his ever-present hat covered one eye.

She'd seen Adven without the slouch hat only once, startled by the long scar that rippled across his left cheek at an angle to his hairline. The puckered scar closed an empty socket where his eye had been, compliments of an angry bear.

As if feeling her gaze, Adven looked at her, a smirk on his face. He pushed away from the wall and strolled towards her. The men and women in the room turned to see what had caught his interest.

Tray's face lit up and Kai looked like he wanted to leap up and follow Adven.

"What's my least favorite tree singer doing here?" Adven said in his gravelly voice. He waved her outside and followed.

Mayten wrinkled her nose. She knew for a fact she was the only tree singer Adven liked. "I need your help."

A wicked smile tipped his lips. In the past, that smile would have terrified her. "Tray told me the good news. You've really stepped in it this time, sister."

"I want you to come with me. Tray and Kai, too."

He laughed. "When do you leave, next month? A few weeks? You know we're basically at the king's disposal and can't make alternate plans without his approval."

"Tomorrow." Mayten held her breath. "I head to the Ocean Clan tomorrow."

She stifled a nervous giggle. Should she widen her eyes, try to look like Wollemi when he wanted a second sweet roll? She gave herself a mental shake. Adven would think she'd gone nuts.

"Tomorrow," he said so loudly heads turned. He kicked a rock.

She stayed quiet, afraid to say more. Hoping beyond hope that he'd agree to come or to let some of his questers come.

Adven started pacing, his boots kicking up dust clouds with each step. "The thing is, Sandy just came in from the Sun Clan. There's been some trouble there and I need to send a team to gather information. Kai is needed at the Ocean Clan for his sister's joining ceremony. He and Tray could join you for a couple of days but there's no way I can spare them longer than that. I'll need them with me when I reach the Sun Clan. They could help you get settled and oriented to the place. Maybe introduce you to some people. They've both been there before and could show you around. Would that help?"

He stopped pacing, looking down at her with his good eye.

Disappointment flooded Mayten again. Her sisters could show her around. She wanted *support,* someone she knew—someone who knew *her*—by her side.

She wanted Cather.

Mayten nodded. "That would help. Thank you." At least she'd have two friends with her for the first part.

And she wouldn't be traveling alone.

"Okay, fearless warrior, hang in there. I need to get back to the briefing." He slugged her softly on the shoulder and headed back inside.

"Fearless warrior, right." She started to kick at a rock, then thought better of it. No need to break a toe. If she wanted to delay the journey, she likely needed to break her skull—or at least a leg.

"Mayten, wait up!"

She turned to find Tray and Kai jogging toward her. "Adven said to come talk to you. Did he agree to let us help you with the competition?"

She studied their faces. Tray looked excited, but Kai was studying her face, and his eyes mirrored her concern.

"Solis wants me to leave tomorrow. Take the barge to the Ocean Clan. She wants me—and my team—to start there."

"Tomorrow?" they both said at the same time.

She nodded. "Tomorrow. Adven said you can go for a few days, but then you have to go on to the Sun Clan. Something's happening there?" She turned the statement into a question and raised an eyebrow.

Tray shrugged. "Some weird things are happening on that part of the island. We need to gather more information. See if we can figure out just what's going on." He seemed proud and excited, then caught himself. "I'm sorry we can't do more to help."

Kai took her hand. "I'm glad to join you on your trip to the Ocean Clan. My whole family will be there for my sister's joining ceremony. I'm afraid I won't be much help either. You can come to the ceremony, though. That would be great!"

She nodded, forcing a smile. The day had started so well.

"What about Cather?" Tray asked.

Mayten's smile faded almost as fast as it appeared. She shook her head. "Her ma said no traveling."

Tray's face fell. "I'd better go see her, then. The market barge leaves after first morning bell if they get it loaded tonight."

"Will you be coming with Cather to the naming ceremony this evening?" Mayten asked.

"Right," Tray said, pointing at her. He'd obviously forgotten. "I'll be there." He turned and dashed down the lane.

Kai took her hand. "Do you want me to walk you home, maybe stay awhile?"

"Thanks," she said, pulling her hand away. "But I need some time to think."

His smile faded.

"I'll see you tonight," Mayten said. "And we'll get to travel together. It will be good to see your family again."

He brightened. "It will."

Mayten walked home, her feet seeming to drag. She had so much to do before the barge left in the morning and no energy to do more than crawl into her soft bed and cry like a baby.

Fearless warrior indeed.

CHAPTER SEVEN

The evening passed in a flurry of activity. After Mayten told her family she'd been ordered to leave early the next morning, they decided to focus on the naming party first, then turn their attention to packing and preparing for Mayten's trip.

Tables and chairs borrowed from neighboring homesteads and delivered earlier were arranged outside for the naming day celebration. It was not a sit-down meal but more of a gathering with close friends and family bringing stews and breads to supplement the fruits and vegetables Mayten's family had in abundance.

Sweet and savory smells drifted around the bustling yard. Tray arrived with an egg dish his mother had prepared. Cather showed up with him, a tray of beautiful cheeses in hand. Her family must have bartered their healing services.

Mayten's stomach growled.

Kai had purchased hard candy from one of the merchant shops in town. He set a full basket on a side table and everyone—including Mayten—dug in. A real treat as no one in their clan produced sugar. It had to be imported from the Ocean Clan.

Da and Ma stood behind the guest of honor's chair, a toddler-size chair raised high off the ground that Ma had requisitioned from the carpenters. This chair had been through a lot of children, allowing each to sit at the table with the rest of the family.

Da placed his hand on the toddler's black hair. Ma followed suit as family and fifteen friends gathered around.

Mayten liked this part of the naming ceremony when the parents touched the child. It felt intimate although the ceremony itself seemed unnecessary. Her siblings were her siblings, not some unrelated children.

Da lifted his chin. "Let me introduce to you the beloved youngest boy of the Singer family—Aster Singer."

He winked at Mayten who clapped so hard her palms stung. Then it was time to eat and enjoy watching little Aster dive into his food and presents.

Mayten smiled as Kai walked over to her, followed by Cather and Tray.

"Happy Naming Day," Kai said.

"Happy Naming Day," Cather and Tray echoed.

"Thank you. Someone else is having fun, too." Mayten nodded at Wollemi who was busy helping Aster pull wrappings off his presents. A stack of hand-carved toys and crocheted and knitted animals was growing beside Aster.

Kai bumped Mayten's arm. "Naming Day at my house is a bit anti-climactic."

Mayten burst out laughing. "I never thought of that."

Naming the boys Thomas and the girls Thomasina would definitely take the suspense out of the ceremony.

Cather giggled and Tray gave a quiet snort.

Kai's ears turned pink, but he joined in.

Cather took Mayten's hand. "Tray told me you have to leave tomorrow. I'm so sorry I can't go with you."

Mayten hugged Cather tight. "Won't be the same without you," she whispered in Cather's ear.

"You have us," Tray said.

Mayten managed a weak smile. "Yes, and I'm glad of it. But . . ."

Kai squeezed her hand. "I wish we could stay with you." He looked like he wanted to say more but Tray slapped his shoulder.

"Adven wants us back. We'll see you in the morning, Mayten." He turned to go and then looked back at Cather. "Are you coming down?"

Cather looked at her friend then at her love. Mayten could tell she was torn between staying with her or spending some time with Tray before he left. Who knew how long it would be before he returned?

"You go, Cather. I've got to help clean up this mess, then get packed. It's okay."

Cather sighed, and gave Mayten a final hug. "I'll come see you off in the morning."

She followed the boys down the path, taking Tray's hand when she reached his side.

Mayten felt like a heavy blanket had just been dropped on her shoulders. It seemed they had all grown up overnight, with cares and responsibilities they never could have imagined.

CHAPTER EIGHT

For the second time in her life, Mayten found herself walking in the dark with her family as she prepared to head out on a journey. Last night, she'd found out Wollemi was also going. Her parents had decided to let him visit the Star Singer who lived with the Ocean Clan.

Last time, her hands had shook so hard she'd barely been able to lift her pack. This time, Wollemi's hand was the hand that shook, not hers. Knowing he was scared made her somehow feel braver.

Anatolian pranced around them all the way to town dashing to the front of the family and then to the back as if trying to keep them all together. Perhaps he thought he was the one going on the adventure, but Ma had not offered to let him go this time. With the classes, he was needed to help herd, protect, and calm the students.

Mayten would miss his gentle presence, but he might not have enjoyed being on the water. In fact, she wasn't sure *she* would enjoy being on the water. The family hadn't attended a summer solstice gathering since Mayten was ten, what with the fever winter and Ma always being pregnant. When they had attended, they'd walked.

They reached the dock just as the sun rose into the sky. Bells rang as though bidding them farewell. The chill air held the stench of wet mud and fish mixed with the scent of fresh-cut wood from the sawmill.

There were no crowds to sing them off this time, though Cather, Tray, and Kai huddled on the shore near the dock. At the end of the dock, a half-dozen bargemen worked hard moving crates and boxes and strapping them securely in place. These wares would be sold or traded to the other clans. She couldn't make out the men's faces in the dim light, but she heard their grunts as they tied down the load.

The barge was longer than she'd thought, with crates and boxes stacked like steps—up from the front, then back down in a flat-topped triangle. The flat profile reminded her of an arched door—rounded in front and square in the rear. There wasn't much in the way of sides to keeping crates—and people— from sliding off and she didn't see any seats.

Mayten felt extra thankful Tray, Kai, and Wollemi would be with her. The idea of getting on this odd-looking barge alone, with men she didn't know, shook her confidence.

Two men stepped off the dock in front of them. One was an older man the size of a bear with a grizzled beard and bulging muscles in his arms. The other was younger, perhaps in his twenties, with a lean body and high cheekbones and a strong chin.

"Time to load up," the older man said. "And just to be clear, we only got the news last night we'd be taking passengers and we already had a full load. So don't whine if you get to feeling uncomfortable."

He was clearly not happy to have them.

Ma stepped up, spine straight, and put a hand on Wollemi's shoulder. "I'm sorry to add to your load, Barge Master, but my son will be going as well. He can sit with his sister."

"If he falls into the drink, don't blame me."

Mayten shivered. Was falling out of the barge a possibility? Did Wollemi know how to swim well enough to survive if he went overboard? Did she?

"Don't mind Transom here," the younger man said. "No one will be falling overboard. I'm Rill. Who are our passengers?"

Mayten raised her hand, as did Kai, Tray, and finally Wollemi.

Rill grabbed Mayten's hand. "I'll take the pretty one and the squirt." He grinned at Mayten. "You two will get a front row seat."

Front row? Mayten's eyes widened as she pulled away to hug her family and Cather.

"You're in our hearts," each said as they made their good-byes.

Transom barked. "Enough already. You," he pointed at Tray, "you're in back with me. You're Adven's kin, aren't you?"

"Yes, sir," Tray said, hopping to the back of the barge.

"And you, Princeling," Rill said with a smirk. "You can ride on top of the load."

Kai scowled.

These two must have met before, Mayten realized, maybe on an earlier trip. That was the only explanation. Otherwise, how did Rill know Kai was a prince and why did he dislike him? The 'top of the load' did not look very comfortable.

Rill led the way down the dock, then jumped onto the barge, holding out his arms. Mayten lifted Wollemi to him, then handed him her pack and the hamper. She took his hand so he could pull her up, startled when he grabbed her waist.

"Get on up, *boy*," he called down to Kai.

Mayten frowned at the rudeness, growing more and more certain Rill and Kai had crossed paths before.

Rill showed her a long box short enough for her to sit on, though Wollemi's legs were too short to touch the deck. She propped her pack behind her back and did the same with Wollemi's and tried to get comfortable as Kai scrambled up to the top of the load, a frown on his usually placid face.

Transom untied the rope binding the front of the barge to the dock, then tossed the rope to Rill. He moved to the rear, untying the final rope and tossing it to Tray before leaping aboard.

And just like that, they were heading down the river. Rill moved from side to side across the front of the barge wielding a long pole that he used to push the barge away from the dock and guide the craft into deeper water. Once they cleared the docks, Rill lifted his pole out of the water and rested it against the cargo. He stood, hand on the front rail, his eyes on the river ahead.

Trying not to focus on the water slipping by, Mayten pulled Wollemi close on the seat. They both turned and waved at the family and friends on shore. Her throat tightened, watching her parents grow smaller and smaller until the barge rounded a bend and they vanished from sight.

Rill lifted his hands in the air and yelled. "Hiya!"

The barge surged forward.

Heart skipping, Mayten gripped Wollemi and glared at Rill. "What was that? What did you do?"

"Just encouraging the river to push us along." He turned and leaned against the railing as if commanding the river to make a huge barge speed through the water was no big deal.

It was her first chance to get a good look at the man. She studied his reddish-brown skin and sensual full lips, his short, cropped hair curled tight to his skull, and long thick lashes framing his eyes. His square jaw looked as if it had been chiseled from stone.

Mayten found it hard to take her eyes off him. She'd never seen anyone quite so magnetic.

He caught her staring and grinned. Her face flushed with heat.

"So, what emergency calls the four of you to the Ocean Clan with no warning?" Rill asked.

His loud voice grated on her nerves. He was likely used to shouting at Transom or other barge workers.

Mayten expected Kai to answer, but the prince remained quiet. Unsure how much she wanted to share with this stranger, she kept her answer short. "Kai and Tray are going on a quest. Wollemi and I are going to see our sisters."

Rill raised an eyebrow as if he didn't quite believe her. He crossed his arms over his chest, pulling his shirt tight and revealing a well-muscled chest and arms.

Lean but strong, she decided.

"Did someone die? Have a baby? Why the rush?"

"I'm going to train to become a star singer," Wollemi said, his voice thin in the river air. "Mayten's going to find the next king!"

She winced.

Rill pursed his lips. "Find the next king? How so?"

With a sigh, Mayten gave a quick summary of her assignment.

Rill listened intently, occasionally looking over his shoulder as though making sure they were heading the right way. He stared into the distance after she finished, apparently thinking about what he'd just heard.

Tray's voice rose somewhere in the rear, likely peppering Transom with questions.

She tried to relax and enjoy the view. The trees lining the shore slipped by, slowly changing from familiar to not-so-familiar.

Occasionally they'd pass someone traveling on the river path. Some people were pushing carts full of goods. Some traveled in groups, some alone. Once in a great while, threads of a tune would reach the barge.

According to Solis, the trip to the Ocean Clan could take two days on foot while the barge would only take five hours, including a stop for lunch.

"Interesting," Rill said, interrupting her thoughts. "Perhaps I'll apply."

"Pfft." She could picture Kai rolling his eyes, though she couldn't really see him behind her, perched on top of the crates and boxes. It was the first sound he'd made since they'd left the dock.

"What's wrong, Princeling?" Rill raised an eyebrow. "Don't want the competition?"

"I've no interest in being king," Kai said, obviously irritated.

"Good," Rill said. "More room for the rest of us. But I have one more question for the beautiful lady."

Mayten could almost feel waves of anger coming off Kai.

Rill's face turned serious. "How did a young lass like yourself end up with this huge responsibility?"

Mayten was trying to figure out how to answer when Wollemi spoke up. "She saved the forest."

"Saved the forest?" Rill said, looking her over from head to toe, then dropping his arms and straightening. "Wait! Are you the one who killed the evil singer?"

Mayten rolled her eyes. They could probably hear the man all the way back at the docks.

"That's her," Tray yelled from the back of the barge.

"I didn't do it myself," she said. "Kai was there. And Tray and Adven. There was a whole group of us."

Rill shook his head. "Wait until I tell the guys about this. Not only beautiful but brave and wise. I feel like I'm among royalty right now and I'm not talking about the Princeling up there."

Mayten felt her face flush with heat again, this time with embarrassment.

Wollemi glanced up at her, his face glowing with pride.

"I want to hear every detail of that story," Rill said, turning away. "Hang on!" He grabbed his pole, spinning to face forward. Ahead, the water churned and dropped, snatching the barge and flinging it forward at an alarming rate.

Rapids.

Stomach roiling and heart pounding, Mayten pulled Wollemi tight and they clung to each other as sprays of foam flew over the front of the barge, soaking them through.

After a moment she realized Rill was using the river itself to help navigate through the enormous boulders. He'd use the pole, pushing the barge away from a boulder when they got too close, then hold up his hand as if to physically move . . . move what? The boulders? The barge?

Was Transom doing the same in the back?

She'd rarely thought about the working of gifts other than her own. Watching Rill work with the river was fascinating.

Once she'd stopped being scared.

The front of the barge dipped low. Mayten stared at the water spinning in a circle. A twig caught in that circular current, spinning around and around, closer to the middle.

The twig vanished, swallowed by the angry river.

Wollemi shrieked.

"Whoa," Kai yelled.

Mayten glanced over her shoulder, sick with panic when she didn't see the prince. Hand on a crate behind her, she stood and breathed out a sigh.

Kai had pressed himself flat on the box he'd been sitting on. His knuckles were white from clinging to the rope that tied the cargo to the barge.

His face had gone pale green.

She sank back onto her seat, taking a deep breath as the barge rode high, then dropped again. In the rear, Tray whooped and hollered.

Wollemi started to giggle. Mayten watched his fear turn to glee, her stomach lurching with the barge's movement.

A nervous laugh burst from her lips and she found she might actually be enjoying the crazy ride.

Rill turned back to them, grinning widely. "Now, that's the way to ride the rapids!"

They all started to laugh, though Mayten cut her laughter short when she realized that somewhere above her, all she heard was moaning.

CHAPTER NINE

When the water calmed, the bargemen landed on a small beach for a meal break. The river road was nowhere in sight.

"Bushes are over there if you need them." Rill handed her the hamper, then pointed at the heavy brush growing between the trees. Eat while you can. It'll be awhile 'til we arrive."

Kai scrambled off the barge, heading for the brush. His face had gone from green to white.

Mayten and Wollemi found a fallen log in the shade of the pines. She handed her brother a hunk of bread and a slab of cheese from the hamper her da had filled. The scent of tree sap and duff calmed her. It was a lovely little area to rest in after being bounced around by the river.

She'd barely had a chance to relax before Transom ordered them back on the barge. The rest of the trip was a repeat of the morning with Rill asking questions, telling stories, flirting, and guiding the barge easily through each change in the river's mood. White water rapids or sluggish calm, nothing seemed too big a challenge for the capable bargemen.

After a bit Mayten found herself brooding over the dream she'd had last night. Something about that dream troubled her down deep, in the same way her spirit had felt troubled during her blight quest. She'd taken that journey to discover what was hurting the trees.

Her current journey was completely different. There was no danger—to people or trees.

Then why was this sense of dread still with her?

"Have you heard any news about the Sun Clan?" she asked Rill. "Any trouble they might be having?"

"Of course," Rill said. "Wave runners pick up news every time we dock. We share what we hear with the wind catchers and they do the same."

Wave Runners? Wind Catchers?

She'd heard her da speak of wind catchers, but had never heard of wave runners.

Rill must have seen her confusion. "Me and Transom are wave runners. Those with our calling generally man the barges. We know how to run with the river and how to encourage the barge to move faster. That's why we can get to places so quickly. Wind catchers serve on the big ships. The wind catchers know how to move the wind into a ship's sails and work with it. Manipulate the wind, so to speak, so their ships sail true. I imagine it's a bit like what you do with the trees."

"I see," Mayten said. Running and Catching didn't sound anything like what she did with the trees. She *talked* to her tree aunties and uncles. She didn't manipulate them.

She sighed. There were so many gifts she didn't know anything about. How was she supposed to interview candidates for the king when she still had so much to learn?

"The news from the Sun Clan is sort of mysterious," Rill continued. "Could be the water. The Sun Clan has had trouble in the past, running low on water. They don't get a lot of rain, like the Forest Clan or the Ocean Clan. I do know people have been getting sick, though no one knows why. That's about all I've heard. Heave to."

They rounded a bend and the barge slowed. Wollemi stood on the seat next to Mayten. She wrapped an arm around his waist, holding tight so he wouldn't fall. She gazed in astonishment at the docks directly ahead, an assortment of small boats and barges tied alongside each dock. Late afternoon sun glistened off the river, casting shadows that seemed to flow with the current.

Wollemi turned to her, his eyes wide with wonder. "I didn't know it would be so big!"

Mayten nodded. Not only were there more docks than she'd ever seen before, the number of people set her head spinning.

"Sorry to say that I must leave you all here," Rill said as he guided the barge up to a dock, deftly weaving between the other barges already there. "We can't get you any closer to the ocean. The big ships would likely smash us to bits. If you follow that road, it will take you to the Ocean Clan proper."

Anxiety swept through Mayten. She'd enjoyed Rill's capable manner and felt safe with him nearby. She clenched her jaw and straightened her shoulders.

Time to be an adult, take care of Wollemi, work on the king's assignment.

Transom leapt from the barge to the dock and quickly wrapped a rope around a short post. Rill did the same at the front.

Rill touched his forehead with two fingers in what looked like a salute. "I will see you again when I apply for that competition. Being a king would be an easy job and I wouldn't mind the rest. I could get myself a beautiful queen like you and spend my later years producing lots of children."

Mayten's face heated. She knew the job of king was not as easy as Rill made it sound but she didn't feel like arguing.

Kai scrambled off the cargo, leaped onto the dock, and took off down the road.

"You're welcome, Princeling," Rill shouted. He held out his hands and Mayten handed Wollemi to him. Her brother wobbled a bit, trying to stand steady after the movement of the barge. She handed Rill the hamper, pulled on her pack, and took his hand as she stepped down to the dock.

Tray slapped Transom on the shoulder and shook the older man's hand before strolling over to her side.

"Thank you both," he said, offering Rill his hand. "Please forgive my quest brother. He's just nettled you flirted with his girl."

"His girl?" Rill raised an eyebrow and glanced at Mayten.

She shook her head. "Nothing official."

Rill grinned. "Until we meet again, then." He gave her another salute and turned back to the barge.

Tray took her arm, picked up the hamper, and headed for the road. "What was all that about?"

Wollemi dropped behind. Mayten slowed to take his hand, really looking around for the first time. Besides all the boats and barges, there were people everywhere, in all the clan colors—the brown and green of her Forest Clan, the yellow and orange of the Sun Clan, the blue and white of the Ocean Clan, and some folks with no clan affiliation—all swarming like bees around the docks.

"Rill is harmless." Mayten said, feeling more than a little overwhelmed. Booths were set up along the riverbank where she imagined some of the sales and bartering took place. The smell of fish and fried food filled the air, making her stomach rumble. Voices rose and fell with talk of commerce, intermingled with joking and laughter. She wished they could stay and explore. She reluctantly turned her attention back to Tray. "He was just trying to rile Kai."

"Well, he sure managed that," Tray said. "I thought you two—had an understanding."

"Nothing spoken." Mayten tugged on Wollemi's hand. Her brother kept stopping to gawk at the people.

"I'm here to do a job for the king," she said. "I have to focus on that and not silly crushes."

Tray was silent as they followed the road away from the docks. The air grew quieter as they found themselves among trees—large maples, and oaks. The smell of ocean brine mixed with the cherry scent of the maples filled her with a sense of peace. They passed a lot of people coming and going. Some pushed wagons, some pulled carts, and some had animals Mayten had only seen in books—horses and mules—that must have been shipped to the clan to pull carts for the merchants.

"Look!" Wollemi said, his voice filled with awe.

They stopped and gazed between the trees where glimpses of blue could be seen.

The ocean.

Wollemi had been only two when they'd last visited the Ocean Clan. She'd been young herself and had only vague memories.

Mayten studied her brother's face as they continued walking. Judging by the joy in his eyes, he'd remember this visit for a long time.

Each time they caught a glimpse of the water, he shrieked. "It's so blue," he said. "It's so big!"

The road left the trees behind, revealing a broad vista spread before them. Long docks jutted into a sea so dazzlingly blue she could hardly look at it. Large vessels bobbed in the harbor, beautiful ships with billowing sails and carved figures on their bows, some women's bodies, some mythical creatures.

Her eyes must be as big as her brother's, Mayten realized. But she wasn't surprised. It was quite a sight, after all.

Beyond the docks stretched a sandy shore where children and adults played in the waves. She'd never seen so much sand! The shoreline near the Castle was rocky and constant-ly pounded by storm-driven waves. This shore hosted sand that looked so soft her toes ached to walk in it. Warm sun heated her head.

"I want to swim!" Wollemi said. "Please!"

"I'm sure we'll have a chance to swim," Mayten said with a reassuring smile. "But first we must find the twins."

The road curled away from the vista and up a short hill. She paused to catch her breath at the top of the hill, surprised to find the town center so different from what she was used to. Here one broad street ran along the base of small hills with rows of shops branching off like a tree. Homes rose on the hills, surrounding the center like protective arms.

"Is this it?" Wollemi asked. "Is this where the Ocean Clan lives?"

"Yes," Mayten said. "It's where our sisters live."

"I just thought it would be bigger, especially with all those ships and stuff."

Mayten touched his curls. "You know the island isn't big enough for cities. Just the three clans—Forest Clan, Ocean Clan, and the Sun Clan—along with the Castle Keep."

Wollemi nodded. "I want to see them all."

Mayten smiled at her brother's fearlessness. She'd not been like that before her first quest.

The air felt soft against her skin and smelled of exotic flow-ers that seemed to grow everywhere, dotting the world in pur-ples and pinks.

The trees were different too. Towering palm trees mixed with a variety of plants and strangely shaped hedges. The hedges reminded Mayten of the king's garden at the Castle Keep. The king's daughter Nan had shaped those hedges into fantastic animal figures.

They reached the first row of shops and Tray stopped. "Do you know where your sisters' shop is?"

"I'm sure we can find it," Mayten said. "They are crafters and it's a small shop. I'll ask around. A pair of twins married to brothers can't be too common."

"Great." Tray handed her the hamper, looking relieved. "I need to get up to the Questing Lodge. I'll check in with you later."

"Tray." Mayten stopped him. "Please tell Kai that Rill was just joking. I didn't mean to hurt his feelings. And I'm hoping to see his family."

Tray nodded and took off at a jog.

Mayten headed for the closest shop. Teas and herbs hung in bundles from the ceiling, filling the air with a spicy aroma. That should have made the shop pleasant. Instead, the interior felt dark and close. The odd sense of foreboding that started with her dream crept over her, urging Mayten to leave the shop, to step outside and bask in the sun.

An older woman with a broad backside stood behind what appeared to be a sales counter. She wore an apron over her clan clothes.

"Excuse me," Mayten said, her eyes adjusting to the dim light. She pulled Wollemi behind her, moving out of the way of a young lad who had his arms full of small packages.

"Yes?"

"I'm in search of my sisters, Acerola and Zigba. They're twins and own a—"

"I know who they are," the woman said in a harsh voice. "Are you the one the king sent to find the candidates? The one who saved the forest?"

Mayten nodded, not knowing what to say. The lad stopped at the front of the shop, listening.

She swallowed, trying to wet her suddenly dry throat. "I'm here to meet the rest of my team. Could you point out my sisters' shop, please?"

The woman turned to the boy. "You hear that, Owen? She's the one who comes from the king. This slip of a girl. Who'd of thought it?"

Owen nodded and took off running. After a moment, she heard him shout. "She's here, she's here, the king's girl is here!"

Mayten's stomach tightened. "Merchant?"

The woman stepped up and took Mayten's hand. The merchant's hand was small and papery, dark from the sun. She tugged Mayten toward the back of the shop.

"You must be tired from your long voyage. Come, sit for a minute, and have a drink. I make a special juice that is good for restoring your energy."

Mayten glanced at Wollemi who shrugged. Maybe this was part of the clan culture, she decided. Invite strangers in and serve them right away.

She'd have to ask her sisters.

Though Mayten wanted to find the twins before doing anything else, she also didn't want to give offense. They followed the woman to the back of the store where a small table and chairs sat waiting. The woman practically pushed Mayten into a chair, gesturing at Wollemi to sit in the other. Without a word, she set out two glasses, filled them with something thick and orange, and placed slices of a cake that smelled like spices in front of them.

"You don't need to go to such trouble," Mayten said, trying to keep the dismay from her voice. "We just need to find our sisters."

"Eat," the woman ordered.

Mayten and Wollemi shared a look. They lifted their glasses and sipped. It was a fruit juice—sweet, cool, and delicious—that Mayten had never tasted before.

"This is good," Wollemi said. "What is it?"

The woman ruffled his hair as he started shoving large bites of cake into his mouth as if he hadn't eaten all day. For a growing boy who hadn't eaten since lunch, it probably felt that way.

"It's mango juice, a clan specialty. And the cake is spice cake. My name is Coriander Merchant. I didn't get yours."

Mayten had just put a forkful of cake in her mouth. She quickly took a sip of the thick juice and swallowed. "I'm Mayten Singer and this is my brother Wollemi. Thank you for your kindness. This is a welcome gift after our journey."

Coriander smiled, hands on her generous hips as she observed them. "You'll be looking for likely youngins for the contest, right? Well, I want to recommend my two daughters, Cumin and Pepper."

Mayten tried not to choke.

"Cumin is tall and strong and whip smart," she continued. "Pepper is pretty as a picture and good at cooking and sewing. They are fifteen and sixteen and I hope you'll think kindly of them when they come to apply."

Looked like this hospitality was more about introducing the woman's daughters than it was about welcoming strangers. A commotion at the front of the shop caught the merchant's attention. People were gathering outside, squinting into the dark interior.

Mayten leaned over to Wollemi. "We'd better get out of here," she whispered.

He shoved the rest of his cake in his mouth. When Mayten stood, he grabbed her leftover cake and shoved it in his pocket.

"Thank you, Merchant. I'm afraid we must be going. My sisters are expecting us." Mayten shouldered her pack, lifted the hamper, and grabbed Wollemi's hand, towing him toward the front of the shop.

Coriander followed close on their heels. "Cumin and Pepper. You'll remember, right?"

"Of course," Mayten said, dragging Wollemi into the sunlight. The crowd of people—dressed primarily in blue and white—parted for them.

"Welcome to the Ocean Clan," someone said.

"Hello, I'm Hering," said a man with a broad chest.

"This is my son Cotton," said a woman as she thrust her child forward.

Mayten pulled Wollemi close as the people crowded around. One young man stood flexing his muscles. A young woman did a running flip, almost kicking a boy in the head.

Mayten glanced around, frantically looking for an escape and trying not to panic.

"Get back, get back," a familiar voice said.

Mayten sagged in relief as a tall woman muscled through the crowd. Her sister Zigba with Acerola at her heels.

Acerola threw an arm around Mayten's shoulders and raised her voice, addressing the crowd. "Is this any way to welcome our guests? Now let them be. They've had a long journey, and they need to rest. I'm sure Mayten will let you all know very soon when the interviews will start. Until then, let us have some time with our family."

The crowd dropped back as Mayten and Wollemi were ushered up the hill.

Mayten glanced back over her shoulder. Coriander stood outside her shop, a smug smile on her face.

The twins led them away from the town center, down a cart path that wound between houses. She was startled to realize the houses basically looked the same—all made of beige-colored mud with dome-shaped roofs.

"You two sure know how to make an entrance!" Zigba said with a wink.

Mayten had to agree. If their greeting was any indication of what was to come, she definitely had her work cut out for her.

CHAPTER TEN

Mayten breathed deeply as she sat around the table with Wollemi and her sisters after a wonderful evening meal. Their husbands had gone to close the shop and ready it for the morning.

Zigba and Acerola were identical twins. Both had toast-colored skin with a light smattering of freckles across their noses and brown curls they kept pulled back in handkerchiefs.

Just like Wollemi's freckles, Mayten realized. With her sisters gone for so long she'd never really noticed her brother's resemblance to the twins.

Zigba finished clearing the table, grabbed a folded paper off the counter, and sat back down, handing the paper to Mayten. "This came for you this morning."

She had a small scar on her upper lip. Without that scar, Mayten wouldn't be able to tell her twin sisters apart.

Suddenly, she found herself thinking about Hunter, the woodsman who had died on their quest last spring. He'd had a crush on Zigba long ago. Her chest ached thinking about the good-hearted man.

"Me?" Mayten took the letter, staring at the wax seal with a sun pressed into it. "I just got here."

The letter had her name scrawled across it. She looked at her sisters who shrugged.

Mayten broke the wax seal and unfolded the paper. "We regret to inform you that Anteny Weaver will no longer be able to join you in fulfilling the king's request," she read out loud. "Anteny has taken ill. We would send a replacement but there are currently a lot of sick people here and we are unable to find a suitable replacement at this time. With best wishes. Joshua Leader. PS: We hope you will consider joining us after your time with the Ocean Clan. We could use your help."

Mayten looked up, dread seeming to darken the warm kitchen. "What on earth is going on? I keep hearing about something bad happening in the Sun Clan. Have you heard anything? Do you know what kind of sickness it is? I'm not sure we should go if everyone is getting sick."

Acerola shook her head. "We don't know. We keep hearing bits and pieces, but nothing definitive. *Something* is causing people to fall sick. I think you should stay away."

"What if it's like the fever winter?" Zigba added.

Mayten's stomach churned just thinking about the fever winter. She sat back in her chair, rereading the missive. "He's asking for my help, but I know nothing about healing. How could I help?"

The twins shrugged again.

Mayten exhaled, forcing herself to think. "I still have Santana Merchant to help me. Can you introduce me to her tomorrow?"

The twins exchanged a glance and anxiety clawed its way up Mayten's spine.

"Santana is engaged to a Sun Clan man. She went for a visit and was supposed to be back by now. No one has heard from her."

Mayten swallowed hard. Who would help her if Santana was sick? Her hands shook.

Acerola reached out, laying her hand on Mayten's. "You've got your family. We're here to help however we can."

Mayten blinked rapidly, nodding. "Thank you."

"Always wanted to save the day," Zigba said, obviously trying to shift the mood. "What can we do to help you with this quest?"

"Quest?" Mayten hadn't thought of the assignment as a *quest*.

Acerola picked up where her sister left off. Finishing each other's thoughts was a long-time habit of theirs. "The king sent you away, traveling far from home on a mission to find candidates for his training program, isn't that correct?"

"I guess so."

One of the babies cried from the baskets near the twins' feet. As one, the twins bent down, lifted the boys who stretched and yawned, and efficiently attached them to their breasts.

Mayten had almost forgotten the babies, they'd been so quiet.

"That sounds like a quest to us," Zigba said, completing her sister's thought.

"I guess it is," Mayten said. What would the king say if he knew her team had gone from three to one? Would he want her to continue?

Relief swept over her in a giant wave as she remembered the joining ceremony. She'd ask him then. Hope fluttered in her chest. Maybe he would postpone the whole thing.

Her sisters waited patiently. Sounds of suckling babes filled the room. She could sit here for the rest of the night listening to those sounds.

Joining ceremony or not, she still had a job to do.

Mayten swallowed a sigh. "We were supposed to interview the applicants. I've got a list of questions . . ." An image of the spice merchant's face flashed through her mind. "I need a place to conduct the interviews. Someplace private. After everything that happened today, I think it's better if we're not out in public."

"You can do it here," Acerola said.

"While we're at the shop," Zigba agreed.

"Thank you." Mayten smiled at her sisters. That was one worry off her mind. "Then we were supposed to talk to people who know the candidates, ask them for references, you know—"

Both her sisters' foreheads creased and their mouths turned down.

"What?"

"You saw what happened today," Acerola said.

"Their friends won't tell the truth," Zigba added.

"Then what should I do?" She'd thought checking references would be a great way to cull the candidates, especially if there were a lot of applicants.

She'd also thought she'd be working with a team.

Both women looked thoughtful. Suddenly, they turned to each other and smiled. "Mantica!" they said at the same time.

"Mantica?" Mayten echoed, mystified.

"She's a wise old woman," Acerola said.

"Lived here forever," Zigba said.

"Knows everyone," Acerola said.

"She'll tell you the truth," Zigba said. Both women unlatched their babies and put them on their shoulders to pat until the boys both burped and were attached to the second breast.

Mayten's shoulders relaxed. Talking to one old woman would be much simpler than trying to interview all the candidates' friends and relatives. She nodded.

"What about me?" Wollemi gave her that look, the look that pleaded with her to remember something they'd already talked about.

"I'm sorry, Wollemi," Mayten said. He'd been so patient. She looked at each of her sisters in turn. "Wollemi would like to swim in the ocean."

"Don't forget about the star gazer," Wollemi reminded her.

Mayten rubbed his shoulder. "Ma said there was someone here Wollemi might talk to about possibly training with, someone who is an expert with the stars."

Acerola nodded. "As far as swimming goes—the bakers next to our shop have two boys who love to swim. I'm sure he can swim with them." She nodded at Wollemi. "Are you a good swimmer?"

He nodded, wide-eyed. "I love to swim."

"He played in the lake with Anatolian for hours last summer." She'd almost forgotten that trip to a nearby lake.

"And we can introduce him to the star gazer on our way to the shop," Zigba said.

"Yippee!" Wollemi bounced once in his chair. Then he yawned so wide Mayten couldn't see his face.

"Time for bed," Acerola said, unlatching her babe and burping him again.

"You've had a long day. Swimming will wait until tomorrow," Zigba agreed as she did the same.

Mayten couldn't argue with that. The day of travel and the news about her team had knocked her down hard. She'd love to sleep.

A knock sounded at the door and Acerola jumped to her feet. She pulled the door open, revealing a glum-looking Kai.

"Hello, Prince Thomas. Good to see you again. Would you like to come in?" The sisters had met Kai when he'd come back from the quest with Mayten.

Mayten saw him wince. He'd confided to her that he enjoyed being away from the castle and being called by his nickname Kai, instead of Thomas, as it seemed to separate him from his father and from being a prince.

"No, thank you. May I speak to Mayten for a minute? I won't keep her."

"Of course." Zigba beckoned to Mayten and turned back to the table.

Mayten approached slowly, embarrassed about what had happened with Rill. She could tell by Kai's pinched face he was still angry.

"Kai, I—"

"My father wanted me to make sure you'll come to the joining ceremony tomorrow at noonday." He said this fast, as though he couldn't wait to be gone.

"That's very kind," Mayten said. "I'd love to come. And Kai—"

"I'll come get you." He turned and strode out into the night.

Mayten watched him go. She had hurt him and hadn't meant to. She wanted to run after him, but decided not to. Maybe he just needed time to calm down.

A good night's sleep would be best. Otherwise, she might say something she'd regret and make the situation worse instead of better.

CHAPTER ELEVEN

Mayten woke with a start. Had someone called her name? No one was there but she had that same feeling of disquiet.

The twins had left with their husbands, Wollemi in tow, after a chaotic breakfast. When they were all gone, she'd climbed back between the soft sheets of the bed she'd shared with Wollemi and dozed.

A soft purring sound drew her attention and she found an orange cat snuggled close to her side. She hadn't known the twins had a cat. "Hello there. Who are you?"

She rubbed the soft fur, and the buzzing purr grew louder. "Aren't you a sweetie."

Resting her hand on the cat's warm body, she let her mind wander over the past few days, lingering on the upcoming joining ceremony.

King Redmond was quite a character with his rust-red beard, broad nose, and booming voice. He had the same cute gap between his front teeth that Kai did.

The queen had been sick during their visit to the Castle, but Mayten had met all the children. She smiled.

"Let's see if I can remember all of them," she said to the cat.

"The eldest daughter, the one getting married today, is Cherry. Her hair is the same rust red as the king's beard." Had Cherry met her sisters yet?

She held up one finger and continued.

"Kai is the oldest son. Then there's Nan, short for Banana. I can't wait to see her." She ruffled the cat's ears. "She hated me at first, you know."

During the quest, a lot of people seemed to dislike her. It had taken her some time to understand why. Except for whispered gossip about witches and magic, tree singers were unknown to most everyone outside the Forest Clan.

"Nan is not pretty like her sister—she has large, buck teeth—but she is brilliant. She's a botanist, you know. Came up with the idea of sharing methods and techniques of how the different gifts are used and adding in the science that might affect each gift."

She couldn't wait to hear how the preparations were coming at the castle.

The cat pushed her ribs with a paw as if asking her to continue. Mayten chewed her lip, struggling to remember who was who in the king's family litany. "Then there is Blue, short for Blueberry. He's about Wollemi's age. Then come the twin girls, Lemmy and Limey, and a little boy—what was his name?"

The cat meowed.

"Raz! That's right—for Raspberry. And there's a newborn baby girl, little Plum."

She grinned at the cat. "That's all of them, except for the queen. I never learned the queen's name."

Cather had spent most of her time trying to help the queen. She should know the queen's name.

The front door slammed open and footsteps pounded down the hall. Wollemi threw open their bedroom door, a triumphant look on his freckled face. "I knew it! Zigba said you'd be up, but I said you might be lazing. It's time to get ready to go to the ceremony. Hey, where'd you get a cat?"

He dashed up to the bed and ruffled the cat's fur.

"He—or she—was here when I woke up."

He snuggled his face into the cat's side. "I miss Squeaker."

Squeaker was Wollemi's tabby cat, who loved to chase mice through the fields. Wollemi loved that crazy cat, mice and all.

The orange cat stood, stretched, then hopped off the bed and marched away as though he—or she—had had enough cuddling for one day.

Wollemi watched the cat go, then turned back to Mayten. "The twins said the queen's daughter invited them to the ceremony and they'll meet us there. I get to go, too! Now get up, lazy."

Mayten laughed. Had she ever been that energetic? She could use a bit of that now. She threw off the covers. "The twins get to come? And you?"

He nodded. "The man getting married is a friend of theirs and he invited them. When he found out about us being here, he invited me too! Acerola said you'd fix me up."

Mayten took a closer look at her brother. He was wet, not dripping wet but wet enough. His swimming suit had dried with a white crust. She reached a finger out and touched his face. "Looks like someone fulfilled your swimming request."

Wollemi nodded, his head bobbing up and down so fast she thought it might fall off and roll away. "The water has salt in it! I got some in my nose and it burned. But the waves are fun to jump, and Terrell showed me how to lie flat and ride the waves to shore!"

Someone had told her the ocean was salty, but she'd never experienced it herself. "We'd better get you washed."

She led him to the washroom and was surprised to see no bathtub but something like a metal disk coming from the ceiling. When she turned a handle, water streamed from it. It was cold, but it would work. Wollemi stripped down and jumped in and out of the stream, shrieking loudly. He rubbed at the salt, trying to get clean while Mayten found him some appropriate clothes.

She helped him dry and attacked his wild curls. A futile task. The curls would spring up as soon as they dried, but she had to try.

She changed into her dress, thankful her mother had insisted on her packing more than pants. She added her clan apron. Both had survived the trip mostly unwrinkled.

No time to re-braid her hair, so she undid the braids and found some oil to finger comb through her curls. Her hair fell in spirals down to her shoulders and looked decent enough. She'd have one of the twins braid it later.

Then she rubbed the oil into her arms, legs, and face and chased Wollemi until he stood long enough for her to rub some on his face.

They were pulling on shoes when they heard a knock at the door. Mayten fastened her last sandal, then rushed to open the door. Kai stood outside, looking regal. He'd tied his long black hair back, and wore a soft pair of white pants topped by a billowing white shirt, the long sleeves and neckline bright with embroidery. They stood, staring at each other.

"You look . . " Mayten stuttered. "Good."

"And you," Kai said. He clamped his mouth shut, frowning in a way that made his thick eyebrows turn into one long line. So, he *was* still mad at her.

"What about me?" Wollemi jumped up and down next to Kai, oblivious to the tension.

"You look great." Kai smiled and took Wollemi's hand, leading him down the walk. Mayten closed the door and rushed after them down the flowered path and up the hill toward a stand of palms and other exotic trees.

Wollemi adored Kai, one of the reasons why Mayten had come to trust the prince. Her little brother had an uncanny way of judging people.

"I got to meet the star gazer today," Wollemi told Kai. "His name is Lynx and he's from a family of Star Gazers. Do you know how rare that is? He told me I could train with him if I want to, but first he has some tests for me to see if I have the gift."

Mayten was happy to listen as Wollemi continued. She enjoyed watching Kai's attentive face as much as she did Wollemi's animated face. The pair had developed a bond following the quest.

Wollemi's enthusiasm broke the awkwardness between her and Kai as the boy prattled on. It was hard not to laugh at his stories.

Mayten hadn't given much thought to their surroundings until she realized they were walking with a crowd of other people. Her skin crawled as people pointed and whispered. Fortunately, no one approached them.

They crested the hill, joining a line of chatting people. She was shocked to see such a crowd. Then again, this was the king's daughter.

Palm trees stood like elegant sentries around an arched entrance. Beyond the entrance, she made out an area overlooking the sea. The space was big enough to hold her entire homestead along with the community building! Wooden poles defined the large square. Each pole was adorned with a hanging basket filled with colorful flowers. Bees buzzed inquisitively in and out of the flowers.

Lilacs covered the archway, filling the air with their sweet scent. Mayten drew in a breath of their sweetness as she followed Kai and Wollemi through the arch.

Everything was so beautiful, so perfect . . .

A breeze whispered through her hair, brushing strands against her cheek, and everything around her darkened. A feeling of doom—the same feeling she'd had in her dream—swept away the sense of peace and joy she'd just had. A sudden desire to press her hand against a nearby palm started her feet moving back toward the entrance, but Kai's firm hand kept her moving forward.

Mayten drew in a breath, then another, forcing herself to remain calm. She'd never had a dream affect her so, but this was not the time to try and figure out what was going on.

Kai paused after they'd made it through the entrance, giving her a chance to pull herself together. She studied the tables piled high with food and gifts lining each side of the square. At the far end, the ground sloped down to a flat area where the ceremony would take place.

And her stomach sank. She'd been so busy with the king's assignment she hadn't thought to bring a gift.

Sunlight glinted off the ocean waves, sparkling like stars in the endless sea. The view washed the darkness away. She'd never seen anything so lovely.

She thought about the Forest Clan's community square. In contrast to what lay before her, her community felt small and drab and uninspired. The few joining ceremonies she'd attended within her clan had been small family affairs held on the pledging family's homestead.

This was so much more.

Then again, what was more special than the joining of the king's daughter?

In a far corner, musicians played stringed instruments, filling the air with sweet music that wove through conversations as people milled around, talking happily. She scanned the crowd, looking for familiar faces. Kai's hand pressed warm against her back as he pointed at a group gathered near the flat area and they walked toward it.

Children raced in and out of the crowd, heads crowned with rings of flowers. One suddenly stopped. "Mayten!"

It was one of the king's twins. Based on the green color of her dress, Mayten thought it must be Limey.

"Mayten!" a chorus of young voices echoed. And just like that she was surrounded by children hugging and tugging and grinning at her.

Mayten suddenly felt light as a sprig of spring grass, the last vestiges of doom brushed away. She bent down. "Limey, you look lovely. You too, Lemmy. Blue, how handsome you look! Raz, you've grown."

They all responded with such joy that Mayten's worries seemed inconsequential.

They had greeted her this way the first time she'd visited the castle and their love had confused her then. Turned out they'd never met a tree singer and were so excited. But they knew her now and still they wrapped her in love as only children could.

"Hey, everyone!" She waited until she had their attention. "This is my brother Wollemi." She pulled him close to her side. "He's about your age, Blue. Maybe you can let him play with you?"

Blue nodded as Limey stepped up to Wollemi and tapped him in the chest. "You're it."

The children ran off screaming, Wollemi running happily after them.

Mayten shook her head. Children were so accepting. They had none of the fear or distrust adults had.

"Mayten?"

Mayten spun at the familiar voice. "Nan!"

Kai looked troubled as Mayten threw her arms around the older girl who looked a bit taken aback. Nan was the most reserved person she knew.

"You look beautiful," Mayten said. She studied the botanist—the shapely gown flowing off her shoulders, the ring of flowers in her hair. She looked like a princess.

Nan smiled shyly. "And you look completely different."

Mayten laughed. She'd worn pants on the quest and had kept her hair pulled back out of the way.

"Agreed," Tray said, stepping up beside her. "You almost look like a girl."

Mayten smacked his arm playfully.

"Seriously," he said. "I didn't even know you owned a dress."

"And your hair's down," Kai added. He stepped up beside Tray and was trying to smile. "It's, it's . . ."

"Quite a picture," Nan finished. "How about you two let me have some time with my friend before the ceremony starts."

She dragged Mayten off to one side, away from Tray and Kai and the crowd.

"Do I normally look that bad?" Mayten asked.

Nan laughed. "They're just being boys. Ignore them. You look fine in pants. Now, tell me how the school is progressing."

Mayten laughed. "I wanted to ask you the same. Ma and I are training ten children. Only five of them are old enough to be considered for the school, though, and only two or three of those are showing real progress. Cather's family is helping train healers with about the same success. How is it at your place, Nana Banana?"

Nan's eyes widened. "I'll kill him. He wasn't supposed to tell you."

Mayten laughed as Nan glared at the crowd. "Did he tell you his nickname is Kiwi?"

Mayten nodded. "Actually, he's adopted Kai for short. He spells it K-a-i. I think he's glad to get away from the fruity nicknames."

"I guess I can't blame him for that," Nan agreed. "Anyway, Ma has thrown all her energy into planning the school. She's requisitioned a large building with different classrooms and a meeting hall. She's also planned dorms for the children to stay in. She seems so much better after spending time with Cather."

Mayten smiled. Cather had determined the Queen's poor health was due to having so many children combined with depression brought on by losing babies during the fever winter. She had given the queen herbs that could keep the woman from falling pregnant again. Now the queen had the energy to put into a new project.

"I can't wait," Mayten said as a horn blasted and the crowd fell silent.

"Oh," Nan said, oddly out of breath. "That's my cue. I'll see you after." She dashed off toward the flat area.

Mayten scanned the crowd until she found her sisters, Wollemi standing between them. They gestured for her to join them.

"I didn't bring a present," she whispered to Acerola.

"Don't worry. We put in a bunch of our handmade goods and added some from Da's hamper, so you're covered. We put your name on it too."

Mayten sighed in relief. "Thank you." She waited a heartbeat, then added, "You have a cat?"

Zigba smiled. "That's Pumpkin. And I'd say she has us. She just showed up one day and refused to leave."

Music started up, the stringed instruments joined by flutes and hand-held harps. A beautiful voice rose with the music, quieting the crowd in an instant.

Mayten's heart soared. No one else but Nan could sing like that. Nan had a voice like a nightingale.

The ceremony had begun.

CHAPTER TWELVE

Mayten and her family had a good view from the side of the gathering where the land sloped up a bit. The queen and king stood near the far edge of the flat area. A few feet beyond the royal couple, the land dropped away. Evening sunlight turned the peaks of waves into glittering diamonds.

The king grinned widely at the family gathered in front of him. Everyone was dressed in white. The men wore white pants and flowing shirts with embroidery along the necks and cuffs. Nan and the queen wore off-shoulder gowns and flowers in their hair. The men's hair was unadorned.

Cherry and her mate—a sailor if Mayten remembered right—looked like something from a fantasy book. The sailor stood taller than the king and had brown hair and skin along with a cleft in his chin but he didn't seem all that spectacular. The princess was exquisite with her cascading rust-red hair. Her dress flowed to the ground and was covered in beautiful embroidered designs.

But it was the look in her eyes that captured Mayten. Cherry glowed with happiness whenever she looked at her mate.

Did Mayten feel that way when she looked at Kai? She liked him a lot, but she was nowhere near ready to consider marriage.

The king's family moved into a circle, holding hands to say Thanks-Giving, signaling those nearby to form circles and do the same. Mayten looked for Tray, but he was busy with a group of men and women across the glade. Other questers?

After Thanks-Giving, the king and queen joined the sailor's parents, working together to tie a rope around the couple's wrists, binding them together.

The couple raised their twined wrists into the air and everyone shouted with joy.

Family members crowded around, hugging the new couple, laughing as the couple tried to return the hugs with twined wrists. Eventually, their wrists were set free, and the feasting began.

Mayten held her plate of food, cheeses, exotic fruits, sweet nut breads, and thin cuts of meat as she wound her way through the crowd. She was hoping for a chance to talk to Kai and smooth things out. She spotted him surrounded by a collection of lovely young women, who seemed more than happy to chat with a handsome prince. He glanced her way and his eyes met hers. He said something to the girls she could not hear and headed toward her. As he approached, she felt a hand on her arm.

She turned to see King Redmond's radiant smile. "Mayten, I'm so glad to see you. Can I pull you away for a moment?"

Mayten glanced over her shoulder as the king took her arm. He shook his head. "Thomas won't mind if I steal you away for a moment."

She raised her eyebrows at Kai, who shrugged as she let herself be led to an area set up with tables and chairs. The king held a chair for her, waited until she was seated, then moved to the nearest chair and seated himself. People glanced their way, whispering behind their hands.

Mayten was getting used to being an object of curiosity, but she didn't like it. She focused on the king and tried to ignore the gawkers.

"So," the king said in his booming voice. "How's everything going?"

Mayten's stomach clenched. "I don't know if you've heard, but both the Ocean and Sun Clan members who were supposed to join me here are unable to come. I was thinking maybe we should postpone?"

"What happened to them?"

She filled him in, telling him what she knew about the sick man and the missing woman. He rubbed his beard, a thoughtful look on his face.

"That is very unfortunate. I'm waiting for reports of what is happening in the Sun Clan. Any information I've received so far is as sparse as feathers on a baby bird. No matter. Tell me, what ideas do you have so far?"

Her stomach churned and her mouth went dry. She'd barely had time to organize anything. How could she satisfy the king? "I got here late yesterday," she finally said. "So there's not much to report."

"Nonsense," he bellowed. "I chose you because I knew you'd come up with a plan. Now, what have you got?"

Mayten took a deep breath. This was just like reporting to Solis, wasn't it? "I've come up with a list of questions to use while interviewing the applicants. Friends and family helped with the questions before I left home. And Solis approved them."

His eyes lit up.

"Letters and posters went out to the clans after Solis sent out her own notice letting the clans know I'd be coming."

He nodded.

"I put the age requirements from fifteen to thirty-five like you suggested and stated those requirements on the posters."

"Seems reasonable."

"I had intended to ask for references from the applicant's family and friends following the interviews, but my sisters recommended a wise woman in the Ocean Clan who knows everyone. We hope she will agree to help me cull the list."

She paused and they both stared out at the ocean. Finally, she drew in a breath and looked directly at the king. "Don't you think it would be better to wait until we can get a new team together?"

The king tilted his head back, a thoughtful look on his face. He tapped his fingers on the table. "Let me hear the rest of your plans. Then I'll decide. The wise woman sounds like a good idea. Friends and families aren't the best people to give honest feedback. An objective outsider would likely be better."

"That's what my sisters said."

"I met them," King Redmond said with a grin. "Your sisters, that is. You know I'm partial to twins. And that little brother of yours feels like an old soul."

He grinned in a way that made his otherwise large features quite handsome. The space between his front teeth made him seem younger, and his eyes twinkled like those of a mischievous child.

Mayten couldn't help but smile back. She'd been terrified when she first met him but she'd seen how kindly he treated his wife and children. He was a good man—and a good king.

"Continue," he said, the smile fading from his face.

"I was thinking of holding some kind of athletic games to challenge the candidates' physical fitness."

The king rocked back in his chair and tugged on his beard. Mayten held her breath.

He leaned forward and looked into her eyes, lowering his voice. "You know, Mayten, a leader doesn't need to be physically strong. Of course, a slovenly or lazy person won't do, but I'm more concerned about mental and emotional fitness. Someone who can lead others, but not out of arrogance. Patience, kindness, and integrity are important, but physical obstacles can be overcome."

"Should I not hold an athletic challenge, then?" Mayten wasn't sure how else she could find capable candidates.

The king laughed. "By all means, have contests. It will be fun. Good healthy competition always brings out people's core values. But watch your contestants closely. Don't let them know what you're really looking for: how they treat others, if they have anger issues, or if they're sore losers."

Mayten loved that idea.

"As for postponing—I think you should proceed. You have wise advisors in your family and your plan is sound."

Mayten's heart sank. A tiny part of her was excited about this challenge, though she still felt completely unqualified. "What if I choose wrong?"

The king patted her hand. "The men and women you choose will meet with me at the summer solstice gathering. They'll be rough stones, so to speak. I want you to bring me those with potential. I still have years to watch and train them before deciding on a successor. The clan elders will have a say too, but that's down the road. All you have to worry about is finding me a bunch of promising rough stones. Don't be so worried. I trust you." He smiled warmly and Mayten sagged in relief.

"Now, how is my son doing?"

Mayten stared at the king. Did he know about their fight? "Kai?"

The king tilted his head. "I've heard several people calling him that. You wouldn't believe how hard he fought to get away from his nickname."

Mayten laughed. "Ki is what he fought against. Evidently, adding an 'a' made a difference in his mind."

"But does he seem happy as a quester? Will he give up this silliness and come home?"

Mayten hated to disappoint the king, but she had to be honest. "He seems very happy in his training."

The king sighed. "We miss him. His mother especially. When he comes home, all he talks about is quest business and then he's gone again."

Mayten understood. She barely had time with Kai even when he stayed with the Forest Clan.

"It will be good for his mother to have him for a couple of days before we return." The king slapped his hands on his knees. "How are things between you two?"

Mayten sucked in a breath and felt her face flush with heat.

King Redmond laughed. "It's obvious he likes you, Mayten, or he wouldn't be hovering over there, waiting to talk to you."

Mayten turned and saw Kai kicking the dirt with his boots. "We, um, had a bit of a—disagreement, I'm afraid. I need to straighten it out."

"Then go. I'd be happy to have you as part of our family."

Mayten started to stand but the king took hold of her wrist. "You are young. You are incredibly gifted and have a great responsibility that will need your entire focus for the next few years. I love my son, but don't tie yourself too tightly to anyone right now."

"Yes, sir. My father said nearly the same thing." She stood, hesitating for a moment. "Thank you. For trusting me."

Mayten turned away, feeling better than she had since receiving the king's assignment. He seemed to have confidence in her.

And he'd said almost the same thing about Kai that her father had.

They were both right. She had a job to do. When this assignment was over, the school needed her attention.

Romance could wait.

CHAPTER THIRTEEN

Mayten drew in a deep breath and tried to relax, thankful her sisters trusted her with using their house. The rooms were quiet without her twin sisters and their babes. She'd been using the living room to interview the candidates, seating the candidate on the couch and her across from the couch in a chair. A low table sat between them with two soft chairs to either side.

Pumpkin curled on a chair to Mayten's right in the living room. The cat had attended each interview, serving as her silent partner. Mayten swore the cat was sizing up each candidate herself.

"This was harder than I thought," she told the cat. "Of the five candidates we've interviewed so far, two were tongue-tied, one spoke in a monotone so boring I almost fell asleep—and you did—and this last one was so full of himself I wanted to punch him."

She'd sent the last candidate home after a frustrating session where she asked the questions and he proclaimed his opinions. Or stared at her as though she were crazy.

Pumpkin meowed as if agreeing.

She shook her head. How could anyone be so arrogant? "I'm pretty sure he was the one flexing his muscles outside the spice merchant's store when I first arrived. 'The king would be crazy not to want me!' indeed." She shook her head. "Only one woman has been worth passing through to the next stage."

She stalked around the small living room to get her blood circulating. Her sisters had insisted on taking signups at their shop, assigning each of the candidates a specific time to come up to the house. According to the sundial, she had one more candidate before her noonday meal break. After that candidate she'd stretch her legs a bit, walk down to the shop to join her sisters and their husbands for lunch.

She'd check on Wollemi, too, though he'd seemed quite content when they'd headed out after breakfast. He was still a bit shy, being in a new place, but he enjoyed following the star gazer around, playing with other children, and splashing in the ocean.

She walked to the kitchen and found some dried fruit to nibble on. At Pumpkin's insistence, she slipped the cat a small slice of cheese, letting her mind wander back to the previous night. The joining party had gone on for hours with an entire second meal served in the late evening.

Mayten had finally gotten a chance to talk with Kai, only to be cut short when his mother came looking for him. The short time they'd had before the interruption had been awkward. She'd apologized again and found out that Kai was terrified of his new assignment.

It was the first time he'd been involved in a potentially dangerous quest. She could tell he wanted someone to tell him everything would be all right, but she couldn't be that someone. Not when she felt the same way about her responsibilities.

His mother had interrupted them before they could get things straightened out. For a moment, she'd even thought he might kiss her.

A loud knock shook the door and Pumpkin jumped back into her chair. She ran a hand over her hair, glad to be back in her comfortable clothes with her hair pulled out of her eyes in braids. No matter what her friends said about how she looked in the dress, it just wasn't her.

She opened the door to find a man holding a baby in his arms. The baby looked about a year old and was fast asleep. She raised an eyebrow.

"Are you here for the interview?" Maybe he was just a neighbor who needed to borrow something.

"Yes," the man said, lifting his hat a bit. "I'm Chamfer and I'm sorry to bring the babe to this interview, but my sister didn't get back from the catch in time to take him."

"No problem at all. Please come in. I'm Mayten Singer." She stepped back, allowing him to enter, then gestured at the small couch. "You can put the baby down if you'd like."

"Oh, I would, Miss, but I'm afraid then he'd holler." He perched on the couch with the baby sleeping on his chest. "Little Arbor prefers to be held. I wonder if it's because his ma died in the birthing of him and now he just wants to be up."

Mayten's heart went out to the man. She sat in her chair and studied the kind face, light skin, and freckles. Her throat tightened as she realized this man reminded her of Hunter.

She shifted her thoughts, forcing them in a different direction. She hadn't considered the fact that candidates might have children or be married. She chewed her lip, reviewing the king's letter in her mind. He hadn't said anything about children or marriage. She'd have to clarify that the next time they spoke.

The man noticed Pumpkin watching him. "That's a fine-looking helper you have there."

Mayten laughed. "She's a good judge of character." She picked up her papers and glanced at the questions. "Please tell me about yourself: your age, what you do for work, family, and why you're interested in this competition?"

"I'm Chamfer Builder, Miss Singer. My trade is assembling wood planks into barges and ships once they come down from your clan. I'm thirty-two and, as I said, my wife died when the babe was born."

His face pinched with grief. Again, Mayten thought about Hunter, and—heartsore—waited for him to continue.

"My sister is a fisherwoman, and she helps me all she can. As to why I want to be in the competition—it's hard to say. I saw the sign. Thought it might be good to do something new. Maybe get away from here and all those sad memories."

Mayten nodded, unsure if that was a good reason to join the competition. She certainly felt for the man.

She started the list of "What if" questions her family had compiled, asking how he would handle difficult situations, like a disgruntled worker or a gossiping cook. His answers were practical examples from his own life experience and Mayten was impressed with his understanding of human nature. She enjoyed the time so much she was startled when the front door opened and Wollemi peeked in.

"Time to come down for lunch."

"Oh my, is it that time already?" She stood. "Mr. Builder, it was very nice to meet you. I'll be posting the next phase of the competition at the end of the week. Thank you for your time."

"Thank you, Miss." He tipped his hat, adjusted his still-sleeping child, and followed her to the door. Pumpkin jumped off the chair and rubbed against his legs as he left.

Mayten wanted time to ponder the discussion she'd just had with the young father, but Wollemi danced on his feet, impatient for her to follow him.

"One second." She went back to her interview notes, marking the builder's name with a 'yes' and adding, *He's a good man and deserves a chance at a fresh start.*

She let Wollemi drag her down the hill to the shops, chagrined to find the Spice Merchant standing outside her shop, waving vigorously at Mayten. The woman pulled two young girls through the shop door, probably the daughters she'd told Mayten about.

Mayten gave a small wave then whispered to Wollemi. "I can't believe some of these people."

He wrinkled his nose. "I've had people pestering me about the competition, too. That lady tried to get me to come in for more cake. I said no thanks."

"I'm sorry, Wollemi."

"It's okay."

No one else tried to stop her, although several people looked like they wanted to. Her sisters must have made it very clear she was here to do a job and that job would be done in an orderly manner.

Too bad she couldn't take her sisters with her to the Sun Clan. Not only were they busy, she couldn't take a chance they'd get sick. She'd have to find someone else to help her organize the Sun Clan interviews.

A tall lanky girl ran up to them as they approached the shop. Her short brown hair stood up in spikes as if the wind was constantly tugging at it. The girl looked too young to apply for the competition, but somehow she looked familiar.

Is this the girl from my dream?

Mayten looked longingly at her sisters' shop door, then turned back to the girl with a quiet sigh.

"Hi, Wollemi," the girl said. She glanced at Mayten and then at the ground, as if afraid to meet Mayten's gaze.

Mayten was shocked to see Wollemi's face soften in adoration.

"This is Flurry," he said in a rush. "She's training to be a Wind Catcher! Flurry, this is my sister Mayten."

Did her brother have a crush on this girl, a girl who was obviously older by more than a few years? "Nice to meet you, Flurry. Aren't you young to be a Wind Catcher?"

"I just turned thirteen so I'm not official but my ma and da are wind catchers, so I've been training since birth."

Mayten could certainly understand that, having been raised in a third-generation family of tree singers.

"She's really good at it." Wollemi added.

Mayten studied her brother's face. "How would you know that?"

Wollemi grinned. "She took me out on her skiff and there wasn't any wind at all, but she sailed us all over the cove."

Mayten's eyes widened. "You wore a float, right?"

Wollemi rolled his eyes as if his sister was missing the point.

Flurry came to his defense. "Of course he did. My da always says, 'Safety first and safety last.' It's part of our code."

"I'm glad to hear that," Mayten said, stroking Wollemi's curls.

He grabbed her hand and pushed it away, which was unlike him. Was he afraid she was treating him like a baby in front of a girl he evidently *liked*?

"The wind speaks to Flurry, like the trees speak to you," he said. "She has something important to tell you."

Zigba opened her shop door and stepped out, squinting in the sun. "Wollemi, Mayten, come and eat!"

Wollemi glanced at Zigba, then back at Mayten, concern written on his face.

"Can this wait until this evening?" Mayten asked the girl.

Flurry shook her head. "Our ship sails in an hour. I won't be back for four days."

Once again, her strained face reminded Mayten of her dream. "Wollemi, go in and tell them to start without me. I'll be in shortly," Mayten said.

Wollemi grinned and gave Flurry a quick hug before dashing into the shop.

"Let's sit in the shade for a moment, shall we?" Mayten led the way to the side of the shop where they sat in the shade, leaning against the cool clay of the building.

"What is it that burdens you, Flurry?" She knew this girl from someplace, Mayten was sure of it.

Flurry's eyes closed as if she were trying to sort her thoughts or get up her nerve to speak, Mayten wasn't sure which.

Finally, she said, "Wollemi told me about how you were barely an initiate when you got sent on a quest, and how you didn't feel ready but still you were able to defeat the threat to the trees."

Mayten nodded. "With a lot of help, yes."

"He said that too. That's why I wanted to talk to you. I need help."

"Go on." The girl was clearly distressed and Mayten's stomach was rumbling for food, but she needed—*wanted*—to give her time to tell her story. She remembered how frustrating it was when no one gave her time to listen to the trees on the quest.

She reached out and patted the girl's knee, giving what she hoped was an encouraging smile. "Tell me."

That seemed to be what Flurry needed. She began to talk so fast Mayten found it hard to keep up. "I know I'm young but sometimes I feel like the wind talks to me in ways that others don't hear. I mean, I think they could hear it if they listened but grownups—" she looked at Mayten and stopped.

Mayten didn't feel like a grownup at all. She nodded, hoping she sounded encouraging and not judgmental. "Grownups are busy so they don't always listen."

The girl's lips parted but no words came out.

"What is the wind telling you?" Mayten asked.

Flurry's face lit up in a grin that showed her teeth. The two front teeth crossed at the tips making her look like a scamp.

"I knew you'd understand! We all know there's trouble in the Sun Clan—that's my clan, by the way—but no one knows what it is. You know everything is connected, right? The wind, the water, the land, the trees . . ."

"Yes, they are," Mayten agreed, glad someone so young understood this truth. She hadn't understood it until halfway through her previous quest and she'd been fifteen.

Flurry leaned in toward Mayten as if sharing a secret. "The wind says the water is in trouble."

A shiver ran up Mayten's spine. "The water?"

"She tries to show me but all I see is blackness."

"She?" Mayten asked.

"The wind," Flurry said. "She wants me to understand but I can't. I told Ma and Da, but they just shook their heads. I've wanted to talk to you for so long and when Wollemi told me you were here, I knew I had to find you, that you could ask the trees and figure out what the wind is trying to tell me." She bobbed her head once as if that settled the matter.

"Oh my." Mayten blinked. Had the trees been trying to talk to her and she hadn't been listening? Was that where the feeling of disquiet—and doom—came from? What caused that weird dream?

But what did the girl want her to do?

"I admire your faith in me but that's not how it works. I can't just ask any tree. It's best if I talk to the trees near the problem, the Sun Clan's trees—if they have any. I can't go now. I'm need-ed here, maybe for weeks."

The girl's chin dropped and she blinked rapidly as though fighting tears. Mayten reached out and touched her arm. "I promise you I will spend some time talking to the trees here and listening, though I'm not sure I'll get an answer."

Flurry's lips trembled.

Mayten wanted to help her. No one should carry such a bur-den alone. "Keep listening while you're gone and see if anyone else has more information. When you come back, we'll meet again and talk. How is that?"

Flurry's lips pinched together as if this was not the answer she'd hoped for. She stood slowly. "Thank you, Mayten. I'll go now so you can eat." She turned before Mayten could say an-other word and jogged down the hill toward the shore.

Mayten stood, staring after the odd girl. What did it all mean? The darkness, the wind, the hints of doom? How was she supposed to deal with such a nebulous mystery when the king had given her this task? She had enough on her hands, without adding someone else's problem to her own. She sighed.

It wouldn't hurt to listen.

CHAPTER FOURTEEN

Mayten loved her sisters' shop. The building was split in two—her sisters sold their knitted goods out of one side while Dado and Mortise sold handmade wooden toys, spoons, and bowls out of the other.

Both sides were cozy and had distinct smells. The woodshop smells reminded Mayten of home. The knitted goods were beautiful. With giftings that allowed the men to listen to the wood and the women to listen to the yarn, the couples were able to create not only functional but lovely and imaginative things.

Along the back of the shops was a long room where they could sit, rest, feed the babies, and eat. When they were not selling, they were working on new items. Mayten had never known how busy her sisters were until she'd spent this time with them.

She'd never known how well they cooked, either.

Full after another wonderful midday meal, Mayten stepped out of the twins' shop and blinked at the sun. A vague sense of doom lingered after Flurry left, dampening Mayten's spirit. She couldn't think about the darkness or the doom right now. She needed to get back to their house for her last two appointments of the day.

"Hello, beautiful," a familiar voice said.

Mayten squinted into the sun. Her breath caught when she finally made out his face.

Rill.

Her body warmed at the sight of him, a new sensation. One she wasn't sure she liked. "Hello, Rill. What are you doing here?"

"I'm here for my appointment." He gave her a wide grin.

Mayten frowned. She needed to keep a clear head, but Rill's close presence—his dark gleaming skin and strong arms straining at his cotton shirt—was proving a distraction.

She cleared her throat. "So you are."

Should she get one of her sisters to do the interview with her? Was it proper to be alone with this man?

She gave herself a mental shake. She'd already been alone with several men during this interview process. She was just being silly. The interviews were a part of her job and she would not shirk her responsibility. "Come along, then."

She headed up the hill, Rill close to her side. Did he know how his presence made her tingle? Did he have this effect on all women?

She needed to be careful. She was here on the king's business and couldn't afford to let some girl crush—or whatever this was—get in the way.

She glanced over her shoulder, consumed by the sudden feeling that someone was following them.

Except for a single handcart and a few merchants involved in their own conversations, the road was empty.

"How has it been going for you so far?" Rill asked, grinning at her startled expression.

Did the man never stop smiling?

Mayten cleared her throat. "I've just gotten started, but it's been—interesting."

"Interesting?"

"Yes, that's all I can say for now." She pointed at the house. "This is us."

He followed her inside and again her eyes had to adjust. She was not used to extreme contrasts between bright and dark. In the forest, the light seemed softer, kinder as it filtered through the trees. Here everything seemed either light or dark with no in between.

"Have a seat over there and I'll be right with you." She gestured to the living room, dismayed when Rill took the chair she usually sat in instead of the couch.

She made a mental note to be more specific next time.

She could not let this man fluster her. She went to the kitchen, got two glasses of water, and placed them on the small table in front of him. Since Pumpkin occupied the chair on Rill's left, she took the chair to his right, moving papers, pen, and inkpot within reach on the table. She settled in the chair, pleased to note Rill shifting his chair toward her.

At least they were on a slightly more equal level.

Pumpkin looked back and forth between Mayten and Rill as if sensing something between them. Yes, something in that stunningly handsome face seemed to pull at her, like a bee to a flower, but she had work to do.

"Let's jump right in," she said before he could start the teasing she saw in his eyes. "Tell me about yourself: your age, work, family, and why you're interested in this competition?"

"Okay. My name is Rill Wave Runner. I obviously use the waves to maneuver the barge. As far as family, I have none."

"You have none?" Mayten's chest tightened. Her family was everything to her.

"Not by birth, anyway. My folks died in the fever winter and my sister sailed off with a trader who came from Caspia, leaving me alone. Fortunately, I have some friends here in the Ocean Clan who welcomed me and have treated me like one of their own. It's the closest thing to home I've got."

Mayten was temporarily speechless. She'd heard of many children dying in the fever winter but not adults. "That's just awful. I'm so sorry."

He shrugged. "It is all that it is. And my age," he said with a wink, "is twenty-five this month."

She'd thought him older. His wind-roughened face looked too mature for twenty-five. Or perhaps it was the loss that showed in his eyes when he thought no one was looking. Still, he had ten years on her.

"I'm going to ask you a series of what-if questions to see how you handle practical conflicts that come up in life."

He smiled, sat back in his chair, and put his hands on his knees as if preparing for a challenge.

She glanced at her paper. "What would you do if someone you worked for or with had a complaint about you?"

He bellowed a laugh, so loud and long Pumpkin hissed and jumped off her chair. "Old Transom has a complaint about me every three minutes. I mostly ignore him."

Mayten remembered Transom with his grumpy face. Couldn't very well blame Rill for ignoring the grouchy man. "Does anyone else work for you or with you? Or do you work for anyone else?"

"Nope, Transom and I are partners. Most Wave Runners stick with their partners. They learn each other's ways and listen to the waves—to the *water*—together. It's hard to explain but losing your partner is difficult, like losing an arm or a leg. Together you make a complete pair."

Mayten made a mental note that Rill had failed to answer the initial question—*What would you do if someone you worked for or with had a complaint about you?* "If you won this competition and went to train with the king, would you be willing to leave Transom?"

Rill's face grew serious. His eyebrows knitted into a scruffy line. "That's a hard one. Mostly I was applying for a lark. I wanted to see you again." He grinned, but the grin fell flat as though he'd been trying to flirt but lost the heart. "Sometimes I feel like I might be meant for more, you know? When my folks died, I was pretty lost. I became a Wave Runner because Transom snatched me up. It was his way to keep an eye on me, to make sure I didn't 'sink into the depths,' whatever that might mean. It wasn't really my idea. When you came along, though . . . when I found out about the competition . . . I started to think that . . . maybe . . . there might be more."

He paused and took a long drink of water.

This was the first vulnerable thing she'd heard him say. Why shouldn't he have a chance to see if there was more for him? she decided. He was strong and likable. He'd make a good leader.

A knock at the door startled her and she jumped to her feet. It wasn't time for her next appointment yet. She went to the door and opened it to find Kai standing on the porch, a big grin on his face.

"I wasn't sure when you'd be done. Can we talk?" He stepped forward but she held up her hand to stop him.

"I'm sorry, Kai. I'm still doing interviews."

He glanced around her, his grin fading when he saw Rill.

Mayten's heart squeezed tight as Rill gave Kai a pirate's grin and waved. "Hi, Princeling."

Kai frowned, his eyebrows pulling together in the middle. "Interviews?"

The accusation in his voice made her spine stiffen. "Of course. The same thing I've been doing all day. I have one more after this. I could meet you after evening meal if you'd like."

He nodded once, still frowning, then turned and left without a word.

Mayten shook her head as she moved back to her chair. "Why do you do that to him?"

Rill's eyebrows shot up. "Do what?"

Mayten's mouth tightened. "You know exactly what."

He shrugged. "I guess because I can. He's an easy bird to ruffle. Must be his life of luxury. It hasn't prepared him for the real world. And—I don't like that he treats you like you're his property."

"He does not."

Rill raised one eyebrow.

Mayten wrinkled her nose. Was it true? Did Kai treat her like a possession?

She settled in her chair and pushed the thought away. Best get back to the interview. She'd deal with the princeling later.

By the evening meal, Mayten was practically falling asleep in her soup. Doing all those interviews hadn't been as scary as she'd feared but focusing intensely on people all day was exhausting. She yawned, then thanked her sisters and wandered outside to try and wake up.

The air still felt pleasantly warm even though the sun had slipped from the sky. The far-off sound of waves lapping against the shore and the cool ocean breeze caressing her face helped ease some of the day's stress. She settled on the front step and was just starting to relax when she heard footsteps approaching. One look at the sour expression on Kai's face chased away any patience she had left.

"Don't you scowl at me, Kai Redmond. I was doing my job and that's all. You have no right to come at me with accusations."

He threw his hands in the air. "What accusations? What did I accuse you of?"

"The way you acted when Rill was here. It was embarrassing."

He turned and headed back in the direction he'd come. "I'm embarrassing to you now, am I? You'd rather be with that brute of a man?"

Mayten dragged herself to her feet and ran to catch up with him, careful not to bruise her toe on a rock in the evening light. "That's not what I said. I said I was doing my job, a job your father gave me. I was doing interviews. I did seven today and I'm exhausted. You could show a bit of kindness."

He stopped and looked at her, his face softening. "I'm sorry. He just . . . I just get so . . . Argh." He stomped and started walking again. This time she stayed by his side.

After a few strides, he stopped and turned to her. "I just want some time with my girl before I leave. Is that too much to ask?"

She took a breath, ignoring the "my girl" comment. "I'd like time with you, too, Kai. I feel like we've hardly had any time together. Can we go somewhere and sit?"

He reached for her hand and she let him take it. They walked up the hill toward the gathering place where the wedding had been and settled on one of the benches.

"That's better," she said as they sat. She sighed, letting her stress slide away as smoothly as light slid down the ocean waves. "Thank you."

He turned to face her, taking her hand in both of his. "The thing is, I'm scared."

"Scared?"

"When I think about the quest you led last year. How brave and confident you were. At the time, it never occurred to me how young you were and how dangerous the situation was. You just handled it."

She smiled gently. "I was none of those things, Kai. I was so scared I could hardly breathe most of the time, and I was sure I was doing everything wrong. There was not one part of me that felt brave or confident. I just did what I had to do. One day at a time."

He shook his head. "We're leaving tomorrow afternoon. I have no idea what we're going into, but the news doesn't sound good. I always pictured myself dealing with difficult situations like—I don't know—like my da, I guess. Instead, I feel—shaky. Maybe I'm not really cut out to be a quester. Tray seems excited about everything, and I just miss my home, my bed, and my horse."

"I'm sure your da wasn't always so—kingly. He had to grow into the position, like everyone else. And you'll grow into questing. Tray's from a questing family. Trust me, growing up with a family with a focused gifting, that gifting is in your blood. While I had a lot to learn in order to use my gifting, I never had to *think* about it—the gift was just there. *You* have to learn it all from scratch. Just let the other questers take the lead. Give yourself time to learn."

He nodded. "I suppose so. It's just when that . . . *bargeman* . . . calls me Princeling, it pokes at exactly how I'm feeling. Like I'm nothing but an entitled child."

She stroked a hand down his cheek. He didn't make her blood boil, but he was special to her. Very special. "I'll miss you."

He smiled and touched a finger to her cheek. "That's what I needed to hear. I know I can be brave if I know you'll be waiting for me."

She leaned forward and placed a kiss on his lips. Just a small one, for reassurance. His eyes widened and his face flushed.

This wasn't the time for promises, but she could share her strength with him. She scooted closer, turning to face the ocean, and placed her head on his shoulder. "Look!"

The sun was turning the sky orange and red. "Tomorrow you'll have good weather for your voyage. My da did some time on a ship and he always said, 'Red sky at night, sailor's delight'." She yawned.

"You're tired. But can we sit like this for a while longer? Just like this so I can remember it all?"

"Of course."

His arm wrapped around her shoulders and she snuggled close to his warmth.

This is the last time either of us will feel safe.

The thought came out of nowhere like a hammer blow.

CHAPTER FIFTEEN

Mayten forgot the sensation of doom as the week went on. Her routine settled into a rhythm. She enjoyed breakfast with the family where she got to know her new brothers and the babies—even her sisters—a little better. She felt more connected to her sisters after seeing them in their new home.

Their husbands—Mayten's new 'brothers'—were surprisingly different. Acerola, older than Zigba by minutes, was the organized, bossy one. Her husband, Dado, was her opposite. He was a large man with a kind voice and a broad smile.

Zigba, was chatty as a magpie while her husband, Mortise, was tall, thin, and quiet.

Breakfast on the fourth morning was the usual chaos with Zigba rushing around putting food on plates as fast as Dado cooked it. The smell of savory bacon made Mayten's stomach growl in anticipation. There was a mound of scrambled eggs and a large pile of pancakes. A bowl of cut fruit balanced the hearty meal.

"I swear you've grown a foot since you came, Wollemi," Zigba said, putting a second stack of pancakes on his plate. "Don't they feed you at home?"

Wollemi grinned and shoved a huge spoonful of eggs into his mouth.

Mayten studied her brother. He *did* look taller. The sun had warmed his skin, increased his freckles, and lightened his hair. He walked differently too with the bouncing step of a carefree child. Perhaps he'd needed this time away. While he was loved at home, spending most of his time with the two youngest siblings, he didn't have many friends. His other siblings, including Mayten, were quite a bit older.

Here he had friends to swim with and a mentor who loved the stars as much as he did.

"How is it going with the Star Singer?" Mayten asked.

"*Chief* Star *Gazer*," Wollemi said, his eyes growing huge.

Mayten smiled. Looked like her little brother had found a mentor.

She knew that feeling. Her mother had been her mentor and still was. While her earlier relationship with her mother as mentor had been strained, she remembered the awe, respect, and fear she'd felt at the time.

"What is he teaching you?" Zigba asked as she finally sat to eat. Dado sat too, settling across from Acerola with a smile. For a big man, he moved very gracefully.

Wollemi tilted his head, apparently thinking the question over. "He talks, I listen. Tonight he says there will be no fog, so he wants me to go with him to practice gazing."

The table went silent.

"Gazing?" Zigba asked.

Wollemi shrugged as if it was the most obvious thing. "At the stars, of course. You have to get to know them before you can listen."

Everyone nodded, though Dado's look of confusion was mirrored on other faces. Star Gazers were rare. Mayten had never met one, so this was all new information. But Wollemi had been obsessed by the stars since he was old enough to talk. Apparently, he'd found his place in the world.

"And," Wollemi said after swallowing a forkful of pancakes. "He said the Sun Clan was the best place to see the stars. The climate is drier, you see. Fog and clouds don't get in the way of viewing. He's going to write Ma and Da and get their approval for me to go with you, Mayten. If you agree."

Mayten glanced at her sisters. She couldn't let Wollemi come with her. Couldn't take a chance he'd get sick. "People are sick in the Sun Clan and no one knows for sure why. Maybe it's better not to come this time."

"Aren't you going?" he asked.

"I suppose so but…"

"Then I'm going too." He dove back into his food with determination.

"How is your search going?" Zigba asked. She always seemed to know when to change the subject. She pushed her plate away, lifted her baby, and put him to her breast.

Mayten shrugged. "Pretty good, I guess. I think I have ten solid candidates so far. How many are left to interview?"

The whole process was exhausting, but she didn't want her sisters to feel they needed to help any more than they already were.

Acerola looked at Zigba and raised an eyebrow. "Nine more?"

"Yes," Zigba agreed. "You should be able to finish by tomorrow."

"Take the next day off to rest," Acerola said. "That will be a market day for us."

"All the makers bring their goods to the shore to sell," Zigba added.

"You might enjoy coming down to see it all," Acerola finished. She wrinkled her nose. "What happens after the interviews, some kind of race?"

"A physical competition." Mayten looked at her new brothers. "The king says the physical competition isn't that important and it should be fun. Any ideas?"

"This clan's giftings should be taken into account," Mortise said. "We are a clan of woodworkers, seafarers, swimmers, growers, sheepherders, and makers. Your competition should reflect that."

That was the most Mayten had heard the man say at one time. "Sheepherders? What do they do?"

"Herd sheep." Mortise gave her a lopsided grin. "Though the dogs they train actually round up the sheep. I'd love to see those dogs compete someday."

She'd never heard about dog competitions but didn't think a dog herding or sheep shearing competition would work, not for her purposes, anyway. "So, swimming competitions, maybe a rowing race. Should we have them build something?"

"What is the purpose of these competitions if the king doesn't really care?" Mortise asked, his narrow brow wrinkled.

"To see how the candidates work in a competitive environment," Mayten said. "According to King Redmond, a lot can be discovered about people's personalities during competitions. How they handle winning and losing, for instance."

She'd never participated in any sort of competition, but what the king said made sense.

"We could rope off some lines in the cove for a swim race or a boat race," Dado said. "You should have some competitions that stress individual skills and some competitions that stress group skills."

"A sandcastle build." Zigba grinned like a child.

"For working alone." Acerola nodded.

"Maybe a tug-of-war?" Mortise raised an eyebrow.

"You all have such good ideas." Mayten sighed, then gave Dado and Mortise a hopeful look. "I hate asking for more help, but would you mind running the competitions for me?"

She held her breath as the brothers looked at each other and then broke into grins.

"We would love to!" Dado said. Mortise nodded in agreement.

Mayten let go of the breath she'd been holding. She was grateful for this family, so glad she had started her quest here.

She had to admit—Solis had been right. At home in the Forest Clan, she would have been torn between responsibilities that would have distracted her. Going to the Sun Clan first would have been terrifying—she knew no one in that clan.

Here in the Ocean Clan, she felt safe and supported.

As they stood to clear the dishes, Wollemi put his hand on Mayten's arm. "Flurry will be back today. Have you listened to the trees for her?"

Mayten felt as though she'd been gut punched. She'd completely forgotten. "I'll go out now. I've got some time before my first interview."

Wollemi pursed his lips, evidently disappointed. He nodded and stepped to the sink. It was his turn to wash and her turn to dry. They worked in silence until they had most of the dishes done.

"Go now," Wollemi said. "I can finish. Please. She was so upset when she came to me. I've been trying to see if the stars had anything to say, but I don't know enough yet."

Mayten put down the dish towel. Her little brother was such a serious soul. "Thank you. I'll listen, I promise." She squeezed his shoulder before heading out the door.

She stepped out into the morning mist and shivered. The air felt colder here, mostly because of the damp. By afternoon, when the fog and clouds burned off, the temps could get too warm. As soon as the sun went down, however, she'd start shivering again. Hard to believe the Ocean Clan and the Forest Clan were on the same island.

Would the Sun Clan be even more different?

She'd find out soon enough.

Time to listen to her trees.

Pumpkin at her heels, she headed for what appeared to be a small gathering place and found a copse of oak trees away from the stately palms. She felt more at home with the oaks. It had been a while since she'd listened alone, she realized as she settled under a medium-size tree. She'd been so busy teaching back home. Now she was doing interviews.

She'd almost forgotten how much she loved connecting with her trees.

Mayten took a deep breath and quieted her mind, shutting out the noise of birds and chipmunks around her. "Hello, Uncle."

"Hello, Daughter."

A wave of homesickness swept over her as strong and fast as a summer storm.

"I miss my family," she blurted without thinking. A weight settled in her lap as Pumpkin curled up and started purring. The cat's warm body and rhythmic purr soothed her ragged nerves. She took another deep, calming breath and *listened*.

Like Pumpkin, the tree sensed her stress and sent images meant to calm—Ma with the students, Da playing with the little ones, Cather coming by the homestead to get vegetables, Oleaster in the fields.

She wondered for a moment how the tree had known the members of her family. She'd never spoken to this grove. She shivered, realizing that Ma would have sent them, likely days ago, knowing Mayten would check in with the trees at some point.

Seeing the faces of her family, knowing that all was well, calmed her nerves and helped her breathe more deeply.

She sent images back—Wollemi swimming and playing with his friends, studying with the star gazer. The twins, their husbands, and their babies around the table. Tray and Kai leaving on their quest. The king's family at the wedding.

Satisfied she'd taken care of her family first, Mayten turned her thoughts back to the Sun Clan.

Since Mayten had never visited the Sun Clan, she had no images to send, no way to ask Ma if she had more information.

How would she find out what was wrong with the Sun Clan? Asking the trees general questions, like "What is bothering you?" usually resulted in tons of images, a mistake she'd learned when she first started questioning the trees. She had to be more specific.

"Thank you, Uncle. Now I have a question." She visualized the Sun Clan's colors—yellow and orange like the sun—and then visualized a barrel of drinking water.

She held her breath. Until the trees answered, she never knew if she'd asked the right question in the right way.

A wave of blackness washed over her, leaving her feeling slimy and gross as if she'd been covered with something sticky. A rotten smell filled her nose, a stench she couldn't identify.

Then came images—fish, birds, big cats, people—all dead or dying.

She shivered and hugged her arms around her chest, rocking to soothe herself.

What was going on? Where did the darkness come from? And that stench? That slimy feeling?

Pumpkin put a paw on her chest and softly meowed.

Mayten opened her eyes as the green-eyed cat pressed her nose and cheek to Mayten's face. "Did you see that? Everything's dying."

CHAPTER SIXTEEN

Flurry didn't show up at midday, leaving Mayten relieved yet confused. She couldn't shake the images the tree had shown her. Darkness wrapped up in rotten stench played through her mind, followed by images of dead fish, dead cats, dead people, the images refusing to leave while she conducted her morning interviews.

And beneath it all lingered the question: What would she say to Flurry? What *could* she say?

Obviously, something was wrong, though she wasn't certain the wrongness originated within the Sun Clan. As Flurry had pointed out all things on the earth—including the wind, water, land, and trees—were connected, something Mayten learned during her last quest. If one of those elements was affected, everything was affected.

The uncle tree had indicated something was wrong with water. But what? What on earth could cause an imbalance in water, of all things?

It was impossible to tell, she decided.

"It's not my problem anyway," she reminded herself. Except she knew it was. Just as the tree blight had been her problem. Tree singers bore a responsibility to care for the land, not just the trees she held so dear.

She sighed. So far, this last day of interviews had gone well. She'd met with the daughters of the spice merchant. Coriander Merchant's daughters Pepper and Cumin had interviewed well, and she was glad to add them to the list. Maybe now their mother would stop showing up at random places, giving Mayten hopeful glances. The woman was unnerving.

A sigh escaped her lips at the sound of knocking. Two more interviews left. She was ready for the interviewing process to be over.

She opened the door . . .

And found an angel standing on the porch.

Chocolate skin, soft, curly hair topped with a black cap, and the bluest eyes she'd ever seen.

Her breath caught in her throat. She stared at the young man who looked to be her age.

The young man stared back.

Part of her brain reminded her she needed to stay professional. The other part noted that this was no man. This was a storybook hero.

Pumpkin meowed, breaking the spell Mayten seemed to have fallen under. "I'm sorry, are you here for an interview?"

"Yes." The young man yanked off his cap, keeping his gaze on the floor. "I'm Lan Shepherd."

His voice was husky as though it hadn't been used in a while. He held out a hand, white muslin sleeves rolled up to his elbows revealing muscled forearms. She was surprised to find his hand incredibly soft.

She stepped back from the door. "Please, come in. Take a seat on the couch while I get us some water."

She was thankful she'd developed the ritual of filling a water glass for each person who came for an interview. It gave her a minute or two to compose herself.

It was his eyes, she decided. On an island with various shades of brown skin and brown eyes, blue eyes were rare. His were exceptionally blue.

She handed him the water glass and settled in her chair, lifting her pad of paper and pen as though wielding a shield and sword. She needed to remain professional, but this boy/man was breathtaking.

"I'm Mayten Singer and I have some questions to ask if you don't mind." She tried to smile but her lips felt stiff and unreal.

Lan nodded, shifting uncomfortably on the couch.

"Could you tell me a bit about yourself—your name, family, work, age, and why you want to be considered for this competition?"

He smiled then, deep dimples on both cheeks that made her stomach tighten. "Well, as I mentioned, I'm Lan Shepherd."

"Yes, you did. Go on." Pumpkin gave her a stern look. Mayten needed to get control of herself.

"I work up at the ranch," he gestured toward the mountains, "with the sheep."

"Right, the ranch. To be honest, you're the first rancher I've met in the Ocean Clan. Can you tell me more?"

He seemed to relax.

"The ranch has been in our family for generations. You should come see it. It's a beauty. We raise sheep for the wool your sisters and the other crafters use to make clothes. We have a large band of sheep, the biggest in the clan, five hundred at last count."

"I would love to see that." Mayten knew nothing about sheep. In fact, she'd never even seen one, except as meat on her table and in pictures.

He grinned. "Then you must come for a tour, and I'll show you about. I'm always at the ranch. Except tomorrow as it's Market Day."

Mayten's heart skipped a beat. "I plan to see the market too."

"Come by our stall. If Da's okay with it, I'll take you up to the ranch."

Mayten felt a little flutter in her stomach. She didn't want him to think she was using her position to gain favors, but she would love to see a ranch. And she wouldn't mind more time with this fellow.

She was torn by guilt. Would it give Lan an unfair advantage over the others if she spent time with him?

If she used the time to ask more questions, to understand his character better, it would likely be all right.

Pumpkin left her interview chair and jumped into Lan's lap. He smiled and stroked the cat gently, murmuring something Mayten couldn't hear. Pumpkin purred and rubbed her head against his hand.

"She likes you," Mayten said.

"I have a way with animals, always have. It's part of the gifting. I can tell you this is a wise cat, one who can read people well. Now, my age is seventeen. My family . . . let's see—there's Ma, Da, the grands, and I'm the youngest of four brothers. And that leads to the why of wanting to join the competition. I love the ranch, the sheep, and the clan, but I'm not exactly indispensable at home. The two oldest are married with kids. They're both content to work the ranch as my da ages. I think I'd like to see more of the world."

That made sense to Mayten. He was a very down-to-earth sort of guy. "Can you tell me about a time you had a conflict with someone you work with and how you resolved it?"

He grinned. "Being the youngest of four brothers, I've had a lot of conflict. Usually, we manage to work it out without coming to blows." He chuckled. "Mostly I try to keep the peace and just walk away or do what they ask but I've had to stand up to them a time or two when they try to give me the short straw. Like when it's lambing season, they'd try to give me all the midnight shifts and such. I called a family meeting, which is something my da says anyone can call anytime. So I called one and we discussed it and now we rotate the shifts day and night during lambing."

"Your da seems like a wise and fair person."

"Oh he is. I want to be like him someday."

Looked to her like Lan was well on his way.

At the end of the interview, she told him the list of finalists would be posted on her sister's shop tomorrow and the competitions would be held at the shore the next day. He stood, set Pumpkin on the couch, and followed Mayten to the door.

"I look forward to seeing you tomorrow, Mayten Singer," he said as he replaced his cap. "Whether I make the list or not, I hope to show you my home."

Pumpkin was suddenly next to her, watching Lan clomp down the steps. Mayten shut the door and leaned against it.

"Well," she told the cat. "That was something, wasn't it?"

Before Pumpkin could answer, another knock rattled the door. Mayten groaned. This should be her last interview—her final interview. Then it would be time for the evening meal and her stomach was already growling.

She opened the door and found a rather round woman with bright red hair, not rust red like the king's but red like Hunter's.

Mayten's heart squeezed.

Even though Hunter had been a woodsman, he'd been the palest person she'd ever met, the pale skin marking his family as more recent immigrants to the island. This woman looked like she could have been his sister—light skin, freckles, and green eyes.

Behind the woman stood Flurry.

"Can we talk yet?" Flurry asked.

Mayten swallowed a sigh. "I've got one last appointment. Can you come back in half an hour? Walk me down to the shop for the evening meal. You're welcome to eat with us. My sisters are working late tonight to prepare for Market Day."

Flurry nodded, her mouth pressed tightly in a straight line. No wonder she and Wollemi were friends. They both acted like the weight of the world was on their small shoulders.

Mayten wanted to take that weight from the girl in some way, allow her to be a child while she could.

But how?

Mayten ushered the red-haired woman into the room and started to close the door, stopping short as Pumpkin slipped out.

Odd. The cat always stayed with her during the interviews.

The red-headed woman perched on the couch, looking like she'd be more comfortable in a knitting circle than in a competition. But the king had said integrity, kindness, and leadership were more important than physical strength. Mayten had to keep an open mind.

"I'm Mayten Singer," she said as she took her chair and picked up her pad and pen.

"Aren't you, though, and doesn't everyone know it? I'm Purl Leader." A smile lit up her round face, creating deep dimples that made Mayten instantly comfortable. "You're just a wee lass. To think of all you have done. This must be quite a burden for you."

The lilt of her speech was so much like Hunter's Mayten found herself staring at the woman.

"Are you okay, love?" Purl asked.

Mayten shook her head. "I'm sorry, you remind me so much of a friend of mine. He—he died earlier this year."

"Are you talking about my cousin, Hunter?" Purl's eyes glistened.

"Hunter was your cousin?" Mayten's breath caught in her throat. She didn't know anything about Hunter's relatives.

"Yes, lass. He's the main reason I've come to see you. That and me ma."

"Your ma?"

"She's the clan leader here, off to the castle on clan business. She wanted me to check in on you while she's gone. See if you need anything."

Mayten had heard the clan leader was away but hadn't known the leader had a grown daughter or that she was related to Hunter.

"I miss him. Hunter." She said the words before she thought about it. "He was so kind to me."

Purl smiled, the expression tight and sad. "He was a good man."

"I was with him, you know. When he was dying."

"I heard that. I was hoping you could tell me the story so I can tell Ma the details, you know."

Mayten's heart squeezed. It was hard to talk about what happened to Hunter. He'd been the woodsman on their quest, the same age as the twins. She'd found out that he'd harbored a secret love for Zigba when they were young. He was kind to Mayten, unlike the quest leader Adven who'd been a bear. While Mayten didn't want to relive the experience, she felt she owed the story to his cousin.

She took a deep breath and began to tell the story of Hunter's death.

Purl nodded as she spoke.

A thought came to Mayten as she neared the end of the story, something that might bring the family some comfort. "We did Thanks-Giving with him before he died. He was awake for it. Able to thank the Great Hunter."

A small smile crossed Purl's face. "I didn't know that. Thank you."

Mayten nodded. "He passed a day later. Adven, he helped um…" She hesitated to share what she knew about the quester's code.

"Ease his passing?" Purl finished the thought for her.

"Yes," Mayten said, thankful the woman seemed to know the tradition. It was something she hadn't known before the quest. There were herbs to help when an injured person was dying and there was no hope for them.

Purl nodded. "We were grateful to hear it."

Mayten paused, then added, "Is that why you came, or did you also want to enter the challenge?"

"Oh yes," Purl said. "I definitely want to enter the challenge." She grinned, flashing her beautiful dimples and Mayten laughed, readying her pen. She liked Purl. Whether the woman qualified or not, maybe they could be friends.

She took more time with Purl than she had with the other candidates, surprised by the wisdom the woman shared while answering the 'what if' questions. Purl had grown up with a clan leader mother, that much was evident. Purl definitely qualified. They said their goodbyes as Mayten ushered the woman out the door.

Flurry sat on the bottom step, orange cat curled in her lap.

"Oh honey, I'm sorry to keep you waiting," Mayten said, guilt replacing the pleasure she'd felt during Purl's interview. "Come on, then."

Flurry stood, setting Pumpkin gently on the ground.

Purl headed up the hill with a wave and Mayten and Flurry started down. The air was just starting to cool as day gave way to evening.

"Did you find out anything new on your trip?" Mayten asked.

"Not really." Flurry frowned. "My parents treat me like a child. Whenever they talk about important things and I come into the room, they stop."

Mayten knew that feeling well. She'd been kept out of some important conversations in her time. "So, nothing new?"

"Only that something is wrong, something that affects everything. People are starting to suffer. Evidently, my clan is low on water. I didn't think we were in a drought, though."

Mayten considered the girl's words in light of the images she'd received from the tree. Did any of it fit?

As they walked downhill to the shops, she ignored the birdsong and puffy white clouds, sharing what she'd learned from the oak. She stopped outside her sisters' shop and turned to Flurry, taking hold of the girl's shoulder.

"Flurry, you are like Wollemi, wise and thoughtful beyond your years. You pay attention. You *listen*. Tell your parents that something is happening with the water. Tell them to look, to *listen*, for something that indicates blackness or death. Tell them I said it was vital that they take you seriously."

Flurry nodded. "I will."

She waved at the shop. "Stay and eat with us."

The girl shook her head. "I've got to go." She turned toward the docks.

Mayten touched her shoulder. "Remember, Flurry, you've got the gift of speaking. It's time to use your voice."

The girl nodded, a look of grim determination on her face, and ran down the hill, her thin, deer-like legs flying.

Flurry was so young. Could she learn to trust herself, a skill Mayten had almost taken too long to learn?

CHAPTER SEVENTEEN

Flurry ran straight back to the ship, which was sitting at the Ocean Clan wharf, known as the Deep Dock. This dock, the largest on the island, with several jetties where most ships were able to pull right up in the deep water, unlike her home marina in the Sun Clan. There, they had to unload one ship at a time.

Her feet slapped against wooden slats as she raced down the dock. She bolted up the gangway, leaping onto the ship's deck. She headed to her parents' room on the top deck where her father would be standing at the map table. She knocked, and heard a gruff, "Come."

Her da didn't like to be interrupted but her talk with Mayten had strengthened her nerve. She had to do this—had to get her da to *listen* to her—before she backed out. She pushed open the door. He stood where she'd expected him to be, leaning over his maps at the large oak table they used for meetings and eating together as a family. He didn't look up.

"Da?" she said without stepping inside.

He glanced up, a distracted look on his dark, sea-weathered face. "Good, you're back. We have to take a quick run up to the Castle. I was about to send your brother out to fetch you."

"Can I talk to you for a minute?"

He took a breath and moved to a bench, gesturing for her to sit.

The quickest way to get her father's attention was to talk about his mother, the family matriarch who still lived with the Sun Clan. He loved her and missed her deeply when they traveled.

"What is it?" he asked, a frown on his face.

She swallowed. "I'm worried about Grandma."

His eyes narrowed. "Your grandma? Why?"

"She's at home, and we keep hearing bad things are happening in the Sun Clan. I worry she might be sick."

He shook his head. "Nothing can take out your grandma. She's as strong as a mast."

"But the wind—" She tried to steady her breathing.

He didn't roll his eyes but she bet he wanted to. "I know, the wind tells you things. My little seagull, you know that only the oldest wind catchers can talk to the wind."

Flurry's throat tightened. Mayten said to use her voice, to be strong. "The wind *does* talk to me, Da. And it's telling me there is something very wrong with the water in the Sun Clan. Maybe there's a drought?"

"No drought that I've heard of, but there is talk going around. People are making all kinds of suppositions. You know gossip is unreliable."

Flurry stood, heart racing. "It's not gossip, Da. The wind tells me things."

Da stood and walked back to the map. "We've been over and over and over this before, Flurry—"

"I've been talking to Mayten, you know. The Tree Singer."

He paused, looking her in the eye for the first time. "The one from the song? How?"

He turned and gestured for her to continue, joining her as she went on. "She's working here, gathering names for the king's replacement or something like that. I've met with her twice. I asked her to listen to the trees and she did. Da, Mayten Singer confirmed what I'm hearing."

"Which is?"

"Things are dying, Da. The animals and the earth and maybe the people. It's all connected."

He scratched the stubble on his cheek. "That sounds serious. We'll be back with the clan in a week or so and we can check on Grandma. Meanwhile, I'll ask around, see what I can find out. Does that help?"

"Yes. Thanks, Da." She felt a weight lifted from her shoulders. If her father said he'd do something, he did it.

"Okay, skedaddle. We've got to get going." He flicked his hand toward the door. She'd been dismissed.

She went to her favorite place at the railing where the wind could ruffle her hair and caress her face. She loved the view here at the stern, loved the salty brine smell. It was a view, not of where they were going, but of where they had been. Something about watching the wake left by the ship calmed her. She heard orders being shouted as they prepared to set sail.

Why was it so hard for her parents to believe her? She felt like her parents and brother and sister came from one kind of people while she came from a completely different kind. They understood hard work and they loved being outside, working with the wind. But she loved just *being* with the wind. The wind was her friend.

The wind listened.

Her brother Cal was the only one who understood her and he was off on his new ship. With his new bride.

Were there others like her who thought of the wind as their friend? Others who did more than just work with the wind?

Mayten said she had a gift.

Did she truly have a gift?

A soft breeze caressed her cheek as though trying to comfort her. "I'm sorry. I'm trying to hear you, trying to get help. Is there anything else you can show me that might help?"

Flurry closed her eyes and *listened*. The image of blackness assaulted her, leaving her breathless for a heartbeat. Then the blackness resolved into a shape—roundish with jagged edges. She strained to see more detail, but all she could make out was what looked like a bit of depth in the middle.

Is that a cave?

The breeze tickled her hair.

Yes. It was definitely a cave.

She had to tell Mayten.

She spun on her heel. She had to get back to the dock. To warn Mayten.

The loading dock creaked and groaned as it pulled up and her parents took position on the deck.

She was too late.

CHAPTER EIGHTEEN

The sisters had sent Mayten back to the house following the evening meal. "You're exhausted," Zigba said, raising her finger to stop Mayten's protest. "We're fine here. Almost ready for Market Day. Wollemi can help finish up."

So she'd headed back up the hill, enjoying the evening breeze and singing birds as she walked.

Pumpkin greeted her as she stepped through the door.

Mayten sighed. "We did it, Pumpkin. We made it through the Ocean Clan interviews. Let's see who we have in our 'proceed to contest' pile." She walked to the living room, gathered her papers, and curled up on the couch. Pumpkin snuggled close to her side.

She went through the papers, one by one. "We've got Gale Sailor. She was the first one we picked. It seems so long ago. She's thirty-five years old . . . Oh, I remember her. She's from one of the big ships, said her body's wearing out. I liked her."

Pumpkin purred as Mayten absently stroked her soft fur, moving down her list. "We've got Chamfer Builder, that single father you liked so much. And Rill, of course. There's Purl, Hunter's redheaded cousin. And the daughters of that spice merchant, Pepper and Cumin. And those young brothers, remember? They were twins, Butch and Skinner, my age really, but seemed so young. But they were sweet and had good an-swers. And Lan Shepherd. You loved him."

Pumpkin meowed as if to say, "It wasn't just me."

"All right, *we* liked him."

She studied the list again. "That's a good variety of men and women of different ages. I think we did well. We do have an uneven number, which doesn't work for some of the challenges the brothers are planning. Is there anyone else who deserves a second chance, maybe another girl, to make it even?"

She flipped through her notes again, anxiety tightening her stomach. This was all so . . . much. "There was that one woman, Sugar Baker. Her answers were okay. She was just rather quiet. We don't have any women in their early twenties, so let's give her a shot."

Pumpkin sat back on her haunches and washed her face.

Mayten laughed. "I'm done, too. I'll write this list up and the twins can post it tomorrow, maybe in their shop and down at the market stall. I'll include a note at the bottom about the contests. That way the word will get out."

Satisfied, she re-wrote the lists and put the pages firmly on the table. She was about to congratulate Pumpkin for a job well done but the cat was fast asleep on the couch. "You've got that right, don't you?"

She stretched out next to Pumpkin, pulling the cat to her chest. When she closed her eyes three faces floated into her mind—Lan, Rill, and Kai. Each was attractive in a different way. Rill made her feel things she'd never felt before, Lan put butter-flies in her stomach, and Kai was just, Kai. Though each showed interest in her, she needed to focus on the king's charge.

She floated off to sleep, handsome faces dancing through her mind. Just before consciousness faded, those handsome faces turned dark.

CHAPTER NINETEEN

The day was already warming, sending tiny rivulets of sweat trickling down Mayten's sides. She wished she'd worn sandals instead of her boots, but their walk had started off cool enough to chill bare toes.

She stopped to catch her breath at the top of a small rise, setting two woven baskets on the ground and stretching the ache from her hands. Her nephews slept in those baskets, swaddled in snug blankets.

Wollemi bounced from foot to foot beside her. They'd seen this harbor with its beautiful ships from a distance but had not visited this area.

"We're not supposed to swim there," Wollemi said. "Too many ships. We swim in a cove around that bend." He pointed at the far end of the harbor where a massive boulder jutted out of the glistening water.

Mayten nodded, wiped her hands on her tunic, and picked up the baskets. "Looks like there's a whole market down there."

They headed down the hill and joined a bustling crowd, all headed toward the harbor's shore. She glanced in each basket periodically to make sure the babes stayed safely tucked in.

The cacophony of Market Day drifted toward them—merchants calling to one another, hammering, the rustle of so many people gathered in one place. Ships with billowing sails lined the harbor. Outside the harbor, more ships bobbed on the waves. Small boats packed with people and goods headed to shore.

"Look at all those ships," Wollemi said. "How did they get here? I thought our island was protected."

Mayten understood. The island was surrounded by enormous boulders that could break a ship to pieces if someone tried to come in unassisted.

"The sailors from the island know the safe channels well. It's the unknown traders who have to be guided in. Those must be trading ships, friendly to the island." She paused a beat, then continued. "The Ocean Clan has the biggest harbor with the most docks so that's why it seems like a lot. If you look closely, you can see some of the ships are actually from other clans."

The scents of roasting fish, baked bread, and ocean brine blended into a pleasing mix. Zigba and Acerola were around somewhere, though Mayten suddenly wondered how they were going to find them. The twins and their husbands had left while it was still dark to set up their tents and wares.

"How will we ever find them?" Wollemi asked as if reading her mind.

Mayten hoisted the baskets and moved toward the rows of tents. "Zigba said they were near the middle. Let's head toward that blue tent on the end and find someone to ask."

She glanced at the babies who were starting to stir. "Never mind. Let's head for the middle. Keep fingers crossed we find their tent before these boys start wailing for milk."

They were almost past a green tent before she recognized the pungent scent of spice drifting from the tent. She stifled a groan. Of course, they had to pass the spice lady's tent.

Pepper and Cumin were busy setting out bottles of spice on a waist-high counter, speaking to each other in low voices. They caught sight of Mayten and squealed before dashing around the counter to hug her.

"We saw the list," Pepper said, her smile taking up her whole face.

"Thank you," Cumin said.

"You both did well during your interviews." Mayten frowned. Did they think the process was over? "Making it on the list just means you're entered in the competition. There's no guarantee you'll make it all the way through."

"We know." Pepper bounced in place. "Are you looking for the twins? We can help you. Ma?" She turned and yelled at her mother who was watching with a smug smile.

"Go on, now," Coriander said. "Help her carry those babes."

Pepper and Cumin each grabbed a basket from Mayten and led the way along the row of tents. Merchants still setting up hurried to get their goods in place before the majority of shoppers arrived.

"Didn't I tell you, Mayten Singer," the spice merchant yelled after them. "My girls are special!"

Mayten lifted her suddenly weightless hand. "You did, and thanks for your help."

The girls chattered as they walked between tents displaying beautiful jewelry, tasty treats, and lovely crafts. Wollemi looked longingly at the food stalls.

Pepper pointed. "See that stall with the paintings? That's Matte's tent. He wasn't on the list."

Matte. The boy who flexed his muscles outside Coriander's store the day she and Wollemi arrived.

Mayten clenched her jaw when she saw Matte inside. The boy had his arms crossed over his chest, glaring as they walked by. He ducked around the table and stood in front of her, puffing out his chest.

"You must have made a mistake," he growled. "Picking these two fluff brains over me."

Mayten's heart thumped against her ribs. Would this boy attack her? In front of all these people?

She took a breath, remembering how full of himself he'd been during his interview. She'd handled him then. She'd handle him now. "I suggest you step back, Matte."

"Why? Why'd you pick them and not me?" His face was red and blotchy.

She hated confrontation, but she was the king's representative. She straightened her spine. "You seem to think you're the strongest, the smartest, and the most deserving person on this island. That's not the kind of person the king is looking for. Now, please move out of our way."

The boy's mouth fell open and Mayten pushed past him, waving for the girls to follow.

After a few steps, she heard him racing to catch up, stopping in front of her once again.

This boy was not used to losing.

Merchants were gathering outside their stalls, curious to see what was causing all the commotion.

"I'm sorry, Matte. The list is final."

He stamped his foot and bumped her with his shoulder. "Change the list."

Mayten studied the boy's hard eyes as Wollemi stepped up to her side, his small hands clenched into fists.

She waved Pepper and Cumin on. "Girls, could you take the babies to my sisters, please?"

The girls moved several steps away but stopped to watch.

"Matte, I am the king's representative. This kind of behavior will certainly not win any points with King Redmond. If you ever want to work for him in any capacity, you need to change your attitude immediately."

She grabbed Wollemi's arm and shoved past Matte, heart in her mouth. She'd never had to stand up to anyone like that before. She refused to look back, but she could practically feel the boy's glare burning a hole in her shoulders.

"Don't you worry about him," Pepper whispered as Wollemi took off running, headed for the twin's tent five spaces away. The girls linked their free arms through Mayten's and hurried her up to the twins, quickly handing the baskets over the front table to the waiting mothers. Then they waved at Mayten and ran back to their tent, no doubt to fill their mother in on what had happened with Matte.

Her family's tent provided shade for four tables in a U shape. Two long tables ran into the tent while two shorter tables formed a counter across the front. Colorful cloths of red and deep purple had been spread over the tables with merchandise arranged on top of the cloths. Two of the tables—one long and one short—featured the twins' knitted hats, gloves, socks, and baby clothes. The other two held the husbands' woodworking.

Chairs had been added at the entrance of the tent with mats to lay down on and baskets filled with food toward the back of the tent.

"This is lovely." Mayten said. Her voice was still shaky.

"Thank you," Zigba said. "Are you okay? You look rather pale."

She lifted her baby and sniffed its diaper. "This one needs a change and a feed. Mortise, can you mind the store? Mayten, come with me. Tell me what happened."

"Just a run-in with an unhappy applicant who didn't make the list. I'll be fine. I'm sure Wollemi will be glad to tell you all about it, especially if you bribe him with food."

Zigba narrowed her gaze at Mayten, then went to the back of the tent with the baby.

Acerola lifted her son from his basket, looking Mayten over as if checking for blood. Seeming satisfied, she headed after Zigba.

Wollemi followed them in. "That guy was scary. You want to bribe me with food?"

Mayten groaned. She was going to regret that "bribe" comment.

She turned to the merchandise her sisters had on display. Sweaters hung on a rack to one side of a long table. The display reminded her of a rainbow—so colorful and organized. Considering how many boxes the sisters packed last night, there were likely extra sweaters—extra everything—stored in the boxes she could see at the back of the tent.

Wollemi perched on one of the boxes, waving his arms wildly as he told the story of their confrontation with Matte.

Mayten fingered a beautiful scarf. "How often do you do this? Sell your goods at market?" she asked Dado.

The large man looked up from a toy he was staining. "Twice a month until the weather changes and keeps the ships from coming. The winds can be brutal and too dangerous for the ships to risk running onto the rocks."

"How do you sell your goods, then?" People milled around the sandy paths between tents, so she moved inside by the sweaters, trying to stay out of the way.

"Traders we trust take our goods—goods from the entire clan—to warmer places to sell. We mostly spend the time resting and resupplying our wares for the warm season."

"How long is that?"

"Oh, about two moons," Mortise said, winking at her as he carefully set another armload of wooden bowls on the table. "We shutter the shop for a whole moon during winter solstice. It's a festive time for rest and catching up with all of our neighbors."

"You should come visit around then, Mayten," Dado said. "Everyone is much more relaxed."

"That would be nice."

They all worked so hard. It was good to know they took time for a break. "Would you know where the shepherds' booths would be?"

Soft heat spread up her cheeks as she asked, but she'd promised to visit Lan.

"That's easy." Dado pointed to the far end of the market stalls. "Just head that way and follow your nose. They're in the hot food section. They make a lamb stew that everyone will be wanting around midday."

"Thanks. When do you need me back to help?"

"If you come back as the sun is setting and take the babes back up to the house, that would help. Otherwise, you are free to enjoy the day."

"Thank you. Do you want me to take Wollemi with me?"

"No. This is your break before the competitions tomorrow. We'll keep an eye on him. And Mayten, this is a small town. The way you stood up to that bully—word will get out about that. People will respect you more."

Mayten nodded. She took a deep breath and headed toward the far end of the tents. Two weeks of interviews were over, she reminded herself. She had a whole day to do whatever she wanted.

She wove through the crowd, noticing smiles directed her way. From people who'd made the list, she realized, and their families.

There were also some glares. Likely, those who hadn't made the list and *their* families.

By the time she reached the food stalls, Mayten was feeling more than a little uncomfortable. Being a leader was hard. The same people who'd been trying to impress her before had started snubbing her. Looked like making decisions had also made her enemies.

The enticing aroma of onions, garlic, and meat flavored the air. Her stomach grumbled as she glanced at the various offerings—baked goods were particularly enticing as was what appeared to be vegetables and meat speared on long sticks. She didn't linger—too many merchants were still working on getting set up.

Lan's stall was easy to find, a wooden structure they must have brought to the shore in pieces and fastened together on site. Stools had been set out so people could sit and eat at a counter if they wanted to. A smiling sheep graced a sign above the stall. The scent of lamb stew wafted on a gentle breeze.

She spotted Lan off to the right side of the stall. He lifted a large pot onto a spit positioned over the coals of a fire, then moved on to lift another pot onto its spit over a second fire. He repeated the chore several times, pausing to wipe sweat from his forehead when he'd finished. A few other men worked behind the counter, chopping vegetables and meat and tossing them into the pots. With similar skin coloring and hair, these were likely his brothers. They were all handsome, but none had Lan's startling blue eyes.

As though sensing her presence, he turned and met her eyes. A wide grin spread across his face. He quickly wiped his hands on a cloth tucked into his pants and spoke to a sturdy-looking man behind the counter. The man glanced at her and nodded to Lan who pulled the cloth from his pants and folded it, placing it on the table before joining Mayten. "You came!"

"I did. This is quite a setup you've got here."

He glanced down, looking embarrassed. Was he shy or humble or both?

"Da said I could take you up to the ranch if you have time. This is a good time for me to take a break."

"Are you sure?" She gestured at the stall. "It looks like quite a lot of work."

He nodded. "We've been here since before dawn, building the fires so the stew can simmer. We won't start serving for another two hours, and it won't get busy until midday, so I have time to show you around if you'd like."

"I'd like it very much. I've never seen a ranch or a sheep for that matter."

His head came up, eyes wide. "You've never seen a sheep?"

She laughed. "We don't have sheep in the forest. An occasional bear or mountain lion, even some wild hogs, but no sheep."

He led her away along the shore to a different hill than the one she'd come down with Wollemi. A sandy road led away from the town center and had barely any traffic. Sand changed to dirt as the road climbed. Cheatgrass sprouted here and there. What started as sparse clumps thickened into an abundant field. Lan turned off the road, following a small path winding through the grass.

Short of breath, Mayten tried to find something to say. Nothing came to mind beyond keeping up with Lan's long legs—and the fact she was glad she'd chosen to wear trousers as well as boots.

"We have mountain lions that cross the mountain sometimes to try and take sheep but mostly it's the coyotes that run in packs we have to worry about," he said after the silence grew uncomfortably long.

"I've never seen a coyote either," Mayten managed to say. Her face heated from more than the exercise. What a stupid thing to say.

The path grew steeper, the cheatgrass changing to lush green grass as they hiked up one rolling hill, then another. Mayten relaxed as the silence went from awkward to companionable, though she couldn't put her finger on when it changed.

She'd spent two weeks mostly sitting and her body needed this exercise. It felt good to stretch out her legs and explore the land.

She found her thoughts drifting to the talk she'd had with her father before starting this trip. The world was much bigger than she'd known, and this was only her island. When she'd gone to the castle, the Keep—with its beautiful gardens, guardhouses, and stone structures—had seemed so big and different than anything she had known. Now she was here, learning about a new clan, meeting new people. How much more was there to discover—to explore—on her little island?

And what of the worlds that lay beyond it?

She was panting a bit when they reached the top of the next hill. Lan stopped, pointing down. "There she is. Our ranch."

Mayten's heart filled as she gazed down on lush green grass and what seemed like an endless number of sheep in pens. A ranch house perched on a small rise beyond the pens. "They're beautiful! I love their little black faces."

Lan grinned, grabbed her hand, and started running down the hill. She ran after him, laughing as they went, and felt all the heaviness lift off her shoulders.

He stopped when they got to a fence made of wooden logs. She marveled at how the logs crossed each other in a way that kept them standing. Lan stepped over a low spot between the logs and guided her through.

"Can't they get out?" she asked.

He stooped as sheep gathered around them and stroked their wooly backs. "They're not that smart. The dogs keep watch, though. Occasionally a young one will get out, but the dogs let us know."

"Dogs?" Mayten couldn't see any dogs.

"You'll meet them. Sheepherding dogs about this tall." He held his hand level at his knee. "They're very good at keeping the herd together."

A sheep nuzzled Lan's leg and he stroked its head. "This is only part of the flock. We have other grazing areas. Do you want to pet one?"

"They don't bite, do they?"

He laughed and Mayten couldn't help smiling. When he laughed it was as if his whole body laughed, a contagious sound.

"No, they don't bite. Come here."

She stepped close and he took her hand, setting her palm on the fleece. The wool of the sheep was deep, and her fingers sank to her knuckles. A chill ran over her skin at the touch of his hand.

"He's so soft and fat." She forced herself to focus on the sheep's round belly and cute face.

"That's because he's a she, a ewe, and she is carrying a baby lamb. It will be born during the winter. In fact, we'll have a batch of them born in the winter."

She liked his gentle patience. "When they have babies—lambs—is it a busy time for you?"

He nodded. "Lambing is busy. Shearing—that's when we shave off their coats—is even busier. We have people who process the wool, wash it, collect the oil, and spin it into the yarn your sisters use. Throw in tending to the lambs whose mothers don't feel like mothering. It's always busy here."

"I never knew so much went into the yarn my sisters use."

"Our sheep provide more than just yarn. Take a look when we get back. We've got four stalls. We sell the lamb stew you smelled as well as yarn—your sisters often visit the yarn sellers. We also sell butchered meat, dried meat, and oil."

They were surrounded by sheep now. She felt slightly nervous but took heart at how happy and calm Lan was. She drew in a breath, surprised at how little the field smelled. Slightly gamy smell, but not bad. "I thought the smell would be stronger than it is."

"We try to keep the sheep clean. Being outside helps." The pregnant ewe butted his leg for more petting. He scratched her head.

"They like you." Mayten gave the ewe's head a quick scratch, then pulled her hand away. There was an oily feeling to their fleece that she wasn't sure she liked.

"I like them, too. Let's go up to the house so you can meet my ma."

He led her slowly through the sheep, touching the ones who came close. She let him help her back through the fence, thrilling at the warmth of his hand in hers. He kept hold of her hand as they strolled up to the large ranch house. It was wider than her homestead but she couldn't tell how far back the building went.

They climbed the porch steps and Lan stopped to take off his boots outside the front door. "Ma will skin us if we bring lamb stink in here."

Mayten took off her boots, wondering if they smelled after walking through the sheep. She followed him inside.

"Ma," he yelled as they entered a large room with an empty fireplace and soft-looking chairs. A rich, yeasty aroma permeated the room, reminding her of mornings waking to Da's baking.

"In the kitchen," called a woman's voice.

He led her through an open door into a large kitchen with a huge table running down the middle. It reminded her of the kitchen back home but was even bigger. A stout woman with her hair covered in a kerchief worked at the stove. A large tray of bread rolls—the source of that wonderful smell—sat on the counter beside the stove.

The woman turned toward them, face flushed from the oven's heat. She had the same startling blue eyes as Lan, but her skin was much lighter, a warm toast color. She smiled. "And who's this?"

"This is Mayten. She's the singer running the contest for the king."

"Welcome, please take a seat. I've got some butter, jam, and mango juice to go with this hot bread. I'd like a rest myself."

Mayten liked Lan's mother at once. She seemed warm and kind and her eyes held the same look of joy that Lan's did. "Thank you, Mrs. Shepherd."

"Call me Kara. Now help yourself." She placed plates and food on the table and poured juice into ceramic mugs. "Tell me, how did my youngest do at your interview?"

"He passed to the next level," Mayten said, taking one of the plates. She raised her eyebrow and gave Lan a questioning look. She'd assumed his family knew.

"I did?" Lan said. "I didn't have time to look this morning."

"Of course you passed," Kara said, her face glowing with pride. She pushed a crock of butter toward Mayten. "How could you not?"

In Mayten's experience, all parents thought their children were special. In this case, she had to agree.

"What's next?" Kara asked.

"Tomorrow there will be some physical challenges at the cove. My sister's men are setting everything up. They've assured me it'll be fun." She spread butter and jam on her bread, then took a large bite, savoring the sweet taste of strawberries.

"I'll have to come see. What time will it be?

"Midday," Mayten said after a swallow. She took another bite of the still-warm bread. "This is amazing."

"I'm glad you like it. I'll bring a hamper," Kara said. "We'll make a party of it. What kind of challenges will there be?"

Mayten took a sip of juice. The mango clashed with the strawberry in a tangy, but not unpleasant way. "I wish I could tell you, but the announcements are to be made to all the contestants at the same time."

"That's fair." Kara nodded. She turned to Lan. "Would you take some of this bread back to the men and save me a trip?"

"Sure." Lan grinned. "We'd better get going. I can practically hear the empty bellies from here."

Mayten watched curiously as Kara loaded a large tubular-shaped woven basket with bread. She wrinkled her nose, puzzled by the two long straps hanging off one side of the basket. They made their way to the front door and put their boots back on. Then Lan took the basket and pulled it onto his back like a pack.

"Take this," Kara said, slipping a small clay bottle into Mayten's hand. "It's oil from the sheep. Makes your skin very soft."

Did Lan use this oil? Or were his hands so soft from working with the sheep?

"You'll need it when you visit the Sun Clan," Kara continued. "That's where my people hail from. The air is very dry."

"Thank you." Mayten tucked the bottle into a pocket. "And thank you for the food. It was delicious. I'll see you tomorrow."

Lan whistled as they left the house and two dogs ran up. They were small compared to Anatolian and very fast. Their coats were mostly white with black patches of short hair, similar to Tray's dogs but with long tails. They circled around Lan's feet, yipping and whining. Mayten bent down and tried to scratch them as they dashed about.

"Meet Bud and Carla," Lan said. "The best sheepdogs around."

"They have a lot of energy," Mayten said as she stood.

"Go to work," Lan said firmly, flicking his hand. The dogs sprinted off toward the sheep.

"And they're very well-behaved."

"Working dogs," he said. "They earn their keep. You can trust me on that."

On the walk back, Mayten told Lan all about Anatolian and how he helped keep the homestead safe. Lan told stories about the ranch dogs. When they got within a stone's throw of the crowds who were now busily making purchases, Mayten slowed to a stop, suddenly reluctant to face the smiles and the glares again. "I'm going to leave you here and head home. I think I'd like some time alone before tomorrow. Thank you for sharing your home with me."

"Of course." He grinned. "I enjoyed your company."

"It was fun and your ma is great." Mayten gave him a smile, ignoring the fluttering in her stomach. She turned away, thinking about what she needed to do next—

"Lan, where were you?"

Mayten glanced back to see a pretty girl with thick black braids run up to Lan and take his arm, looking back at Mayten with a frown.

She should have realized. After all, he was old enough to pledge. Her spirits fell a bit as she started up the hill toward home.

It's no big deal. I'm too busy for a relationship, anyway. I'm just overly tired. I'll have a long nap and some snuggle time with Pumpkin.

She had several hours before she had to help her sisters. Tomorrow would be a new day with troubles of its own. But as she reclaimed her bed and began to drift off, the looming presence of doom, dark and sinister, slipped into her mind.

CHAPTER TWENTY

ayten was surprised at how organized Dado and Mortise were when she went down to the cove the next morning, especially after a long day at the market. She met them an hour before the start of the games and found they had already set up three staging areas.

It was a perfect morning. The fog had already burned off, but it wasn't too hot. The sky shone a robin's egg blue against the darker waters of the cove.

"Here, you can take notes on how the contestants do." Dado handed Mayten a flat, rectangular writing board with paper affixed along with a small inkpot and pen. It was like a little table she could hold in her hands or on her lap.

"Thank you," she said, grinning so wide she thought her cheeks might split. "Did you make this?"

He nodded, his cheeks blooming red as a summer apple.

"It's great!" She gave Dado an awkward hug, then stepped back, cradling the table box in her arms. She looked at both brothers. "Why don't you walk me through the competitions?"

Dado gestured at five small rowboats drawn up on the shore. "First is a boat race around a buoy. The contestants will pick partners, push the boats out, then row around the buoy and back to shore."

"Sounds like it'll be fun to watch." Mayten gave an approving nod. "It will also give me a chance to see how the contestants work with each other."

Dado nodded.

Mortise pointed to a rope lying on the sand a distance away from the boats. "Next, they'll form two teams for a rope pull contest."

He went over and drew a line in the sand under the middle of the rope. "The team that is pulled across this line first, loses. But we didn't know if you wanted to choose the teams or let contestants choose their own teams?"

Mayten rubbed her chin, considering. "If we choose the teams, the sides will be more even so it will be a tighter competition. If they choose the teams, it might be enlightening."

"Or," Dado added, "you could pick two captains to choose their team members."

Mayten thought about what it would be like to be the last person picked. She didn't like that idea. "I think I'll choose the teams."

Dado pointed at ten sticks they'd pushed into wet sand about four feet apart further down the shore. "This will be the sandcastle building area. It will be a timed build. They can use anything found in nature, but nothing made by hand to build their castles. This will be an individual event."

She studied the waves for a moment. Yes, this was a cove, mostly protected from big waves. Still . . . "Isn't there a tide? Will that destroy the castles?"

"We're at high tide now. The water will be going out until the tide shifts much later today. The castles should be fine until the next high tide."

She nodded. "This is perfect. Thank you both so much."

A noise caught her attention and Mayten turned to see people coming down to the beach, surprised to see families with children along with people carrying hampers and blankets. "I'm surprised so many can come in the middle of the day."

"The entire town takes the day after market off," Mortise said.

"We need to keep the crowds out of this area." Mayten said.

Dado and Mortise looked at each other and grinned. They raced to opposite ends of the cove, lifted long sticks connected by a light rope, and stuck them in the ground. They pushed two more sticks into the sand. The two sticks had also been tied in a way that helped the rope stay off the ground. It made a visual barrier for the people to sit behind and watch.

The brothers had thought of everything.

The twins walked up, babies in their baskets and Wollemi at their heels. Wollemi carried a large lunch basket and all three had blankets draped over their shoulders.

Her stomach fluttered as though filled with butterflies. Thank the Singer, Dado and Mortise were running these events.

She noted the position of the sun straight overhead and handed a paper with the contestants' names to Dado. He grinned at her, then turned to the crowd.

"Welcome to the first, and possibly first annual beach games!" he called, his voice loud and strong. "These games are part of the selection process for the king, but if all goes well, maybe we'll do them yearly for the fun of it!"

The crowd cheered, the sound so loud Mayten was tempted to cover her ears.

Dado held up his hands, waiting for silence. "Gale Sailer, Rill Wave Runner, Pepper and Cumin Merchant, Lan Shepherd, Sugar Baker, Butch and Skinner Butcher, Chamfer Builder, and Purl Leader, please come forward."

One by one, the contestants slogged their way through the sand, ducking under the rope to stand before the two men. Parents and friends clapped and cheered.

Rill winked at Mayten as he passed and her face grew warm. Lan gave her a shy, dimpled smile.

Dado held up his hands again to quiet the crowd. "You'll pair up for the first test," he told the contestants.

Mayten watched carefully as he explained the rowing challenge and the contestants paired up. The two sets of siblings, who also happened to be the youngest contestants, paired immediately. Rill grabbed Gale Sailor's hand. They probably knew each other, a major advantage as they were both seafaring folk.

Lan and Sugar looked at each other shyly and became a pair, leaving Chamfer, the single father, with the red-haired Purl, daughter of the clan leader.

Mortise positioned the pairs in front of the rowboats. Dado raised an arm, then dropped it. "Go!"

The crowd yelled and cheered as the teams scrambled into the boats.

Rill and Gale were off like a flash, rowing like they'd been born to it. Lan and Sugar took longer to coordinate their rowing. Mayten was surprised to see Chamfer and Purl working together and making good time.

The two sets of siblings had been busy kicking sand at each other when Dado yelled, "Go!"

Mayten bit back a smile as the young ones tripped over each other, trying to get into their boats.

The crowd shouted. Mayten glanced up, shocked to see the first boat approaching the buoy.

The hair on her arms rose as Rill and Gale rounded the buoy first, Chamfer and Purl close behind. Lan and Sugar trailed by a boat length but seemed to be gaining.

The siblings' boats were neck and neck when Skinner used his ore to splash water at the sisters' boat. Pepper stood up, swaying as the boat rocked. She planted her hands on her hips. "Knock it off—"

The boys' boat hit the girls' boat and Pepper went over the side.

The crowd groaned and Mayten's heart leapt into her throat. What if the girl got hurt, or killed? How would she explain that to the king?

Pepper's mother stood up, yelling at the boys. Cumin screamed, searching the water frantically for her sister.

The boys laughed, using the distraction to pull ahead.

Rill and Gale changed course when they saw Pepper go into the water. Working together, they retraced their path, rapidly gaining on Pepper and Cumin's boat.

Safety first, safety last, it's part of our code, Flurry had said.

Cumin sat in her boat, tears streaming down her face as Gale grabbed the side of the boat, holding it steady while Pepper pulled herself back aboard.

Chamfer and Purl caught up just as Rill and Gale let go of the girls' boat and started rowing again.

The cheering grew to a roar. Mayten swallowed, then swallowed again, trying to get moisture back in her mouth.

Gale and Rill's boat touched the beach a few feet ahead of Chamfer and Purl. The pair quickly dragged their boat on shore and slapped hands in victory before turning to greet Chamfer and Purl. Lan and Sugar pulled up next, laughing as they tumbled out of their boat.

Butch and Skinner dragged their boat up on the sand, glaring at each other.

"Couldn't you flirt later?" Butch yelled. "You ruined it for us!" He stood with clenched fists as though ready to punch his brother.

Skinner shoved Butch and stomped away.

Mayten made notes, pleased to have her portable table at hand. Skinner and Pepper would likely be the first to be eliminated. She needed mature people to recommend to the king and these two were definitely not mature.

She'd wait and see how they did in the other events, though.

She was impressed with Rill and Gale, willing to sacrifice their lead to make sure Pepper was okay. That showed good leadership.

Better to break up all the pairs for the pulling competition. A good leader didn't get to choose who they worked with all the time.

Another cheer drew her attention. Gale and Rill stood in front of the boats, grinning and bowing as Dado raised their hands high. The crowd held their cups high, acknowledging the winners.

"We'll take a short break," Dado said. "Meet back here in fifteen minutes for the next competition!"

The girls dragged their boat on shore, miserably watching the other contestants head off to their families and friends. As soon as their boat was out of the water, the girls ran to their mother's blanket. Coriander put an arm around Cumin and shook a chastising finger at Pepper.

Mayten shook her head, tucked her table board under her arm, and squished her way through the sand to her brothers. "Well, that was interesting."

"Enlightening," Dado agreed.

"Have you decided on teams for the rope pull?" Mortis rubbed a hand across his glistening forehead.

Mayten nodded. "Let's split up the pairs and see what happens when the siblings are apart."

"Sounds good," Mortise said. "And now for a drink."

Mayten followed them to the colorful quilt her sisters had spread out on the sand. The twins handed them each a cup of juice and a roll filled with sliced meat. Mayten hadn't realized how thirsty she was and gulped the sweet juice, letting a dribble slide down her chin. She flopped down on the blanket and took a bite of her sandwich.

"That was exciting!" Wollemi said.

Mayten nodded, but was too busy eating to say anything.

It barely felt like they'd sat down when Dado drained his cup and stood. "Ready for round two?"

"Ready," Mayten said, swallowing her last bite of sandwich. She jumped to her feet, drained the last swallow of juice, and handed her cup to Zigba. "Thank you."

She followed the brothers to the rope pull area, feeling more like a waddling duck in the deep sand than the king's representative.

Dado quieted the crowd and once again called the contestants forward. Pepper had the good grace to look embarrassed as she walked slowly across the sand, but Skinner still wore a scowl on his face.

Dado stood at the midpoint of the rope and deepened the line in the sand on either side of it with his foot. "Each team will control one side of the rope. Lift together, pull together, and try to drag the other team across this line. Three members across the line and your team loses."

He called out the team members and the contestants lined up.

Pepper, Butch, Lan, Purl, and Rill picked up one end of the rope. Rill positioned each person on the rope with himself at the end, serving as an anchor. He'd placed Lan directly in front of him.

Cumin, Skinner, Sugar, Chamfer, and Gale picked up the other end of the rope. Gale took the lead on her side, putting herself and Chamfer as anchors on her end of the rope, with Chamfer at the end.

Smart. Mayten jotted a few notes. The teams looked evenly matched.

Dado held one hand high, then dropped it. "Go."

Rill shouted. Muscles tightened and feet dug into the sand. The crowd roared, cheering for their favorites. Over the chaos rose the voices of Gale and Rill shouting encouragement to their teams.

Purl's foot slipped. Lan reached forward, supporting her with one arm.

That shows kindness and compassion. She jotted another note. Leadership seemed to be a combination of strength, support, and compassionate action. Mayten added those things to a growing list of things to look for.

Cumin was starting to weaken. Mayten could see her legs shaking and the girl's feet starting to slide. Chamfer's voice rose above the crowd's cheers. "Come on, Cumin, you're doing great. You've got this."

Cumin gave a curt nod, firmed her jaw, and pulled. Encouragement. Mayten added to the list. Sugar surprised Mayten by propping Skinner up, muscles in her arms bulging.

Must be the baking.

The rope moved one way, then the other, neither team willing to give way.

"On three, pull," Rill yelled. "One, two, three." His team gave a huge yank on the rope knocking Cumin to the ground, and she was dragged across the line.

The crowd groaned. Mayten held her breath as the teams struggled. Cumin stayed on the ground, shoving with her feet. Sugar fell and did the same.

Other competitors ended up in the sand, shoving backwards as hard as they could with their legs.

Judging by the look on Pepper's face, the girl was running out of steam. Same with her sister and a few others.

Mayten was trying to be objective but seeing Rill and Lan on one team made her secretly hope they would win.

Rill's voice rang out again. "On three. One. Two, Three!" His team hauled on the rope. Cumin screamed, dropping the rope and clutching her hands in pain.

The rest of her team tripped and stumbled as one by one they were yanked across the line.

Mayten let out a breath, set down her writing board, and joined the cheering, clapping so loud her hands stung.

Rill's team jumped up and down, grinning and hugging each other. He surprised her again by leading his group over to the losing team, shaking hands and slapping shoulders.

Skinner refused to shake hands and stomped off again.

Chamfer and Sugar stopped to see if Cumin was okay, clucking sympathetically over her blistered hands.

Gale, big smile on her face, slapped Rill playfully and congratulated the winning team.

The king was right. A lot could be told about people when during—and after—competing.

The young girls and Skinner were definitely not mature and that was hampering their chances.

Was *she* mature enough for the things the king kept asking her to do? What was it that made a person mature, anyway?

Dado asked the winning team to take a bow and they received cheers from the crowd. During the cheering, a woman with muscled arms marched up to Mayten, face red and angry. "This is clearly not fair. My son Skinner wasn't given a chance. The other team had two strong men on it. I think you should mix up the teams and do it over."

Mayten's heart stuck in her throat. What could she say to calm this angry woman?

She took a deep breath, reminding herself the king had put her in charge. She could see her brothers turning toward the commotion and didn't want them to interfere. If she was in charge, she needed to act like it. "I'm sorry you feel that way, Mrs. Butcher. However, the king asked me specifically to arrange these games not to prove physical strength. These games allow me to observe how the competitors work together as well as how they act when they win or lose."

She paused, letting the woman think. No one could say Skinner had acted well in the games so far.

"Well, well," the woman sputtered. "I still don't think it's fair." She turned and stomped off, looking very much like her son.

Mayten took a shaky breath as Dado laid a hand on her shoulder. "You okay?"

Mayten nodded. She picked up her writing board and added one more thing to her list. *You can never please everyone.*

Another recess was called and Mayten and Dado joined Mortise.

"This is going well."

Mayten, still a bit shaky, realized he was right.

"The next competition is the sandcastles," Mortise said. "After that winds up, do you want to announce the winners of the day? The ones who get to meet with the King?"

"No, I'm getting a better sense of each contestant, but I'll still be meeting with Mantica before I announce the final candidates. Just congratulate everyone at the end, then tell them a list will be posted by the end of the week? I don't know when Mantica can meet with me."

The men nodded, and they all returned to the blanket for more snacks and drinks. Wollemi was full of energy. Mayten couldn't help laughing as he demonstrated the entire rope pull, explaining each movement as if they hadn't just watched.

All too soon, their break was over.

"Ready?" Dado asked.

The three stood and walked under the rope separating the crowd from the contestants. Dado called the contestants forward and explained the final set of rules.

"Contestants are to stand behind the sticks and build whatever kind of castle or home they want. I know most of you have never seen an actual castle, so just be creative."

Mayten watched as the contestants moved toward their sticks. Sugar and Lan headed for the same stick and Sugar immediately moved over.

Is she too timid? Mayten wondered.

Dado raised his arm, and dropped it. "Go!"

Each person approached the task differently. Several started digging big pits in the sand. Sugar walked around, gathering sticks, shells, and rocks. Rill seemed to be going for height. Instead of digging a pit, he piled up sand. As soon as he started shaping it, however, his castle toppled over and he'd have to start again. He laughed whenever it happened which Mayten thought was a good sign.

Each contestant seemed to be enjoying the event so much Mayten wanted to join them.

How long had it been since she'd kicked off her shoes and let herself play?

They had no sand in the forest, but she'd spent many hours building houses from sticks, leaves, and rocks when she was little.

As the creations emerged, Mayten was amazed at how different each one was. The contestants worked hard and fast but also seemed to enjoy the task, except Cumin who frustrated herself to tears, and Skinner who finished early and spent time kicking sand at his brother who scowled at him in return.

Dado gave the contestants a warning, then a few minutes later called, "Time. Step back from your creations. The judges will visit each of you. You can explain what you've made at that time. After the judging, everyone is invited to view the finished creations. You've got until the tide washes these efforts away."

Mayten joined Dado and Mortise and began the judging.

Pepper was first. She pointed to a small mound with a large fenced-in area. "This is my dream home. A small house on my own island with the man of my dreams."

"Nice," Mayten said. She made a note beside Pepper's name. Her "castle" was uninspired and rather selfish.

Cumin's was next. She kept her gaze trained on her creation. Mayten's heart went out to her. She was too young for this challenge.

"Mine is a family compound," she said. She pointed at the small round huts she'd made and the fence that encircled them. "I'd like to live near my ma and sister forever with our families."

And so joining this competition *had* been their ma's idea.

Skinner had drawn a battlefield with a lot of small lumps representing people on each side and small sticks for weapons. "I want to join the king's guard and defend the castle," he said with a grin.

Great Singer help us. Mayten nodded. "Interesting."

Butch, Chamfer, Purl, Rill, and Gale had all tried their hands at actual castles, some with more success than others.

Butch's was most interesting as it had a moat with alligators made of sticks in it, which he said he'd read about in a book. "Moats were filled with water to keep out invaders and alligators were like giant lizards," he said, face filled with pride and perhaps a tad of uncertainty.

Mayten liked that he was a reader. He was definitely the most thoughtful of the Butcher twins.

Lan smiled as the judging team approached, his blue eyes the color of the sea. "This is a ranch where all the animals can live happy lives."

He pointed out different corrals for sheep, goats, pigs, horses, cows, and a large pen for chickens. He used stones for each kind of animal. Bigger ones for the larger animals and tiny pebbles for the chickens. A large rectangular ranch house sat overlooking the corrals, with sticks representing people watching over the herds.

Overall, Mayten thought it was very well done.

The last one was Sugar's. Her castle had levels with each level smaller than the one below it.

"It's a cake castle," she said shyly. "I love to make cakes and tiered cakes are my specialty." She'd added shells and seaweed to create patterns and swirls.

"It's lovely," Mayten said. "I'd love to see one of your real cakes."

Sugar blushed down to the collar of her shirt.

Mayten led Dado and Mortise a distance away. "I don't know how to decide. They all did a good job."

"How about we choose more than one winner," Mortise suggested.

Dado brightened. "Great idea! Butch had the best sandcastle, but Sugar's was the prettiest."

"And Lan's was the most interesting," Mayten said.

"Most creative," Mortise agreed. "Three winners then?"

Dado and Mayten nodded.

Dado walked toward the contestants.

"Family and friends of our fine contestants." Dado's voice was still strong. Her throat would be sore by now. "We invite you to step up and see these wonderful creations. All our contestants have done an outstanding job. But first, we have two announcements."

Cheers and hoots rose, building to a dull roar. He raised both hands and waited for the crowd to quiet again before continuing.

"A list of those chosen to meet King Redmond at the Summer Solstice celebration will be posted at our shop by the end of the week."

Mumbling rose along with a few frowns.

"Why take so long?" someone shouted.

"The king's representative has a few more tasks to check off her list before she makes a final announcement." Dado raised an eyebrow as though daring the crowd to complain.

He gave a curt nod when the crowd remained silent. "Now for the winners of the sandcastle contest!"

He walked over to Butch. "For the best sandcastle, including a moat with alligators, Butch Butcher!" He raised Butch's arm and the crowd cheered. "You'll have to ask Butch about those alligators—it's quite interesting."

He patted Butch's shoulder, then walked over to Lan. "For the most creative creation, Lan Shepherd!" He lifted Lan's hand and the crowd cheered. His four brothers made loud hooting noises, which made everyone laugh.

Dado gave Lan an approving nod and scrunched his way through the sand to Sugar's creation. The poor woman looked like she was going to pass out.

"And for the loveliest creation, with her tiered cake castle, Sugar Baker!" He lifted her hand and the crowd roared its approval. Sugar ducked her head.

Mayten grinned, pleased the woman had won something. She might not be the best candidate for the king's consideration, but she wasn't the worst.

Dado waved and the crowd hurried forward, some stopping to congratulate the winners while others surrounded the castles.

Mayten helped the brothers pick up the fencing and ropes. It had been a fun day without too many mishaps. Relieved and more than a bit grateful, she finally felt like she could narrow the list, with Mantica's help of course. Maybe she'd talk to her brothers and get their thoughts. She was glad she hadn't had to do all this alone.

She shivered, realizing her trip to the Sun Clan was drawing near. How would she pull the same thing off without the help of her family?

The sense of doom returned, sweeping over her like an enormous wave.

Would there even be a Sun Clan to visit?

CHAPTER TWENTY-ONE

The twins invited Mantica over for dinner the next day. Mayten waited on the porch, too nervous to sit inside. She crossed her arms, pinning her hands to her sides to stop their trembling. The aroma of stew and fresh bread drifted from the house. Normally, her stomach would grumble at the smells. Now she just felt sick.

Dado went down the steps, offering the approaching woman his arm even though she was using a hand-carved cane that looked to be made by either Dado or Mortise.

The woman herself resembled an ancient oak with long gray ropes of hair and weathered dark skin as if one of her auntie trees had come to life.

Mayten stayed back as Dado led the woman into the house, helping her to a chair at the table. Her heart thumped against her ribs as though trying to escape. She drew in a deep breath, then another, and forced herself to walk into the house.

She hadn't been this nervous during the interviews. What was it about this woman that had her so on edge?

She'd handled bullies and disappointed contestants, she reminded herself. She could handle this old woman.

Mayten waited until Mantica was settled before she approached. Zigba had warned her that Mantica didn't see well anymore, so she squatted beside the woman's chair and looked directly at her. "Mantica, I'm Mayten Singer. Thank you for agreeing to help."

The woman gazed at her for a moment, her brown eyes faded as though the color had been leached out of them by the sun. The wizened old woman put birdlike hands to Mayten's cheeks and held them there as if reading her soul.

Mayten tried to hold still under the penetrating gaze. Her heart fluttered. *What can she see? Does she know how inadequate I feel?*

Mantica nodded once as if confirming something, then turned to Zigba. "I smell stew, let's eat."

The strong voice didn't seem like it belonged to such a tiny woman. Mayten flinched at being dismissed so quickly. It was like being with Solis. The Forest clan leader was quick to give orders but slow to give praise.

Mayten took her seat next to Wollemi, who kept peeking through his bangs at Mantica.

Acerola and Mortise put food on the table and then took their seats. Everyone passed their bowls to Acerola who filled each bowl with stew from the enormous pot set before her. Mortise handed out hunks of bread and Zigba circulated with a large bowl of green beans. The food smelled delicious and Mayten's stomach rumbled but she didn't think she could eat a bit.

When everyone had bread on their plates and stew in their bowls Mantica raised her hands, palms up, and gave a blessing. "This house is full of love and laughter. I can feel it. I ask the Great Weaver to pour wisdom into the hearts of all this night, and especially this young singer who is out of her depth."

She lowered her hand and began scooping up her stew into her mouth, smacking her lips and humming in appreciation after each bite.

Mayten blinked. Out of her depth? *The king chose me. He doesn't think I'm out of my depth. He didn't think I was out of my depth on the first quest.*

Indignant, she watched the woman eat. Hard to believe the woman wasn't choking. Didn't she have anyone to cook good meals for her at home?

A quick glance at Wollemi diffused her indignation. He was trying so hard not to laugh. She focused on the beans beside her bread. The last thing she needed to do was laugh at the woman who already thought she was out of her depth.

"So," Mantica said, pushing away her empty bowl. "Who is this silly fellow?"

She picked up her bread and pointed it at Wollemi.

"This is our brother Wollemi," Mayten said, scooping her first bite of stew. "He's come to shadow the star gazer."

Mantica tilted her head. "Come here, boy."

Wollemi's eyes grew round. He scooted off his chair and walked around the table, stopping next to Mantica's chair. She put down her bread and cupped his face in her hands just as she had with Mayten.

After a moment, she nodded and turned back to her bread.

Wollemi glanced at Mayten, wrinkling his nose like he always did when he was uncertain. She tilted her head toward his chair, so he sat back down, staring at the woman.

Zigba reached out and squeezed Wollemi's hand. "Would you like more, Mother?"

"No, I'll wait for dessert." She jerked her chin at Mayten and stuffed a chunk of bread in her mouth, somehow managing to talk and chew at the same time. "Tell me what you have discovered about the people here."

Mayten wasn't sure what the woman was asking. "It's been wonderful to visit the Ocean Clan. People have been very welcoming."

"Not everyone, I hear." Mantica grinned, revealing a missing tooth.

Mayten's cheeks warmed. Dado had predicted word of her confrontation with Matte would get around. Was Mantica teasing her or mocking her?

Before she could answer, the crone continued. "I'm talking about the king's list, girl. That's why I'm here, isn't it?"

"Of course," Mayten said. She scooted her chair back and stood. "Let me grab my notes."

She rushed to the living room where she had set her notes in neat stacks. So much for sitting around the room discussing her notes after a nice meal. She brought them back to the table and sat down. "Do you want me to tell you who I think should go forward so I can get your opinion?

Manteca shook her head. "Tell me what you went through—who you started with and how you picked them and how you winnowed them down. In other words, how did you get to this list you have."

"Okay." Mayten pushed her stew aside and spread her notes on the table. Zigba gave her a look that said, "I'm sorry" and took her stew back to the pot on the stove.

"Well, first I did the interviews . . ."

Mantica interrupted. "Start with how you let people know about the contest. I want to know where you met, what you asked them, and on what basis you decided to eliminate people?"

Nervous sweat tickled Mayten's sides. Evidently, this woman doubted she'd done a good job. As she walked Mantica through her process, however, her confidence grew.

"Show me the questions," Mantica said.

Mayten bristled at her tone but handed over the list of questions.

Mantica held them close to her face, reading each one, then nodded. "What happened after the interviews?"

"I went through the list and eliminated those I didn't think fit the king's criteria." She read the list of the people she'd eliminated after the interviews. The woman tilted her head and nodded without a word.

"That left me with ten who would continue on to the physical competitions, Gale Sailer, Rill Wave Runner, Pepper and Cumin Merchant, Lan Shepherd, Sugar Baker, Butch and Skinner Butcher, Chamfer Builder, and Purl Leader."

Mantica raised a finger. "Why Sugar Baker?"

Mayten decided it was best to be honest, no matter how foolish it sounded. "Sugar's interview answers were good, but she was rather soft-spoken, so I had originally eliminated her. Then when I realized I had an uneven number of contestants, I added her back in."

"And how do you feel about her now?"

"She did well in the competition. But she is still very soft-spoken and shy. She's the only one I'm undecided about."

"Why didn't you eliminate her? Don't you trust your instincts?"

Mayten thought before she answered. Why *did* she want to keep Sugar?

"I am trusting my instincts," she insisted. "I was a bit like her when I was called on my first quest. On that quest, I learned that leadership can be something that rises within a person as they are tested."

Mantica nodded. "Who have you eliminated from the ten?"

Mayten took a deep breath and reminded herself to stay calm. "Skinner Butcher. We all agreed he was not a good candidate."

"And his twin, Butch? What about him?"

"I thought to keep him." Mayten had seen nothing wrong with how Butch handled himself during the competitions.

Mantica tilted her head. "Anyone else?"

"Both Pepper and Cumin Merchant. Pepper is too flighty, and Cumin is just too young."

"Cumin is your age, is she not?"

Mayten straightened. "I don't think she wants to leave her mother. In fact, I think putting the girls' names on the list was Coriander's idea, not theirs."

Mantica nodded. She wrinkled her nose. "I don't know why I'm here," she said to the table at large. "This girl has made sound decisions. The king chose well."

Relief flooded Mayten with warmth. "Thank you, Mother. I couldn't have done it without my family. In fact, Dado and Mortise did such a good job I wondered why they didn't add their names to the interview list—or the names of my amazing sisters."

Mantica lifted her eyebrows, glaring at the couples around the table. "What answer do you have for the girl?"

They all spoke at once.

"Oh no," Dado said.

"I'm happy here," Zigba said.

"I already moved once," Acerola said.

"Not me," Mortise said.

Mantica started laughing. She laughed loud and hard, showing how few teeth she had. Everyone joined in and Mayten found herself chuckling.

"Would you like dessert now, Mother?" Acerola asked.

"I thought you'd never ask!"

That brought another round of laughter.

Mayten didn't know what to think of this old woman, but she didn't seem so scary now. As they enjoyed their cobbler and milk, Mantica talked about her daughter, her grandchildren, great-grandchildren, and the weaving she loved.

As Mantica stood to go, she gestured for Mayten to come near. Again, she cupped Mayten's face in her birdlike hands. "I hope there are two things you have learned here you will never forget."

Confused, Mayten stayed silent.

"I know you realize how big a challenge this task is. Never be afraid to ask for help as you have here. And always trust your intuition. You have a gift for it. I believe it comes from your training as a singer. In listening to the trees you have developed a great intuition about people. Trust that."

"What about Sugar? Was I wrong to add her?"

Dado held Mantica's shawl up and the old woman dropped her hands from Mayten's face. She wrapped the shawl tightly around her shoulders. "If Sugar is not meant to be in the competition, she will take herself out of it. But it doesn't hurt to help her see she is more than she thinks she is. I appreciate your heart in that. Now I must go. Dado, you will walk me home."

"Yes, Mother." The large man took her arm and helped her out the door.

As the door closed behind them, Mayten sighed.

"That was wild," Zigba said. "I had no idea she was like that."

"You must be starved," Acerola added. "Sit down and eat."

Mayten sank into her chair. Now she had to post the list and ruffle some feathers.

CHAPTER TWENTY-TWO

Mayten stayed close to the twins' home the day after they posted the list. She wanted to avoid running into anyone who was mad about being cut, mainly Coriander Merchant and Skinner Butcher whose brother got to go without him.

Purl made a surprise morning visit, assuring Mayten a ship would be ready to take them to the Sun Clan in two days. She also gave Mayten the name of the clan leader who'd agreed to let her stay with him during her visit.

Mayten kept a low profile, helping around the house, and running errands for her sisters during the busiest part of the day in hopes no one would see her.

Until Wollemi grabbed her arm. "You promised to go swimming at the cove with me and today's our last chance. Come on. You promised!"

She stared into the face of her little brother. All the time at the beach had browned him like a berry and the freckles on his nose had multiplied. How could she refuse a face like that?

"Let me get my suit on and I'll meet you by the door."

She dressed quickly in her swim tunic and short leggings and grabbed one of the sisters' handmade throw blankets. Wollemi stood by the door with a bright smile. When they left the house, he took her hand.

"I'm glad you're coming with me to the Sun Clan, little brother. But I still don't know if it's the right decision. I'd never forgive myself if something happened to you."

Wollemi wrinkled his nose. "Nothing will happen," he insisted. "I really want to see the stars, and this is the only chance I'll get until I'm older."

She wanted to pick him up and carry him to the barge and send him home, but the decision was out of her hands. She'd not been able to persuade Wollemi not to go. Besides, her parents had sent their permission. They would be going together whether she thought it wise or not.

She glanced up to find they'd reached the outer edge of town. "Do you mind if we don't walk by the spice shop? I'd like to avoid that one if I can."

"Sure, I know a path that goes behind town. I didn't like that spice lady, either."

While she'd spent two weeks involved with interviews and competitions, Wollemi had gotten to know the Ocean Clan people. Several greeted him by name, nodding at her with respect.

"What do you think of star gazing now?"

"I love it. The chief star gazer gave me charts to keep up my studies while we're with the Sun Clan. Maybe I can come back to study with him after the summer solstice." He looked up at her, eyes glowing. "The stars are so beautiful."

She squeezed his hand. That was how she felt about the trees.

The nose-tickling scent of cloves almost made her sneeze and she realized they were behind the spice merchant's shop. She picked up her pace, practically dragging Wollemi after her. "Promise me one thing."

Wollemi looked at her, concern in his young eyes. He nodded.

"You won't do anything—go anywhere—without telling me first."

He nodded again. "And you won't be alone. Kai and Tray will be there too. But I imagine they'll be fighting the black thing."

Mayten froze, pulling Wollemi to a stop. She squatted until she could look him in the eye. "The black thing?" she asked, heart pounding so hard it seemed the world could hear it. "What do you know about it?"

"The chief said the stars were uneasy and when I tried to listen, all I could sense was something bad and black." He looked at her with knitted brows. "We'll be careful, Mayten, won't we?" He threw his arms around her waist and hugged her tight.

He was wise for a child, wiser than many adults, but he was a child. She forced herself to stay calm. "We will. You'll be gazing at the stars at night, and I'll be working on the interviews and competitions during the day."

He nodded, and they went on. The path turned to sand and her feet sunk in with each step as they got closer to the beach. The smell of brine wafted on the breeze. She gasped as they rounded a large palm tree and the cove lay open before them, blue and sparkling in the morning light. Several children were already playing on the beach. They waved to Wollemi as he helped Mayten spread out the blanket. She kicked off her sandals.

Then Wollemi dragged her down to the water.

"Come on," he pulled her into the water. She shivered as cold waves dashed against her feet, her calves, and her thighs.

"Follow me. I'll teach you to ride the waves." Wollemi dove in and she followed, the salt water burning her nose.

When they were out beyond the shallow waves he paused, treading water. She was still able to stand. "When the next wave comes, swim hard toward shore and the wave will pick you up and push you."

She glanced around, suddenly nervous. The ocean was so much bigger than the lakes and rivers she'd swum in. Something tickled her calf and she stifled a scream.

Something was swimming with them!

"Swim!" Wollemi took off. After a heartbeat, she followed, not willing to be left behind. To her surprise, the wave did push them all the way to shore. Her anxiety faded as they rode the waves over and over, laughing and choking on salt water and jumping waves they didn't ride.

When was the last time she'd felt this free?

One ride landed her in a tumble, and she came up spitting salt water, her nose burning. She stumbled out of the water and collapsed, legs splayed in front of her. She shook her head to clear the dizziness and wiped at her eyes. A shadow cast a chill over her. Startled, she looked up.

Rill grinned down at her. He held out a hand to help her up.

Embarrassed, Mayten ignored his hand and struggled to her feet, wiping seawater from her face and nose. "What are you doing here?" She winced, realizing how rude she sounded, but Rill didn't seem to notice.

Wollemi raced up and Rill scrubbed his wet curls. "I was looking for you and this little scamp to say goodbye. Finding you both here saves me a walk up the hill. This letter is for you, Mayten."

He held out a letter, his gaze traveling over her water-soaked clothes. The short leggings and sleeveless tunic clung to her like one of those barnacles Wollemi always talked about. She felt her face warm as she took the letter. She sighed, noting Solis's seal. News from Solis was rarely good.

She broke the seal and read.

"What does it say?" Wollemi asked.

"She says she heard all about the competition from Rill and that it was a job well done." Mayten gave Rill a nod. "Thanks for telling her about it."

Rill pursed his lips. "That woman terrifies me, but there were orders to report to her as soon as I showed my face around the Forest Clan."

Mayten laughed. "At least I'm not the only one she terrifies."

She reread the letter to make sure she hadn't missed anything. "The best part is she's confirmed our stay at the clan leader's house. His name is Joshua Leader."

She glanced from Wollemi to Rill. "He's the one who told me that the rest of the team couldn't come. I wonder if this means the situation with the sickness has improved. Solis says he'll meet us at the dock."

"Yay!" Wollemi raised his hands and did a little dance, then jumped when a girl tapped him on the shoulder.

Jasmine, if Mayten remembered right.

The girl beckoned, urging him back into the water. He gave Mayten a pleading look.

"You go on," she said. "I'll wait here. Can you sit awhile, Rill?"

"I was hoping you'd ask." His smile grew as she led him over to their blanket. He plopped onto the blanket and scooted around in the sand until he was comfortable. "I've one question for you."

"What's that?" Mayten used her hands to brush more water and sand from her legs. She hoped he wasn't about to ask anything personal. She didn't need any complications like romance just now. Besides, she wasn't sure she liked him that way. He was charming and attractive but more of a flirt than boyfriend material.

"Did I make the cut?"

She looked at him, confused. "For the contest? You passed with flying colors." She thought a moment. "That's right—you left before I posted the results."

He grinned even wider. "That means I'll get to see you at the solstice celebration if you catch another barge on the way home."

"Don't be silly. It means you'll get to talk to the king and if he agrees, you'll enter his training program. How do you feel about that?"

His eyes smiled in a way that made her stomach warm. "I like the idea of talking to the king *almost* as much as getting to see you again."

"You're a terrible tease." She turned away, furious that she couldn't stop her face from flushing.

"But I'm not teasing. But I know you have other concerns and I'm not in a hurry." He leaned in and kissed her cheek.

Her hand flew to her cheek as he stood.

"I'm off. If you want to send anything home to your family or to Solis, I'll be glad to take it."

She swallowed hard, struggling to get her emotions under control. Carefully, she stood. "Thank you, Rill. That's a good idea. I'll ask my sisters if they want to send anything home. I'll prepare an answer for Solis tonight."

He nodded, and with a wave, turned and walked away.

Mayten shook her head. That man made her body warm in ways she'd never felt before. But he was right. She had no time to think about that now. She needed to pack and write some letters home and put together a report for Solis.

"Wollemi," she called, waving until she had his attention. "I'm going back to pack."

"Okay," he yelled. "Don't forget midday meal."

She hadn't noticed it was practically midday. She needed to change before lunch at the shop. Her last lunch. She would miss her sisters and brothers. She would definitely miss the babes. She would also miss this beautiful place. Now that she'd been here, though, the Ocean Clan didn't seem so far away. She could come again.

Maybe next time she'd be free of the overwhelming sense of doom that never quite left her alone.

CHAPTER TWENTY-THREE

After lunch, Mayten packed, wrote a few letters, then tackled her reports. She was in the middle of her report to Solis when she felt a strong pull from the oak tree.

Had Ma sent a message? Her stomach clenched—or was there news about the Sun Clan?

She slid on her sandals and opened the door, intending to go sit with her trees.

Instead she found Lan at the door, his hand raised. He'd been about to knock. Good thing she'd opened the door when she did. Getting rapped on the nose was not part of her afternoon plan. "This is a surprise." How could she send him away without hurting his feelings?

He smiled, the dimple in his cheek making her heart skip a beat.

Then again, did she really want to send him away?

"I was hoping to see you before you left and didn't know how long I might have. I hope you don't mind."

"I'm leaving in the morning." The look of disappointment on his face hurt her heart. She hated disappointing people. "I'm headed up to spend time with the trees. Would you like to walk with me?"

"I'd like that." He held out a small cloth bag. "Ma sent more lamb oil and a cake. She says you need to put more meat on your bones."

She took the bag from him and peeked inside. "Thank her for me. My skin needs the oil. I went swimming today, and it feels like my shoulders are burned. I'm not sure the cake will help with my bones. I got my ma's frame and she's still a stick. Hang on."

Stop blabbering. He'll think you're an idiot. She stepped back inside and placed the bag on the kitchen table.

"No sampling before I get back," she warned Pumpkin before heading back outside and beckoning to Lan. He walked beside her up the hill. Mayten was absorbed thinking about what messages the trees might have for her—good news, bad news—

"I like your bones just the way they are," Lan said as if the words were hard for him to get out. "I think you're beautiful."

Mayten swallowed, her cheeks flaming with heat. "Thank you."

She turned as if to admire the trees that grew along the path, feeling an awkward silence building between them. "These are so different from our trees at home," she said, trying to change the subject. "This one with the purple flowers is like a lavender cloud. It smells so sweet." Without thinking she added, "I noticed the beautiful girl with the braid at the competition. Is she your girl?"

Her cheeks grew even hotter. Why had she said that?

He dipped his head. "She's a family friend and would like us to be together, but I've never felt that way about her."

Mayten nodded, not sure what else to say. They walked the rest of the way in silence.

When they got up to the tree she'd communicated with— her *uncle* tree—she laid a hand on the rough bark and grinned. "This is my oak tree."

"*Your* oak tree?"

"Well, not mine exactly. This is the tree I communicate with." She felt awkward. It was always hard to describe her gift to people outside of her clan. Would he think her strange? "Look, I need to listen to the tree for a bit before I head to the Sun Clan."

"How does it work, the listening?" he asked.

Mayten relaxed. She thought about the young students at home and how she'd been teaching them. "I have to shut out all noises first—that took a while to learn. Once things are quiet—inside and out—I listen. The trees send and receive images. It's not like speaking with words. It's their own way of communicating."

He nodded. "Sounds like me with the animals. They don't speak in words, but they communicate. That cat of yours is on her way to you right now. She thinks you need comforting."

She loved the fact he communicated with animals . . .

"Pumpkin? Comfort? How do you know?" She looked back down the path and thought she saw a swish of orange tail disappear behind a bush.

He shrugged. "It's sort of like you described—images that let me know what the animal wants to tell me. I can 'see' her coming up the trail. The feeling I get is concern for you. I get the sense she purrs to comfort."

Mayten watched the trail for a heartbeat, then two. Sure enough, Pumpkin was heading her way. "The purrs *are* comforting. I'm going to miss her."

Pumpkin dashed the rest of the way to them, weaving around Lan's legs as soon as she arrived.

Mayten laughed. "Are you sure she didn't come to see you?"

He picked the cat up and stroked her face. "Maybe a bit of that. But animals are a good judge of character. You probably already know that if your dog doesn't like a person, you should trust your dog's opinion. Ravens not only judge character, they remember slights. If you make friends with a raven, you'll have a friend for life. If you anger one, they'll never forget it."

"How curious." She loved talking about this with him, with someone who felt the whole world was alive and able to communicate.

"Give a raven a peanut or a shiny trinket and they'll love you forever. They are very smart. Not like my sheep, who are a bit dim." He shuffled his feet, glancing around as if he was getting uncomfortable.

"I'll see you at the summer solstice. You get to meet the king, you know."

He sighed. "That's wonderful and dreadful at the same time. I'm excited to meet him, but scared I'll get tongue-tied as I sometimes do."

"Just be yourself. King Redmond is larger than life, but he's good and kind. It would be wonderful for you to get into his training. You'd learn so much from him."

"And I'd get to see you more. You'll be at the castle too, won't you?"

"I suppose I will, eventually. The king wants my help in starting a cross-training school for some of the giftings. Like tree singers learning to heal and vice versa. Those with gifts have always focused on that gift, but the king feels it might benefit everyone if we learn from each other. Since you already listen to animals maybe you can listen to trees too."

He smiled and she felt herself melting. "Then, Miss Singer," he put Pumpkin down, took Mayten's hand and tenderly kissed her palm, sending a tingle up her arm. He looked shyly into her eyes. "I'll say goodbye for now."

"Goodbye, Lan."

He tipped his hat and headed up the hill.

She stared after him. How much would it brighten her days if that smile was around all the time?

She shook herself and turned back to the tree. Yes, she'd been kissed twice in one day by two very different fellows. One older and dangerously alluring. One her age and charmingly sweet. A year ago, she'd never have believed this was her life. She was glad her da had told her to keep an open heart and that she had other—more important—things to do.

Mayten settled at the foot of the tree, her back to the broad trunk. Pumpkin crawled into her lap. The hard earth pressed against her backside, connecting her, grounding her. She drew in a slow breath, held it for a heartbeat, then let it out, repeating as she focused her mind and blocked the sounds around her.

After what seemed an inordinately long time, she began to see images, messages from the tree. There were no new messages from her mother except an image of the family saying Thanks-Giving. The circle looked small without her and Wollemi. She missed her father's deep voice and the way he looked at each of them with love when he spoke.

She sent a message to her mother—Wollemi playing in the surf, his tanned face smiling, the twins and their families in the shop, and her brothers running the competitions.

Then she asked the tree about the Sun Clan.

And received the same response—blackness, water, and that bone-chilling sense of doom.

There was something more this time, an image that looked like . . . a cave?

Chills raced up and down her spine. She hated caves. At least, she thought she hated them. Since she'd never been in a cave, it was hard to really hate them.

What I hate is the idea *of caves.* Caves were dark and scary, not peaceful like the inside of a burned tree. Creepy things lived in caves, didn't they?

She'd send Tray and Adven if any caves needed exploring. They were the adventurers, after all. Exploring new things was what questers did.

Satisfied she'd learned everything she could from the uncle tree, she said her goodbyes and headed back to the house.

CHAPTER TWENTY-FOUR

After the craziness of Market Day, the harbor seemed almost deserted. Clouds perched like puffy birds along the horizon, their vibrant white seeming to make both sea and sky bluer than blue. Three ships were pulled up to the long docks, two along the dock closest to where Mayten and her family stood. One ship—a beauty with sleek lines and pristine sails—bobbed at the end of the furthest dock.

A gull glided overhead, its lonely cry echoing the sadness in her heart. She would miss the gulls and the scent of the ocean. A couple walked hand in hand along the sandy shore where children and adults would be playing in the waves later in the day.

Too cold for swimming as far as Mayten was concerned. The sun had just started its daily climb.

The twins stood near a stack of small packages. Once they'd said goodbye to Mayten and Wollemi, they'd head to the barge docks with packages they'd prepared for Rill to take back to the Forest Clan, sending the family beautiful woven scarves and sweaters. Winter was just over the hill and warm sweaters would be more than welcome. They sent Mayten's warm clothes with Wollemi's. Those clothes would go back with the rest. Jackets weren't needed in the Sun Clan or so she'd been told.

Mayten hugged her sisters and brothers and placed soft kisses on the babies' cheeks. Seemed like she'd barely had time to spend with them. Her throat tightened, not knowing when she'd see them again.

She was surprised to see so many familiar faces. Butchers, bakers, builders and more. Had these people come just to see them off?

Wollemi waved to his new friends, his face crinkled in a way that meant he was holding back tears. He had so few friends at home.

Pepper and Cumin ran up and hugged Mayten.

"No hard feelings?" she asked.

Both girls shook their heads. Pepper whispered in Mayten's ear. "We didn't really want to go. It was Ma's idea."

"I'm scared of the king," Cumin added.

She squeezed the girls one last time and spotted Flurry skipping toward them. She smiled at the girl's impish face which split in a wide grin.

Flurry grabbed her hand and pulled her toward the lone ship at the end of the furthest dock. The closer they got, the more imposing the ship appeared. Soon they stood at the loading ramp, shivering in the shadow of the enormous hull.

"Is this your ship?" Mayten asked, studying the ship in awe.

The girl flushed with shy pride. "It is. Meet the *Lady Grace*."

"Wow!" Wollemi said, craning his neck to stare up.

Mayten relaxed a bit. At least they knew one person on the ship.

The *Lady Grace* was huge compared to the barge which had seemed big enough when they'd first seen it. Flurry led them up the loading ramp and onto the ship. Mayten gawked at the enormity of it all. And everything seemed so clean—from the polished deck to the white sails.

"A beauty, ain't she?" Flurry said. "These long poles are the masts. They hold up the sails."

Workers darted about the deck, some carrying boxes, others handling ropes. "Those folks are loading the wares and tying everything down so nothing will move in a storm."

A storm? No one had mentioned the possibility of a storm.

Overhead, sails billowed and snapped as the ship rocked from side to side. Mayten grabbed Flurry to steady herself. All this rocking and bobbing—no wonder they had to strap things down.

A breeze ruffled her hair and she shivered, regretting the sleeveless tunic she'd worn for the trip.

No one on the ship wore a sweater, just cotton work clothes. Wollemi was wearing shorts. She glanced at him but he didn't look cold. Too bad she didn't have some of his . . . what? Fortitude?

She rubbed her arms and thought warm thoughts.

"Come to the railing and say goodbye. It's tradition." Flurry dragged them over to a rail about waist high. Below Mayten could see her family, distance making them look rather small. Zigba waved, then pointed at the basket and wrinkled her nose.

Mayten chuckled. She was going to miss her sisters and their sometimes-stinky babes.

"Come on." Flurry turned away from the rail. "My da is giving the signal to raise the loading ramp."

Mayten gave one last wave, throat tightening as everyone in the crowd twaved back. Vibrations ran beneath her feet as the huge loading ramp thudded against the side of the ship and was secured fast with ropes.

Flurry continued her commentary. She seemed quite a different person here, perhaps because she felt more at home on water than on land. "We'll stop at the Sun Clan for trading before heading off to foreign ports. We'll stay a bit extra as my grandma is there and we want to make sure she's okay with all the strange things happening." The girl quickly looked from Mayten to Wollemi, worry creasing her forehead.

"It's okay," Mayten said. "He knows something weird is happening there. If you have time, maybe we can talk more about what we've been hearing."

Flurry's face lit up. "That would be great. I've got something to tell you."

"I've got something to tell you, too."

Wollemi turned from the railing. "Have you always lived on a ship, Flurry?"

"My family's home is with the Sun Clan when we're not at sea but we've been wind catchers for three generations. Our ship is named after my grandma who still lives at the Sun Clan." She waved her hand at the front, then the rear of the ship. "She's almost three hundred feet from bow to stern. See those three sails?" She pointed to the huge billowy sails, bunched partway up three long poles. "It takes a lot of people to hoist those up, but the wind catchers keep them filled, even when there's low wind. Watch now, see how my ma and da direct the wind."

Mayten watched as several people pulled ropes attached to the sails, lifting them halfway up the masts as the man and woman at the front waited, feet spread wide. The couple seemed somehow familiar though she had no memory of meeting them.

Flurry's parents?

The man was bearded with dark skin, muscled arms, and long black hair held back in a tie. The woman almost matched him in size, but her hair was a lighter brown, and cut short close to her head, like Flurry's.

"See there," Flurry pointed at the couple. "Ma is giving the signal for the apprentice wind catchers to direct the wind to back the ship from the dock."

The woman raised her thumbs toward two men at the opposite end of the ship. Both men were about Mayten's age, one tall and thin, one short and muscled. Together they stepped forward and lifted their hands.

The breeze intensified and filled the partially lifted sails.

The ship slowly moved backward.

Mayten's stomach jumped. Hard to believe such a large ship could be driven backward by a simple lift of the hands.

Once the ship cleared the dock, everything stopped.

"What's wrong?" Mayten asked.

"Nothing's wrong. The ship docked bow in, you see. Now that we're clear of the dock, we'll turn the ship. The apprentice catchers will send the wind from aback the sail, the side of the sail we don't usually use."

The men changed position, moving to either side of the sails. They lifted their hands again.

The world shifted as the ship slowly spun until it was facing the open sea.

Wollemi's small hand slipped into hers.

Mayten's breath caught. "It's all so . . . magical."

"Just wait." Flurry smiled as the ship stopped again. Men and women began pulling on ropes at the bottom of each large mast.

Mayten's mouth dropped as the sails stretched like enormous tablecloths, then snapped tight white and huge against the blue sky. Flurry's parents stepped away from the railing and stood behind the first mast. They looked up at the mast's sails and lifted their hands in unison.

Wind roared across the water, catching the sails with a jerk that made Mayten grab the rail. Her braids whipped around her face, stinging her cheeks and neck. She clenched Wollemi's hand but was too scared to speak as the deck rocked beneath her feet.

The ship slipped through the water, faster and faster, until they were practically flying over the waves.

Mayten squeezed the rail with her other hand until her knuckles turned white. How did anyone get used to the feeling of moving so fast? Wind tugged at her hair and pressed her pants tight to her legs.

"Ow!" Wollemi shook his hand free.

Mayten gave him an apologetic smile. "Do you know how to do this?" she asked Flurry. "Make the wind blow?"

The girl's smile dimmed. "My parents think I'm too young to learn yet."

Mayten studied the wind catchers' faces. Both were tight with concentration. Was it hard to call the wind?

She'd had to focus very hard trying to heal Rafe the woodsman's leg during their last quest. But that had been different somehow. What the wind catchers were doing seemed so powerful.

"It must be thrilling to hold that kind of power in your hands."

Flurry tilted her head. "We don't hold power exactly. I don't think anyone can force the wind to do anything. We work *with* the wind."

Mayten nodded. That made sense. She was learning that there was a give and take—a working together, not a conquering—with all the gifts.

"Come," Flurry beckoned for them to follow her. "I'll give you a tour of our home."

Flurry chattered like a magpie as she led Mayten and Wollemi around the ship, pointing out different parts, explaining how things worked, and introducing her to everyone they met. In the middle of the ship was a small cabin with windows. "My folk's room. It's like the brain of the ship where decisions are made."

There were so many people and words Mayten didn't know she began to feel dizzy. *Bow, stern, abaft, anchor, beam*—the words blurred together like a multigrain porridge.

Just when she thought there couldn't possibly be more, Flurry led them below deck. They had to climb down a steep ladder clinging to handrails lest they pitch off the ladder.

"These are the rooms you'll be sleeping in tonight," Flurry said, stopping before a small door. Through the door was a room with hammocks hung two to a wall, six in all, swaying with the motion of the waves. "Wollemi, this is Bailer. He's the cabin boy."

A skinny boy not much older than Wollemi was just leaving the room carrying a mop and bucket. He stopped, a quizzical look on his narrow face.

"Bailer, this is Wollemi. Would you please take him under your scrawny wing? Show him where to put his things and show him to the mess? I need to spend some time with his sister."

Bailor gave an impish grin. "Sure thing. You'd like to help me clean a bit, wouldn't you, Wollemi?"

Wollemi nodded but looked at Flurry with lips pressed tight.

Flurry patted him on the shoulder. "Don't worry. Mayten will be helping me with my chores too. Nobody gets a free ride. You be nice to him, Bailer."

Wollemi followed the boy with a backward look at Mayten. She gave him a reassuring nod. "He'll be okay, won't he?"

"He will. Bailer's a good kid. He'll be glad not to be the youngest for a change."

Flurry led them down the narrow hall to the next room which was almost identical to the one they'd just left.

"You can put your stuff on that hammock." She gestured to the swinging bed on the bottom to the right.

"I'm feeling a little queasy," Mayten admitted. She hadn't felt it up top in the fresh air but the closeness here made her stomach slosh a little. "Would you mind if I rested a bit?"

Flurry's lips pursed and then turned up in a tight smile. "Of course, I forget it often takes people time to get used to the swaying. Do you mind if I stay with you? If I go up, my folks will put me to work."

"That's fine. I wanted to talk to you, anyway."

Flurry brightened. "I'll go get you some water and salt biscuits from the galley. They'll help settle your stomach. And try to focus your eyes on one spot. That helps." She was out the door before Mayten could reply.

Mayten breathed deep, grateful for the sudden quiet, and sat on the lower hammock. Down here, the chaotic noise was muted. Orders were being shouted above, ropes dragged as they were moved, boots thumped across the deck, and water rushed against the hull. Fear clenched her stomach as she listened to the creaks and groans. The *Lady Grace* was a sound ship, she reminded herself. It had done this trip lots of times.

Right?

She shoved the fear down, focusing on the room around her. She wasn't nauseous, not really. Just dizzy from all the newness. It felt good to sit still, even though she knew they were flying through the water, a thought that threatened to let the fear loose again.

Flurry came back with water and two biscuits that were more like crackers—salty and crunchy. They didn't have much flavor, but she imagined that wasn't the point. Flurry took a seat on the hammock next to her. "How are you feeling?"

"Much better." Mayten was surprised to find it was true. "I listened to the trees before I left. The only new information I got was the image of a cave."

"A cave? That's what I got too! And I did tell my da what you said. My family wants to meet you. We can wait until midday meal if you'd like. That would be in another hour. The mess—that's where we eat—can be loud, though."

Mayten shrugged. "What do you think is best?"

Flurry blinked. "I've got two older brothers and an older sister. I'm not used to being asked my opinion."

Mayten grinned. "I've got four olders so I know what you mean. I'm asking you since you're the one who knows what's best."

Flurry grinned back. "Then I think it would be best to meet in their captain's cabin before the mess. It'll be quieter. I'll see if they want anyone else to join us."

With that, she was out the door again, leaving Mayten alone with her thoughts.

The problem of the sickness in the desert wasn't her main concern, no matter what Flurry thought. Mayten would tell the clan leader and Tray and Kai about the messages both she and Flurry had received—the cave, the blackness, the water. They'd take it from there.

She had to start interviewing candidates.

Mayten closed her eyes, enjoying the gentle sway of the hammock.

The next thing she knew Flurry was shaking her awake.

"Sorry, I got pushed into duty. My folks will meet with you now. Do you feel up to it?"

Mayten sat up, rubbing her eyes. "Yes, I'm fine. I didn't realize I was even tired. My grandda, when he was alive, used to rock me and I'd fall asleep in his arms. Being here reminds me of that time."

Flurry nodded. "It's always been that way for me. Some people don't take to sailing and end up spewing over the rail."

She held the door open for Mayten, then led the way back up the wooden ladder. Mayten clung to the handrails as she climbed, shocked when they reached the top before she expected. Fresh air slapped her in the face, bringing her fully awake. The wind tasted of seaweed and salt.

Flurry led her to the cabin she'd pointed out earlier. It was darker inside, but the air was still fresh with the windows open to the sea. As Mayten's eyes adjusted, she found a dark mahogany table with charts laid across a beautiful finish. The seats and benches positioned around the table were anchored to the floor as was the table itself.

"They'll be right in." Flurry stacked the charts into a tidy pile. "As I said, this is the brain of the ship where decisions are made. My parents are the captains, of course. That is where they sleep." She pointed at a curtain drawn closed at the back of the room. "Their bed is back there. The rest of the crew sleeps below. Let's sit." She moved around the table and Mayten followed.

The cabin door banged open and four people came in, arguing about some navigational things Mayten could not follow. She recognized Flurry's parents plus a younger man and woman who must be Flurry's siblings. They all had the same look—short, muscled, and swarthy. Only Flurry was tall and thin.

"Ah," her father said in a booming voice. "So this is Mayten the fabled Singer." He held out his hand.

Mayten flinched at the title but took his hand. "I don't know about fabled, but I am Mayten Singer. It's nice to meet you."

"I'm Khamsin. This is my wife, Breeze, my daughter, Sirocco, and my son, Theo." The four took seats around the table as the introductions were made.

Theo looked to be about her age, maybe a bit older, and took after his father, stocky with long black hair pulled back.

He kept looking at her so intently that it made her skin crawl. She nodded and glanced away from his piercing gaze.

Sirocco was older, closer to twenty, and she had her hair cropped short like her ma, with tattoos of fish running up her muscled arms. She looked like someone you'd want on your side in a fight.

"You know our Flurry." Khamsin nodded at Flurry.

"Yes." Mayten agreed. She felt so out of her element.

Mayten realized the family was waiting for her. She lifted her chin, determined not to appear intimidated. "Flurry came to me with her concerns about the Sun Clan and asked me to listen to the trees to see if I could get more information."

"She's a sly one, that one is," Breeze said, frowning at her daughter. "But I suppose it was a good thing to do. Did you get anything useful from the trees?"

"We all heard what you did about the blight," Theo said, leaning forward. "We know you can glean from them."

Glean? He must mean gathering information from the trees. She'd never heard it put that way.

Sirocco punched her brother's arm. "Theo's had a bit of a crush on you since he heard the new song."

Mayten's face flushed hot.

Theo's mouth tightened. He slugged his sister back. "I just think it was brave, what you did."

Sirocco smirked and rolled her eyes.

"Enough," Breeze said. "Let the girl talk."

"What song?" Mayten asked.

Theo's face radiated excitement. "Haven't you heard it? It tells the story of your last quest—the harsh weather, the death of your friend, and the evil singer. And how you led the others as the evil singer tried to drain your energy. And how you killed him. And how the trees sang your praises."

"Where did you hear this song?" Mayten felt irritation beginning to build. Few people had heard all those details.

"Sailors are great for collecting songs," Sirocco said. "We heard it came out of your own clan, from your sister."

Mayten's jaw tightened. She should have known. Taiwania had questioned her at length about the quest. Seemed she'd finally written her first song. Would have been nice if she'd said something.

"Well," Theo said. "Is it true?"

Mayten frowned. "I've not heard the song, but from what you said, it sounds pretty much like what happened."

Theo slammed his fist down on the table, causing Mayten to jump. "I told you! Sirocco said it couldn't be true, but I knew it was."

"I didn't say it wasn't true." Sirocco punched her brother's arm again. This time it was Breeze's fist that hit the table.

Sirocco closed her mouth.

Mayten could see why Flurry barely got a word in. "Isn't someone missing?" She looked around the small group. "Another brother?"

"Ah, that's our Helical. Cal we call him," Breeze said. "He's off on his wedding trip with the king's daughter, Cherry. You were at the wedding, weren't you?"

"Oh, yes. I'm sorry, I didn't realize." Mayten remembered the tall, handsome man who had indeed looked a lot like Flurry.

"Nothing to be sorry about," Breeze said. "It was a busy day for all. And most people don't recognize us when we're dressed up. Now, what do you have to tell us? The midday bell will ring shortly."

"To put it simply, I've seen what Flurry's seen—the cave, the darkness, and the water. My little brother, who will one day be a star gazer, saw the same thing. He's here on the ship."

"I saw him." Theo grinned. "Bailor finally has someone to boss around. They were scrubbing the deck when I came in."

Mayten closed her eyes and reminded herself that her brother was in safe hands.

According to Flurry anyway.

"The cave is new. Flurry and I both saw it." She forced her thoughts away from Wollemi. "I'll give all this information to the clan leader and the questing team when we reach the Sun Clan. Maybe they'll have an idea where this cave might be. Whatever it is the darkness represents, it's affecting everything—water, plants, trees, even animals."

"That's basically what we're hearing, except the cave." Khamsin nodded. "There are caves on the way to Table Mountain. I think your plan to share the information is wise. The Sun clan leader, Joshua, is a good man. He'll know what to do."

A bell rang and chaos erupted around the table as everyone stood.

"Time to eat." Flurry practically had to shout over the noise of the bell. She headed out the door, Mayten following close behind. They hurried downstairs to a long room that had to be the mess and joined the line of sailors, all smelling of sweat and sun. The men and women were of different ages and skin tones. Some men were bearded, some clean-shaven. The women all looked strong and serious.

She was handed a metal plate as she followed the line. A scrawny man with a ladle dumped beans on her plate followed by a crust of bread.

A burly man with kind eyes wearing a dirty apron handed her a mug. In his large hands the mug looked tiny. He smiled at her, revealing a missing front tooth.

"Thank you," she said as she followed the others to one of two long tables. She was glad to see Wollemi and Bailor down at the end of the table, already tucking into their food.

The room grew noisier as people joked and laughed and ate. She took a tentative bite of beans. Although the meal was simple, it was flavorful. She watched as those around her used their bread to sop up the bean sauce.

She leaned towards Flurry. "There are a lot of people in here."

At least twenty people. All breathing the same air.

Suddenly, she longed for the forest. *Her* forest. She missed her auntie trees.

She missed her family.

"It's only half the crew," Flurry said, talking as she chewed. "The rest come in at second bell. Then there's the kitchen help. About forty-five in all. We don't get long to eat before the second shift, so eat up."

Mayten noticed some people, including Bailer and Wollemi, were already handing back their plates and forks. She dug into her food, wondering how she would ever finish.

Flurry's brother Theo stood, banging his empty plate with his fork. Everyone who was about to leave stopped and looked at him. He pointed his fork at Mayten. "Hey, everyone. This is Mayten Singer, the one from the song."

Mayten's whole body flushed with heat.

People shifted, mumbling among themselves.

Theo banged again. "Turns out she's never heard the song. So tonight, I suggest a singing."

The room filled with a thunderous cheer.

Mayten wanted nothing more than to hide under the table.

CHAPTER TWENTY-FIVE

Nighttime on the ship was an experience Mayten would remember for a long time. The air was chilly, but the sea was as smooth as a polished table. Flurry led them past two older women holding up hands toward the sails. Even with no discernable wind, the ship continued to fly across the water thanks to the wind catchers.

They joined other sailors gathered in the bow. Everyone was bundled in blankets. She nodded at various greetings, relieved when Flurry sat cross-legged on the deck and pulled a blanket tight around her shoulders. Mayten followed her example, glad for the blanket Flurry had thrust at her when they'd left their room below deck.

Wollemi sat next to her, eyes lifted to the sky, his own blanket pulled tight. The look of wonder in his eyes was something she didn't think she'd ever forget.

Mayten understood that look. She felt it every time she talked with her trees.

She leaned back, resting her head against the short wall that enclosed the deck. A "gunnel" according to Flurry.

In the Forest Clan, the sky was hard to see at night, blocked out by giant trees. But here, there was nothing to block her view.

The stars clustered together like sugar crystals, more than she could ever count. She'd never seen so many stars.

A single note drifted on the breeze, drawing Mayten's attention. She searched the crew gathered on the wide deck, the folks leaning against the rails. Everyone's attention was focused on a man sitting on a stool. He had his back to the sea and held a stringed instrument Mayten had never seen. It looked like a small guitar.

When he opened his mouth and started singing, Mayten realized this was the same man who'd served her dinner, the one with the missing tooth. Though he did not look like a singer with his large hands and gruff face, his tenor voice was clear and beautiful. He sang several songs, the crew clapping and singing along.

Then he strummed a slower note, and everyone grew silent. He stopped playing and sang without background music.

> *"In the forest clan lived a girl who sang.*
> *Sang strength into the trees."*

Mayten's stomach tightened. This was the song Tawania had written. About her. She wrapped her blanket tight as Wollemi scooted closer.

> *"Her life was quiet, her homestead true,*
> *She'd no desire to leave."*

> *"But the trees were hurting, they asked for help.*
> *The king called her to rise.*
> *A questing team was formed to go*
> *And healing was their prize."*

"She heeded the call
And joined the quest,
Facing the unknown foe.
Traveling far and farther still,
Such a long way to go."

Mayten shivered. She'd wanted nothing more than to stay home with her trees when the king called her to the quest.

"As they forged ahead, she faced her fears
Through wind, and rain, and death.
Thanks-Giving done, she kissed his cheek
Held as he took his last breath."

Well, that was poetic license. She'd actually left Hunter with Adven who had stayed with him until he died. A tear slipped down her cheek as she remembered the angst-filled night.

"To the castle and beyond they went.
To where the trees lay dying.
She listened and learned through their stories and tears.
And joined them in their crying."

"A stab from an enemy is bad indeed
But one from a friend is worse.
As the evil singer revealed himself
For eons, he'd plied his curse."

Mayten felt the sting of the truth. She'd trusted the man who'd turned out to be the evil singer. It was the last person she'd expected.

"Our quiet girl who longed for peace
Joined hands among her friends.
Together they saw evil die
It's not how this story ends."

"The trees rejoiced, they sang and shared
This story far and wide.
How the quiet girl became a sign
Of love worked side by side."

"We share the song of one who sang
Through fear, and foe, and pain
Alone we are not strong enough
Hold hands and form a chain."

Then he repeated,

"Alone we are not strong enough
Hold hands and form a chain."

Mayten let out a breath as the last note slipped into the night. The crew members clapped and some banged cups on the deck. Several people pounded her back as everyone stood and stretched.

Apparently, the nighttime sing was over. Hardworking folks needed their sleep.

She made her way to the singer who stood with his back to the crowd. Before she reached him, Theo blocked her path. "Would you like to stroll the deck with me?

The way he looked at her made her shiver. It was like looking into the eyes of a predator who wanted a meal.

Her back tightened. "No thank you, Theo. I need to talk to the cook and then I'm off to bed."

He frowned and stomped off.

She approached the singer who stood wrapping his instrument in a cloth. "Thank you for the song."

The singer/cook turned to her, his grin wide enough to show his missing tooth. "Did I do your story justice, m'lady?" He bowed as if she were royalty.

She grinned. "You have a beautiful voice. But . . ."

"But?"

"It just seems so fanciful the way you sang it. Like something of a fairy tale, when in truth it was dirty and sweaty and I was scared and—"

He laughed a warm laugh, patting her shoulder with a plate-sized hand. "That's the way of all stories, dear. They take on a life of their own. But the moral's a good one, eh? And true?"

"It is." Mayten nodded. "It's very true. And thank you again."

"Good night, m'lady," he said with a grin and a bow.

Mayten turned at a touch on her shoulder.

"Let's go down and get some sleep," Flurry said. "Wollemi's already gone down. We arrive in the morning."

In the morning.

The song was a good reminder. She'd get others to help her. She wasn't in this alone.

CHAPTER TWENTY-SIX

The sky outside the small porthole was still pitch black when the morning bell rang. Mayten woke groggy. With Flurry peppering her with questions about the song, it had taken a long time to fall asleep.

Once again, her dreams had been filled with watery darkness.

After breaking their fast, she helped Flurry wash down the deck with seawater. When they finished with the deck, they scrubbed dirt and grime off the railings. She was almost too warm working in soft loose pants and a light sweater.

Sometimes, she and Wollemi would be working in the same area, and they'd roll their eyes at each other and smile.

It wasn't so bad to be outside working. The last weeks had involved a lot of sitting. The only thing she didn't like was Theo lurking nearby. She continued to ignore him.

The morning turned from warm to hot as the sun rose and she peeled off layers until she was wearing a sleeveless top with her brown clan trousers. Theo walked by with his shirt off, flexing his muscles as he went.

Work done, she stood in the bow of the ship with Flurry watching as they approached the Sun Clan's docks. Mayten's stomach tightened into a cold knot. She didn't know what she was expecting but this was definitely not it. She studied the shore with its empty white sand. Up a long sloping hill she could see shapes she assumed were buildings. "Where are all the trees?"

"Trees?" Flurry looked at her in confusion. "There are no trees. It's a desert. Mostly sagebrush, cheatgrass, some cactus. Up there," she said, pointing at mountains Mayten hadn't noticed, "is where our crops are grown. Table Mountain. They grow corn and potatoes, onions, squash, and beans up there. That's all I ever ate until I started traveling to other places."

Something else seemed missing as they neared the dock. Mayten frowned. "Where are the people?"

"Now *that* is a mystery," Breeze said, moving up beside Mayten. Deep lines creased her forehead. "The docks are usually swarming with people."

"Stand by to dock," she shouted, glaring at the crew.

Sailors got busy securing the sails and throwing ropes to the dock hands waiting for them.

"There's the harbormaster." Breeze pointed to a woman on the dock. "I'll ask her what's happening."

Breeze ran down the loading ramp and hopped onto the dock before the ramp was all the way down. The harbormaster, a woman wearing what looked like a bright yellow loosely wrapped robe with a hood that covered her hair, held up a hand. "The Clan is under quarantine. We don't know what is causing the sickness here. Enter at your own risk."

Breeze stopped before reaching the harbormaster and appeared to be asking questions Mayten couldn't hear over the sounds of the ship docking.

"Quarantine?" Mayten glanced at Flurry.

"I've never heard of that before, have you?" Flurry wrinkled her nose.

"Once, when we had the fever winter. You'd be too young to remember." The cold feeling in Mayten's stomach turned to ice.

"Do you think the fever has come again?" Flurry asked. "I lost my baby sister to that. I'm old enough to remember that much."

"I'm sorry. I lost two myself. I hope it's not that." A lump of fear lodged in Mayten's throat as she watched Breeze speaking with the harbormaster. Breeze gave a sharp nod, then dashed up the ramp to her husband.

What if she or Wollemi got sick and didn't make it home?

What if she died without fulfilling the king's wishes?

"Attention," Khamsin yelled, voice loud enough the entire crew turned. All activity ceased and everyone gathered around. "Here's the scuttle. There's a sickness in the Clan that is not understood. For right now, those who are sick are kept separate. Either in their own homes or in the community rooms. It is not the same sickness we suffered during the fever winter. It does not appear to be contagious though no one knows why people are getting sick. Each of you can make your own decision. We'll only be here a few days and we have enough food and water if you want to stay aboard. Some of you, like me, have family here and will want to check on them. That's up to you. Breeze and I will be going up to check on my ma. You children," he gestured at Flurry and her siblings. "Stay here for now. We'll send word if it's safe to come."

Flurry turned to Mayten. "What will you do?"

If she stayed on the ship, she'd be neglecting the king's orders. If she went ashore, she'd risk getting sick.

What would her mother advise?

Fear and duty warred within her. She had to tell the clan leader what she'd seen about the cave, but she had to protect Wollemi.

"Mayten," Breeze walked up and gestured for Mayten to follow. She led Mayten to the railing and pointed at a man waving up at them. He wore the same bright yellow clothes as the harbormaster with an orange sash across his chest. His dark-skinned head was completely bald, and he had a bushy mustache. "That's Joshua, the clan leader. I think he's here to get you."

Mayten blinked, glad the choice had been made for her. "Thank you." She smiled at Breeze, then looked down at Wollemi. "I think you should stay on the ship, at least until we know what's happening."

Flurry put her hand on Wollemi's shoulder. "He can stay with us until my da says it's okay."

Mayten lifted Wollemi's chin. "I'd feel safer if you stayed?"

Her brother looked about to argue. Instead, he threw his arms around her. "Don't get sick."

"I won't." She kissed the top of his head. Trying to look brave, she gave him a shaky smile, picked up her pack, and slipped it on.

"Thank you for everything," she said to Breeze.

"Blessings as you go," Breeze said.

Flurry wrapped her arms around Mayten. "Be safe, Mayten."

Startled, Mayten returned the hug. "You be safe too, Flurry. I hope to see you soon."

She released the girl and headed slowly down the ramp, listening to the wood thud beneath her boots. The sound changed from a dull thud to a haunting echo when she stepped from the ramp onto the dock itself. The ship rose tall beside her, water glistening between the dock and the ship's hull.

For some reason she felt like she was heading into danger worse than she'd faced when she confronted the evil singer. But why? As far as she knew, the sickness affecting the Sun Clan hadn't killed anyone yet.

Had it?

The sound changed again when her boots stepped onto the road. The hard-packed dirt was so . . . solid. The ground seemed to tilt and sway beneath her, but Mayten had learned from her time on the barge, that sensation would pass. She walked up to the man who pulled his hood over his head. It was then Mayten noticed how hot the sun was. "I'm Mayten Singer."

"You are, and I welcome you." His voice was warm but there was a tightness around his eyes that belied his smile. "Let's get you out of the sun."

He led her up the road toward a group of houses halfway up a sloping hill. "I'm sure the harbormaster told you of our concerns. This entire situation is so strange. My wife is ill and confined to her room, but I am well. I believe it will be safe for you to stay with us. I'm not sure how you will complete your task in this situation, however. But I'm sure you're tired and thirsty. We can discuss it more over a cool drink. Is your brother staying on the ship?"

Mayten's head spun trying to keep up with the man's words. "Wollemi is staying on the ship for now."

She hadn't realized she was thirsty until he'd mentioned it. Now her throat felt parched as if the air was sucking the moisture from her. "I would love something to drink."

The road was bordered by rocks, the ground so dry, it was a wonder anything could grow. Yet bushy plants studded the landscape and tall pole-like plants stretched arms to the sky. Many of the plants had needles sticking out all over them. Those spikey plants must be the cactuses—cacti?—Flurry had mentioned. No wonder the girl had a hard time describing them.

Homes slowly grew larger, round and low to the ground, like bubbles on a pond. The homes were all white. In fact, there was very little color anywhere, save for the clothes and beautiful embroidery she saw on the sleeves of the few people they passed on the way.

They stopped at one of the small dwellings, identical to the others. The path to the door was lined with rocks. In fact, rocks seemed to be the major decorating medium.

"Welcome to my home." Joshua led her through an arched door.

The first thing she noticed was how much cooler it was inside. As her eyes adjusted to the dim interior, she could make out the ceiling arching high overhead. Wooden beams bent around the inside of the ceiling, holding up something that looked like clay. The ceiling was painted white, but it appeared slightly different than the outside of the building.

Did they use cloth with the clay outside?

The walls themselves were painted with fanciful designs, similar to the embroidered designs she'd been seeing on their clothing.

"Sit here," Joshua Leader said, gesturing at a small table. He pulled off his sash and hooded garment, hanging them on hooks near the door.

Mayten sat, resting her hands on the table. While different from what she was used to, she could feel comfort in the air. Along the back wall sat a stove made of clay. Next to the stove was a large basin for washing. Shelves lined with food stood against the adjoining wall. Behind her was a living area with stuffed cushions stacked to resemble couches.

Joshua placed a clay mug in front of her.

"Thank you." Mayten took a tentative sip. She was glad it wasn't water, since the images she'd been receiving indicated water was part of the problem.

Perhaps there was something in the water?

Mayten took another sip. She needed more information.

"What is this?" The drink had a very mild taste, rather nutty and slightly sweet.

"It's juice from the fruit of a cactus. We use different cactus plants for many things, including medicines and soaps. Some cacti have roots to boil. Those are eaten like potatoes, but we also harvest some of the fruits to make juice. It's good for you. My favorite." He sighed.

"We've always been a healthy people." He shook his head. "I don't know—" His voice caught and he cleared his throat. "I just don't know what is happening to us."

CHAPTER TWENTY-SEVEN

Mayten felt Joshua Leader's pain as she would her own. Frown lines creased his forehead and dark shadows underlined his eyes. This man carried the burden for the whole clan along with the pain of his wife's sickness.

"The sickness didn't come on all at once," he said. "It built up over time. Feather, that's my wife, has been lagging in energy for about a month. Lately, it's gotten worse. Now she can't even leave her bed. She has no interest in eating, and I can barely get her to take a sip of juice. She's wasting away and there's nothing I can do."

He looked down at the table, studying the grain. "Every household has been struck, but not every member of every household. We don't know if that means it's contagious or not. Overall, my clan's energy seems to be leaching away. Our main export is our decorative cloth, but scarcely anyone has the energy to weave or embroider. We've still got plenty of food coming from Table Mountain, but when so many people aren't eating, the food starts to rot. We could export that food, but ships have started avoiding our harbor."

Mayten breathed slowly, forcing herself to relax. She needed to distance herself from his pain. "Has there been a drought or any problem with your water?"

He shook his head. "We have plenty of water this year and last year we had good rain. We've had years with no water, but not recently."

What would happen if this sickness reached the Ocean Clan? Or the Forest Clan? Would this be a repeat of the fever winter even though it seemed to move a lot slower?

Should she insist Wollemi go home?

The clan leader studied her with weary eyes. "I keep thinking I should just put you and your brother on the next ship home."

She shook her head. "No, I want to help. Do you have children to help with your wife?"

"It's hard to keep young adults here after they've gotten a taste of other clans. I have a son at the King's castle. He works in the garrison as a soldier. One daughter is a sailor, and two other daughters married into the Ocean Clan. Now it's just me and Feather, thank the Great Leader. I don't want them here. Not now. Not when we don't know what's causing the sickness."

In her heart Mayten knew the king would want her to help in any way she could. If she had to skip the interviews, so be it. "What can I do?"

He barked a sharp laugh. "Figure out what's causing the sickness."

He paused, still studying the table. "If I hadn't been so preoccupied, I'd have stopped your visit. People are so excited about the competition. In fact…" He reached into a pocket in his billowy shirt and pulled out a piece of paper. "I wrote down a list of people I thought would be good candidates. I did that before Feather got worse. And I'm sorry about your team members. Santana Merchant and Anteny Weaver are both sick and in seclusion. "

Mayten swallowed twice, trying to clear the lump from her throat. "Thank you."

She took the note from his shaking hand. "Have your healers had any luck with this sickness?"

He shook his head slowly. "We only have three healers. Two of those are sick. Our remaining healer has never seen anything like what's happening. She's trying, but . . ."

Mayten had once managed to set a broken bone, but this was completely different. "I could send for our clan healers. Our healers are strong and very knowledgeable. We have a whole training program for healers."

Hope flickered in his eyes. "Would you do that? It would take time for a message to reach them, and for them to get here, but it's a good idea."

"I'll write a letter as soon as I'm settled." She paused, then went on. "I've been listening to the trees. They are anxious but don't have any real answers. The wind catchers are trying to help, too. Even the star gazers are seeking answers. Besides a thick blackness, some of us were given an image of a cave. Does that mean anything to you?"

"We have a lot of caves, up under Table Mountain." The sorrow on the man's face made her stomach squeeze tight. "Most of my people are sick, though. I have no one to investigate." He raised his head and looked at her. "Maybe that's something you can do?"

His face brightened. "Those questers who arrived a few weeks ago. They should be able to help, right?"

Mayten nodded. "I know them. I should be able to convince them to go with me. They're here to help figure out what's going on."

Mayten had never seen a cave. In fact, the idea of going into one scared her—all that darkness and . . . bats.

"Joshua," a weak voice called from the back of the house.

"Excuse me." He refilled his mug. "Remember, don't go out in the heat. Always cover your head and always carry water.

Keep an eye out for snakes and some of the lizards here can get pretty big. Rest now, help yourself to whatever you need, and I'll see you when the day cools."

He gave her a rueful smile and headed down the hall.

Mayten unfolded the paper in her hands. There were fifteen names—men, women, boys, and girls. She sighed. At least she wouldn't face the king empty-handed.

Joshua had left bread and cheese on the table which she'd ignored until now. She broke open the roll and put a thick slice of white cheese inside to make a little sandwich. Next to the bread was a small pot with a knife in it. Inside the pot was a yellow sauce with black specks. She grabbed the pot and sniffed, wincing at the strong, spicy smell. She added a thin layer of the sauce to her sandwich and found it quite delicious. Quickly, she made a second.

As she swallowed the last bite of her first sandwich, she thought about the king and his expectations. She could practically hear him: "What have you discovered?"

How was she going to tell him she'd found qualified applicants in the Ocean Clan, but no one for the Sun Clan? At least she had this list. Hopefully, it would be enough.

Quietly she explored the house, discovering a bathing room and three small rooms in a row that butted up against the backyard. Doors to two of the rooms stood open. One remained closed. Behind the closed door she could hear low voices.

Through one of the open doors, she spied a mussed bed. The other open door revealed a tidy bed. Figuring that Joshua must be sleeping in the mussed bed to limit his exposure to Feather, she put her pack next to the tidy bed.

A door in her room led onto a covered porch. She eased the door open and stepped out into the shade. The air was hot but under the wood-lattice canopy that ran across the entire back of the house, it felt nice. The air was dry and smelled of dirt and a slight sweetness she couldn't identify.

Along the back wall, other doors opened onto the porch. Two had to lead to the other bedrooms.

Chairs had been set out along the wall. She pulled one close to the porch rail and sat down, chewing on her sandwich and studying the unfamiliar landscape. As she munched on her bread she noticed crows in the wiry bushes growing along the perimeter of the porch.

On second thought, they were too big to be crows. Ravens? She'd seen ravens at home but never near their homestead, probably because of Anatolian.

The birds croaked at each other. One separated from the flock and hopped up on the railing. It crooked its head as if studying her. She crooked hers back with a smile. There were myths about ravens being harbingers of doom, bad omens, but Lan said ravens were smart. They were also good friends.

If you make friends with a raven, Lan had said, they never forget.

"Right now I could use a friend." She tossed the bird a piece of bread. He gobbled it up and looked at her expectantly.

"Aren't you a hungry boy." She threw him another chunk which he ate just as quickly.

"How does one tell a boy raven from a girl raven?" she asked the bird. He cocked his head and blinked.

"How about I call you Ebony? It's the blackest wood I know and you're the blackest bird I've ever seen. What do you think?"

Their gazes locked. She couldn't look away from the raven's black eyes. The world seemed to spin—

Blackness swept over her so strong and fast she almost fell from her chair. She blinked, struggling to see through the vision. A sense of doom, the vague outline of something that might be the opening of a cave . . .

And the vision was gone.

Leaving Mayten dizzy and slightly nauseated.

The raven stared at her for a moment longer, then bobbed its head. She tossed it another chunk of bread and gave a nervous laugh. "I think Joshua is right. I'm starting to feel this heat. I think I'll lay down."

She tossed the last piece of bread to the bird and went back into her room to rest.

It felt like she'd barely fallen asleep when she woke completely disorientated and tangled in her sheets. She thrashed about, sure she was caught in something trying to drag her down. It took her a minute to remember where she was. Had she been dreaming again?

She perched on the edge of the bed and drew in great gulps of air to slow her racing heart. Slowly, her head cleared enough she could make out clanking noises coming from the kitchen. She wandered out of her room and found Joshua filling a mug from a pot he'd pulled from the clay oven. She joined him at the table.

"I hope you got some rest." He placed a cup of something warm before her. "Our habits here might take some getting used to. Because it's hot during the middle of the day, we eat our big meal early and use the cooler evening hours to work. That," he pointed to the cup he'd handed her, "is tea with a bit of a kick. It's called yaupon. The native island peoples used to drink it. It's like the imported teas or coffees we drink to wake us up. Since it grows wild here, we end up drinking yaupon more than anything else."

"Thank you." Mayten took a tentative sip. It had a soft, sweet flavor, definitely better than coffee which she'd never liked. "It's good and I could use a little wake-up."

"I hope you don't mind simple fare." He turned to the oven and took out two plates he must have been keeping warm. He set a plate in front of each of them. On each plate were slices of meat, some beans, and an ear of corn.

"It looks great. We don't get much corn back home."

"Corn grows well up on the Table. This year it's better than ever. Dig in."

Mayten did. The pork was tender, the beans were salty and filling, and the corn was the sweetest she'd ever tasted. "I'll write that letter and take it to the harbormaster after I eat. Hopefully, someone will be going to the Forest Clan and can deliver the letter."

"Thank you." His forehead furrowed. "I've got to go out and check on the villagers, see how things are progressing. I'll check on Feather before I go. She sleeps most of the time, so you don't need to worry about her." He sighed and pushed his plate away, leaving the food half-eaten.

Mayten felt helpless. There had to be something she could do. "After I see the harbormaster, I'll go by the questers' lodge and see if I can find my friends."

Joshua nodded. "Take one of those hoods by the door to cover your head and remember to always carry water. Use the leather bladders hanging by the hoods. You can fill them from the pitcher on the counter next to the oven."

He finished his food, looking as though he forced every bite, then rinsed his plate in the sink and grabbed his hood and sash. "I'll see you tonight."

Mayten watched the door swing shut, suddenly missing her family so much it hurt. If there'd been any trees around, she would have spent time talking with them. But she hadn't seen anything that resembled a tree since arriving. Thorny bushes and even thornier cactus but no trees.

Maybe she should try talking to a cactus?

The idea seemed ridiculous at first. But the more she thought on it, the more she grew to like the idea.

It was a place to start.

Following Joshua's example, she cleaned her plate and put it away, then went to her room to write the note. Once she gave the note to the harbormaster, however, she had no control over how long it took to reach her clan.

Mayten sighed and sat down to write. She could only do what she could do.

A quarter hour later, she filled a bladder from the pitcher, then studied the coverings hanging by the front door. All of the hanging garments were made of light cotton and covered in beautiful embroidery, some large and some small. She chose a smaller one with ravens across the front, the embroidery as intricate as if someone had studied the birds for a long time.

Was Feather a friend of the ravens? Had she fed Ebony her bread too?

Mayten slipped the garment on, feeling a bit silly as she drew the hood up and smoothed the soft fabric. She slipped the water bladder strap over her shoulder, grabbed the letter, and headed out the door.

The air had cooled, reminding her of the time of evening in her clan when activities were winding down. Here folks seemed to be waking up. She couldn't see much of their faces or even tell their sex in the large, hooded garments everyone wore as they hurried about their business.

Standing outside the front door, she looked down the road, counting houses as far as she could see so she could find her way back. Joshua's home was the tenth house up from the first intersection. There were houses below that intersection all the way down to the docks. Perhaps some of them were shops?

There were more houses than she remembered during their walk, but each looked so similar she was glad she'd taken a moment to get her bearings.

Movement caught her attention. She glanced back, surprised to see Ebony hopping along the road a few feet behind her heels. Maybe with Feather sick, the bird was lonely.

"Coming along for the walk?"

The bird tilted its head but didn't answer. She was surprised at how well it kept up, hopping along the ground and occasionally taking to the air.

Ebony followed her all the way down to the dock. The *Lady Grace* bobbed gently alongside the dock, the only ship there to be seen.

The harbormaster's shack was a small red wooden building halfway along the wooden dock. The door had been cut in half to provide a half window. She stopped at the window and Ebony flew up to the sill.

"Hello," Mayten called. Even though the shack was small, the interior was dark enough she couldn't tell if there was anyone inside.

"Hello," echoed Ebony.

Startled, Mayten stared at the raven.

Ebony stared back.

"I'm here." The woman she had met earlier moved into the light.

"Hi, I'm Mayten Singer. I was wondering if you have any ships headed to the Forest Clan?"

"Heading home, are you? Wise move, that."

"No, I've got a message for the clan, a letter asking them to send healers."

The woman took the letter Mayten held out to her. "There's a ship scheduled to pass through tomorrow. It's headed to the

Ocean Clan. You know the letter would have to go by barge from there. No ship sails direct to the Forest Clan."

Mayten nodded.

"I can't guarantee the scheduled ship will actually stop," she continued. "With word getting out about the quarantine, some ships are passing us by. There are those who will stop for news, though. I'll try to get your letter on a ship soon as I can. We need all the help we can get."

"Thank you. I appreciate it."

"That your bird?" The woman nodded at Ebony who promptly nodded back.

"Not exactly. I'm staying with Joshua Leader. This guy kind of adopted me."

"Feather is a great bird lover. She's got a whole flock of ravens hanging around. This is probably one of the young adults. It looks too young to have mated yet. Maybe he's got a crush on you!" The harbormaster laughed, the sound loud and somehow out of place in a town under quarantine.

Mayten couldn't help but smile, though. Ebony bobbed his head as if in agreement and they laughed again.

"Thanks again for helping with the letter." Mayten turned to go, then turned back. "Can you tell me how to find the questing house?"

"Straight up past the round houses. Look left and you'll see it. It's like three round houses fastened together."

"Thanks." Mayten headed back up the dock, Ebony hopping beside her.

She'd just stepped back on hard ground when she heard her name called. She turned to find Flurry and Wollemi running towards her, her brother stumbling over a too-long sun garment. Ebony croaked and flew off, returning a moment later and landing on her shoulder.

"What are you doing off the ship?" Mayten demanded.

"Nobody else is getting sick." Wollemi shoved the hood back on his head only to have it slip back over his face.

"Ma said we can come as long as we stay away from those who are already sick." Flurry shoved her own hood off her head—at least she tried to.

"Is your grandma okay?" Mayten asked.

The girl nodded, hood slipping forward over her eyes. She reached up and tugged the hood back with a frown. "She's fine. I'm so glad we found you. We have to do something, don't we?"

Flurry ran her hands up and down her arms as though cold even though Mayten was sweating.

Wollemi tugged at Mayten's cloak. "Why's that bird on your shoulder?"

Mayten laughed. "This is Ebony. He seems to have adopted me." She thought a moment. "I'm going up to the Questing Lodge to see if Adven and the other questers are there. Do you want to come? Maybe they've figured something out."

Flurry slipped her arm through Mayten's and Wollemi moved to her other side. Together they headed up the road.

It felt good to be with friends, Mayten realized, her mood lightening. If they all worked together, perhaps they'd find a way to beat back the darkness.

CHAPTER TWENTY-EIGHT

Mayten, Wollemi, and Flurry stood in front of the questers' lodge which looked like a group of three connected mushrooms, one in front and two toward the back with enough room to walk between them. Much to Mayten's relief, the evening air was cooling. She knocked on the door of the first building, excited to see her friends.

No one answered.

"Maybe they're all out while it's cool," Mayten's stomach tightened.

Flurry frowned. "Maybe they're all sick. Should we go in and look?"

What if Flurry was right? What if Kai and Tray were lying in bed with no one to care for them? Mayten reached for the door—

"Who goes there?"

She knew that gravelly voice.

Mayten turned to see Adven coming up the road, hat canted over his face, Tray and Kai by his side. Kai's quirked eyebrows and Tray's impish grin were all she needed to feel her stomach relax. She dashed toward them, dismayed when all three took a step back.

They didn't recognize her!

She yanked back her hood and flung her arms around Adven. The chief quester sputtered but didn't object. Tray grabbed her in a bear hug, swinging her in a circle before releasing her to Kai who kissed her cheek with a happy grin and sparkling eyes.

"What about me?" Wollemi said.

Kai grinned, then reached out and mussed Wollemi's hair.

Adven laughed. "All right, all right, you'd think we'd returned from war."

Mayten grinned, overjoyed at seeing faces she loved like family. "Feels like it's been years since I last saw you. And it feels like there *has* been a war with half the clan under quarantine. I was worried you were all sick."

"Who's this little scrap?" Adven growled. Flurry froze, then glanced at Mayten, eyes wide.

Mayten took her arm. Adven could be scary if you didn't know him. "This is our friend, Flurry. She's a Wind Catcher and has been helping me."

Adven nodded. "You're a scrap of a thing, but we'll take all the help we can get." He tipped back his head and glared at the sun. "Let's move to the covered patio. Kai, why don't you bring out some juice? Tray, grab the charts. We'll catch you up on what we've got so far, which I'm afraid isn't much."

The two disappeared inside as Adven led Mayten and the others around the first building to a covered porch much like the one at Joshua's house but this one had a shade cloth that hung between the three dwellings with tables and benches underneath. "All the local questers are down with the sickness. We've been okay so far."

They sat around a worn wooden table. Wollemi sat next to Mayten on a bench that looked as worn as the table. Flurry sat to her other side.

After a minute, Kai joined them, setting down a tray loaded with cups filled with cactus juice. He sat on Adven's right, taking up most of the shorter bench. "Have you gotten used to the taste of this yet?"

"I had my first cup today," Mayten said. "I think I prefer the Ocean Clan's mango juice."

Wollemi nodded so hard it looked like his head might fly off.

Kai laughed. "That's tasty stuff, it is. But this is good for you. At least they say it's good. Doesn't seem to be helping with the sickness, though."

Tray came out with enormous rolls of parchment—the charts?—and laid them in front of Adven before taking a seat across from Kai.

"First things first." Adven lifted his cup. "I hear a toast is in order. Rill Wave Runner had nothing but praise for the competitions you held for the Ocean Clan!"

The questers clinked their cups together. "To Mayten."

Mayten's face heated. Hard to believe she was getting compliments from a man who used to be grumpy as a bear with her. "My sisters and their husbands helped. I couldn't have done it without them. I'm afraid that won't happen here, though, with so many clansfolk sick. The clan leader gave me a list of names, so I have a place to start. Question is—*should* I start?"

Adven shrugged.

Mayten turned to Tray. "I've sent a note home asking Solis to send healers. They only have three healers here. Two are sick and one can't figure out what to do. Maybe Cather will come."

Tray's face lit up, then fell. "I'm not sure I want her here with everyone sick. But I'd love to see her."

Flurry sat quietly, watching closely but not saying a word.

Probably why she seems so wise for her age, Mayten realized. The girl listens and observes better than most.

"Excuse me," Kai said. "Is that your raven?"

Mayten glanced at the empty end of the bench just beyond Wollemi. She hadn't even seen Ebony land.

"He's one of Feather Leader's flock. Been following me around since I got here."

Wollemi stroked the bird's shiny head.

Kai tapped his cup with a finger. "We use ravens to send messages sometimes. There was a man that trained them to do it, though I'm not sure how."

"Really?" Mayten frowned at Ebony. "That's amazing. I've heard they're very smart."

"Enough blather," Adven said. "Let's get to it before it gets too dark to see."

He took one of the rolled parchments and spread it out on the table, anchoring the corners with their cups. The parchment was larger than the paper she used for her notes, being almost the size of her portable desk/table.

"This is a list of the entire Desert Clan population." Adven sat back. "We've interviewed at least one person from every family. Most families have been affected but not every family member got sick, so we don't think the sickness moves quickly from one to another. They all eat the same food and drink the same water. None of the folks we interviewed have traveled to other lands since this began."

Mayten nodded. Flurry chewed her lip as though deep in thought.

"The exception is the farmers on Table Mountain," Adven continued. "They seem particularly hearty. According to them, it's been an exceptional year for the crops. We figured perhaps their physical labor keeps them strong. Except for the farmers, the majority of Sun Clan members are rather sedentary—weaving and working with cloth." He scratched a whiskered cheek. "The sickness doesn't come on fast. Most people reported feeling tired, then they started sleeping more and more. Three people have died—just went to sleep and didn't wake up. We're fortunate there haven't been more."

He unrolled the second paper. "This is a map of the area. You can see that people down here . . ." He drew his finger along the bottom part of the map that showed the shoreline and docks, then up the road Mayten had traveled earlier, pointing to the clusters of homes on each side of the path. ". . . live close together. Not so on the mountain." He pointed at the top of the map where lines indicated farmland. The houses were larger in that area and more spread apart.

"Having large farms keeps the people separated. That could be another reason they are healthier. Considering the sickness is not contagious, spacing shouldn't make much difference, though. We're *still* at a loss as to why people are falling sick. What do you have?"

Mayten bit her lower lip. Her news didn't feel all that special after hearing everything Adven's group had accomplished.

She took a deep breath. "It was Flurry's idea to have me listen to the trees. She'd been listening to the wind and had seen something black that was affecting not just people, but plants and animals too." She smiled down at her brother. "Wollemi received similar impressions from the stars."

"When I first listened to the trees," she continued, "they gave me the same visions. Have you noticed anything different during your explorations? Anything unusual going on with the plants or the animals?"

Tray and Kai both shrugged. Adven frowned, a thoughtful look on his face.

During their last quest together, she'd discovered that Adven had a bad history with tree singers. He hadn't even listened to her at first. Now he seemed to be listening.

"I've been here two weeks," Adven finally said. "Tray and Kai have been here less than that. I haven't noticed anything other than everything's so blasted hot and dry." He glanced at Tray and Kai. Both shook their heads.

"Frankly," Kai said. "Everything is so barren, I'm not sure I'd notice if the plants or animals were hurting."

Tray nodded.

"We can investigate." Adven blew out a breath. "Any hints on where to start?"

"During my second conversation with the trees, I received an impression of something that might have been a cave. Flurry has recently seen the same thing. Have you come across any caves while you've been tromping about?"

Adven pulled the map closer. "There are caves all along this ridge." He pointed to the straight lines drawn under Table Mountain. I'd say at least six. What do you think?"

He looked at Kai and Tray. The pair leaned in, studying the map.

Tray pointed at the lines and nodded. "They are caves, but they're not evenly spread out or anything. Some are big, and some are small. I've only peeked in. Not going to catch me in one of those caves without a lamp. There are a lot of snakes here, most types hazardous to your health."

Kai nodded.

Adven pursed his lips. "We've got things to do today, but we can spend the night canvassing the town again. We'll ask about the plants, animals, and caves. Tomorrow morning before first light, let's meet back here. We'll go up and search those caves."

He nodded at Mayten. "I'm assuming you want to go with us?"

Mayten returned the nod. Of course she wanted to go.

"I'll go too," Flurry said.

Mayten gave her a smile. She was a brave one, that was for sure.

"I want to come," Wollemi said, sitting up tall.

"No," said Adven. "I honor your bravery, Wollemi. But it could be dangerous. We need more information before we can let you come with us."

Wollemi's face fell and his lower lip pushed out, showing his disappointment. Mayten understood. She'd been ignored and pushed aside many times—simply because she was too young.

But it *was* best for him to stay. Who knew what they'd find in those caves?

"All right then." Adven rolled up the map. "I suggest you rest up. Tomorrow bring water and lanterns or candles if you can. Throw in some food. Who knows how long we'll be." He gave the map a light tap with his finger. "At least we have somewhere to start."

Something had been bothering Mayten ever since they'd arrived. She held up her water bladder. "Do you think we should be drinking the water? We keep hearing there may be a problem with the water, but Joshua Leader says that it's fine."

Adven wrinkled his nose. "It smells strange, but everyone says the water always smells this way. Plus, everyone is drinking it and only some are getting sick, so I'm not sure water is the problem."

"It's too hot and dry not to drink something," Kai added. "And there's not enough juice to drink all day. It's more of a treat."

Mayten nodded, trying not to wrinkle her nose. She didn't think of the juice as a treat.

The group broke up, Flurry heading to her grandma's, Tray and Adven heading inside. Kai grabbed Mayten's arm as she and Wollemi turned to go.

"It's good to see you," Kai said. "It's been hard being here, wondering how you are and dealing with this heat." He looked tired and hot. His cotton shirt and pants were rumpled and sticking to his sweaty skin.

She pushed dark strands of straggling hair off his forehead. "Your home is near the ocean. I'm a forest person. Neither of us is used to this."

"I've almost shaved my head three times since I've been here. I might yet." He grinned.

"Don't." She tugged at the tail of his hair. "I like your hair."

He pulled her into a hug and lifted her chin for a light kiss which Mayten wasn't expecting. She pulled away quickly.

"Ew!" Wollemi said, startling them both.

Kai laughed. "Sorry, Wooly-man." He softly punched the boy in the arm before turning back to Mayten. "I'll keep it just for you, then."

He stepped back. "It's too hot to even hug you."

She laughed. "I'll see you in the morning."

She, Wollemi, and Ebony turned toward home.

CHAPTER TWENTY-NINE

That night after a small meal of fresh tomatoes, cucumbers, cheese, and bread, Mayten sat on the back patio with Wollemi. Feather was sleeping and Joshua was off doing whatever it was he did. Mayten and Wollemi took turns throwing scraps of bread to Ebony then switched to tossing a small ball of yarn when the bread ran out.

Ebony seemed to enjoy playing with the yarn, bringing it back so they could throw it again.

"You are a smart one, aren't you?" Mayten said.

Ebony's squawk was like a gurgling croak which made them laugh.

"Smart boy," the raven croaked.

Mayten could feel her eyes widen in shock. "You *can* talk."

"Smart boy talk," Ebony agreed.

Wollemi gaped at her. "How many words do you think he knows? Has he said anything else?"

Mayten nodded. "I heard him say hello, but I didn't think he could actually *talk*." Her mind raced. "You heard Kai earlier, didn't you? He said the castle uses ravens to send messages."

He nodded. "I wonder how they do it. How they train them."

An idea was forming in Mayten's mind. What if she could use Ebony as a messenger?

But how?

Lan said he received feelings and images from animals the same way she did with the trees.

"Wait right here." Mayten jumped up and ran to their room, grabbed paper, pen, and ink, then rushed back outside.

Hands shaking, she tore off a small scrap of paper and spread it on the table. Then she carefully dipped pen in ink and wrote:

Let me know you got this. M.

She showed the paper to Wollemi. "Help me tie this on his leg."

Wollemi gently lifted the bird onto the table. Ebony looked back and forth between them as if trying to figure out what was happening. When he spied the rolled note in Mayten's hand, he stopped moving and stood still, lifting his leg out to her.

Mayten laughed. "Looks like he knows how to do this. Now we just have to figure out how to get him to go where we want."

It took a few tries but they finally secured the note so it wouldn't fall off or hurt Ebony's leg.

Images were likely the best place to start. "Let's both think of Flurry, see if we can send images of her face to Ebony. Ready?"

Wollemi nodded.

Mayten envisioned Flurry with her skinny fawn-like legs and spikey hair and tried to send her vision to the bird. "Ebony, can you take this to Flurry? To Flurry?"

The bird just stared at her.

Keeping the vision firmly in her mind, she laid her hand on Ebony's head the same way she did when she talked to her trees. The bird's head was soft and smooth, not at all like tree bark, but she hoped the contact helped. "Take it to Flurry."

Ebony fluffed his feathers, then hopped away from her hand and out of Wollemi's grasp. He looked at them and she could swear he winked. Then he hunched down and took off, creating a small wind with his powerful wings.

"Do you think he understood?" Wollemi asked.

Mayten shrugged, not wanting to show too much excitement. The more she thought about it, the crazier the idea seemed. "Maybe he just got hungry. If it works, though, we could try to send a message to the healers in the clan. If ravens can fly that far, that is."

"I wonder if they can take a message to someone they've never met?" Wollemi frowned.

Mayten sighed. That was the big question, wasn't it? "It's probably a stupid idea. But it's worth trying. If this works, Ebony could probably get a message to our clan faster than a letter could travel. Think of it—first, a letter would have to get on a ship, sail to the Ocean Clan a day and a half away, then transfer to a barge headed the right way. Birds fly over the mountains all the time. If Ebony understands and can fly that far, he'd likely make it in much less time. Flying over the mountains is a more direct path than going around the island. He might make it in a day or maybe two."

Wollemi nodded. "If it works, what should we write?"

Mayten took a second small scrap of paper. "The what is fairly simple. But who should we send it to?"

"To Solis?" Wollemi suggested.

Mayten studied the end of the pen. "The clan leader might be too busy to notice or sitting inside her office with the door closed. Maybe Cather? But she might be teaching healers. Same with Ma. If you were there, I'd definitely send it to you. You'd pay attention to a bird."

He nodded. "I would. I bet Da would too."

A croak startled them as Ebony landed on the table next to Mayten and held out his leg. Mayten gasped and undid the yarn holding the same uneven scrap of paper she'd written on. Her stomach dropped. "Looks the same as when he left. I'm guessing he didn't make it to Flurry."

Disheartened, she opened the note and turned it to show Wollemi. That's when she noticed a word that hadn't been there before—

Yes. F.

Wollemi let out a whoop before Mayten could shush him. He lowered his voice. "It worked!"

Mayten stroked Ebony's head, more excited and—yes— more hopeful than she'd felt since arriving. "You *are* a good boy, a smart boy, aren't you?"

"Good boy. Smart boy." Ebony cocked his head and glared at her with one beady eye.

"I think he wants a treat," Wollemi said. He dashed in the house and back out, holding a chunk of bread. He broke off a large piece and held it out to the raven.

"Treats are good," Ebony said, his bird voice sounding eerily like a small child with a cough.

They laughed. Ebony bobbed up and down in what Mayten could only assume was some kind of raven victory dance.

"Let's send a note to Da, then." Was she sending this lovely bird into harm's way? What if Ebony got hurt or lost or something?

But what if he got through?

She wrote a note using the smallest print she could manage. *Da, we are fine. Need Solis to send healers to Sun Clan fast as possible. Please. M&W.*

They tied it as carefully as they could, aware it might slip off Ebony's leg if it was too loose, but not wanting the yarn to be too tight. He held perfectly still while they fumbled with the tie.

Finally, Mayten straightened. The note would either stay or it wouldn't.

"Let's think of Da." She stroked Ebony's silky head and focused on images of the Forest Clan, their homestead, and Da. She let the image of Da linger on his tall frame and dark skin, his curly hair and deep voice, his love of flowers, and even his kitchen and cinnamon rolls. "Please, Ebony, go find Da. Take the note to Da."

The bird jumped from the table and strutted around, then bobbed his head and sprang into the air, wings flapping hard as he gained height. They watched until he disappeared into the darkening sky.

"Do you think he'll make it?" Wollemi asked, his eyes glistening.

Mayten studied the sky where Ebony had disappeared. Had she just sent their bird friend on a dangerous journey?

Another thought niggled at her mind—did ravens even fly at night?

She shivered, hoping he would be okay, then straightened her shoulders. "I guess we'll have to wait and see. But Ebony's smart. He knows how to take care of himself."

Were those words for Wollemi or herself?

They went inside and Mayten wrote a quick note to their host, who was still out visiting families. She deftly outlined the plan for their trip to Table Mountain and propped it on the kitchen table.

Wollemi smiled, his face a bit wistful as he watched. "I wish I could go with you tomorrow."

She grimaced and put her arm around her little brother. "I'd like it if you could. But Adven has been leading quests for a long time and I trust his instincts. Now, it's been a very long day and I have to get up early. I'm going to bed."

"I'll be in later," Wollemi said. "The stars are coming out and I want to watch them."

CHAPTER THIRTY

In the morning, Mayten slipped out of bed, careful not to wake Wollemi. She found an oil lamp on the table in the kitchen, along with matches and a full bladder of water and several sandwiches left for her by Joshua Leader. She pulled the hood robe over her clothes, shoving the hood off her head as it was still dark. She placed the sandwiches in a pocket of the robe, the strap of the water bladder over her shoulder, and lit the lamp, storing the matches in another pocket. Cold air rushed in when she opened the door. Mayten shivered. It had been so hot yesterday, but now she didn't seem able to get warm.

A light hovered before her about ten feet down the path. Flurry waved, looking almost ethereal in the glowing light. Mayten blew out her own lantern—no use wasting fuel. She moved cautiously down the dirt road, moving faster the closer she came to the lantern light.

"You ready for this?" she asked Flurry.

The girl nodded, though her face reflected Mayten's anxiety. Together they headed up the hill to the meeting spot.

Mayten missed having Ebony hopping along behind her. She hoped the raven was okay.

At the top of the hill, Flurry's bobbing light revealed three figures standing outside the questers' lodge. Tray and Kai gave Mayten quick hugs and greeted Flurry warmly.

"Did you bring food, water, lights?" Adven asked.

"Yes," Mayten and Flurry said at the same time.

"Then let's go." Adven headed up the road at a pace that almost had Mayten jogging to keep up.

It was too dark to see much but the exercise was welcome. Mayten found herself warming up as she followed Tray and Kai. Adven was out in the lead. Flurry stayed close to Mayten's side.

The sun was starting to rise, taking the chill from the air and flavoring it with the smell of sage. Adven stopped at the base of a large cliff that led, Mayten assumed, up to the Table. He pointed to the right. "Kai, you take the girls and explore the caves to the west."

Mayten studied the path he'd indicated, noting dark depressions that could be caves notched into the cliffs. A shiver ran through her. Was this where the darkness was hiding?

"Tray and I will head east and work our way back toward you. Plan on meeting back here in say, three hours, before it gets too hot. Got it?"

Kai headed west, Flurry behind him and Mayten following. She was glad not to have to figure this out on her own. It felt safer to be in a group. Who knew what they'd find in those caves—if anything.

The air heated as the sun rose, and Flurry and Kai turned off their lamps. Mayten sipped a bit of water. This terrain was so different than any Mayten had seen in the other three clans she'd visited. It was barren, hot, and dry without trees for comfort. Rock-pebbled sand stretched as far as she could see, undulating at times, but never really breaking its monotony. Sagebrush took turns with another type of bush with thorns as long as her finger. Scraggy cheatgrass stalks waved forlornly in a tiny hot breeze. Thorn-laden cacti—short, fat, and round—hid like mice beneath bushes while their taller brethren reached for the sky.

Somewhere in the maze of thorny life, a lone bird sang. The notes warbled up and down, then slowly died away, lonely and sparse as the landscape.

"Stop." Kai held up a hand as he took a step backwards, almost running into Flurry. "This is the time of morning snakes like to sun themselves on the trail. Since these snakes aren't exactly friendly and their bites can be deadly, I think we'll slip around that one. Okay?"

He pointed to what looked to her like a curly branch on one side of the path.

Mayten bit her lip. All the forest snakes around their homestead were mostly shy. Only a few posed any threat to hikers and she knew which of them to avoid.

Anatolian always let her know if she misjudged a particular snake.

Mayten took Flurry's hand and Flurry gave her hand a reassuring pat. "The snakes are not looking to harm anyone. We just need to respect their space."

"If you say so." Mayten lifted her chin, but she didn't let go of Flurry's hand.

Kai navigated carefully around the snake, Mayten and Flurry close on his heels.

Mayten shuddered as they passed the innocent-looking reptile, suddenly glad Anatolian wasn't with her. If he'd been bitten, she'd never be able to carry him down the mountain. That dog weighed almost as much as she did.

No matter which way she looked at it, the snake resembled a curly branch. "I probably would have stepped right over it."

"It wouldn't have bitten you," Kai said. "Even if you stepped over it. Snakes only bite when they're coiled, at least that kind."

Flurry shook her head. "That's a myth, Kai. No matter the type, snakes can bite if they're not coiled. They just have a shorter striking distance."

"Oh." Kai sounded a little embarrassed to be shown up by a girl.

Mayten sighed. Flurry was so at home in this desert. Even Kai seemed comfortable with the strange surroundings. "Do you mind if I walk between you two?"

"Sure." Flurry gave her a quick smile. "I don't mind being in the back."

They followed the path along the bottom of the cliffs as the sun continued to rise. How were they going to search for three hours? As far as she was concerned, the air was already uncomfortably warm.

She squinted at the cliffs ahead, trying to make out any caves. If she was right, there were at least three caves not too far ahead that would be large enough.

She kept her eyes roving between the path and the cliff, watching for snakes. Once she thought she saw something much bigger than a snake moving alongside the path. The animal ducked behind an outcropping of rock and disappeared. Coyote?

Several lizards skittered off the path, setting her heart skittering along with them. A huge lizard lumbered by. The creature reminded her of the stories Butcher told about the alligator that lived in castle moats, but those stories hadn't been true. Had they?

She jumped as something—a dog?—yipped.

"Coyotes," Flurry said. "Don't worry. They won't hurt us."

The yips were joined by other yips, yowls, and howls.

Flurry grinned. "They had a successful hunt. That's their way of celebrating."

Mayten probably *had* seen a coyote by the rocks and Flurry's words weren't comforting. Gooseflesh grew on her arms as images of snakes, coyotes, and dark caves danced through her mind.

Eventually, they came to a good-sized cave. They stood in the entrance and peered in, but it was so black inside, they couldn't tell how far back the cave went. The air oozing out of the cave felt cool and a bit . . . slimy.

Could this be it? The blackness she kept seeing?

"I'll go in first," Kai held up his lantern. "I'll call you if it's big enough for you to join me."

His voice shook a bit, but he clenched his jaw and lit his lantern. As far as she could tell, none of them were used to walking into dark caves.

She glanced at Flurry, then quickly lit her lantern and fell into place behind Kai. He shot her a grateful look and walked in.

Mayten's heart pounded so hard she barely noticed the sound of a soft breeze where a breeze shouldn't be. Flurry crowded close, though she hadn't lit her lantern. She muttered something Mayten couldn't understand.

"What?"

What? What? What . . .

The word echoed through the cave over and over before fading away.

Before she could apologize, could explain she hadn't meant to be that loud, Kai cried out.

The soft breeze exploded into a cacophony of tiny flying creatures, brushing past their heads and blasting from the mouth of the cave like a storm wind suddenly set free.

She and Flurry ducked as hundreds of the little creatures swept into the sky.

"Bats!" Flurry said with a grin.

Wasn't that girl afraid of anything?

"Those were bats?" Mayten asked, struggling to keep from sounding like a frightened child. She ran her hands over her braids to be sure nothing was tangled in her hair.

Flurry nodded.

Kai's face was white as her mother's good linen and most of his hair had escaped its tie. He started to speak, stopped, and started again. "They should be gone. Let's get a better look."

Flurry lit her lantern. Together the three of them studied the walls and floor as they moved further into the cave.

She was shocked to find the cave was only as deep as their family kitchen, about ten feet. She held her lantern high, studying the ceiling while the others inspected the walls.

No more bats, thank goodness. But her nose burned. "What is that smell?"

Kai lowered his lamp, illuminating odd-looking stone beneath their feet. "Bat poop."

"Ick," Flurry said, lifting her feet. "That's disgusting!"

Kai moved the lamp around the cave. "Is there anything of interest in here—according to your visions, that is?"

Mayten was feeling something, but not necessarily from this cave. There were whispers of . . . a taint?

But not here.

She shrugged. "Other than how black it is. I don't think so. Could the bat poop be causing some kind of trouble, though? Don't bats carry disease?"

Kai shrugged and turned back to the opening. "Let's go check the next cave."

Mayten took deep lungfuls of air and grounded herself in the songs of birds and the sweet smell of sage as they continued their exploration. She was grateful to be out of the dark and away from that eye-burning stink.

The next two caves were smaller, the back of each cave visible from just outside the entrance.

The fourth cave they approached looked deep. A shiver went up her spine. She was not looking forward to exploring this cave.

Did that mean this was the cave she was looking for?

Kai stood at the entrance, a frown on his handsome face. "I'm not excited about disturbing more bats."

The whispers grew stronger. She looked at Flurry who stood, face lifted, as though listening to the wind.

Flurry nodded and Mayten took a deep breath. "Let's all go in again. I'll lead."

She lit her lantern and stepped around Kai, bracing herself for the onrush of bats. The lantern shook in her hand as Kai and Flurry crowded in behind her.

She took five steps in and stopped, listening for some hint of danger. The cave had a musty smell she couldn't identify.

Whispers drew her forward like a magnet. Something was rustling over the ground, though it didn't really sound like water.

She took a few more steps, throat tightening. The ceiling lowered, forcing her to bend her neck so she didn't whack her head on the stony ceiling. She held her lantern in front of her, arm stretched to its limit.

There was something dark on the floor—

The floor moved.

Mayten lowered the lantern and immediately wished that she hadn't. Fear bolted through her as she recognized the creeping, crawling creatures with enormous tails seething across the floor.

Scorpions!

Something skittered across her boot and she nearly dropped her lantern.

"Out!" she hissed, afraid if she yelled—if she screamed—she'd antagonize the scorpions. The hissing and rattling grew louder. Sounded like there were thousands of the creatures in this cave.

"What is it? Why did you stop?" Kai asked.

"Do *not* come any further." Mayten tried to keep her voice from shaking. "Back out slowly."

She held out her free arm, herding her friends behind her. She backed out of the cave, hoping none of the scorpions followed. She stumbled outside, ecstatic to be back in the sun. She set her lantern to one side, brushed off her legs and feet, and shook out her hair, shivering convulsively despite the heat of the day.

"What was it this time?" Flurry asked, her voice high and thin.

Kai watched Mayten, eyebrows drawn together.

"Scorpions." Mayten turned a circle. "Are there any on me?"

Flurry inspected her from head to toe, shaking her head. "You're clear."

She and Kai examined their own clothes.

Mayten took a gulp of water, hands shaking.

"First bats, now scorpions," Kai said. "This is getting creepy." He looked at Mayten, then at Flurry. "Your call. Do we go on?

Mayten met Flurry's gaze.

"I think we need to go on," Flurry said. "I'm feeling *something* though I can't say what it is."

Mayten turned back to Kai. "Same here. Let's keep looking."

The next cave looked deeper than the last, but the ceiling was lower to the ground. They'd have to hunch over to enter.

"I guess it's my turn," Flurry said.

Mayten couldn't let the girl do it. She'd gotten her into this mess. "No, let me go first." She hoped Kai would object and insist on going first but he said nothing. So she lit her lamp and bent down.

The whispers were there again, even stronger, accompanied by a stench worse than bat poop. Surely there would be some clue inside.

She took a few steps, then a few steps more, pleased to find the cave opened up. The interior didn't smell like bats or scorpions.

"No bats, no scorpions, though there is something that smells rather bad." Her voice echoed off the walls. "And you can stand up in here."

What *was* she hearing, besides her heart, that is?

It sounded like water, but that's what she'd thought last time. The ground was dry around her feet. She took three more steps, growing confident the sound was water.

But what was that smell?

"Look at that," Kai said. He moved up behind her and pointed his lantern at the back of the cave. Water tumbled down the back wall, sending mist billowing into the air. The damp felt good after the heat outside.

"Where does it go?" Flurry swung her lantern around so fast, Mayten felt a bit dizzy. She blinked and willed the sensation away.

Mayten moved her lantern slowly, following the water from the fall . . . back into the ground.

A tiny pond—no, smaller than a pond, though she wasn't sure what to call it—captured the flowing water.

And that was that. No more flowing water.

Only a dead rat along the water's edge.

"This explains your rotten smell," Kai said with a grimace.

Mayten's stomach seemed to shrink in on itself. A dead animal. Just as the visions had predicted. "I suppose so."

She lifted her lantern, illuminating first one side, then the other side of the cave. No sign of other creatures, living or dead.

"Either of you know where that water is coming from and where it's going?" Mayten asked.

"The source is likely overhead, on Table Mountain," Flurry said. "The town gets its water from streams that mostly flow down from the mountain where most of the rain falls. The mountain folk use most of the rainwater. Our town gets whatever comes down in streams, both above and underground. Most of above-ground water evaporates along the way. Looks like this is one of the underground streams."

Mayten frowned in confusion. "Why would the mountain folks get more water? They're not that far from you."

"Grandma says we're in a rain shadow. The rain clouds drop their rain on the way up the mountain, the top of the mountain gets what's left. By the time a storm gets down to the desert, the clouds are mostly empty. Sometimes even the Table doesn't get much. Those are drought years when food is scarce. It's one reason my da took to the sea. That way he can always bring in goods for the Sun Clan, drought or not."

This cave *was* significant but Mayten wasn't sure why. One dead animal wasn't nearly the disaster the visions had shown.

Disappointment filled her. She took another gulp of water, then stared at the falls. This would be a good place to refill their bladders.

"Does anyone need to refill?"

"Mine's still full," Flurry said.

Kai shook his water bladder. "I'm good."

Mayten shook her water bladder, and sighed in relief. She really didn't need to refill either.

Although there was nothing visually sinister about this cave, the hair on her neck prickled. What was she missing?

They looked around the cave one last time and went back into the sunlight.

Kai looked up at the sun, then pointed at the fork ahead. One path curved to follow the bottom of the ravine while the other snaked up the cliff. "This is where we turn and head back."

They walked back in silence. Kai took paper and pencil from his backpack and made notes. Some of the fissures they passed had trickles of water that indicated the possibility of springs or flow from up on the mountain.

"There you are," Adven said.

Mayten jumped so hard she almost bit her tongue. "Where did you come from?"

Tray stepped from behind Adven. "Find anything helpful?"

"Bats, scorpions, and water," Kai said. "You?"

"Most of our caves were shallow and empty. Sounds like you've had more of an adventure."

Mayten shook her head. "Not one I'd like to repeat."

She was disappointed and a little embarrassed that they'd found nothing helpful. "I'm sorry I dragged you all up here. It was a waste of time."

Adven pursed his lips. "Looking at the caves was something we hadn't thought of and it needed doing, so don't think twice about it."

"What now?" she asked.

"Now we go home for the afternoon rest. The day's already hot." He beckoned to them and headed back down the path.

That was it? Weren't they going to go up to the mountain? See what else they could find?

Mayten didn't follow. "I wonder . . ." Adven stopped and looked back.

She cleared her throat. "I wonder if I could go on up to the Table. I'd like to see it and maybe talk to some of the farmers."

"If you do, you'll have to stay until it cools off again. It will be dark before you get back."

"I'll go with you," Flurry said. "I know how to walk in the dark. Besides, we have our lanterns."

Adven tilted his head. "I have work for Kai and Tray so I can't leave them with you. The people up there are very friendly, so I imagine you'll be okay."

"Thanks," Mayten said. She wasn't sure why she wanted to go, but it felt important, and old lady Mantica had told her to trust her instincts.

Adven took off without another word.

Mayten straightened her back and watched the men leave. Then she nodded at Flurry and they headed up the hill.

CHAPTER THIRTY-ONE

Mayten and Flurry struggled up the road which was barely more than a path. How did the farmers get their produce down such a narrow road?

Even through the hood she could feel the sun's burning heat. Sweat trickled down her neck and back as the road grew steeper. Heat radiated off the rocky cliff on their left. On their right, the edge of the road was lined by rocks and boulders. Beyond that ridge of stone was . . . nothing.

Mayten let her hood drape forward, blocking her view of that treacherous edge. She focused on putting one foot in front of the other. Two wagon ruts had been worn into the rocks and sand. At first, she tried following one of the ruts, but that proved more difficult than dodging fist-sized stones that threatened to bruise her feet even through the boots.

They finally crested the edge of what turned out to be a broad plateau. "Table Mountain" had been appropriately named. The land was flat as far as she could see, with row after row of various plants in different stages of growth.

To the west, majestic mountains reached toward the heavens. "This is beautiful."

"Agreed," Flurry said as they paused to catch their breath. "I'm surprised my gran never brought me up here, or my folks, for that matter. It's so green."

"Look," Mayten pointed. "Trees!"

An orderly line of evergreen trees stretched along the far side of one of the fields. The sight of trees filled her with the same joy she felt when coming home to her family. "I wonder if they're being used as a windbreak to protect the crops. Trees don't normally grow in a line like that."

Could trees planted in a line talk to each other as easily as trees that grew naturally? She started toward the trees, feeling a strong desire to connect with them.

Flurry took hold of her arm. "There's a ranch house." She pointed at a building beyond the edge of a cornfield. "Maybe we should head there?"

Mayten shook off her disappointment. *I'll find time to visit you before I leave,* she silently promised. "Probably a good idea. I'm beginning to melt."

The air was moist compared to the air of the desert below but she still felt like she could drink an entire bucket of water. She took a long swig from her water bladder as they started around the cornfield toward the ranch house.

The closer they got, the bigger the ranch house looked. Lan's home was large in comparison to Mayten's homestead, but this house was even larger. The building spread wide to either side with corrals close by and barns in the rear. There were also round buildings on stilts she didn't recognize.

Flurry pointed at one of the round buildings. "What do you think those are for?"

Mayten frowned. "No idea. Should we just walk up to the door and knock?" She felt her back tighten at the thought of knocking on a stranger's door.

"I guess."

Before they reached the house, a man wearing dirt-coated coveralls waved at them from one of the corrals. "Hello, strangers. Welcome."

As they drew closer Mayten guessed that the man was middle-aged, judging by the scruff of gray beard covering the lower portion of his dark face.

"Hello," she said. "I'm Mayten Singer and this is Flurry Wind Catcher. Might we rest in your shade for a while?"

The man pulled off his gloves and slapped them across his thigh, sending dust flying in a billowing cloud. "I'm Clavis Grower and I'll do you one better. Come inside and join us for the midday meal. Then you can rest and tell me what you're doing out in the heat."

Mayten relaxed as she followed the man to the house and up steps to a porch that wrapped around either end of the house. Rocking chairs of all shapes and sizes sat around the porch. He stopped in front of a wide front door and stepped out of his work boots.

"Should we take our shoes off?" she asked.

"No, not to worry. You haven't been shoveling bat guano. My wife doesn't like the smell. Can't say as I blame her." He shucked out of his coveralls and tossed them over the porch rail, then led them inside.

Mayten and Flurry shared a look. Was it normal for folks to go around in what appeared to be cotton undergarments when strangers came to call?

They both checked the bottoms of their shoes and followed the man inside, staying close together. It took a minute for Mayten's eyes to adjust to the dim interior. She had to keep her jaw from dropping as she gazed at their surroundings.

The inside was lovely and lived in, a cozy combination. They stood at the junction between a large room with a fireplace and soft-looking couches and chairs to the left, and a dining room with a large wooden table to the right.

Big families and working families seemed to have long dining tables in common, she realized.

"Honey," Clavis Grower called. "Look what I grew in the field."

The woman who came from the back of the house had dark skin, wavy black hair, and a round face. She resembled the island's original inhabitants, reminding Mayten of her sister Taiwania.

"What is this?" she asked. She winked at Mayten. "You growing girls now?"

"This is my wife, Honey," he said, looking a bit embarrassed. "I'm afraid you'll have to remind me of your names again. I'm terrible with names."

Mayten dipped her head. "I'm Mayten Singer and this is Flurry Wind Catcher."

"Oh my," Honey said. "I can't say as we've ever had singers or wind catchers up here, though we have had some questers lately. Are you here for the same reason they are? Trying to figure out this sickness?"

"Yes," Mayten smiled. "We don't have much to go on, but we're trying to help."

"Good. Hang your cloaks and water bladders on those hooks by the door. You can help me put the food on the table, while Clavis gets the plates and silverware. The crew will be in shortly and they are always hungry."

Crew?

Mayten and Flurry followed Honey into the largest kitchen Mayten had seen outside of the castle keep. This kitchen was well-used, with battered iron pots instead of the beautiful brass used in the castle.

One middle-aged woman and two older men wearing similar cotton undergarments and looking flushed from their work stood at the stove, filling serving platters with food. The filled platters were handed to Honey and the girls.

Workers or part of the family?

Her stomach growled at the intoxicating smell drifting up from the corn on the cob stacked precariously on the platter in her hands. The sandwiches she and Flurry shared on the way up to the plateau seemed hours ago.

Besides corn, there were piles of green beans, salad, and a platter of the darkest sliced tomatoes she had ever seen. Several platters held a yellow bread she couldn't identify placed beside enormous crocks of butter.

They made another trip to the kitchen and were handed platters of fried chicken that soon joined the rest of the food.

After they'd laid out all the food, Honey told them where to sit. The kitchen workers joined them at the table as men, women, and a few children stomped in from the porch, shoeless. When everyone had taken their seats, there were at least twelve at the table.

Honey had taken a seat to Mayten's left. She held up a cup of cactus juice. "Please welcome Mayten Singer and Flurry Wind Catcher to the table today. Thank you all for your hard work. And we thank the Great Grower who sustains us. Let's eat."

Mayten was shocked as everyone piled food on their plates and dug in as if they hadn't eaten in a week.

"They work hard during the fall harvest," Honey said. "You must forgive their manners. Please, eat."

And Mayten did. The corn was the best she'd ever eaten, each bite sweet and juicy. She picked up a square of the yellow bread and studied it.

Honey leaned close. "It's cornbread. Spread a little of this on it." She slid a butter crock in front of Mayten.

What appeared to be regular butter had a sweetness to it that made the bread melt in her mouth. Flurry took a bite and they turned to each other with wide eyes.

"This food is amazing," Flurry said.

Honey smiled. "Everything is grown here on the Table—butter from the cows, honey from our local bees, and all the vegetables you can eat."

"What do you eat when you're sailing?" the boy next to Flurry asked, speaking with his mouth full. His black curls were sticking out in all directions and a leaf had been trapped in his hair.

"Silas, swallow first," Honey said.

Mayten smothered a grin. How many times had her own mother given the same instruction at her family's table?

Silas swallowed, still looking at Flurry.

"A lot of fish." Flurry's lip pulled up in disgust. "And dried beans, onions—you know, things that keep. Ship meals are nothing like this." She lifted a drumstick and took a big bite, rolling her eyes with a happy sigh.

Honey smiled, then shifted her gaze to Mayten. "What do tree singers eat over in the Forest Clan? Is that where you're from?"

"It is. My da is a great cook. He's especially good at cinnamon buns and soups. It's colder in the forests, damper. Warm foods are always welcome. My brother sings vegetables—he's a grower like you all. But no one grows corn. I think the weather is too cold. This is wonderful. So sweet and juicy. Do you help your crops by singing?"

The table fell silent and everyone stared at Mayten as though she'd grown a second nose.

Clavis set down his fork and smiled, but his eyes looked tense. "No, our gifting is more in the soil. We're always working to improve the soil, listening to it so to speak." He chuckled. "It's a bit of a competition between the farms, to see who can come up with the best soil."

He nodded as though that was that and everyone went back to eating.

Mayten was mystified by the sudden tension around the table. Were they hiding something, or was she just jumping to conclusions?

The boy seemed to have no qualms about sharing their secrets.

"We're having a bumper crop," Silas said. He looked to be about nine years old. "Da says it's the new fertilizer he's mixin' with the bat guano."

The boy shoved a giant scoop of beans into his mouth.

Honey blanched. "I'm sure the girls don't want to hear about bat guano while they're eating."

Had Clavis tensed at the boy's words?

"Bat guano?" Mayten wrinkled her nose. "I think we smelled some of that in a cave down below. It stinks. You put it on the crops?"

She sat back, eying her plate as though it might turn to dung at any moment.

"Aye," Silas said. "Always have."

He shrugged, looking as though he'd been farming for decades. "Makes good fertilizer. I've had to muck it out of the caves, though, yuck!"

"That's enough of that," Honey scolded. "Let the girls eat."

She pointed down the table at a man they'd seen in the kitchen. "Bran's made a cake and you don't want to miss a slice of it. I'd love to taste one of your da's cinnamon buns, Mayten. They sound lovely."

Bat guano or not, the food was delicious, she decided. She was already so full she didn't think she could take another bite. Someone set a slice of cake in front of her and she felt a bit nauseated. One bite of the lemony goodness, though, and she ate the whole slice.

Everyone helped clear the table but when Mayten offered to help with washing up, Honey shook her head. "We've got a schedule. Each member of the crew takes turns at the chores. You girls go on and find a comfy spot in the living room. You'll be wanting a rest after that meal."

Mayten couldn't disagree. She yawned, watching as the dining room emptied and people disappeared, either out the front door or toward the back of the house. She and Flurry headed to the living room.

Large but cozy, the living room looked—lived in. Two long couches held throw blankets draped over the back and small pillows at each end. She took off her boots and snuggled onto one of the couches, pulling the throw over her legs. Flurry followed her lead and soon Mayten felt herself drifting into sleep.

Something banged and Mayten sat up, rubbing sleep from her eyes and trying to figure out what had woken her. Flurry sat up at the same time, looking as disoriented as Mayten felt.

Silas stood beside a pile of discarded boots at the front door.

How long had he been there staring at them?

"Da said I could give you a look around. Everyone else has gone back to the harvest."

Mayten nodded and pulled her boots on, wishing she'd had more time with one of the grownups. Had they sent the boy on purpose, hoping to avoid her questions? "Thank you, Silas. We'd appreciate that."

"Gets me out of the harvest." The boy grinned.

She couldn't help but grin back.

Honey stepped into the hall. "Can I get you girls anything? I hear Silas will be showing you around. You'll probably want to use the facilities before you head back down the mountain. Silas can show you."

"Thank you," Mayten stood. "We'd like to ask folks some questions about the sickness before we go."

"Trust me, Silas will talk your head off about any subject. He's the third generation here, my grandson. If you have more questions he can't answer, just have him come and get me. I'll be helping at the harvest until then."

"Thank you so much for everything," Mayten said. "You've got a wonderful place." She returned her blanket to the couch back and adjusted the pillow.

"And delicious food," Flurry added as she folded her own blanket.

"I'm glad you like it. You're both welcome anytime. I've got to get out there now before we lose too much sun." She waved and headed out the door.

They donned their hooded robes—what Honey called "cloaks"— slipped their water bladders over their shoulders and followed Silas outside. It was cooler now, the sun heading along its western path. Mayten pulled her hood down and noticed Flurry did the same.

Silas led them toward the barn where they'd first met Clavis.

"What are those round buildings?" Mayten asked, pointing at the tall structures she didn't recognize.

"That one's our water tank." Silas nodded at the building she'd pointed to. "Every farm up here has one." He waved at the mountains to the west. "The rain dumps up there. Is that where you live?"

"Maybe, I'm not sure," Mayten said. She'd never seen her own mountains from this angle.

"It rains a lot up there. We get some good rain down here, but not always enough for our fields during dry years. During a good storm, we open the top of the water tower and it collects rain. During dry years, when we need more water, we open the spigot and water the fields. The water is sweet and good to drink too. We collect it in rain barrels and cisterns all over the mountain."

He paused for a moment, then pointed at another round building, slightly different from the first. "That's a corn silo. What corn we don't immediately eat or sell, we take off the cob and dry out to use later. That's where we store it."

"Makes sense," Flurry said, rubbing her spiky hair.

Mayten gestured at the fields. "How many farms are there?"

"Twelve." Silas grinned. "Not all grow corn, beans, and squash like we do. There's a dairy farm up here and a chicken farm. We trade for what we need. There's also an orchard with lemon and orange trees, a farm that grows mostly wheat, and a farm that specializes in cotton. There's even one grower trying to grow rice. I'm not sure that's working, though."

As they walked, Silas pointed out different sections—the cornfields, the barn, the windbreak trees, and the farms off in the distance. Mayten gazed at everything in wonder. It had been less than a year since she'd been called on her first quest. Before that, she'd seen nothing outside of her own homestead.

Now she'd visited every clan—she'd even been to the castle itself— Every place had its own . . . personality, she supposed. Until this trip, she'd never understood how diverse their island home was.

When they reached the field being harvested, she stared in fascination at the workers cutting corn off the stocks with small knives. They tossed the cobs over their shoulders into baskets held by straps on their backs. They worked steadily and quickly.

"We make a lot of things out of corn," Silas said. "Corn cider, cornbread, cornmeal for baking. We even use the husks and the stalks. What we can't use the animals eat. Corn is amazing."

Mayten laughed. "You're quite a corn expert, Silas. Can you tell us what you know about the sickness? I heard it hasn't spread up here."

"That's true." The boy tugged at his lower lip. "Da says it's because we're such hard workers, and we eat really well. Of course, the folks in the desert eat the same food we do—we trade with them for clothes and such. But nobody I know is sick."

Something niggled at the back of her brain, but she couldn't grasp it.

And the sun was getting lower. Time to be heading back. She was not going to have a chance to listen to the trees. *I'm so sorry. Perhaps another time.*

"Thank you for showing us around," Mayten said. "Thank your folks again for us, will you?"

"Of course. I'll walk you to the path if that's okay? That way it'll be dark before I get back and I won't have to work." He gave her an impish grin.

"That would be great." This little fellow made her miss Wollemi. She wondered how he was faring back at the house. There were no children to play with down below as everyone was home in quarantine and he was probably bored out of his mind unless Ebony had returned.

Silas said goodbye at the junction with the downward road. The sun was going down and in the twilight, Mayten could see bats swooping after bugs.

How long would it take a raven to fly to the Forest Clan and back?

CHAPTER THIRTY-TWO

Mayten and Wollemi were woken by a tap on the bedroom door.

"Come in," she said. Wollemi groaned and rolled over.

Joshua stuck his head in the door. "Sorry to wake you but there's someone at the door for you and I've got to dash."

"Thanks, Joshua. I'll be right out." She looked out the window, wincing when she noted how bright it was outside. How long had she slept?

She'd been exhausted by the time she and Flurry got down the mountain. She'd given Joshua a brief update, watching his face fall when she had no new information. She felt like she'd failed, though she and Flurry had only gone up to the farms to talk.

"Wollemi," She shook her brother. "I'm late for a meeting with the questers. Do you want to come?"

He nodded and sat up, eyelids drooping. Perhaps the heat was getting to both of them.

They tumbled out of bed, pulled on their loose cotton clothes, and headed for the front door, only to stop when they saw Flurry standing in the living room.

"Are you two okay?" Flurry asked.

"We're fine," Mayten said, "just worn out. Why?"

"Adven wanted us to check in before it got hot, so I waited at the questers' lodge but you never came."

"Is it really that late?"

Flurry nodded.

"Guess we'd better get going." Mayten grabbed her hood and water bladder, throwing a second hood and bladder to Wollemi who looked like he was sleepwalking. She snatched a hunk of bread off the table and followed Flurry out the door. The girl paused and pointed at the raven waiting outside on the path.

"He's been waiting too."

Mayten's fuzzy head cleared. "Ebony!"

She kneeled and Ebony hopped over to her, lifting his leg to show a thin strip of paper wrapped around it.

"Did you make it all the way to Da?" she asked, stunned.

Ebony bobbed up and down as though nodding.

She untied the ribbon and removed the note, then stroked the raven's sleek head. "You're such a good boy, a smart boy."

"Smart boy," Ebony croaked. "Smarrrt boy."

She started to break off a piece of bread, but Ebony grabbed the whole chunk and flew off.

Mayten laughed. "Guess he's hungry."

"What does it say?" Flurry asked.

Wollemi walked up, tugging her arm down so he could see as she scanned the note.

Mayten gently shrugged him off. "It's from Solis, our clan leader. 'We are sending our best,' she says."

Tears burned Mayten's eyes and her entire body seemed to relax. "Thank the Great Singer. Solis will likely send my friend Cather or her parents. They are the best healers we have."

She stood and headed up the road, Flurry and Wollemi on either side. "I'm going to have to give Ebony an extra treat today."

Wollemi's face was flushed and he was breathing hard before they'd walked halfway to the lodge.

"Are you okay?" Mayten asked. "Did you stay out too long in the sun yesterday?"

He shrugged but kept trudging after them. Her stomach clenched as she watched him closely.

"This walk didn't bother you yesterday," Flurry said. Her face was pinched with concern.

Mayten shared a worried glance with Flurry. "Maybe it's the heat. We are not used to this heat. I'm feeling it too. Saps your strength."

She took her brother's hand, suddenly worried that she'd somehow exposed him to the sickness that seemed to be affecting so many people.

"Drink some water," Flurry said. "And eat something."

"Not hungry." He paused to chug water, wiped at his forehead, and started walking again. "I'm okay."

They walked the rest of the way in silence, Mayten trying not to worry. She was tired, too. It had to be the heat.

Relief helped her perk up when they reached the questers' house. When no one answered their knock, they walked around back and found Adven, Tray, and Kai leaning over the map on one of the tables.

"'Bout time you got here," Adven growled.

"Sorry," Mayten said. "We're having some trouble with the heat."

They took seats on the benches and Mayten sighed. "And we didn't learn anything new yesterday, I'm sad to say."

"They fed us well," Flurry added.

"Did that little scamp tell you what he did yesterday?" Adven pointed at Wollemi slumped on the bench.

Mayten studied her brother. "No . . ."

"He followed us. After I told him to stay put."

"What?" Shock hit Mayten like lightning. It was so unlike Wollemi to disobey.

"He came running down the trail after us when we were about halfway down." The look in Adven's good eye could've fried an egg.

Mayten had been on the receiving end of that look many times. A shiver went down her spine. She shook her head. "What were you thinking? Anything could've happened to you!"

Wollemi nodded, laying his head on the table. "I'm sorry."

She took a deep breath. "It's no wonder you're exhausted. Not only was it a long hike—I'm worn out, too—but we saw snakes and all kinds of nasty things."

She'd even glimpsed a coyote—or so she'd thought. Had it actually been her brother hiding behind a rock?

Her throat tightened. There were so many dangerous creatures hiding in those rocks.

Mayten rubbed his back, then remembered the note. She took the slip of paper out of her pocket and handed it to Tray.

He read it and grinned. "They're sending their best healers! That means Cather and her family, I hope."

Adven reached out and took the note, studying it with a frown. "How did you get this news so fast?"

"Seems my new raven friend, Ebony, is a message bird—" Mayten gasped as Wollemi started to slide off the bench.

Kai caught him. "I think we'd better get you back home, little man." He felt Wollemi's forehead and gave Mayten a worried look.

Mayten jumped to her feet. "It can't be the sickness, right? That comes on slow. It's the heat. He has heat sickness."

No one answered, though Adven shared a look with Tray and Kai.

Kai lifted Wollemi in his arms while Mayten followed close to his side. Her stomach roiled, making her glad she hadn't eaten any of that bread.

"We're coming too," Adven said. "We need to continue this conversation."

Kai carried Wollemi all the way back to Joshua Leader's house and set him on the couch without saying a word.

Flurry brought Wollemi a cup of cactus juice while Mayten stuffed a roll with sliced meat and cheese.

Eyes half closed, Wollemi sipped at the juice and nibbled on the sandwich.

Adven glared down at him, hands on his hips, then turned his glare on Mayten. "Tell us exactly what happened yesterday, step by step."

He pulled up a chair and sat, waving at the others to do the same. Flurry found a chair, Tray dropped to the floor. Mayten and Kai flanked Wollemi on the couch.

Kai kept his arm around Wollemi. The boy rested his head on Kai's shoulder, trying to keep his eyes open as Flurry and Mayten quickly gave Adven a report of their time on the mountain.

Adven scratched his cheek. "When we saw you, Wollemi, you were coming down from the caves. Did you go into any of them?"

He nodded without lifting his head. "I needed water, so I went into the water cave and filled my bladder."

Flurry closed her eyes, pinching the bridge of her nose. Then she straightened in her chair. "When I first listened to the wind, water kept showing up. I thought the wind was trying to tell me something about the lack of water—the Sun Clan always has issues with water—but when we got here, everyone seemed to have plenty. Then Mayten and I both received images of a cave and dead animals and—doom, I guess. There was only one cave with water in it. The one he used to fill his bladder."

Adven lifted Wollemi's water bladder from the table where he'd dropped it. He opened the bladder and sniffed. "It doesn't smell any different than the water down here which has always smelled weird to me, anyway. Is it the same water they drink on the mountain?"

Flurry's eyes got wide. "No. They collect rainwater. The boy who showed us around said it's sweet."

Adven pursed his lips. "So, they don't drink the same water as you do down here."

Flurry nodded. "But that's nothing new. We've been drinking the water that comes down the mountain for years."

"Something has changed," Adven said. "But what?"

CHAPTER THIRTY-THREE

They sat together in the living room, Wollemi still laying against Kai's shoulder.

If I hadn't brought Wollemi here, he'd be safe. I knew something was wrong and yet I let him come. Mayten tugged at her braids, stood, and started pacing.

She should be able to figure this out. The King trusted her, after all. She was in charge, responsible—

Flurry jumped to her feet. "Silas said they were using a new fertilizer to mix with the bat poop, and it was giving them the best crop ever. It has to be that fertilizer."

Mayten thumped her forehead with her palm. "You're right."

Tray sat up straight. "So, they spread the fertilizer, the water leaches off the crops and into the streams that come down the mountain and it's making people sick."

Frowning, Kai put his hand on Wollemi's forehead. "But why did he get sick so fast? Everyone else got sick gradually."

Flurry leaned forward. "By the time water reaches town, it's been diluted. One stream joined by another stream and so on, eventually becoming the river that supplies our water. Wollemi drank straight from the source."

Mayten's throat tightened. She'd brought her brother into this mess. What if he died?

Mayten refused to leave her brother's side. Wollemi slept off and on for the next few days and when he woke, she sat at his bedside, wiping his forehead and forcing him to take sips of cactus juice. He hardly moved when he slept, lying perfectly still like he was under ten blankets and not just one light one.

When he slept, Mayten paced his room, barely sleeping herself, worried that he'd slip away in the night. She couldn't bear the thought of losing another sibling, especially Wollemi.

If the unbearable happened, if she did lose her precious brother, it would be her fault.

On the third day, there was a tap on the door and Cather walked in. Mayten rushed into her best friend's arms. "It's my fault. I shouldn't have brought him. You've got to save him."

"Shh," Cather said, brushing Mayten's braids back off her face. "It's not your fault."

Cather pulled back, looking at Mayten. "When was the last time you ate? When was the last time you slept?"

Mayten slumped into the chair with a shrug. Cather found a cup by the bed and poured Mayten some water. "Drink this while I check on him. Then I'm taking over here. You, my friend, will go get something to eat. Then you'll get some sleep."

She moved to the bed across from Mayten and placed her hands on his chest. Her eyes closed while she *listened*. Wollemi looked up at her through half-open eyes. He smiled. Then his eyes closed again.

"Can you help him?" Mayten set the cup back on the little table. Yes, Cather had just arrived, but she *had* to know.

Cather came around the bed and took her hands. "We'll do everything we can. Ma and Da are out gathering the information we need for healing. I need you to eat and sleep so you don't get sick too." She lifted Mayten's chin. "Can you do that for me?"

Mayten nodded and Cather led her to the couch in the living room. She disappeared into the kitchen, reappearing with a cup of cactus juice. She handed the cup to Mayten along with something soft and sweet.

"Your father sent these cinnamon rolls." Mayten's eyes welled with tears as she lifted the roll to her nose and breathed in the little bit of home.

"Joshua says they are seeing signs of improvement in everybody now that they've started boiling the water." Cather sat next to Mayten and watched her eat.

Mayten sat up straighter and took another sip of juice. "That's good news."

Cather nodded. "They are shipping in uncontaminated water and are making more of that cactus juice, which is definitely an acquired taste." She wrinkled her nose.

Mayten set down the juice and took a bite of roll. Suddenly she didn't feel like she was quite so alone. "What did you think of my raven's message?"

Cather grinned, eyes sparkling. "You should have seen your da. I was the only one home when he showed up at our door, that raven hopping beside him. I think your da ran all the way to town. First thing he said was, 'I'm supposed to take this to Solis, but it involves you too, want to come?' I followed him even though Solis scares me silly."

Mayten took another bite of roll and let it melt on her tongue. Solis would scare anyone silly.

"Solis didn't hesitate, though. She wrote that note and sent the raven off, then went straight to my folks. Your da and I had to run to keep up with her long legs. She told us to pack our things, we were getting on a barge the next day. Your da dashed back home and came back with your ma and these rolls. They helped us pack."

Her own barge adventure seemed like ages ago.

"I can't tell you how scary that was," Cather continued. "I've never been on a barge. I squeezed Ma's hand the whole way. After we landed, we had one night with your sisters—those babies are so cute—then we were tossed onto a ship without even a break."

She paused to take a breath. "I thought our quest to the castle was exciting, but this was something else. I can't believe you traveled all that way by yourself! As soon as we got here, we met with Joshua Leader, Adven, Tray, Kai, and your little Flurry. She's a cutie."

She stopped and her face took on a glow. "When I saw Tray, the trip was all worth it." She glared at Mayten. "The note didn't say who was sick, so I was terribly worried."

Mayten flinched. "I'm sorry. I didn't think about that."

Cather shrugged. "Tell me about your raven."

Mayten open her mouth, then closed it as boots thumped on the front porch. A moment later, Adven and the boys flooded through the door, followed by Flurry.

Adven gave Mayten a curt nod. "You're looking better."

"I feel a bit better. It's such a relief to have Cather here."

"Agreed." Tray grinned.

"We need you to come with us." The look on Adven's face would melt stone. "Time we got some real info from those farmers."

CHAPTER THIRTY-FOUR

They planned to leave the next morning while it was dark to beat the hottest part of the day. Cather promised to look after Wollemi. Tray volunteered to stay behind and help the healers.

Mayten woke up feeling as dull and disoriented as she'd felt before she'd slept. She'd only checked on Wollemi once during the night. Cather's mother had been with him at the time and assured Mayten he was going to be fine.

So why was she still so groggy?

Her head cleared a bit after she started walking. The journey up the mountain in the dark wasn't as scary as the first time. She kept her mind off snakes and coyotes, focusing instead on how they were going to get the farmers to agree to stop using the fertilizer.

The sun was fully up when they reached the junction. Mayten and Flurry led the way to the ranch house.

They stopped at the barn and found no one inside or outside so they went up to the house and knocked on the door.

Honey yanked the door open, took one look, and smiled. "Back so soon?"

Mayten nodded and waved a hand at the men. "This is Adven Traveler and Kai Leader. May we come in?"

"You two were here last week, weren't you?" Honey said to Adven. He nodded. She shoved the door wide and stood back, inviting them in.

The house felt cool after the growing heat outside. Mayten drew in a breath. Savory smells from the kitchen teased her nose. "We didn't mean to arrive for another meal. We need to talk to you about the sickness and what we've found out."

Honey led them into the living room with the couches.

"Sit, please," Honey said, drying her hands on her apron. Her graying hair escaped its tie and curled in whisps around her weathered face. "I'm just in from the fields. Everyone except the kitchen shift are still out harvesting. We start very early as you know, to beat the heat. We've heard a bit about the water issues. It's caused quite a stir up here, a bit of division I'd say. Some farmers don't believe it's the fertilizer causing the trouble, some do."

"We were wondering if there is a way to gather all the farmers for a meeting," Adven said. "We'd like to share our findings with everyone at once."

Honey tapped a finger on her chin. "It would have to be tonight, after it's too dark to harvest. I'm sure most everyone would come. Let me just tell the kitchen shift to add some plates to the table, then I'll run out to the fields and get Silas moving. I bet he can get the message to most of the farms before it's too hot. Make yourselves at home. I'll send some juice in for you."

"Thank you so much," Mayten said.

Honey dashed off to the kitchen. Her voice overrode a few other raised voices, then she was out of the kitchen and through the front door.

A grumpy-looking man with calloused hands and bowed legs entered the dining area, carrying a tray with cups and a pitcher full of cactus juice. He grumbled to himself as he set the tray on the long table, leaving without a word. Others brought in a small table and added it to the end of the long table, dragging in chairs and slamming down plates. Mayten and the others watched in silence until the kitchen shift was back in the kitchen.

Mayten leaned forward, keeping her voice low. "Do you think they're mad that we're eating here or that we're calling a meeting?"

"Maybe both," Adven said. "Or maybe it's the disagreement about the fertilizer."

"Plus, it's harvest time and they're all exhausted," Flurry said.

Kai gave her a wry smile. "The last thing they're going to want to do tonight is come to a meeting. And if some don't want to give up fertilizer . . ."

"We could be in for a fight," Adven finished.

Famished workers shoveled roasted potatoes, corn, and beans into their mouths quickly. They seemed eager to get back to work and ate without speaking. It was an early lunch, a much smaller meal than the evening one Mayten and Flurry experienced on their previous visit.

The food had been delicious again, especially the corn, but the mood around the table felt less welcoming. Thankfully, Silas sat at their little table and kept them entertained with stories.

After the meal, Adven volunteered their whole group to work alongside the harvesters until the sun got too high, then join them for the large meal and nap, then work again until dark.

Mayten approached Adven as they headed to the cornfields. "Why are we doing this?" she said so only he could hear. "We're wasting time."

He gave her his one-eyed glare. "They'll listen better if we help."

Mayten rolled her eyes as he stalked ahead. He was likely right, but she couldn't help feeling time was slipping away. She believed Cather and her parents were doing their best for Wollemi, but what if something went wrong?

Silas showed them all how to feel the cob for a full, heavy head, and make sure the silk coming out of the top was long and dry. He demonstrated cutting the cob off the stalk with a small knife and tossing the cobs into baskets slung across their backs.

After an hour Mayten's hands were sore and dry. After three hours she was spent. Thank the Singer they broke before she collapsed. They headed back to the big house with Clavis and Honey while others headed to smaller houses.

Were all those who ate in the big house related?

"Can you believe these workers have been doing this every day for weeks?" Mayten asked Flurry as they settled into their chairs. Those around the table seemed more relaxed than they had at the last meal. Looked like Adven had been smart to offer their help with the harvest.

Once again, the food was abundant, the table laid out with the same foods they'd had on their last visit—with chocolate cake for dessert.

Once they'd all eaten, Clavis put folks to work setting up the barn for the meeting. The sun had slipped from the sky while they were eating, leaving the barn in shadows of gray and black. The farmers hung lanterns on beams. She was surprised they'd bring lanterns into a barn, but they must know what they were doing. Seemed the chances of a fire were greater than if they'd just met outside.

A breeze swept through the barn as someone opened the back door. Mayten shivered at the chill, suddenly understanding the need to be indoors.

Kai helped push hay bales around in something resembling a seating pattern while Adven stood near the front of the barn talking to some of the farmers.

Flurry had found a hay bale to sit on. She leaned back against a wall, looking beat.

Mayten watched as people trickled in from other farms, greeting each other and talking in small groups.

Did they gather like this regularly? Use the gatherings to reconnect with friends they didn't get to see very often?

Silas raced up and grabbed her arm, looking like he'd raced around the barn three times. "People are coming up the path. Lots of them. I saw the glow and went to check it out."

He dragged Mayten from the barn to what she'd begun calling "the junction" that led down to the town and headed downhill. They rounded the first corner and her heart plummeted. A long line of lights wove its way up the road.

Looked like the townspeople had lost patience with their tabletop kin.

She couldn't let them storm into the farmers' meeting. That would put everyone and everything in jeopardy.

Mayten turned to Silas. "I'm going to talk to them. Let Adven know where I've gone."

She straightened her shoulders and started down the path toward the bobbing lanterns, murmuring a prayer under her breath.

CHAPTER THIRTY-FIVE

Mayten stepped carefully, squinting to see the road and trying not to shake. She should have stopped to get a lantern and a sweater. Not only was it chilly, she could hardly see her feet. She stubbed her toe on a rock, almost falling to her knees.

She could do this. She *had* to do this.

There'd been twenty lanterns coming up the path, maybe more. If there were people without lanterns in the group, they would have been as hard to see as the rocks trying to trip her.

"Why did they have to come now?" she muttered, shifting sideways to avoid clipping her shin on a boulder she'd barely seen in time. It would only make the farmers angrier if this crowd stomped into their meeting.

She should have grabbed Kai instead of heading out alone to face a mob of angry townspeople. The fact he was the king's son might have slowed these folks down.

And she was the king's representative, wasn't she? She'd survived the bullies of the Ocean Clan. She could survive this as well.

She got within shouting distance and raised her hand. "Stop!"

The train of lights slowed to a stop, those at the front raising their lanterns to see who was blocking their path.

Her mouth went dry as Mayten realized she'd never *met* any of the townspeople, except the clan leader and the harbormaster.

"Great Singer, I could use your help right now," she whispered.

"Who are you to stand in our way?" An enormous man whose beady eyes seemed to glow in the lantern light stepped forward as though he was going to charge right through her.

"Hold up, Grebo." A stocky woman shoved her way free of the others. "This is the Singer I told you about."

Mayten's heart skipped a beat. Thank goodness the harbormaster was here. She seemed to be the spokesperson for the group.

The woman squared her shoulders. "I'll repeat Grebo's question: Why are you blocking our way?"

"The farmers are having a meeting—" she started.

"Talk louder," a man yelled from the back of the line.

Mayten took a breath and tried to project her voice. "The farmers are meeting with the questers who are hoping to convince them to stop using the fertilizer. They need some time to talk this out."

"That's why we're here, to *convince* them," the same male voice said.

Murmurs of agreement rose from the crowd.

A woman yelled from the back. "It's their fault my kids are sick. Those farmers need to own up to their mistakes."

The crowd shoved forward and Mayten took a step back.

She needed help, but everyone on her team was back at the barn.

There was no one around to help her.

Flurry studied the crowd filling the barn. Clavis got up on a hay bale, raising his hands to quiet the crowd.

These were hard-working people, with sun-darkened skin, muscled arms, and dirty clothes. Some folks sat on hay bales, some leaned against walls, while others crouched on the floor.

She had taken a position against the wall near the front. Kai stood a few paces away. Adven stood near Clavis.

But where was Mayten?

"As many of you know, we have guests from below," Clavis said. "This is Adven Traveler. He's chief quester of the Forest Clan. He's here to tell you what he found out about our water."

Clavis hopped off the hay bale while Adven climbed up.

"Thank you for coming," Adven said, his voice low and calm. "I know you're all tired, so I'll keep this short. Unfortunately, our news isn't good. We've tied the sickness affecting your neighbors in the desert directly to the new fertilizer you've been using. We've come to ask you to stop using it."

Grumbling rose, making the barn seem even smaller.

Alarmed, Flurry slid off the hay bale and grabbed Kai's arm. "That's not how it's done here."

An older man with gnarled hands and stooped shoulders stood, raising an arm in the air. The crowd stilled.

Who was this man?

"First," he said in a voice that carried. "What does a *quester* know about fertilizer?"

Several people chuckled.

"That's right," a young man yelled.

"You tell 'em, Foster."

"Listen to the quester," shouted someone else.

Was that Honey? Flurry scanned the crowd, looking for the woman who'd been so helpful to them.

"Second," the old man said. The crowd hushed again. "Does this quester know we've had our best crops ever? That we grew enough produce to hold us through two drought years? Has he ever had to put his kids to bed hungry?"

"That's right," a woman in the crowd said. People around her nodded their agreement.

"Let's hear what the quester has to say." That high-pitched voice could only belong to Silas.

To Flurry's relief, other people in the crowd seemed to agree.

The farmer raised his hands again. Adven looked about to interrupt, but Clavis took hold of his arm, pulling him down and saying something in his ear.

"Third," the old man said. "Let's see his hands. Do they look like this from hard work? Are they full of callouses?"

"See his hands. See his hands."

Stomping started at the back of the barn, moving through the crowd like a wave. Dust filtered down from the rafters. For a moment, Flurry thought the whole barn would come down on them.

Others in the crowd started arguing with their neighbors, trying to get them to stop.

Flurry looked at Adven's stormy face. Mayten had told her the man had a temper. This would not be the best time for him to lose it.

He held up his hands, trying to quiet the crowd. The stomping ceased but he had to yell over the angry voices. "People are sick, blast you. I know it's a sacrifice—"

A man with a barrel chest stomped forward, stopping within inches of Adven's face. "And what would you know about sacrifices?"

Spit flew in his face as Adven put up his hands to push the man back. She watched in horror as the man grabbed Adven's arms and tried to wrestle him to the ground.

"Stop!" Kai shoved through the crowd, struggling to reach Adven's side. Flurry gasped as a fist caught Kai's cheek. He fell, disappearing beneath the raging crowd. Grunts and screams echoed off the walls, and dust choked the air.

Flurry was torn. She should help, shouldn't she? But how?

More people were pushing and shoving, shouting and yelling. The entire situation had gone from calm to violent in a heartbeat. She had to do something before the melee turned into a real fight.

Flurry jumped up on her hay bale and clung to a nearby post. She needed to find Adven. Needed to help Kai.

She swung around, struggling to make out figures in the milling crowd. If she could only find Mayten, they could work together, find some way to calm this raging sea.

There was still no sign of the Singer. Flurry was on her own.

CHAPTER THIRTY-SIX

Mayten felt like a single leaf trying desperately not to be blown away. How was one teenage girl supposed to stop an angry mob?

The crowd shifted restlessly, the stench of their oil lanterns tainting the air. She blew out a breath. "It won't help to storm into the farmers' meeting," she said, hoping logic would help calm their anger. "Let's give them some time to work things out."

"They've had plenty of time," the harbormaster said. "It shouldn't even be a question. They're our kin. They should do what is right."

Mayten couldn't really argue with that. "I'm not asking you not to talk to them, just wait until tomor—"

The harbormaster moved forward, forcing Mayten back a step. "Move, girl. This isn't your fight."

Mayten caught herself before she stumbled, then drew her shoulders back and stood tall, surprised to find herself looking down at the harbormaster. She needed to find a way to stall them.

But how?

The harbormaster wasn't intimidated. She shoved right past Mayten, stomping up the road as though ready to knock down anything that got in her way. The townspeople followed, some muttering apologies as they stalked past Mayten, some glaring, one even daring to spit.

Mayten froze. She should get back in front of the mob. Force them to stop.

But she couldn't get her feet to move.

When she'd faced the evil singer, she'd thought she was alone when she wasn't. Mayten shivered, remembering the darkness and the oily feel of evil. Not only did her friends help and support her through that confrontation, the trees helped, too, sending her strength and encouragement.

The only trees here were those that had been planted as a windbreak. They weren't in their natural environment.

Everything is connected.

Flurry's words seemed to whisper in the air.

She had felt it, hadn't she? That connection with all life? The connection she felt when she talked to her trees. She'd felt the same connection among the cactus and brush, though she hadn't really recognized it at the time.

Was that why Ebony had come to her? Were they *connected* somehow?

Mayten inhaled, focusing on the feel of the air rushing through her nose. She welcomed the dust tickling the back of her throat, the scent of *dry* that always reminded her of snakes and lizards.

And felt the connection.

:I need help. Please.:

:We hear you, little sister. What do you need?:

Mayten's skin crawled as words—images?—echoed through her mind, whispered by a thousand voices.

What did she need? She needed help. She needed . . .

:Slow these people down.:

Beyond the tromping and muttering of the passing mob, she heard a soft whirring that grew in volume.

Somewhere up ahead a man yelped, followed by a woman's scream. The crowd surged backward, almost knocking Mayten off the road as the dark night came alive.

A soft wing brushed her cheek. :*We come, little sister.*:

Bats.

Heart in her throat, Mayten struggled not to panic, forcing gratitude into her mind instead of fear. These bats had answered her call. They were here to help.

She clenched her fists at her sides, determined not to cover her head like so many in the crowd were doing, and stalked toward the front of the line.

The bats had done their part. Time for her to do hers.

Bats dove and swirled overhead, creating space between Mayten and the townspeople. When she finally reached the front of the line, the bats dove again, one after another, creating a buffer between her and the harbormaster.

To her credit, the harbormaster wasn't cowering with arms over her head. She did duck, though, while taking swipes at the persistent bats.

"What on earth . . . ?" Someone in the crowd said.

"I've never seen the like," another said.

Mayten raised her hands. "The farmers need more time. The bats understand this. Why can't you?"

The harbormaster shook her head while several folks chuckled. "Girl, you're saying the bats don't want us to go up there?"

Of course, no one believed her. "Do you have a different explanation for why a cloud of bats decided to pay your group a visit?"

The crowd muttered, looking at each other and shifting restlessly. No one said anything. Not even the harbormaster.

Shouts carried on the wind, followed by a distant thump. It sounded like . . . was there fighting in the barn?

"We need to get up there," the harbormaster yelled. The crowd surged up the path like an enormous wave.

If these angry people forced their way into the barn and joined whatever fight was going on up there, someone was going to get hurt.

Images of Flurry, Adven, and Kai flashed through her mind. Were they caught up in the fighting?

"Wait," Mayten said. Though she'd shouted, her voice seemed a mere whisper against the crowd's angry muttering. "Please."

"What the—" The harbormaster leaped in the air, shoving back against the man coming up behind her.

Then Mayten heard it. Hissing, almost as soft and quiet as the bats' wings.

A hissing that grew and grew . . .

Mayten shrank back as a snake crossed between her and the harbormaster.

"Shark teeth and tidal waves!" The woman stumbled back further, leaving a wide gap between herself and Mayten.

A gap that rapidly filled with slithering, winding snakes.

Some people crowded closer to see what was happening while others shoved back down the road. In a wave, snakes slithered across the road and into the sagebrush on the far side.

"Snakes don't travel in groups." The man behind the harbormaster stared at the wriggling mass in disbelief.

Mayten tried to keep her voice from shaking. "First bats, now snakes. All signs that you should not be here. Not right now."

She stiffened her arms and legs, willing them not to tremble and tried not to think about what could be happening up in the barn, tried not to picture tiny Flurry trampled beneath a raging crowd.

❧

Mayten or no Mayten, Flurry had to do something. She was kin with these folks. She knew how they thought. They would listen to her, wouldn't they?

She straightened to her full height. Standing on the hay bale, she could see over the crowd. Mostly.

"My hands are full of callouses," she said. But her voice got swallowed in the sounds of fighting. A woman pushed a man to the ground. People were shouting and somewhere in the mess she heard crying.

"Listen to me, wind take you!" Flurry shouted, then clenched her jaw. No one even looked up.

If they wouldn't listen to her, perhaps they would listen to something a bit more insistent. Flurry raised her hands and called the wind.

Windows slammed open just before the barn door slammed closed. Hay and dust lifted off the floor, swirling together tighter and tighter into a man-size dust devil that zipped around the barn, sucking up debris as it moved, then spitting it out again. Gusts strong enough to topple a chair whipped at the farmers' hair and clothes.

Several lanterns flickered and went out.

"It's a tornado!" a man yelled.

"In a barn?"

Someone chuckled.

And just like that, the fight was over.

For the moment, at least.

Flurry lifted her hands and raised her voice. "My name is Flurry Wind Catcher." This time people turned to look at her.

Men and women helped each other up, dusting off their clothes and straightening rumpled hair. Someone helped Kai to his feet.

Was that the grumpy man who'd brought them juice?

Adven forced his way to the front of the crowd, glaring up at her as his fingers probed a cut on his lip.

Flurry ignored him. "I *am* your kin, from the desert below. My family has lived among you for four generations. We sail the *Lady Grace*."

Again voices rose, but not in anger this time. "Lady Grace," echoed off the rafters. Everyone knew the *Lady Grace*.

Flurry showed them her palms. "My hands bear heavy callouses. My family takes the goods you grow and sells them for you. We bring back what you can't grow. All our lives are better for it."

"That's right," a man yelled and others shouted their agreement.

"I've lived through drought years. I've gone to bed hungry."

"Yes, you have." This was a woman's voice.

She couldn't see the speaker but the whole crowd seemed to agree, to confirm that Flurry was one of them.

She blew out a breath.

"Let me tell you what I know about fertilizer." She paused in wonder at the sudden stillness. Even the barn itself seemed to be listening. "Not much."

An old man bellowed a laugh and the tension in the room eased.

"What I do know is this—" Flurry bit her lip, determined to hold back the tears burning her eyes. "People of the Sun Clan, your kin—are getting sick. Some have died." She drew in a breath.

"My friend Wollemi is only eight years old. He loves swimming and stars and people. He helps even if you don't need it—"

Her voice cracked and she tried to swallow the lump lodged in her throat. "He's sick. Really sick."

Farmers shuffled their feet, looked at each other, then glanced away. None of them were willing to meet her eyes.

Flurry drew in a breath. "For years and years, the desert people have gotten their water from the Table. Everyone knows this just as everyone knows it rains up here on the Table, the water filters through the earth and joins underground streams that emerge as larger streams. Those streams join together into a small river, delivering life-giving water to our desert town."

She could see people nodding.

"In all those years, we've never had a problem with sickness from the water." She paused for a heartbeat. "Until now."

Flurry looked around the barn, meeting the eyes of hard-working men and women, wondering how best to say her next words. "I hear this season is the best season you've ever had. I can attest to the quality of the corn—it's tastier than Gram's harvest cookies!"

A light smattering of applause and a few chuckles loosened the knot in her stomach.

"One of the things Mayten Singer and I wanted to find out when we were here yesterday was whether or not something had changed here on the Table. That's when we found out about the fertilizer. You know as well as I do, that fertilizer can work its way through the soil into the ground water. Even though it mixes with other water in other streams that have no fertilizer, that water is making our people very sick."

"But not everyone is sick," an old man said, the frown on his face so deep she could hardly see his lips. "So it can't be the fertilizer."

Most everyone nodded.

"We wondered about that ourselves," Flurry said. "How many of you are familiar with the caves?"

Almost everyone raised a hand.

"Ugh!" Silas shouted. "I hate those caves!"

Laughter rippled through the barn.

"In one of those caves," Flurry continued, "there is water flowing directly from the Table. Wollemi made the mistake of filling his water bladder directly from that water. The sleeping sickness hit him like a boulder. He can't even move his legs."

Flurry paused again, letting her words sink in. "After our last visit to the Table, we decided the problem was somehow connected to the water. We started boiling water three days ago. The clan leader is bringing in water from other clans. If Mayten Singer and these questers hadn't helped us figure it out, if we hadn't started boiling our water, Feather Leader, Brenda Weaver, little Jeimy Sailor, and hundreds of others would likely be dead. So far, we've lost only three, but three is too many."

The old man scratched his head with a gnarled hand. "What do you suggest we do? Give up the very thing that finally helped us out of the hole we've been stuck in?"

"I'm suggesting you at least think about it. Talk among yourselves. See if there's another way to produce great crops without using the thing that's been poisoning your kin."

CHAPTER THIRTY-SEVEN

Alight appeared at the edge of the plateau, shining down at the townsfolk still staring at Mayten. She squinted, trying to see who was there.

"It's okay." Silas's voice was like warm milk on a cold day. "They said you can come up."

Mayten's knees almost buckled in relief. "Looks like they're ready for us."

She trailed the townsfolk up the road, across the farm, and into the barn. Farmers in dusty coveralls and muddy boots turned to look at them. The harbormaster shoved her way to the front of the barn, heading for an old man who stood next to Flurry on a hay bale that seemed too small for the pair of them.

Kai and Adven stood nearby. Flurry looked shaken but okay. Kai was sporting a swollen eye and Adven's lip was bleeding.

The old man held up his gnarled hands. "Hello friends, what brings you up here in the dark?"

"We've come to see if you've decided to stop poisoning us, Acre." The voice belonged to a man with thinning hair and a long beard. He broke away from the townspeople and faced the old man.

The air in the room seemed to stiffen.

"Poisoned?" The old man looked completely befuddled. "Weaver, you think we did it on purpose? We had no idea the fertilizer was causing the sickness."

The farmers shouted in agreement.

The harbormaster stepped up beside the balding man. "When we were sick, did any of you come down to check on us?"

The townspeople nodded, glaring at the farmers who glared back.

"I never had a visit," a woman with curly black hair said.

"No one checked on me," a man to her left said.

Old man Acre shook his head. "We didn't know if the sickness we kept hearing about was contagious. It could have been like the fever winter. We thought it best to stay up here and not expose ourselves until we knew more."

Weaver's face was red as a beet. He tugged his beard so hard Mayten thought he'd pull it out. "You thought you'd stay up here all safe and sound while we died off, when it was you causing the sickness?"

A chorus of angry mutters rose from the townspeople.

The old man held up his hand. "Look, we didn't know. As soon as we understood, we agreed to form a plan to make changes."

"As soon as you knew?" The harbormaster's voice rose to a high pitch. "Do you mean tonight? Did these travelers," she gestured toward Mayten, "have to convince you to do something when we've been boiling water and bringing it in on ships for days now?"

Someone bumped Mayten's arm. She glanced down to find Flurry who shrugged and gave her a 'what do we do now' look.

Mayten rolled her eyes. "I thought I got them settled down."

Voices raised until both sides were shouting and neither side listening.

Divided like this, unable to hear each other, unable to see the other side—there was no chance these folks were going to work things out.

They had to work together.

Mayten leaned down, pointing at Flurry's waist. "Can I use your water bladder?"

Flurry raised an eyebrow but handed it over.

Mayten took the bladder, then inhaled and stepped between Acre and Weaver who looked very close to throwing fists.

Muttering stopped and the crowd—farmers and townspeople—quieted.

Mayten tried not to wonder what would happen if she was the one who got hit. She'd taken a risk, stepping between the two men. Time to see if the risk paid off.

She held up the bladder. "This is water straight from the stream that runs from a cave below us. It's the same water my brother Wollemi drank. He can't even move his legs now. And all he did was drink this water."

She held the bladder toward Acre. "Would you like to drink some?"

He jerked back as if she held a snake, shaking his head. "No, of course not."

She held out the bladder to Weaver. "How about you?"

His eyebrows came down sharply. "No, why would you even ask that?"

Mayten held the bladder high and turned in a slow circle for all to see. "We seem to have forgotten who the enemy is here. It is not the farmers who simply tried something new to help their crops thrive this year."

Grizzled heads throughout the barn nodded vigorously.

"It is not the townspeople who enjoyed that delicious corn." Reluctant nods came from the townspeople.

"It is the fertilizer in the water that is the enemy."

Both groups nodded in agreement.

She looked around the barn, catching a nod from Adven and a look of amazement on Kai's face. "None of us can be responsible for what we didn't know," she continued. "Now that we know, however, we can work to fix the problem."

More nods this time, though faces remained grim.

She turned back to the two men.

"Are the farmers forming a group to work out a solution?" she asked Acre.

"We are," Acre said.

"'Bout time," Weaver said.

Acre placed his hand on Weaver's shoulder. "I'm sorry we didn't figure this out sooner. We were too caught up in harvesting this bumper crop. I admit it and I'm sorry."

The bearded man slapped the old man's shoulder. "And we were too busy eating your corn to think fertilizer might be the problem." He laughed, frown lines vanishing from his face. "It was mighty good corn."

Chuckles and a few belly laughs followed his admission.

"Why don't you choose some folks to help us figure this out?" Acre said. "They can stay at my house tonight."

"I'd like to join you." The words were out of Mayten's mouth before she realized she wanted to stay.

Flurry stepped up, nodding. "I'll stay, too."

Weaver stared at them both, then nodded and turned to the harbormaster. Mayten had been surprised when the woman hadn't pushed her way into the discussion between the two older men.

A few other townspeople chose to stay and the crowd began to disperse, leaving behind a barn full of echoes and dust.

Adven and Kai walked up, Silas trailing close behind.

"Ma says you can all stay the night if you want." Silas grinned from ear to ear, looking as though he'd just been given a treat.

"If you think you'll be all right without us," Adven said, "we'll head back. We've got water to boil and haul in from the ships in the morning."

Kai groaned.

Mayten ruffled Silas's hair. "Thanks for telling me about the townspeople. If you hadn't raised the alarm, things might have been even worse."

The boy bobbed his head. "Anytime. Come on. Ma'll have snacks and warm cactus juice!"

Adven caught her arm as she started to follow Silas. "Keep your eyes open and your back to the wall. Still feels like something's not right up here in the tablelands."

CHAPTER THIRTY-EIGHT

Mayten and Flurry followed Silas and the other leaders back to the ranch house. Before they reached the door Mayten stopped, grabbing Flurry's arm. "I'd like to sit with the trees for a bit. Do you want to come?"

Flurry nodded as Silas bounced up to them. "You two coming?"

Mayten touched the boy's shoulder. "Silas, will you please tell your folks we'll be there in a bit?"

The boy looked at them and back at the group entering his family home. He seemed torn. "But don't you want to hear?"

"We do, and we won't be long. We need some time to listen to the trees and the wind."

The boy's eyes grew wide. "Should I come with you to listen?"

"No, we'd like you to listen to what the leaders say and tell us later. You're good at listening to people and we're good at listening to nature. Both are important. Can you do that for us?"

He straightened at the praise and grinned. "You bet I will!" He chased after the crowd disappearing into the house.

As they turned toward the long windbreak of trees Flurry glanced at Mayten. "Do you think we're missing something?"

"I don't know, but something still doesn't *feel* right."

"I guess not. I was hoping it was the fertilizer but I feel it too. Something isn't right. Whatever it is has to do with the water, though."

"Agreed." The three-quarter moon had just started inching upward, shedding its soft light over the land. Ahead, Mayten could see the trees lining the far side of the cornfield. The fresh smell of cut corn mixed with the earthy smell of soil. "I'm glad to be away from all that commotion. What happened after I left?"

Flurry told Mayten her story while they walked. Then Mayten told her story, finishing as they reached the line of trees.

"Good job though, stopping that fight," Mayten said with a chuckle.

"Good job calling the bats and snakes."

"It was terrifying. I was afraid the scorpions were next!" Mayten shivered. "But I'm glad they came."

Mayten stopped and looked up at the nearest tree. It was tall and thin and didn't look anything like her forest trees back home. But the tree seemed to call to her all the same. She sat on the ground, pressing her back to the tree, then glanced up at Flurry. "Do you want to listen here or somewhere else?"

Flurry glanced around. "I'll just sit on the path. There's a good breeze here." She plopped to the ground and crossed her legs.

Mayten inhaled to slow her breathing and calm her heart. Slowly she shut out the night sounds, the chirping crickets and croaking frogs, until her mind was still. She leaned against the rough bark of the tree trunk and *focused*.

:Hello, uncle.:

:Hello, child.:

Mayten breathed a sigh of relief. The tree was willing to talk with her.

She'd never tried to talk to something that hadn't grown naturally but it didn't seem to matter. She thought carefully about the question she needed to ask. She'd learned the hard way not to ask questions that were too broad. :*I need to know what is poisoning the water?*:

She was shown the same vision as before, only this time there was something different. The darkness within the darkness was indeed a circle. But it didn't look like a cave. What was she missing?

She leaned into the trunk. :*Uncle, is there anything else you can show me?*:

Again the blackness but also the smell. She'd thought it was from the bat cave but the guano made her eyes water. Besides, the bat cave had no water. The scorpion cave had a musty smell, but not like this. The cave with the water hadn't smelled that bad but it did have a smell. This smell being sent to her by the uncle tree was putrid, but she couldn't identify it.

She sat awhile longer but got nothing else. She thanked the tree and opened her eyes. Flurry stood, arms crossed, waiting.

The girl looked as confused as Mayten felt.

They walked back to the house, sharing the visions they'd received. Both tree and wind had "said" the same thing.

"Maybe tomorrow we should look around more," Flurry suggested. "Ask for another tour to farms outside of this corn farm."

Mayten agreed.

When they got to the house, they found the lights were already off. They opened the door, trying to be quiet.

Silas sat on one of the couches in his pajamas. A candle flickered on a nearby table. He stood when they came in, small hands planted on his hips. "What took you so long?"

"Sorry," Mayten said. "Where is everyone?"

"They didn't talk for long. Everyone was tired. They're gonna meet in the morning and make some plans. Did you hear anything from the wind or the trees?"

Mayten wasn't sure what to say. It was late and she could tell the boy was dead on his feet. "Not much. Is there anything else we should know before we all get some sleep?"

He tilted his head. "Just that some of the farmers still don't think the fertilizer is the problem."

"Why not?" Flurry asked.

"Acre said the fertilizer is spread too thin and would take more than a year to get down into the water table." He yawned so wide his jaw cracked.

Mayten touched his arm. "Thanks, Silas. We'll all talk tomorrow, okay? Thanks for staying up for us. We really appreciate it."

He nodded and stumbled down the hall.

Banging pots woke the girls the next morning. Mayten sat up, more than a bit disoriented. It was still pitch-black outside. Had she missed another meeting?

Flurry stood and stretched as Honey came out of the kitchen.

"Oh good. You're up. Can you help me put out breakfast? We don't have a big meal in the morning just some rolls and cheese and coffee. But the leaders want to meet here after the harvest starts so I've added a few things."

They followed Honey into the kitchen and brought out platters with cut-up pieces of apples and small oranges Mayten had never seen before. There were also slices of sweet bread that smelled of cinnamon and carafes of coffee and tea.

One by one, the rest of the family stumbled down the hall, grabbing mugs and sinking sleepily onto benches around the table. Some of them didn't bother to sit, grabbing food and coffee, then pulling on shoes, picking up gear, and heading outside.

Mayten shivered as cold air wafted in through the open door. Outside the sky was turning a lovely orange.

As the workers went out to harvest, neighbors came in and gathered around the table. Honey and Clavis sat across from Acre who sat next to the harbormaster and Weaver. Mayten and Flurry sat together on a bench next to Honey.

Silas poked his head into the room and Honey shooed him out.

"Where did everyone else go?" Mayten asked.

"We sent the others home," Weaver said. "Too many cooks in the kitchen and all that. So last night we decided to choose representatives."

"Everyone here is needed for the harvest," Acre said, scratching his cheek with a gnarled hand. "But I've got to tell you that most of the farmers disagree with the fertilizer idea."

"Silas mentioned that last night." Mayten took a sip of coffee, once again feeling out of her depth with all these older people. They had so much more experience than she did. Still . . .

Acre pointed at the girls with a piece of bread. "Silas said you gals went out to listen to the trees and such last night. Did you get any information?"

Mayten straightened her shoulders. "We did. We'd like to look around more. See if we can pinpoint a location."

Clavis laughed. "That could take a very long time. There are eleven other farms up here and they're spread out like ours. Some even bigger."

"I need to get back to town before nightfall," the harbormaster said. She focused on Mayten. "Any suggestions where we should start looking?"

"You gonna let these little whelps give us directions?" said Acre.

"It's them that figured out the problem in the first place."

Mayten cleared her throat. She wasn't going to be stopped by one man who didn't believe her. "We found the water in a cave at the base of the cliff, about halfway along the path heading west. That's where Wollemi filled his water bottle. Is there a farm that might be above that part of the cliff?"

Honey, Clavis, and Acre looked at each other.

"There's one over that way—Old Dog's ranch," Honey said. "But it's a dairy cattle ranch. They wouldn't even use fertilizer."

"Old Dog died last year," Clavis said. "His son came up from the Ocean Clan to help his Ma. Not sure he's even gifted in ranching, poor fellow. I haven't even met him yet. Have you, Acre?"

The old man nodded. "A couple of times, though we haven't really talked. Didn't see him last night. He's probably still trying to figure out how to work the ranch. I suppose we could give him a visit."

Honey decided to stay behind while the rest of them headed out to see what a visit to the dairy ranch might reveal. The sun-warmed air actually felt good as Mayten followed the others along a well-worn dirt road. They fell into pairs as they walked—Weaver walked with Acre, Clavis with the harbormaster, and Mayten with Flurry.

Flurry leaned close to Mayten. "Do you know what you're doing?"

"No idea, but this dairy ranch is as good a place to start as any."

Mayten's thoughts drifted to Wollemi. She did not want to spend another night away from her brother. She was glad Cather was taking care of him, but a tiny voice in her head kept her wondering if he was really improving. She forced her attention back to the walk, admiring the orchards filled with fruit trees, the fields of enormous red tomatoes, and what looked like vineyards with rows of grapes.

They could smell the ranch before they could see the corrals.

The morning breeze shifted, carrying a stench that nearly made Mayten gag. Cows were smellier than sheep, she decided.

As they drew closer, Clavis pointed out a big corral holding at least fifty dairy cows with a half dozen calves scattered among them. "There's your dairy cows."

He pointed at a smaller corral. "That's the bull."

"Let us do the talking," Clavis said, raising a hand and bringing the group to a stop. "Is there anything specific we should be looking for?"

Mayten licked her lips. "Something round and black with smooth edges rather than jagged edges."

"And a bad smell," Flurry added.

Acre laughed. "That doesn't narrow it down much, does it?"

Mayten grimaced, hoping they hadn't taken this walk for nothing.

"Anybody know the son's name?" the harbormaster asked.

Acre scratched his chin. "Pretty sure he's a Builder . . . Planer Builder, that's his name."

He led them up a path that ended at a large house beyond the corrals. It wasn't unlike Honey's house except for being more run down. Weeds marred the flower beds, and a rocker was tipped on its side on the porch.

Acre shook his head. "Old Dog would never have let this place get run down. He had a lot of pride in this ranch."

They followed Acre up to the door, but no one came to his knock.

"Let's go round back."

The porch wrapped around the house, back stairs leading down to a big yard—also overgrown with weeds. Beyond the yard an open field stretched all the way to the edge of the plateau.

A lanky man stalked through the field, pushing a wheeled cart with a shovel laid across it. He was tall and thin with brown skin and straight black hair. As they approached, he turned toward them and stopped, waiting.

Mayten studied the man as they got closer. He was about the age of her twin sisters, though his face was more careworn. Deep wrinkles surrounded his eyes and he was sweating heavily even though the day wasn't hot yet . . .

Her skin crawled as she noticed something else—the smell of the cows should be lessening as they walked away from the corrals. Instead, it seemed to be growing fouler.

Flurry put her hand on Mayten's arm and sniffed. Mayten nodded. It was the same smell from their visions.

Acre approached with his hand out. "Planer, we've met a few times. I'm Acre Grower."

The man held out his hands, revealing how dirty they were.

Acre nodded and waved at their group. "This is Clavis Grower from the corn farm."

Clavis nodded a greeting.

"These two are from down clan—the harbormaster and Cord Weaver."

Planer frowned. "What do you all want with me? I've got a lot of work to do, and it won't do itself."

Acre held up his worn hands as if calming a skittish dog. "We won't keep you. This is Mayten Singer and Flurry Wind Catcher. They've been trying to help us solve the sickness that's affecting our down clan kin. That's what the meeting was about last night. I didn't see you there."

His weary eyes narrowed. "Had no time for a meeting. Ma's been sick since Da died and I'm trying to keep this place running. What does the down clan sickness have to do with me?"

"These girls have giftings in listening to the wind and the trees, ya see. And they were able to determine the poison is coming from up here on the Table. Gets in the water somehow."

The young man stared at them, uncomprehending. Then he shrugged. "And . . . ?"

Clavis stepped forward. "At first they thought the poison was coming from the new fertilizer we were using but that wouldn't be possible."

The man shook his head. "I don't use fertilizer, and I don't use poison. Now, if you don't mind, I need to get this done before it's too hot."

He moved to pick up the cart.

"Please Mister Builder," Mayten said. "Do you have anything round and black up here, some kind of dark hole?"

He stopped and turned to her, scowling. "Girl, I don't know what you're on about but the only thing in this field is the compost pit." He grabbed the handles and stalked off.

"Well, then. I guess that's that." Acre and the others turned away.

Mayten wasn't giving up that easily. She hurried after the man, Flurry close behind. The further they went, the stronger the smell grew.

At first, Mayten thought Planer was headed for the cliff, but the man stopped in a few more steps. In front of him was a large hole in the ground. He tipped the cart forward, dumping its load into the hole.

Mayten stopped a few feet away, trying not to gag as the most horrific stench she'd ever experienced filled the air.

"Mr. Builder," she said, keeping her voice gentle. "What goes into this compost?"

He scraped out the cart with his shovel and righted it, turning back toward the ranch. "What goes in? What doesn't go in? Cow waste, chicken leavings, food leftovers, whatever needs cleaning. I spend most of my time milking cows, cleaning up after 'em, feeding 'em. Then there's eggs to gather and cookin' to do. Ma hardly cooks anymore."

The others had followed Mayten and heard his answer. They leaned toward each other, whispering frantically.

Planer glared at them. "What are you whispering about?"

"Planer, I hate to tell you but that's a bad mix to have so close to the cliffs," Acre said.

"What do you mean?" he growled. "It stinks worse than the cows and I wanted it as far from the house as I could get it."

"See that stream?" Weaver pointed at a small stream that ran across the field and emptied into the compost hole.

"'Course. That's why I dug it here, so I didn't have to haul water to mix in. I need to get some good soil out of it by next year. Believe it or not, on top of everything else, Ma wants me to plant her a garden."

The confusion slowly cleared from his face, replaced by a look of horror. "Wait. You're saying this pit is what's poisoning the water?"

Mayten's stomach clenched as Acre nodded.

Would Planer be mad? Would he fight them? Deny responsibility?

She was surprised to see his expression crumble. He turned and walked away from them, striding quickly toward the cliff.

Mayten's breath caught. What was he doing?

She chased after him. "Planer, wait!"

He reached the edge and stood, staring bleakly into the distance.

Mayten stopped next to him.

"I tried to do everything right," he said in a tight voice.

She could hear the pain in his voice.

"I don't know what I'm doing. I'm trying to learn. There is no one to help me. I hardly sleep, Ma is no help, and now you're telling me I've poisoned all those people?"

She placed a hand on his shoulder. She needed to reach him. Let him know there was help to be found. "My sisters live with the Ocean Clan. Acerola and Zigba Merchant. Do you know them?"

He swallowed hard and nodded. "They knit and their husbands are woodworkers. The Great Builder knows I miss the ocean. I was never meant to be here. I don't have a gift for cows or growing or any of those things." His voice broke and he glanced down at the ground plunging away just inches from his feet. "All those people are sick and might die because I was too stubborn to admit defeat." He swayed forward.

"You couldn't have known." Mayten desperately searched for the right words, words that would help and not send him over the edge. "No one will blame you."

He sank onto the ground, shoulders slumped in defeat. "I didn't want to admit I'd failed. I wanted to prove myself to my da, even though he's not here. He always wanted me to run the ranch and was disappointed when I chose to be a builder instead."

Mayten sat beside him. "People have been slowly getting better. We've been hauling in water from other clans and boiling the water we have. And if we clean out that pit, the water will be clean again."

He looked at her, his eyes filled with grief. "Are you telling it like it is or just trying to make me feel better?"

"I'm telling it like it is."

He stood, brushing off his pants. He took one last look at the drop-off, then turned.

Acre and the others waited a few paces away.

Mayten leaned close to the man. "We are given our gifts for a reason. You are needed back with the Ocean Clan, not here."

He nodded and lifted his chin. "Guess Ma will have to understand. Looks like I have a mess to clean up first, though."

Acre stepped up and put his arm around the man's shoulder, leading him away from the drop-off and back to the others. "We've got plenty of hands to help."

Mayten and Flurry made it off the mountain before the sun scorched through their hoods. They'd gathered everyone—Adven, Tray, Kai, Cather, and Joshua Leader around the leader's kitchen table.

Mayten looked around at her friends and pride filled her chest as she reported on what they'd discovered. She still couldn't believe they'd actually solved the problem. It would take an enormous group effort, but soon the pit would be cleaned and the water safe to drink.

"Sorry to interrupt." Cather's ma stepped into the room. She looked at Joshua Leader. "I think Feather is ready to sit up."

Mayten straightened, report forgotten. "That's great news!"

Joshua stood and hurried toward the hall. He turned back, his eyes glistening. "I can't thank you all enough." He gave them a shaky smile and vanished into the back room.

Mayten stared down the hall at her bedroom door. How long would it be—

"Time to get you and Wollemi home," Adven said. "People here will heal, but it will take time. Today the healers decided the best thing for your brother is to go home, where the food and water are clean. We'll be taking you both down to a ship in the morning. Cather will go with you. The rest of us will stay a while longer just to be sure things keep moving forward."

Mayten's eyes burned with unshed tears. She sent a prayer of thanks to the Great Singer.

Home.

She and Wollemi were going home.

CHAPTER THIRTY-NINE

Six Months Later

The sun had barely begun to warm the day when Mayten and her family reached the docks along with a flock of Forest Clan leaders. Puffy white clouds dotted the robin's egg blue sky, providing a perfect background for the arrival of the king's two barges. Bargemen poled the crafts into place along the dock. The welcoming crowd stayed out of the way as a team of young men and women helped the family unload their belongings.

As soon as the luggage had been removed, the royal family disembarked. Cather ran forward to greet the queen and help her with little Plum who was now a squirmy toddler. The other young ones, twin girls and two boys, darted through the crowds to Mayten, almost knocking her over.

The twins reached her first, jet-black hair done up in braids.

"We sailed on a big ship," Lemmy said. She crinkled her freckled nose and swung the hem of her lemon-yellow dress.

"And met your friend Flurry!" Limey said, mimicking her sister and swinging the hem of her lime-green dress.

Mayten laughed. Did all twins talk like this, finishing each other's sentences like her sisters did?

"She said to say hi," Lemmy said.

"And she'll be here in a few days," Limey added.

Blue and Raz raced up and stopped behind the twins, bouncing from one foot to another. All four had grown since she'd last seen them. Blue's rust-red hair and freckles would be recognizable anywhere, while Raz was looking more and more like Kai. Same Black hair; same gap-toothed grin.

"We took a barge," Blue said. "I got to ride in the front and help Rill steer."

Mayten glanced at Rill handing down luggage from the barge. He must have felt her gaze and raised a hand in greeting. She returned the greeting, surprised to find that seeing him again didn't bring on the intense feelings it once had.

"Where's Wollemi?" Raz asked.

Mayten glanced around. "He was just—"

Wollemi raced up, tapped Blue on the chest, and tore off again. "You're it," he called over his shoulder.

Mayten laughed, watching them dash up the path toward town. A lump clogged her throat. Six months ago he couldn't even walk on his own. Now he was running around like a wild thing. *Thank you, Great Singer.*

"I wish I had their energy."

Mayten turned at the familiar voice.

"Nan!" She reached out to hug the king's second oldest daughter, then drew back. Nan was not really a hugger. She studied Nan's long face. "You look exhausted. Do you want to come up to our place and rest? It will be a while before they get your tents set up and Ma is inviting your entire family up for the midday meal anyway." She paused a second. "Da is cooking which is always a good thing."

"I'd love it. I'll just tell Ma." Nan turned, waving at the queen.

Looking regal even in plain traveling clothes, Queen Bella glanced at Nan curiously, pausing her conversation with Cather. Cather didn't seem to mind. She was too busy bouncing baby Plum on her hip.

The first time Mayten had seen the queen, she'd been shocked at how much she resembled Kai. The two were near-perfect reflections of each other, though the queen had a few more laugh lines.

"I'm going to Mayten's with the kids," Nan yelled.

Her mother nodded. King Redmond waved as well, then turned back to the clan leaders.

"I'm glad to see Wollemi looking hale," Nan said as Mayten led her up the path toward town. "I heard your brother got quite sick during his visit to the Sun Clan."

Mayten grimaced. "I've never seen anything so strange. Even when he woke up and seemed to be doing better, he couldn't move his legs. I was scared he'd never walk again. It took forever to get his strength back."

They joined the throngs of people moving toward town, some carrying the king's belongings, some preparing for the arrival of friends and family from other clans. As they entered the town center Mayten paused to spread her arms wide. "Welcome to the town center."

Nan glanced around the horseshoe of small houses. "These are lovely. I love pastels and look at those flower boxes!" Her eyes sparkled.

Mayten pointed at a house with the Healer sign above the door. "That's Cather's home."

She pointed at a large wooden stage at the apex of the horseshoe. "We use that stage for all our events." Her heart pounded. "It's where I attended my calling ceremony and where I found out I was going to the castle."

"Seems like so long ago," Nan said.

Mayten nodded. "So much has happened in the past year and a half." She pointed at one of the larger buildings where Cather's training program was held. Solis's office and the town's bell tower shared the same building. "This is the community center. Your tents will be set up next to that. We're still expecting folks from the Ocean and Sun clans. Once everyone gets here this place will be crowded all the time. Ma has asked to use my brother Oleaster's new wing. That'll give your family a quiet place when you need to get away."

"His new wing?" Nan's brow furrowed.

"He and the carpenters spent the spring and winter adding a wing to our homestead. He's joining with his love during the solstice celebration. It's very roomy and he's put in some beds and couches. It'll be a good place for the littles to nap and rest."

"Thank you," Nan said. "I've never been good in big crowds." She took a deep breath. "The smells are so different here, rich and loamy, like a good soil. I can't wait to meet your da and talk gardening!"

"That's a subject he never tires of." Mayten wrinkled her nose. "Let's head up."

As they walked, Mayten told Nan all about her time at the Ocean Clan and Sun Clan, then filled her in on how she, her friends, and family chose contestants from the Forest Clan after they'd returned home. "I'm so glad I had help. It was actually fun. We held competitions in tree climbing, flower arranging, and construction. Participants had to build structures out of wood."

They crested the hill to Mayten's homestead and were greeted by loud squeals, laughing children, and a very boisterous dog.

Anatolian raced down to meet them, wriggling like a puppy around Nan's legs.

Nan laughed, scratching Anatolian's broad head. His curly tail whipped back and forth, stirring up the air in blissful happiness. "It's good to see you again, boy."

She squatted so she was face to face with Anatolian's brown eyes. She reached both hands behind his ears and scratched. Anatolian closed his eyes in bliss. "The kids talked about him all the way here," Nan said.

Mayten sighed. "I really missed him on my journey to the clans. I did have a cat and a bird to keep me company, though. Along with some very handsome men."

Nan's eyes widened and she raised an eyebrow. "What about Thomas? I thought you two were a thing. Where is he anyway?"

"Kai and Tray were sent to make sure everyone gets here safely. They should be back in a day or two." She studied Nan's wrinkled brow. "You know we call your brother 'Kai,' right? That's what he wants."

Nan nodded. "I forgot. I guess if I saw him more, I'd get used to it. When he comes home, he's still Thomas."

Mayten continued up the road. "Kai and I, we're—very fond of each other but have decided to put all that on hold. With the competition and the school and him gone all the time, it's just too complicated. He did come for my birthday celebration in the spring and that was nice. Who knows, maybe we'll end up together. I'm in no rush, though. We still have a lot to do."

"And I have so much to talk to you about. Did you—"

"Here we are," Mayten said. Heat rushed into her cheeks as she realized she'd interrupted Nan. She gestured at the front yard where Da and Oleaster were busy setting up tables and chairs. Strategically placed blankets spread out on the neatly mown grass adding splashes of color to the grounds as well. Apparently, Da was planning for a crowd. She waved at the men.

"Da, Oleaster, come meet Nan."

The two men set down the table they'd been carrying, then brushed off their hands and came over.

"This is the king's daughter Nan, the botanist," Mayten said. "This is my da and my eldest brother Oleaster."

Nan shook Oleaster's outstretched hand.

Her father beamed. "I'm so happy to meet you. I understand we have a lot in common."

Nan smiled shyly. "I'm looking forward to talking with you." She gestured to the flower beds. Begonias, cosmos, impatiens, and zinnias wove their vibrant colors through bushes and grass. "Your flowers are incredible. I have so many questions."

Da laughed warmly. "So do I. Now, though, I have a feeling the clan leaders will be following your father up here. Would you two help us set out the food? Your poor da probably never gets a break, Nan. Might as well make him comfortable."

"Oh, he likes it that way," Nan said. "He's happiest when he's surrounded by kids and has people to talk to."

Anatolian barked as Wollemi and the king's children streamed down the front porch into the yard.

"Wollemi," Da called.

Wollemi stopped in his tracks mid-run as if he'd been turned into stone holding a funny pose.

Da chuckled. "Can you go down and see if you can get Ma to bring the folks up here to eat?"

Wollemi turned abruptly and headed back to town, a cluster of children following behind him like little ducklings.

A glow started deep inside as Mayten marveled at how easily he moved. He'd had a long recuperation but was going to be fine. "He's going to have a great week."

They went into the house where Taiwania stood at the long wooden table in the kitchen, covering dish after dish with towels. Under the table, Aster the toddler stacked blocks for baby Maple to knock down.

"Taiwania, this is Nan, the king's daughter. I told you about her. We're here to help."

Taiwania smiled a greeting and Nan's eyes grew round.

"Oh my, you *are* beautiful. I mean . . ." Nan blinked. "Mayten said you were beautiful, but . . ." Her long face flushed crimson.

Taiwania was used to this reaction from both men and women. She laughed and moved around the table. "That's very kind of you."

She lifted a platter off the table and placed it in Nan's arms. "I've heard you're brilliant, so I guess you've got me beat."

She grabbed a second platter and led the way out the door. After a glance at Mayten, Nan followed.

Mayten shook her head, took two baskets of bread, and went after them. She rolled her eyes at Da and Oleaster who stood at the kitchen door, trying not to laugh. "Just what my sister needs, a bigger head."

The men nodded in agreement.

They'd almost finished setting up when people began to flow into the yard. Joy swelled in Mayten's chest as she watched her family and what felt like her second family meet each other.

It was the perfect beginning to the summer solstice gathering. She looked forward to handing her notes and report to the king.

Between solving the water sickness problem and culling applicants for the king, Mayten was exhausted. Time for her to relax and enjoy the upcoming music, songs, betrothals, and delicious food. She couldn't wait to catch up with her friends — old and new.

Mayten took a tray of wine-filled cups and started toward the Forest clan leaders gathered around King Redmond. His powerful build, bushy red hair and beard, and booming voice set him apart from the others.

"Mayten, so good to see you." His deep voice seemed to reverberate in her chest. He placed his hand on her shoulder. "Castanea, I can't speak highly enough about your daughter. She has done a lot of work this year for all of us, not to mention saving our trees."

Mayten glowed as she saw her mother's eyes sparkle.

The king looked down at her. "Don't you think this week is going to be all fun and games for you," he warned. "We have a lot of work yet to do."

CHAPTER FORTY

King Redmond was right. Thirty-five contestants showed up to interview. Mayten thanked the Singer that there hadn't been more athletic competitions to organize.

She sat to one side of the king, notepad in hand. Solis had volunteered her office, so there was plenty of room. She and the king sat behind Solis's desk while the contestant being interviewed sat across from them. She took a deep breath, hoping the king couldn't hear her heart pounding in her chest.

Had she chosen the right people? Would the king find what he was looking for? She worried about the Sun Clan people who'd been chosen from the clan leader's list.

Rill was the first contestant who tapped on the open door.

"Come," the king said.

Rill walked confidently into the room. He gave Mayten a wink as he settled in the interview chair. He'd been granted the first interview so he could get back to the task of shuttling people to and from the gathering.

"King Redmond," Mayten said, "this is Rill Wave Runner."

The king stuck out his hand. "Welcome, Rill. Thanks for joining me this fine morning. And thank you for bringing half my family over on your barge."

Rill smiled broadly. "Happy to be here, King Redmond."

Mayten couldn't help but smile. Rill was not cowed by the king at all.

The king leaned back in his chair, wincing as the chair creaked a bit under his weight. "Seems you impressed our tree singer or you wouldn't be here today, young man. Now it's time to impress me. What enlivens your soul?"

Mayten's stomach dropped. How would she even answer such a question? What enlivened *her* soul? The trees popped into her mind. When she was among the trees, speaking with them, it was as if she felt her soul unfurl.

She held her breath, wondering what Rill would say.

Rill took his time, brow furrowed as he thought. Finally, he looked at the king. "The wind. The water. And people. Whenever I am with any one of those things, I feel most alive. If I am fortunate enough to be with all three, it's a perfect day."

The king smiled. "A good answer."

He leaned forward, resting his elbows on Solis's desk. "We know what gives you life. Now tell me—what drains life from you?"

Again, Mayten was surprised by the question. She chewed her lip, thinking.

She didn't know what she'd expected from the king—perhaps questions about running a kingdom—but these questions went much deeper, reaching into a person's heart.

That was why he was king, she reasoned. Not only was he friendly and charming, he was wise.

How would she answer such a question?

Being stuck inside while Wollemi was sick—being away from nature and her trees—had definitely drained her.

Also, being around too many people— especially when they talked about nothing important—drained her.

Rill leaned forward, his body mirroring the king. "Unkind people. People who treat others as below them or unfairly." He shook his head. "It hurts to see that."

The king nodded.

Mayten hadn't expected such an answer from Rill. He always seemed so cheerful.

"And Rill," the king said, "when were *you* last unkind to someone?"

The bargeman huffed out a breath and shook his head. "That's easy. I was unkind to your son Kai."

The king's eyebrows lifted. "My son?"

Rill nodded. "During our barge trip to the Ocean Clan. I guess I was trying to put him in his place, thinking he was a spoiled prince, which was unfair as I didn't know him. And, if I'm honest, I can be unkind when I'm showing off. I had a pretty lady to show off for." He gave Mayten a wry smile. "I think I put him down to try and make myself look better. I thought about it almost the entire return trip and feel rotten about how I treated him. I plan to apologize to him this week."

The king sat back in his chair. "A person who can admit when he is wrong and make amends has a teachable heart. Although my boy probably benefited from a bit of that. Being raised in a castle is not the best way to prepare for the world beyond castle walls."

"I haven't always been able to do that," Rill admitted. "To apologize. But I'm getting better at it."

"It's a lifework," the king said.

Mayten fought the urge to shift around in her seat. She felt like she was eavesdropping on a private conversation.

The king steepled his fingers on the desktop. "Now tell me what your deepest heartache is."

Rill's head dropped. When he looked back at the king Mayten was surprised to see his eyes glisten with unshed tears. "My parents died in the fever winter. I miss them every day."

The king nodded. "We lost two children. The fever winter left us all with a communal pain we will never forget. I'm sorry about your parents."

Mayten found herself tearing up. She didn't know of one family who hadn't lost someone during the fever winter.

Rill nodded.

"Final question—what makes you laugh out loud?"

Rill grinned. "Children. I love to watch them play and hear the things they talk about. Their minds are full of curiosity. In fact, your little Blue had me laughing all the way here."

The king grinned back. "Sounds like Blue."

"And dogs," Rill added. "I love dogs. That is one regret I've had in my job. I'd love to have a dog."

Mayten's heart warmed. She never would have thought Rill's answers would touch her so.

The king laughed. "I'm a big fan of children, too. I have quite a passel of them, as you know. After meeting Mayten's dog, Anatolian, they've all been hounding me for a dog." He smiled at his own joke. "I've put a request out to the traders to see what they can find."

The king put his palms on the table. "I'll be announcing the finalists at the end of the week. Though Mayten and I will be discussing different applicants, I'll be making the final decisions alone. With that in mind, I need you to think deeply and honestly about what I ask next. The finalists will have three months to set their affairs in order. They will need to move to the castle before winter comes. They will be in training—leadership and other areas necessary for the working of the island—for one year. Everyone must decide if they are willing to make that commitment, to come live at the castle for the full year."

He paused, looking at Rill who nodded his understanding.

The king nodded back. "Food and housing will be provided, of course, along with a small stipend. After that year, the group will be culled down to about ten people. The rest can either return to their former callings, move into clan leadership training, or whatever they choose. Those who are asked to stay on—and agree to stay on—will continue training for another five to ten years unless something happens to make me leave sooner. Do you understand?"

Again, Rill nodded. He started to reply but the king held up his finger. "I don't want you to say anything yet. I want you to fully understand what I'm asking. Take the fall to think it through. If you stay after the first year, you may be giving up your gifting forever. The options open for you after that will probably be in some area of leadership which might be hard for a man who loves water and wind as you do."

Rill started to protest but the king held up a hand. "Unless you want to be removed from the list right now, don't say another word."

Rill clamped his mouth shut.

"Good," the king said. "You can go now." He stood, offering his hand to Rill. "It has been a pleasure to get to know you, Rill. You seem to be a very fine man."

Rill bowed his head slightly and turned to the door. On his way out he gave Mayten another quick wink.

As the door clicked shut, Mayten glanced at the king and found him staring at her.

"He likes you, doesn't he?"

Her face grew warm. "I think he just likes to flirt."

The king nodded, a thoughtful expression on his face. "He'd be a fool not to. You will have a lot of admirers, Mayten, including my son. I hope you will enjoy the attention and not let any of them win your affection for some time. You have much to offer this kingdom and I appreciate your single-minded focus."

She was tempted to let the king know how much like her da he sounded. Instead, she took a deep breath and let it out, nodding.

"If he is an example of our other applicants, you've done a good job in choosing. Do you have anything to add to what we covered today? Is his flirting inappropriate in any way?"

She smiled. "Not inappropriate. He just likes to tease. I loved your questions though. I wasn't expecting questions that cut straight to a person's heart."

"You think I'm shallow, do you?" He grinned.

"No," she laughed. "That word would never describe you."

She was surprised how comfortable she'd become with King Redmond. At their first meeting he'd terrified her. She'd even thought he might be mad. Now she felt safe in his presence. She loved his children and even got on well with the queen.

The entire royal family was like a second family to her, with the king being a favored uncle.

"What will you do when you stop being the king?" she asked. She'd been so wrapped up in weeding through the applicants for the king, she hadn't given much thought to what he'd do when he no longer had kingly responsibilities.

He tilted his head. "I haven't really decided. I might like to move my family here or perhaps join the Ocean Clan. I'd like my children to grow up around more playmates—that's one reason I'm looking forward to having a school for training at the castle."

He frowned. "Speaking of the school—did I tell you the queen has been pushing the builders? The dorms and class-rooms are almost done. Perhaps we'll start school sooner than we expected. Nan is certainly ready to go. What do you think? Would you be willing to come before winter? I could also use your advice as I train the new leaders."

He gave her a smile that would charm a tree crab. The gap between his front teeth showed.

She'd seen this look before, though. The king wasn't asking—he was telling.

Mayten swallowed, her mouth suddenly dry. She'd been looking forward to working with the students for another year before taking them to the castle. "I'm not sure that the students will be ready by winter."

She wasn't sure *she'd* be ready either but didn't want to say that.

"Your mother's done a great job without you this year. You can bring a couple of the older students with you and she can bring the others later. We'll see if Cather has a few ready as well. The two of you will come, of course. The queen has grown quite fond of your friend."

Mayten smiled but felt her lips tremble.

Leave home after it felt like she'd just returned?

CHAPTER FORTY-ONE

The rest of the interviews passed in a blur, with only a few standing out.

The first was Lan with his beautiful blue eyes and storybook looks. He gave her a shy smile as he sat. She could practically feel his nervousness and silently willed him to be calm.

When the king asked, "Lan, what enlivens your soul?" the shepherd glanced up shyly. "Honestly, seeing Mayten does."

He blushed beet-red. "I mean . . . when she came to the Ocean Clan it was the first time I'd ever *seen* someone from the outside world. Shepherds mostly keep to the hills except on market days. Even then we don't really get to know people. When Mayten came, she spent time with me. I got to show her my life and she told me of hers. It was the first time I understood how big the island is and how much I have to learn. Seeing her again reminds me of that feeling. It makes me feel alive."

Mayten felt her face heat until she was certain she was as red as Lan. She wrinkled her nose when the king glanced her way, annoyed by the sparkle in his eyes.

In her opinion, Lan answered all the questions well. When he left the king grinned at her. "You certainly make an impression wherever you go."

She shook her head, not knowing what to say.

Another interview of note came when Chamfer Builder, the widowed father, was in what she called "the interview seat." He answered the questions nearly perfectly as Mayten knew he would.

She remembered him as a solid man, with compassion and heart. But at the end of the interview when the king explained the commitment, Chamfer sat back with a sigh. "King Redmond, I need to be honest about something. When Mayten had us competing in the games, I was paired with Purl Leader. It was the first time I'd gotten to know the clan leader's daughter."

He smiled then, a huge smile, his eyes distant as if remembering. "The thing is, we've fallen in love. I don't think she's done her interview yet. She is a very capable leader in her own right. But we've decided to announce our plan to join tonight. If we both make the list, we will be glad to come for the year. But if only one of us does, we'll have to bow out."

He waited, his expression hopeful.

The king nodded. "Love is a wonderful thing. And the opportunity for your daughter to have a mother is an equally beautiful gift. I appreciate your honesty and I will let everyone know by the end of the week. We shall see what we shall see."

Chamfer nodded and stood to leave.

Mayten jumped up, walking him to the door. "Such good news! You and Purl deserve all the joy life can bring."

He took her hand and squeezed it. "It's all thanks to you, Mayten." Grinning, he left.

King Redmond chuckled. "I wasn't expecting that."

"Me either," Mayten agreed.

The only other huge surprise was when Sugar Baker came in toting a large bag. Mayten was more than a bit shocked to see the sweet, rosy-cheeked woman. She'd assumed the shy baker would take herself out of the running.

After answering the king's questions, quiet and well-spoken, she raised her chin. "Your Majesty, I'm so grateful to have been chosen for this honor. It has helped my confidence and my sense of self-worth. But what I really love is baking. Creating beautiful works of art with food."

Sugar paused as though gathering her courage. "I really wanted to ask if you might need a baker in the castle kitchen."

Her eyes widened as if she couldn't believe what she'd just said.

The king grinned as though someone had just granted him his favorite wish. "Are you saying you're more interested in a job in my kitchens than training to be queen?"

Sugar nodded and clamped her lips closed, waiting. Mayten held her breath.

His laughter boomed off the walls. "I think we can make that happen. Come to the castle whenever you're ready and I'll see that you're put to work."

Sugar's eyes glistened. "Thank you so much. I promise you won't be disappointed."

She reached into the large bag and pulled out a box. "They're probably worse for wear after the voyage here, but I wanted to give you a sample of my baked goods."

She placed the box on the desk and scurried toward the door. "Thank you again, King Redmond," she said over her shoulder. "And thank you, Mayten, for believing in me."

Mayten shook her head after the baker left. She would never let Sugar—or the king—know the woman had only been chosen to round out the teams.

Mantica, the old wise woman, had been right. The experience had boosted Sugar's confidence.

"What a brave thing to do," Mayten said. "But do you really need another baker?"

He shrugged. "Old Serine has been running the kitchen for decades. Sugar will need every bit of her bravery to face that woman down. But I'll make sure she has a place."

Mayten wasted no time getting out of her chair as the king opened the box. A wonderful smell filled the room. Six different kinds of confections were revealed, each one lovelier than the other. It looked more like a box of flowers than sweets, and the smells of vanilla, chocolate, and cinnamon made her mouth water.

"Oh my." The king reached in and pulled out a triangular-shaped cake covered in purple frosting and topped with small lavender flowers. He pushed the box toward Mayten.

She chose a small round cake with white frosting and a candied curl of lemon on top.

They looked at each other, tapped the cakes in a toast, and took a bite.

Sweet vanilla and tart lemon burst through Mayten's mouth. "This is amazing."

"Mine too," he agreed. "I must say I do believe I've made the right choice with Sugar, no matter what old Serine will think."

He took another bite, his eyes rolling up in pleasure. "I think we're done for today, Mayten. Go enjoy yourself and I'll see you in the morning. And thank your mother for organizing these interviews for us."

Mayten shoved another bite of cake in her mouth and dashed out of the office. She had to find Cather and tell her what was happening with the school.

CHAPTER FORTY-TWO

The last night of the summer solstice clan gathering was to be one long celebration, starting with a communal dinner, then dancing, joining announcements, and new songs.

Mayten's responsibilities were over. Now she could relax and enjoy the evening. She'd talked to Cather on the way home, only to find out the queen had already told her friend about the school. She'd also run into Kai.

A warm flush spread up her cheeks. Great Singer, she had to stop blushing every time she thought of either Kai or Lan.

Taiwania fluttered around their bedroom, as nervous as a magpie. She'd sit on her bed, then jump up and pace the room, then plop onto Mayten's bed, then jump up. She'd been working on a new song and couldn't seem to get the ending right, but she wouldn't share the song with anyone.

Oleaster, her oldest brother who shared Da's kind eyes, was glowing with joy about finally getting to announce his intention to join with Lilium, and Da was in the kitchen loading food into baskets to be carried down to the town center for the evening meal. Ma was off in meetings with the clan elders before the Sun Clan and Ocean Clan departed tomorrow.

Leaving Wollemi and Mayten to mind Aster and baby Maple.

"It's time," Da called as Aster jumped on his new big-boy bed. Mayten had just finished dressing the baby in her pajamas.

She strapped the baby onto her back and Wollemi lifted Aster off the bed, taking his little brother by the hand. They gathered in the front yard where Da had loaded a cart with food and blankets. Oleaster rocked up and down on his toes, grinning.

Mayten walked up to her older brother and touched his arm. "I'm so happy for you."

He pulled her into a hug and twirled her around, the baby on her back laughing. "I'm happy for me too!"

He danced a jig as he released her. "Aster, do you want a piggyback ride?"

The little tyke nodded vigorously and was pulled up onto his big brother's back. The two took off down the trail.

"Let me take the baby. She's probably hungry," Da said, looking around with a frown. "You go hurry your sister, will you?"

Mayten slipped the baby off her back and helped strap her to Da's back. He started down the hill with the cart, Wollemi following behind him.

Mayten waited for her sister to appear. When she finally came out, she looked stunning in her green dress, her hair tied back in a matching ribbon. "Did you finish your song?"

"I did. At least I think so." She smiled nervously as they headed down the hill.

"Sharing a new song is always scary," Taiwania continued. The warm evening light seemed to make her glow. "The last song I shared was with the other clan singers and singing sailors. This is the whole island—and the king!"

"The last song you wrote took me by surprise."

"Were you happy with it?"

"Yes." Mayten surprised herself. She *was* happy. She was also mortified and embarrassed. No need to share all that when her sister was nervous. "You've got a gift, Taiwania."

Her sister gave her a mischievous grin. "I think you'll like this one too."

She gathered her skirts in her hands and sprinted down the road.

Heart pounding, Mayten chased after her.

What did her sister mean?

She tried to catch Taiwania, but the road was crowded with other families heading to town and Mayten had to slow to a walk. She caught sight of her sister's bobbing head too far ahead to catch.

The crowd was full of happy clansfolk. Greetings echoed back and forth. Some folks joined hands, others slapped each other on the back.

One figure was pushing against the tide, coming toward her. Mayten recognized Lan's curly hair. He waved as he approached. "Are you free of your work now?"

"Yes, have you come to rescue me?" His unconscious beauty always took her breath away. He did seem like a prince from a storybook.

He stopped in front of her, and they moved to the side so others could go around them.

"I was wondering if you had time to show me your home, since you got to see mine? Unless you're needed right away."

Mayten smiled. "I have a bit of time, but we'll have to be quick. There is a lot of setting up to do and I've been told I'm not needed. Yet."

She took his hand and led him back up the hill to her homestead. As they approached, Anatolian came out to greet them.

Lan grinned widely and bent down to introduce himself.

"You're a fine one, aren't you?" he said, rubbing the dog's cheeks and ears. Anatolian seemed to agree, wagging his tail wildly.

"I knew he'd like you." Mayten pointed toward the homestead. "This is it. Let me give you a quick tour."

The scent of the roses in full bloom was almost overwhelming as she showed him her father's gardens. She took him through the house, pointing out the kitchen, living rooms, nursery, bedrooms, and the extension Oleaster had built for his new bride.

"The house is so big," he said. "It goes on and on. You'd never guess how big it is from the front."

"My folks have had a lot of children," she admitted. "They just kept adding rooms. When the twins moved out, Da started a library and enlarged the bathing room. Come see the back."

She led him through a back door and out into the orchards, pointing out her mother's seedlings. "Ma plants these to replace what we use for lumber. It's her job to see to the health of the forest. My brother Oleaster manages the fruit trees and vegetables. All with help, of course."

"Is Anatolian the only animal on your farm?" He looked around as if expecting to see cows or chickens.

Mayten smiled. "He is and there's a cat. We aren't a farm, just a homestead. We grow plants, not animals. There are homesteads up here that have some cows, goats, and chickens. We trade with them for what we need."

He nodded, surveying the rows of fruit and nut trees with the pine tree nursery to the side. "It's beautiful here. And it smells better than our place."

She laughed. "We should head down before I'm missed."

They walked in companionable silence until they'd reached the swarm of people heading to the town center. Families with children hurried by. Most were homesteaders from further up the mountain carrying baskets of food and blankets. They nodded in greeting as they passed Mayten.

"You did a good job at the interview," she said as they wove around people, dodging elbows and children. "I don't have any insight into how the king will choose but if it was up to me, you'd be in for sure."

He smiled shyly. "I'd like that. Would you be there too, at the castle?" He ducked his head as though embarrassed.

She liked that about him. He wasn't confident like Rill, or clingy like Kai. His was a quiet presence, steady and kind. Mayten nodded. "Apparently the king wants us to start the school sooner than I'd expected."

He said nothing but she saw the corner of his mouth twitch up. When they reached the town center he said. "I've got to go help my family with food setup, but would you save me a dance?"

"Of course," she said. She glanced into his gorgeous eyes and might have gotten lost if he hadn't tipped his hat and slipped into the crowd.

Mayten sighed. Her father and the king had both warned her to keep her options open and she really was in no hurry to make any decisions about men. She did enjoy the attention, though. And this trip had taught her there were a lot of good men in the world.

She'd been so afraid during her first quest. This time she hadn't been as afraid of being out on her own. She'd learned so much. Trusting herself was something she was still learning.

Someone tapped her on the shoulder and she started, heart leaping into her throat. She spun and found herself facing Kai.

"Hi Mayten," he said with a grin. "I can't chat. Just wanted to make sure you save me a dance."

"I will." She smiled. He bowed and she laughed out loud. Then he was off, probably helping his folks corral their children before the opening ceremony.

She searched for her family among the hundreds spread across the clan center. People had laid out blankets delineating their spaces so she wove around them and eventually found hers. Taiwania was sitting on the ground next to Aster and the baby. "Oh good, you're finally here. I have to go meet with the other singers to—make sure everything is ready." She jumped up, a mischievous smile on her lips and left before Mayten could even ask where her folks and Oleaster were.

Her sister had set out several blankets, piling baskets and pillows around them like a fence to keep her younger siblings inside. Aster played with his blocks and baby Maple practiced crawling to reach her toys. Mayten sighed, stepping over the small fence to sit with her youngest siblings. Wollemi must be off with the king's children while she was left here with the littles. Again.

Maybe going to the castle earlier than expected would be a blessing. Her mother had brought on a girl to help with the children while Mayten was gone. She'd likely bring the same girl back again.

Movement caught Mayten's eye as Solis climbed up the stairs to the main stage. The clan leader wore her white ceremonial robe, the long bell sleeves hanging down by her knees. She raised her arms and called for attention.

Mayten wasn't as afraid of Solis as she'd originally been, but the clan leader had a commanding presence and the crowd quieted quickly. Everyone made their way to their blankets and settled in. She soon found herself surrounded by family.

The clan leader's new apron was embroidered with all the clan symbols instead of all the callings as was the one she wore at regular clan ceremonies. This special apron was only to be worn by the clan leader hosting whatever gathering was taking place. In the center of the apron stood a crown representing Castle Keep. A pine tree represented the Forest Clan, a wave represented the Ocean Clan, and a sun represented the Sun Clan. The symbols hovered around the crown like spokes on a wagon wheel.

The apron had been made—and embroidered—by the hands of artists she'd met at the Sun Clan.

Sun Clan, Ocean Clan—these places had once been foreign to Mayten. Now they were dear to her heart.

Solis lowered her arms. "Welcome, welcome all to the Forest Clan!"

Forest clansfolk roared their welcome and Mayten happily joined them.

"Welcome to those who traveled from the Ocean Clan!"

Another roar erupted from the crowd. Mayten joined the cheer. Her twin sisters and their husbands were in that group somewhere.

"Welcome to those who have traveled the farthest, the Sun Clan!"

The entire crowd roared their welcome.

Mayten found herself joining in, shouting her loudest. Tears burned her eyes. Even though she hadn't known those who had succumbed to the sleeping sickness, she mourned their deaths. She could scarcely believe she'd helped figure out the problem and the solution so more folks hadn't died.

"And welcome Castle Keep!"

Everyone stood, clapping and cheering their loudest. King Redmond waved as he strolled toward the stage.

He was well loved. How could he possibly be replaced?

The king mounted the stairs in two large steps. Solis again raised her hands, asking for silence and motioning for people to sit down. She faced the king as he spoke.

Even from a distance, Mayten could see the king's eyes full of love. "My friends, the last few years have held some challenges. My family and I visited each of the clans and we've been impressed by your strength and resilience. Many of you have suffered loss, grief, and sickness and still you face life with joy and resilience, reminding me that what makes Triggensfeld strong is not her king, but her people."

The crowd roared their approval.

The king waited a moment, then raised his hand, quieting the crowd. "As you know, I'll be retiring sometime in the foreseeable future."

This time the crowd groaned. The king held up his hands. "Thank you, but don't worry. I'm in no hurry to leave. Traditionally, when I retire my family's official leadership will be at an end."

Another groan from the crowd along with a few shouted protests.

"I have begun the process of selecting your new king or queen. I promise to select someone who will rule with the same fairness and humility that you've been accustomed to."

Another raucous cheer interrupted his speech. The king grinned and waited a few heartbeats before continuing. "There are some wonderful candidates who have agreed to come to the Keep for one year to begin training for leadership. What do you say we confirm this list so our candidates can relax and enjoy the evening?"

A few shouted agreement before a hush fell over the crowd. Each clan had candidates on the list.

"Before I read the list, however," the king grinned as the crowd groaned at the delay. "I'd like to thank Mayten Singer and all those who helped her."

Another cheer, this one directed at Mayten. She stared at the ground, wishing she could pull the blanket over her head and disappear.

The king raised his hands and the crowd quieted. "Her original teammates, Santana Merchant and Anteny Weaver were sick and could not help. Thankfully they are well now. Mayten, along with her family and friends, worked hard and sacrificed much to bring us these candidates. She didn't dally and she didn't whine, no matter the obstacles thrown in her way. I have to admit she set the bar high. The level of strong candidates from each clan is impressive."

He raised his hand as the crowd started to cheer. "Will all the candidates please stand?"

Mayten could hardly keep still as one by one, the candidates—candidates *she'd* chosen for the king to review—rose from their blankets. Only three had dropped out, leaving thirty-two in the running.

"I want you to know that every candidate who agreed to the first year of training has been accepted."

Someone gasped behind Mayten. Some of the candidates had bewildered expressions on their faces. Others wore expressions of triumph.

The king raised his voice. "Please join me in congratulating each and every one of these folks. One of them will eventually be your new leader!"

All of them? He'd chosen *all* the people she had suggested. The hard work, the travel, the fear, the sickness, had been worth it.

Mayten leaped to her feet, clapping and cheering as the crowd went wild, shaking hands and congratulating the candidates who stood near them.

CHAPTER FORTY-THREE

The king left the stage and Mayten was surprised to see old Mantica helped up the stairs in her bare feet. Thanksgiving was generally led by the oldest in the family so she must be the oldest person present. She raised her arms in the air and everyone in the crowd followed her example, kicking off their footwear and taking the hands of those nearest to them, then raising their arms in the air.

Her voice rang out, surprisingly strong as she recited the traditional blessing. "Our feet are planted in the earth from which we came."

Her voice faded as memories flowed like a river through Mayten's mind. Lan's family ranch with all its greenery and sheep, the Table farms with their abundant crops . . .

"Our hands reach to the stars which give us hope."

More memories of Wollemi's enthusiasm for "his stars." Her sense of loss and helplessness when he was so sick. Her renewed joy and hope when he began to recover . . .

"We thank you for all we have. We trust you for all we have lost."

Older memories of Hunter surfaced, his laughter and trust. The emptiness she felt inside when she'd known he was dying . . .

"For everything and everyone between the stars and earth, we give thanks to you, Great Maker."

"Great Singer." Warmth flooded through Mayten, raising the hair on her arms and neck as each clansperson chanted the name for God that came with their gifting. Her sense of family—of clan—expanded, wrapping the clans together in Thanks-Giving.

The warmth turned into laughter as Mantica raised her hands, her dark eyes sparkling with mischief. "Now, let the little ones eat first so they stop whining!"

The sense of ceremony ended and parents jumped up to fill plates for their children. There were tables lining the back of the square with food brought by the clan members.

Mayten watched people mingle, some going for food, some just visiting. She tickled the baby's tummy as baby Maple burbled something that sounded like "mmmaaa."

Aster looked up at her, eyes round as Da's wine cups. "Did she say Ma?"

Mayten gave him a gentle smile. "I think it's a bit early for her to talk, but you could be right."

Someone squealed behind her. A lanky, spike-haired girl jogged up, face bubbling with joy.

"Flurry!"

The girl wrapped her in a bear hug so tight Mayten almost couldn't breathe. "Took me *forever* to find you in this crowd."

Mayten gently disengaged herself from the hug, leaving one arm around Flurry's narrow shoulders.

"You've grown taller." When Mayten left Flurry on her ship, the girl had only come up to her shoulder. Now she was almost up to Mayten's chin.

"I have. Ma says maybe I'll be as tall as you."

"You'd better eat then. I was always starving when I was growing so fast. I have to wait for someone to come watch the baby but you might as well go eat."

"I'll wait with you." The formerly reticent girl started talking about her wind catcher training. She chattered non-stop until Da showed up and shooed them off to get food. Wollemi wobbled up, balancing an overloaded plate in each hand. Taiwania followed after him, shaking her head.

By the time Mayten and Flurry filled their plates, most of the families had settled back on their blankets to eat. The setting sun meant new songs would soon be sung.

Taiwania swallowed her last bite of food, then clutched Mayten's hand. "Do I have anything in my teeth?"

Mayten shook her head. "Perfect as usual."

She squeezed Mayten's hand. "Wish me luck."

Taiwania stood and headed for the stage.

Flurry took another bite of bread, watching Taiwania go. "It's like someone took the best parts of all the Island's immigrants and mixed them together in your sister."

Mayten nodded. She remembered thinking the same thing what seemed like ages ago.

A hush fell over the crowd as Taiwania picked a lyre off the stage and settled herself on a stool. She cradled the lyre in her arms, resting the base on her lap. The stringed instrument was made of wood and had a large hole in its center.

Taiwania plucked a few strings and then sang out in her clear voice.

> *"What does the wind have to do with the water?*
> *What does a tree have to do with the sun?*
> *Take out just one and the rest live no longer,*
> *All live in balance, all live as one.*

There once was a girl who could hear the wind's stories.
There once was a girl who could talk to the trees.
They came together to help solve a problem.
A darkness was bringing the Sun to its knees."

A chill ran up Mayten's spine. She reached out and took Flurry's warm hand. A ring of torches exploded into flame around the outside of the town center, sending a chill through Mayten and lighting up the darkening sky. Voices raised along with drums and a flute as Taiwania moved into the chorus:

"What does the wind have to do with the water?
What does a tree have to do with the sun?
Take out just one and the rest live no longer,
All live in balance, all live as one."

The other singers paused, leaving Taiwania alone to sing the second verse:

"The questers they led them up a high mountain,
To caves full of mystery, danger, and gloom
A young boy drank deeply from the black water
A young boy fell deeply into dark doom."

When the chorus came the other singers joined in. Mayten was shocked to hear others in the crowd sing along.

She understood why, though. She could feel the song vibrating through her bones.

"What does the wind have to do with the water?
What does a tree have to do with the sun?
Take out just one and the rest live no longer,
All live in balance, all live as one."

The voices paused again as Taiwania sang the third verse:

"The gifted they knew, it was the black water.
They rallied the clans to bring the clean in.
Together they found the source of the poison
Because of their wisdom, we all live again."

Mayten couldn't help joining the chorus. Flurry's thin voice rose with hers, their two voices entwining as the song lifted to the stars.

"What does the wind have to do with the water?
What does a tree have to do with the sun?
Take out just one and the rest live no longer,
All live in balance, all live as one."

Mayten felt her heart lift with the other voices, bringing a deep healing to her soul. As the song ended, the music's vibrations seemed to linger.

Tears spilled down Flurry's cheeks.

"Are you okay?" Mayten asked.

Flurry shook her head. "I—I can't believe she wrote that. About me. About us. It makes me feel funny. Like I did something special but . . . you were there. You know how it was."

Mayten handed the girl a clean napkin. "I know how you feel. I keep reminding myself that stories are important. We just have to let them be what they are."

Flurry nodded. She wiped her face and stood up, handing the napkin back to Mayten. "I need to find my family."

"Remember," Mayten said. "You are a Wind Catcher. Never let anyone tell you otherwise. And if they don't believe you—have someone sing them your song."

Flurry flashed her impish smile and gave a two-fingered salute. Mayten watched the girl wind her way through the blankets.

There would be several new songs written by other singers this solstice. Some would be sad, some funny, but Mayten was sure none would resonate with an entire crowd as Taiwania's had.

CHAPTER FORTY-FOUR

After the songs, blankets were moved to the edges of the clan center and space was made for dancing. A band assembled on the stage. There were stringed instruments, flutes, and hand drums. Solis moved to the edge of the stage, raising her hands for silence.

"Now is the moment many of you have been waiting for. Are there any here who would publicly like to share their commitment to join? If so, please step forward."

Mayten almost squealed when she spotted Oleaster and Lilium step forward with several other couples, including Chamfer and Purl. She cheered with the rest of the crowd, her voice cracking under the strain.

Solis smiled down at the couples. "We give our blessing to you all and ask that you lead us in the dancing as you move forward into your new lives. May those lives be filled with love and joy!"

The musicians struck up a jaunty tune and the couples lined up to dance.

Mayten turned to find Rill smiling at her, his hand out. "I wanted to get you first before all of your other suiters could grab you."

She smiled and took his hand. Those watching formed two parallel lines, clapping along to the music as each newly declared couple linked their hands together and raised them in the air running between the lines to happy cheers. When the last couple passed through the line, the watchers broke apart and other couples joined the dance, forming lines to swing their partners in one of the island's fun dances.

Mayten and Rill joined the other couples who danced toward each other, slapping hands together then danced away. It was a flirty dance, with couples turning away and toward each other from their right side to the left. Rill—with his dark eyes and bright smile—turned out to be an excellent dancer. He swung her around, laughing and clapping as the song ended.

He led her to the side of the stage. "I hear you might be coming to the Castle with us?"

Mayten nodded. "It's sounding more and more like we'll be going sooner than I expected."

He leaned close, heat radiated off his skin. "I'll be glad for that." He raised his eyebrows in a comical attempt at flirting.

She laughed. He was so silly.

Taiwania walked up and Mayten wrapped her sister in a hug. "That was amazing!"

But Taiwania was not looking at her. She was staring at Rill.

Rill stared back.

Taiwania, who never gave the boys in her clan a second glance, seemed awestruck. While Rill, never at a loss for words, was completely silent.

Mayten struggled not to laugh. Another song started, this time a slower number. Mayten grabbed Taiwania's hand, then Rill's and joined them. "Rill, this is my sister Taiwania. You may have heard her sing."

Rill gulped and nodded.

"Taiwania, this is Rill. You two should dance."

The couple walked to the dance floor, still lost in each other's eyes.

Her twin sisters, Zigba and Acerola, strolled up, taking position on either side of her. They studied the dance floor while Mayten watched Taiwania who seemed to float in Rill's arms.

"What's that all about?" Zigba asked.

Mayten smiled "I think Taiwania might have just met her match."

"Oh my," said Acerola.

"Poor man," said Zigba.

"Actually," Mayten said, "I'm pretty sure he can handle her."

Lan walked up and held out his hand with a shy smile. She waved to her sisters and let him lead her back into the dancing. The music was another fast song. Lan danced with enthusiasm but not grace.

"Sorry," he yelled over the music. "We don't do too much dancing on the ranch."

"You're doing just fine."

"That song about you was beautiful."

Mayten was glad he hadn't said anything about the beauty of the singer. As much as she hated admitting it, she got tired of hearing about how gorgeous Taiwania was. "My sister is very creative."

"That was your sister?"

Mayten braced herself but he said no more. She decided to press. "She's pretty, isn't she?"

Lan tilted his head to one side, reminding her of Anatolian trying to figure something out. "I guess. But not as pretty as you."

Mayten's heart skipped a beat. Lan was a man of integrity. He wouldn't lie to her, would he?

They were out of breath when the song ended and a slower song began. Lan started to pull her closer, but stopped when Theo, Flurry's brother, tapped Lan's shoulder. Kai stepped up and pulled Mayten away at the same time.

"My turn." Kai grinned, gently guiding her into the dance.

Mayten glanced over her shoulder at Lan. He raised a hand and walked away with another shy smile while Theo stood glowering.

She turned her attention back to Kai, grateful not to have to dance with Theo.

"We make a striking couple, don't we?" the prince said, glancing around at the other couples.

She followed his gaze, dismayed to find people staring and pointing at them. She shuddered. "I imagine we do. The Prince and the Tree Singer. Next thing you know my sister will have another song to sing."

"I wouldn't mind." He tugged her closer and rested his head against hers. "Is that Rill I see dancing with Taiwania?"

Mayten nodded, watching the two moving together to the slow rhythm. "Looks like one of my suiters has been snatched away."

Kai pulled back, looking down at her. "Do you mind?"

"Not at all. He was never serious. I tried to tell you."

Kai relaxed and pulled her close. "You did. I just get jealous sometimes. I'm sorry. It's like, I discovered you first, but now you belong to everyone."

"Discovered me?" She raised her eyebrows, not sure how she felt about "being discovered."

Kai flushed. "You know what I mean. Before the Castle, I never really looked at a girl. And I thought maybe you'd never really looked at a boy. Then, when I saw you in that pond. Well, I can't explain what happened. It was like I was seeing for the first time."

She rested her head on his shoulder unsure what to say. The first time she'd seen him, she'd thought he was a lecherous groundskeeper.

"It's okay if you don't feel the same way," he said. "I know you've got important things to do, and I have to learn more about questing. But —please, don't count me out."

She leaned back and looked into his eyes. "I will not count you out, Kai. I couldn't."

❧

Oleaster's joining ceremony was much less grand than the king's daughter's had been but King Redmond and his family stayed the extra day to celebrate with them. The two families plus a handful of friends gathered outside in the warm June evening as the couple pledged themselves to each other. They both wore the simple green of their clan. Da's flowers were in the height of their glory on the tables and in Lilium's hair. Dressed in a simple long dress, Lilium glowed with beauty, love lighting her eyes and her face.

"Are we ready?" Da whispered to Mayten after the hand-fasting was done.

"I think so."

As Da slipped up the steps of the homestead and tapped on the door, Mayten walked to the front of the crowd and stood beside Oleaster and his new bride. She raised her hands and let the cheering die down. Oleaster beamed at his new bride and she at him.

Mayten lifted a glass of wine from a nearby tray and held it high in the air. The guests echoed the gesture and her brother looked at her curiously. Mayten smiled. "We have a special gift for the new couple. The king's newest helper, Sugar Baker, has made you one of her specialties."

Da opened the door and Sugar came out, holding the tallest cake Mayten had ever seen. It had three tiers and was decorated with enough colorful flowers to rival Da's garden. The crowd gave a gasp of appreciation and applause broke out.

Mayten had never seen Oleaster's eyes so wide. He took Lilium's hand and led her behind the table where Sugar placed the cake. Everyone moved closer to gaze at the amazing confection.

Glass still lifted, Mayten said in a loud, clear voice, "To my big brother and my new sister. May your marriage be as lovely and sweet as this cake!"

Everyone clapped again and Sugar turned bright red. Several people approached her while everyone else lined up eagerly, wanting to share in a piece of the beautiful cake.

King Redmond moved up to Mayten's side. "It looks like we've made the right decision about Sugar, eh?"

Mayten nodded.

"You've had quite a year, haven't you?" he asked. The unexpected question brought a lump to her throat.

"Yes." She remembered the fear she'd felt when the king's letter arrived, asking her to find the candidates. The joy of her time with the twins and their families and how they'd helped her with the contest. The uncertainty and devastation of the Sun Clan, then Wollemi's sickness. The way her family and friends rallied to help her choose candidates, both local and for the Sun Clan. The men she'd met and the places she'd seen.

"Do you plan to come to the castle before winter?"

She didn't know she'd made her decision until the word slipped out of her mouth. "Yes."

"Are you excited about it?"

Was she excited? Mayten didn't know. She did know she wasn't afraid. Not after all she'd been through. She knew the Castle, the king's family, and most of the candidates. Still, change was always hard for her. "I've talked to Solis and Ma.

They'll help me decide who to bring with me. And Solis will help Ma with her responsibilities."

The king chuckled. "You are a consummate diplomat. You and Nan are going to do amazing things. No matter where you are or who you're with—you will always be part of our family."

Mayten felt the words like a warm hug. The king had seemed so strange when they'd first met, but now he was more like an uncle than a king. She was not looking forward to leaving her home and family again, but she had time and she would savor it. Every moment.

The king put his arm around her and squeezed her shoulders. "I'd better go congratulate the happy couple and then help my wife pack. We are on the early barge tomorrow."

Cather, Tray, and Kai stepped up as soon as the king moved away. They were all eating cake.

"This is the most amazing cake I've ever tasted," Tray said.

"I haven't had a bite yet, but it sure is beautiful." Mayten eyed Kai's plate.

"Here," he said, holding out his fork.

Mayten took the bite and savored the sweet buttery taste of the cake and the vanilla of the frosting. She rolled her eyes in delight. "I'll have to get a piece."

Cather laughed. "Don't worry, you're going to have leftovers for days."

Mayten looked at the table. Only the top tier and part of the second were gone. They had a lot of cake left.

"I'm sure Da watched Sugar make the entire cake. He'll be trying to reproduce it for the next twelve months, maybe more."

"When you two come to the Castle, Sugar will be there," Kai said, slipping his arm around Mayten.

"Kai and I," Tray said, throwing his arm around Cather, "will visit often."

Mayten gazed around the crowd, stopping to watch her family—Ma holding the baby, Taiwania chasing Aster through the crowd, Wollemi playing happily with the king's children, and Oleaster introducing his new wife to the twins.

"I wish we could just stay like this. Like it is right now."

The air chilled as the sun sank lower in the sky. She tried to fix the image in her mind so she could carry it with her always.

The people she loved and the home she adored.

She had seen a lot of dwellings on her most recent trip—some made of clay, some of wood; some round, some square; large ranch houses and even larger farms—none were as beautiful as her home, tucked into the forest she loved, filled with her family.

Both times she'd come home from a quest she'd felt different—older, maybe even wiser. But home, with this family and these friends, would always be where she felt safest, the most at peace, the most known, and the most loved.

"Home is where the heart is," someone once said.

Right now, her heart was home.

THE GIFTINGS OF TRIGGENSFELD

Tree Singers (includes flower, fruit, and vegetable singers) – Work with nature to help things grow. They do not take energy from nature but join with it and can also learn to listen to, receive from, and send messages through nature. No vocal singing skills are necessary for this gift.

Story Singers – Memorize the stories of the clans to maintain and share important history and life lessons. They generally have beautiful voices and often, but not always, become Clan Leaders. Responsible for creating new songs of important events.

Star Singers – Listen to the wisdom of the stars and can often read portents in them as they become advanced practitioners.

Clan Leaders – Show a strong gift in understanding the community's needs and have leadership skills. They are called by the Clan Council and sometimes, in rare years, spend time at the Castle Keep being trained by the king.

Questers – Those gifted in solving problems affecting different clans. They have the gift of reading nature for directions as well as investigating problems to help find solutions.

Woodsmen/Hunters – Are connected with nature so they can track and hunt, generally on trips with the questers. They can sense the presence of prey and only take what is needed.

Bakers – Have a gifting with food. They can create never-before-seen desserts and confections by listening to the ingredients.

Builders – Their gifting involves listening to wood during the construction of buildings like houses, boats, and ships. Some builders create functional and beautiful pieces of art as well.

Farmers – Are gifted with soil. They use their gifts to grow food and experiment with soil and various fertilizers to enhance growth.

Merchants – They are gifted in creating saleable and tradeable crafts such as woodworking, knitting, and embroidery. They are gifted at selling and trading locally through the ports where ships take their goods to distant lands.

Ranchers – Can listen to and receive pictures or feelings from animals of all kinds.

Wave Runners – They generally work on rivers and understand the currents. They use their gifting to help their barges to move quickly, both with and against the currents.

Weavers – Are found mostly in the Sun Clan weavers work with cloth. Besides sewing lightweight garments for all the clans, they embroidery fanciful and colorful patterns on clothes and the clan aprons worn at official clan ceremonies. They are artists.

Wind Catchers – Can increase or decrease the wind as needed for large ships to move across the ocean. Talented Wind Catchers can receive information from the wind as well and call up wind when they are not on the ocean.

Sailors – Sailors work with Wind Catchers to guide ships but their gifting is in navigation. Maps live in their heads. They are very important to the Island as there are treacherous rocks surrounding the island that only gifted sailors can navigate intuitively. This helps protect the island from unwanted visitors.

THE CLANS OF TRIGGENSFELD

The Forest Clan – Here the forest is managed by Tree Singers. The wood is milled and used for building furniture, ships, and as exports. Most Tree singers live in the Forest Clan but there are people of all giftings scattered throughout the clans. This clan is not on the ocean but has a river that flows to the sea. Barges take people and goods down the river to the Ocean Clan.

The Ocean Clan – Home to Triggensfeld's largest population and biggest port. Large ships dock there to take goods for trading to other lands. They can also take people to the Sun Clan and the Castle Keep. The primary giftings in the Ocean Clan are for merchants. Many goods are created there and sold or traded on market days. There are also ranches above the clan central that provide food and wool.

The Sun Clan – A dry desert-like place and home to the smallest clan. The major gifting in the desert is artistic design. Most garments are woven there, and clan aprons are embroidered at the Sun Clan. High above the clan center is a tabletop mountain that gets more water and has people with agricultural giftings. The abundance of food is also exported. It has a small port.

The Castle Keep—Castle Triggensfeld is not a clan, but the home of the ruling family. It houses a garrison of peacekeepers. The island has few enemies so there is no need for an army. The Keep has beautiful gardens, and hosts visiting guests. It has a small port. Currently, a school is being built to house and cross-train people of various gifts.

ACKNOWLEDGEMENTS

I wrote *Tree Singer* as a stand-alone book, but enough people begged for more. This book is for the fans, those who loved *Tree Singer* as much as I did. Thank you for your faith in me. It means the world to a writer to have people love their books.

Thank you to my family, who are my true north.

Thank you, Theresa Borges and Stephanie Wilden, for my Beta reads and encouragement.

And thank you to Louisa Swann, my stalwart editor who puts her whole heart and soul into my books. She worked so hard on this one amid a difficult year and I'm grateful, even when I get grumpy. And thanks for always pushing me when I get lazy.

Thank you to all my wonderful ARC readers for their love and feedback. And thanks to the #Booktok community of amazing people who support indie authors.

If you haven't listened to the audiobook of Tree Singer, you should. Barbara Bond did a fantastic job bringing the book to life. I cried when I heard her sing the songs I wrote. She will be doing this book as well for which I am eternally grateful.

ABOUT THE AUTHOR

Jacci lives in the Nevada desert with her husband and their dog Rosie. She loves to escape as often as possible to the redwood forests in California to walk among the giants and find peace. She also loves chocolate, babies, and writing books for readers of all ages!

For more on Jacci's books go to:
http://jacciturner.com

Look for Jacci on your favorite social media sites:

Facebook:
https://www.facebook.com/pages/Jacci-Turn-
er/162842543809329?fref=ts

TikTok
@jacciturnerauthor

YouTube:
https://www.youtube.com/channel/UCU37EJn8r6-o32v-
sU697SWg

Pinterest:
https://www.pinterest.com/jacciturner/

Instagram:
https://instagram.com/jacciturner/

http://about.me/jacciturner

Tumblr:
https://www.tumblr.com/blog/jacciturner

Linkedin:
https://www.linkedin.com/profile/
view?id=148218545&trk=nav_responsive_tab_profile

Goodreads:
https://www.goodreads.com/author/show/5347211.Jacci_Turner